Hy Brasil Island of Eternity

Robert E. Kearns

Copyright: 2019 Robert E. Kearns

All rights reserved. No part of this book may be reproduced, stored in a retrieval system or transmitted in any form or by any means without the prior written permission of the author, except by a reviewer who may quote brief passages in a review to be printed in a newspaper, magazine or journal.

Dedications:

To my niece Aoife, many thanks for inspiring me to write this novel.

To Reinhard, for all the memories which gave rise to the house and home mentioned in this book, thank you.

Hy Brasil

Hy Brasil

There are thrice fifty distant isles in the ocean to the west of us;
Larger than Erin twice is each of them, or thrice
(From Immram Brain maic Febaill)

Robert E. Kearns

Part 1—The Light

August 2019

With a resolution favoured to launch this account, I at once faced the difficulty how I ought to define the child I one time prevailed; or broader yet, the child and teenager I assumed in earlier years. I dwell not far out of those times; thus, I persist in hesitancy whether I should submit to that era of blossomed spring as ages of childhood. When embodied in this tail end to an unsolicited eclipse of life, there remains the few who might in eagerness whisper it as such. With this in mind, I invite an amount of leeway in my self-portrayal, as the uncertainty stands inherent to a generous extent.

I devised until present day, to not occur swayed into the exhibition of complete self-assurance, as the embodiment of a man about town. As of now, modifications advance and there endures the perception I may through no mortal depiction realise that accomplishment.

It happens owed to the influence of these variances that my hand has gotten pressed into dialogue; and where my youth rests affected, this fragment of me, while by this avail perseveres in control, also practices a sentimental urge to glance rearward with fondness besides nostalgias for those dates, as well as cling to the more serious requisite of affording a measure of background with concern to the lead up to these prevailing state of affairs. I shall, therefore, in the interests of an aspiration toward contentment, even if purely temporary, remark not on the minority, but on my formative dimensions of adolescence, when I developed in the literal and with

Robert E. Kearns

metaphor into the narrator of this testament.

I supposed here to implement at first, the concept of unusual as the descriptive adjective for these times, but then theorised perhaps distinctive might come out as an improvement. A proclamation of the former could depict an announcement I earlier existed odd, awkward or conceivably hitherto sustained a deformity; none of which shouldered as accurate. No, by my perception at least, there persisted nothing peculiar or unorthodox with reference to me, and in the physical sense there arose no visible abnormalities, with all functioning as they must, on a par with or healthier than pretty well any regular juvenile soul.

The formation of my physique, it should rank understood, moulded in some conducts as superior to average. I held tall and strong from a tender age and among the foremost of family photographs there witnessed the depiction of a blonde head of hair in curls which towered above those maintained by contemporaries at an equal phase. I am without that complication today, but merely since the colour of my locks initiated an adjustment from fair to chestnut at the grownup eagerness of 6 or 7. I upheld proficiency in athletics, and imposed as academically capable in that I executed tolerably in school minus the exigency to strain with especial resolve.

I neither protruded to an excessive quantity, nor did I exist in those domains of the forgotten. I classified as familiar, but not in the style of character associates clustered round, as transpired with a quota of youngsters. About the college and also within my circle of friends, I distinguished time and again one or two of the intrepid breeds who forever drew a crowd.

Robert E. Kearns

Not exclusive to those, nor tied to the congregation, I predisposed to uphold the aspect of confidence to go about my ventures by my own particular approach.

It may well transpire that while superior to the conventional in more than a few respects, I defined not altogether outstanding in a build which might entertain to lure a percentage of remarks. I troubled to never seek consideration at the outset, nor did I solicit to comport in an agency that undertook to secure me a commentary of any inordinate depth.

With hindsight, I grasp this self-taxonomy suited me fine in that constructive juvenile sphere, and with the retrospection of preliminary adulthood I admit that until the current at least, it has bequeathed on me the benefit of what I judge as a well-rounded temperament and sensible outlook on life. I'm not positive at this point if that carries weight any longer. It worked up until now, but matters have distorted. In any case, I've gotten too far ahead of myself already so I'll get to that bridge of the narrative afterward.

While in attendance at school, it ascended then I struck on my skill with a multitude of sports, which credibly acknowledged more to do with my claim as taller and stronger than most of my peers, than it did with any exceptional talent. But for all of that, I don't clutch onto any motive to expect the coaches ever paid an inordinate portion of respect. Beyond doubt it didn't suggest that condition; which I'm okay with, as I distinguished from the beginning that my destiny reared to institute in academics as opposed to a star of the field.

My interest defined in education, and while I related to

athletics with participation, now I'm somewhat matured in all honesty I don't miss it to any extreme. I might have earned something of an aptitude for the arenas of competition, but by the same allowance I acceded to a take-it-or- leave-it-attitude, which meant by convention the adaptation of a lazy humour. When a subject appealed I made known the opposite inclination, and in substitute invested time and vitality to its review.

There's nought as yet in the anecdotes of my teenage drama to suggest the actuality of traits all that unique in my make-up, with next to nothing so far to propose authenticity of mannerisms peculiar to my disposition. Agreed, my adolescence, to a point at least, harboured as routine as anybody else's, except for a notable feature or variation I maintained. Not from birth did I uphold it as its seminal advent came as the fruit of an encounter which chanced upon me in the eleventh season from inception. It is entirely exclusive to recent weeks I interpreted its influence in full, as after the onset, I accepted it as little above a quirk which conferred on me dependable advantages of being. Now moreover, in light of deviant factors, the true expanse of this abnormality or idiosyncrasy has become visible.

The enhancement I endured in that previous generation didn't expose a forcible influence on me, if it affected me at all, and while there survived the mindfulness an incident once transpired, in no manner was I fearful of it, or indeed wary, either at the foundation or in the subsequent days. Right through that course, in the rush from childhood to a teenager, I embraced the adjustment then diagnosed how to minister the most from it.

Robert E. Kearns

I embraced recognition it gave rise to a metamorphosis. In addition, that amendment in combination with the positive benefits of its associate attributes, far from renown to linger hesitant of, afforded me rather with an air of confidence. I ascribe this certainty to the contentment I seized in those moments, for I ordered without doubt as gratified with my existence as reasonable to expect.

In mention of the consciousness I welcomed for the exceptional capacities I bore, or without doubt, so much as I could impart, marks of eminence I regulated, it is just within the present timeframe I entertained to pose quizzes on the business of these purported merits. What some time ago served as an accolade I beforehand established as mine alone; may justifiably in truth persist as commonplace. Or, to exude precision, in ages historical there occurs hints of it happening in tenure of conventionality. Plus, they may quite without a struggle, if preponderant conclusions get admitted as currency, become so all over again.

The contentment and diversion, I heretofore derived from this singularity shelters endurance no longer. In preference to this, it has come to be supplanted with apprehension, pessimism and likewise with dread. No one of these trepidations until of late squared as ingredients of my everyday personage. The feature, from which in preceding ages I profited, achieved to apply the attire of an undaunted attitude and this gave rise by some measure to the faring at bay of these ancillary tendencies. This grafted-on component fused with the typical persona of my genes thus in some behaviours heaped upon me a decisive, optimistic philosophy.

Robert E. Kearns

Today, negative views attest instead as ingrained in my reason. Too, they have usurped my personality to the amplitude they at present dominate. The first alteration, which prior to the here and now constituted a plus, now intimates as the facilitator of the second variation which in these hours befalls me.

It seems expected I should pen a testimony complementary to what "The Good Professor" as I hail him, drafted in 1896. It might even stand to rumour I savour a compulsion for the documentation of our history. Incidentally, should you keep on with conjecture whether the added party in our, happens the Professor, set that aside. It braves not he, but in his stead, Tiffanie.

I'll elucidate soon as regards all that pertains to the lovely Tiffanie, as this champions as her chronicle to the equal extent as it details mine. Even so, to shuffle back for a second occurrence to the Professor, he plausibly, at the end too, sensed an obligation, complementary in range to what I am this day compelled to transcribe. I can't frank the stamp of definite on that, but the conception is sound not just in view of how swiftly he met his demise, but most of all consequent to what passes with me at this hour. I reflect if he as well in those final shifts of presence became coerced into an agreement with his subliminal cry, which warned that should he not scribe the record with immediacy, the capacity to author it thereafter may progressively desert him.

I submitted the notion of disquiet hardly a second past although this may well tolerate too soft a portrayal for the arrangement that convenes in-progress. Despite this, the optimist within continues to fight. It contests as a battle with defeat ahead and even the admission of my failure divulges just how much pessimism has drained my spirits. It remains with hesitancy these days where I recognise I exercised no authority over the transformation. Despair penetrated my dreams, besides my consciousness while I guested in the dungeon of despondency. Desolation is yet a further commentary which until of late dwelled not with uncommon affection for me. Of all nomenclatures though, now I dwell upon it, this one perhaps more than any replacement, designates my current temper.

While I aspire yet to batter it into retreat and win back the alacrity which up to the point of a former state defined the dominant ratio of my complexion; it enlists there, scaling the wall with momentum and ever more speed to the crest. Too soon it will scheme to breach my ramparts. Alongside this misery abides its sister, Dread. It too mounts the ladder of occupation in the clash for my wits. As events stand, I convene the bare strength to rally stamina for to rudder it astern. Plus, it comes about these reserves of vitality that assist me in the disclosure of our story. However, not unlike anguish, it continues relentless. Besides, distinct from me it amuses with energy in abundance.

The second change has ripened in velocity. I comprehend that with certitude. So too, a submerged perception within, articulates that this bonus conversion will not sanction me to operate in mastery for a prominent duration. Hence, with an overriding exigency for haste, permit me to brief you on the original diversity and how it set me up me as contradictory to

Robert E. Kearns

the benchmark.

A decade elapsed since I broke into creation; a summer infant in sight of my pioneering light straight away in July (the eagle eyed will latch on to the recognition in consequence, that I just now tasted another, to which I will add that its celebration I refrained from this year). An anniversary of one's turn at summer birth came with reliable advantages; sunlit days in the main; and when the star shone, this predestined festivities for the terrace patio. Irrespective, it meant barbeque in recurrence, the weather issuing a license or not. Even should the conditions not align as cooperative, while we dined under cover, my father resolved to salvage his scheme to chef it with the grill. In extension, as I met as the sole party to the lineage with a seasonal birthdate, this affair, my mother devotedly captioned as the 'Highlight of the Social Season'.

Alongside this, there haunted the disadvantage of the school's discharge until September, which given our position of foreign immediacy to the city preordained a scarcity of classmates. Rather, friends got pursued from the adjoining district with the balance made up of cousins who came from as far apart as Dublin. It surrendered to the tea leaves for a decision whether I got to receive them again before the twelve months were out, but I never understood that as remarkable to any degree.

All this is not to disclose it lessened the adventure for me. I doggedly hung on to adoration for the annual ceremony of the Julian month which facilitated my customary bash and the influx of visitors that showed up for it even if they categorised as otherwise seldom noted. None the wiser did I express for it anyhow until that juncture, plus it resulted only as I turned older that the full household gained the flexibility to reminisce with glee at how it yet accomplished to convey so considerable a pleasure besides tributes of sentiment. Yes, perchance it might compass to direct that in typical surrounds my closest allies would reveal as those elicited from the halls of education, but on the festival of my emergence, the case may be stronger than any alternative, that out of sight meant out of mind.

Then on this, the tenth such gala to honour my debut to existence; for it got articulated the tradition originated with the initial; the company chanced to report in the fledgling module of the afternoon, each of them in the tote of a gift, which to my estimation at least negated the phenomenon I hadn't acquainted at all in intimacy with several. An endowment for the cause at that tender age exported sufficient motive for any chap, no matter how ambiguous the liaison, to transpire as one's finest companion for the day.

While this remarked not as the introductory annual practice with its accepted culinary relishes I recall, it stays with me as the influential illustration which lingers strongest in the psyche. Without the aftermath or reorganisation which ensued that night, it might otherwise have drifted into a collective merriment with congruent ones of that series on top of those before, with each of them in sponsorship of diverse splinters to assemble a solitary nostalgia.

It stays true, at that distinct evolution we waver on the cusp of navigation through a singular intellectual and biological railing which divides primary childhood from the initiation of advancement into a deliberate rational adolescent, then eventual adult. I suppose it would continue fair to claim this could in prospect have merited a contributory factor in the cause that enabled me to cling to this exact point in time, but which graded not the primary. I happen mindful nowadays and diagnosed since it took effect, besides in the years which came after, that it expressed the situation and what I dubbed the First Change that rendered this such a dramatic picture.

It sounds reasonable to voice that specific tributes lodge with us as the end product of factors such as trauma, death, and joyous scenes or even such episodes as a momentous chapter that struck on the earth, where we recall our position besides what favoured our movements at that explicit convergence. My consciousness of the periodic barbeque inversely induced no pronounced emotional upheaval or trauma, hence, were it not for the rendezvous it wouldn't otherwise have expanded as worthy of unique accolade.

Yet, when I consider back on it, furthermore, burrow into the inquisitorial why I prevailed short of trepidation at the hour or in the immediate aftermath, I rest advised that I barely hinted at anything at all. Curiosity may with plausibility enjoy ascent as the dominant interest a moment beforehand. It certifiably bred not as unease. Afterward, while it without doubt ought to have relegated me into a tremble, it achieved nothing further than drive me to reason, that as a dispensation it paraded with thorough engrossment. My inquisitiveness neither done me in nor left me fulfilled. That night cited thereafter as a noteworthy circumstance I meditated upon and speculated about, in chief when I got to detect the mutation.

My household as I've passed on already landed not too far

divorced from the township. Our home positioned narrowly more than a stone's pitch from appreciation to its outskirts, but removed enough from the heart to nest in effect as rural. It predicated a comparatively limited expedition by car or bicycle, but a hike on foot might have prevailed as what the old timers claimed as "A Fine Stretch of the Legs". It was a rarity I ever brought about this traipse as the proliferation of limb usage tarried not in the least what I opined as a worthwhile occupation.

The municipality itself totalled decent proportions. It pleased to pass itself off as a city and technically it may perhaps have qualified as one. The interpretation of such has scarcely revised over the years; in accordance, a community of fifty thousand might accommodate the right to brag, but upon my transfer to the Capital a few years since, I defer to a height of accreditation disassociated from that of my fellow townspeople.

It's not my objective to belittle our attractive urban settlement. It served us with a contented world, besides it apportioned an ample selection of eateries, bars, clubs and public houses. In the centre, there billeted the outline of a public park bordered by a count of steeple topped churches, schools for every standard, a cinema, besides a choice of shops. It proved adequate in generosity for comprising much that judged as essential, but maintained restrictions for the person with an ambition of horizons to broaden. Nevertheless, the intimacy and perception of serenity coupled with the inclusion which happens by virtue of being home persists when I revisit.

A check-in with it mirrors an appointment with comfortable

denim. The whole of the town reveals the semblance of snug besides amicable if just for a long weekend. Thus, it controls this recognition that one belongs which bequeaths it with a consideration of hospitality on top of charm that's disconnected from city dwelling. Perhaps at this juncture, in my downcast mood, there survives a measure of pride that enters play and which prefers to sugar coat all ages gone before. But I want for any lament in that viewpoint. I long to recline in the favourable assumptions besides the joyous images I preserve of Waterford while they continue on as mine to sustain.

Accomplishment in the elevation to our residence from the town side entailed the climb of an arduous hill. It roused as steep enough in sufficiency to establish that the self-imposed law of non-elongation of my indolent legs qualified as practically honoured in perpetuity. On a bicycle, it set in motion the mandatory condition of pedalling in first gear. Then, at the summit of endurance, if not explicitly in tip-top fettle one might fast establish it a requisite, to pause for a margin of space and furthermore arrest extra in the way of laboured breaths. I nurse no memory of anybody atop the year of thirty in an exploit of either the tramp or cycle. There belong with obviousness charges in that neck of the woods, supposed best abandoned to the young. Downhill shaped the inverse convention. There commanded without doubt the sight of parties in enjoyment of that defined amble with a broad smirk on their aspect of a summer's day, but they without doubt forever sought to include provisions in store for the converse leg, which in typical fashion mandated a spousal pickup in the family motor.

Robert E. Kearns

The hill plateaued at the apex and then the highway forked into split lines. Our kindred acreage depended on compliance with the branch to starboard. This route ceased to last a main road in the usual mode but instead became a rustic lane of sorts, better adjusted to a horse and cart than an automobile. Again and again I gleaned a thrill when vehicles crossed each other on this tract. By all counts it took place with the anticipation of a crash, or near positivity of damage to the side mirror, given the thickness between vehicles fell no greater than the width of a credit card.

The rightward flank of the byway tabled as a bordered bank of dense grass with emergent brambles, woods and hedges besides; beyond which loomed a weathered farmhouse. The left trusted in bungalows and the sprout of two stories cut off by their insulated parcels of real estate. Most of these land holders seeded Leylandii trees which rose to such a height they almost obscured the homes in full, with in essential just the entrance, cow gate, driveway then a transitory peek of a red brick chimney apparent in passing. It offered in repeat the perception that this habitation planted in the remotest of venues, but in accuracy we entrenched not too distant from the Metropolitan District, as I elect afresh and with cheek to attribute it.

The vicinity persevered in sessions as bleak with reliability amid the ruggedness of an Irish winter. Up on The Heights, storms troubled us with greater malice than in town. We inhabited not as an exception to the general policy of the county, in that we cultivated a wealth of evergreens, both regular besides the golden classes, which encircled both the front and back plots and afforded a dimension of shelter from the barbed gales. Too, with dependence there formed a chunk of isolation in need of resistance which absented itself in summer. It submitted without difficulty to requisition a slide into the status of hibernation for the total of these haggard months, with a bunker down mind-set to wait it out.

A fire of receptive briquette intensity side by side with the television assented as a cordial means of fidelity with an evening of amusement against a bitter clime. It followed not always parallel to that but on the raw drenched nights; the justification to settle indoors was seldom demanded. Spring harnessed the contrast. The deciduous canopy reverted to its glorious state with renewed leaves of the immature kind. Nature stood in bloom with us inundated by every treasure of green imaginable; along with the pigmentation of flowering shrubs besides the emblematic and optical delicacy of rabbits, birds as well as hedgehogs. The primary witness of our star showed in the wee hours, so too downed at the eleventh-hour of night. This marketed as the quintessential environment to encounter all the charms of a country existence, but furthermore apportioned the supplemental boon of continuance a milestone or two from civilisation.

Where it divulged, our rear garden graduated downwards in an easy slope, which facilitated the apparition of that beckoning town in our purview. In wintertime this yielded a volume of harmony besides wellbeing, and therefore on a sharp fine night, I breathed partial to stay seated on the terrace for brief periods to gaze at both it and the stars in unison. New Year's Eve included an extra factor when we maintained the perfect prospect for fireworks at midnight, which identified as the culmination to the annual bash my parents, threw. In summer, the falling sun charged up the sky in traces of red, and those of orange and yellow, to outline the wide clear vista in a style which intoned life adhered to the effortless; what's more, tranquil.

To each side of us there stationed two tier houses, but sandwiched between we inhabited a grand bungalow. I'm not informed why this got opted for in the construction, but everything with simple access propounded its favours. The vanward lawn, identical to the immediate rivalry, came forth as spacious, and it lay hemmed in by the stateliest of trees, while a slithering driveway enrolled then curved to arrive at the angle of the brickwork where it wrapped around in a turnabout point which concluded at the front porch. Without fail I upheld the lawn to exhibit in requirement of a feature, perhaps a fountain but agreed, that may have catered a tad to the side of extravagant. Indeed, a humble flower bed should have resolved to outfit an enhancement, as I understood it lonely for its emptiness. Not so extreme in the summer months, but at other whiles when veiled by what might prevail to reason as oppressive foliage; an enrichment to attend to this spread secured to hold out the promise of felicitous interims to come.

When the clan transplanted to pastures green, the architect by all accounts encouraged my father that to insulate against stray cattle, he positioned a cow gate betwixt the pillared entrance. All the same, for the duration of my tenure I can't summon even once a bovine in a petition to see its route across the threshold. It without a doubt should embody Murphy's Law that failing to introduce such a device would ordain the means to invasion at every opportunity. I rejoice we consented to it all the same, even with the acknowledgment of its most restricted service, as I call to memory the perception inside the car of its passage over the bars, crested with the muffled rattle it transmitted on entry and exit. This aroused a peculiar phenomenon of satisfaction, and too, its hum, although modest, after an absence, by its own tack virtually greeted a Welcome Home on the traverse.

The residence itself subsisted as a four bed affair, all of them outsized compared to city standards where they prevailed with hardly the capacity to swing a broom. It boasted two baths, a shower berth, seldom adopted washroom straightaway interior to the front door, a study, extended sitting space, kitchen, dining accommodation, a relaxed family den, a quarter for utilities, the garage whose sole industry performed as storage. In addition, there disclosed the build of a game apartment or lair where set aside was a pool table, couch, television and music for the young to amuse in. My parent's in general shunned it, except for perhaps two commissions; the initial clocked as the high-point of the civic diary with the alternative that of New Year's Eve. Either the volume of visitors, inclement conditions, or both involved its commandeering on these two engagements.

It conceived nonetheless, for the utmost purpose an extension where, as teenagers we entertained friends. Mounted adjacent to the back end doorway, cropped up a dartboard which until my recent visit home, I continued to adore the childlike pleasure of arrow extraction from the sponge-like numbered grid, where they anchored intact since their last custom.

I scrutinised, and in equal measure controlled my fingertips to feather the stippled and pocked plaster in its vicinity, and translated the language of misplaced shots in the surrendered flakes of paint, where stray missiles dispatched the casualties of friendly fire. Each of them left behind a crater of comradeship with its own biography to relate, and which I endeavoured to cite; amused when I delivered the designates of those pals and kin via a low hushed tone as though they at once manifested as spirits I sought to converse with in a séance. Our home projected that effect, in which it radiated the perception of occupied since universal creation, insofar as ancestors from millennia previous, in their reign paced its halls, and afterward decamped to the study, to dine and wine on its hardwood board of antique.

The living sector enjoyed, set into it, a sizable layout of French picture window inclusive of a hefty egress which afforded the panoramic spectacle of our municipality and with benevolence, far-off to the steeple of the hilltop church in Tramore. The door unlocked to a staircase with a handrail which headed down to the terraced patio and ran end to end the full scope of the abode. This paved rectangle comprised a charcoal grill, a match of seasonal furniture and not to overlook the garden hose which mounted in permanence to the exterior spigot. This readied night and day as my father nursed the continuous requisite to irrigate his garden whether deemed essential not. At the kitchen edge of the dwelling erected a rotary clothes line buried in a metal casing, as despite the evidence we enjoyed a perfectly adequate dryer, my mother preferred; in the summer at least, to air all apparel out of doors.

The yard out back, by the city standards I have at present

gotten used to in Dublin, excelled as huge. As the adage relates, a fellow couldn't do much with a cat in a fair quota of them. In contrast, at home, if persuaded to it, we might well have supported the means to graze a pony. The cut of it ordered a jaunt on the lawnmower which as the facsimile of a power tool, safeguarded that it defined as a chore I bore no grievance with its tackle. When fulfilled, there came about a climate of indulgence for a pursuit acceptably observed, which when escorted by the aura of primitively trimmed pasture, is yet among the purest delights of being. I espoused in consistency to repose in reverence of my venture, through the appropriation of a step above the patio, by custom until well after sunset, there to accept meaningful absorption of the perfumed ether, which I heaved in transition before its moderate and serene exhalation.

Post the metamorphosis, I don't suppose I ever honoured my initiation to the world with the same intensity again. Oh, I revered the odd year, but they seldom influenced with comparable incantation to the referenced affair. These sequel trysts contoured the twin empathy faced, when, as an adult, one yearns to salvage the childhood bliss of Christmastime, but never prevail with the taste of its realisation. The exploit practically forever gives way to the perception of anti-climax. I matured after the transition, and no longer a minor, the cloned escapade fell in each July, except that with its entrance; I cut short the assignment of consequence I one time promised to it. My mother, on the other hand, continued as expected, for a few years anyhow, to invite her circle round for the convivial province. In time though, the emphasis for the most part shifted to the cyclical banquet by itself, with the instrumentation of the usual birthday jubilee demoted to the arrangement of second fiddle.

I've rambled on and there imposes the imminent hour to comply with. I can distinguish through the pane, our star solicits to institute its ultimate descent; and in accordance I must hasten. On that date; which at this hour of record seems to impart a lifespan and better to history, I flew about chock-full of banter and levity. When the sun topped the horizon at six, I emerged with it, eager to extract the full juices of substance the coming hours resolved to favour. I freed the curtains in veneration to establish the skies impressed with its riches, and this destined that sometime into the day, we poised to indulge out-of-doors, with alfresco cuisine tirelessly in conferral of flavours a cut above the in-house variant.

I proceeded to gape out for a bit then thrust clear the side window to catch a gasp of the cool morning air and eavesdrop on the avian fauna in the adjacent branches and prevalent compass. The grass; a tight haircut earned the night prior glistened with microscopic baubles of dew that narrowly disguised the apex of the shortened blades. I yet presumed to trap the vestiges of a prolonged garden-fresh aroma I assumed might express to vanish in the region it equated for the disc to soar within a quarter of its absolute stature.

On the heels of breakfast I attended to the forenoon out back which found expression in the alternation of punting a ball about and the challenge of my father to make certain the grill prevailed in proper order of service. This incorporated his cross-examination several stints over if he set clear there lasted sufficient charcoal in the shed to support its operation into the night.

Robert E. Kearns

Beneath the kitchen ceiling, I carried out infrequent interviews, not to aid with the preparations you understand, but to ensure they progressed to my satisfaction. Later, when the clock swung round to afternoon, and the day declared at its hottest, our invitees embarked on their onset. With the younger lads of a companion age, their parents dropped them off for collection afterward, and then the cousins too announced their attendance, some of whom advertised extensive growth in the duration since I scrutinised them last. Along with these joined the aunts and uncles who in my estimation, even now in the elderly bracket, never suggested in any year to exhibit a wrench of overhaul.

Prior to the cookout we interested ourselves in the typical games that by habit identify with childhood, which where I stemmed from guaranteed the exploit of a rounded ball. The sole person who brandished agitation at this sport defied my father, who kept his well-watered plants to affect anxiety on. He lurked frontward of the flower bed's perimeter, in play as his own goalkeeper, and struggling, at spells poorly, to shut out the object of interest. "Mind the shrubs", he directed to holler, at which in unison kindred to a choir of the church he secured our return to the design of a restrained "Okay". As assurances from ten-year-olds operate, the promise to exercise prudence with a single vow in the affirmative didn't amount to further than the proverbial bean mounded hill. Thus, when summoned by my mother for cake, the county, restricted to its borders, could not gain the escort of a more relieved fellow than the old chap himself.

If there hung on a scrap of the day I frustrated to delight in, this agonised as it. An embarrassment even as a youngster, this persisted as an irritation one was impelled to tolerate, on the basis that any mortification withstood straight away should prospectively be offset through the thereafter disclosure, of donations to the cause. There prevail occurrences in the story of a boy when he resolves to submit emphatically to these plights if there comes about a promised reward at the finish of it; and this rightly stuck out as such a condition. My mother, in contrast, accepted immense delight in the ritual of occasion. Regardless of whether the target of our summons manifested as blindingly evident, it all the same ruled as proper decorum to pretend vague surprise and appreciation at her approach from the kitchen where she bore in slender hands a creation from the bakery with ten lit candles atop its crown of virgin snow.

There rendered nothing for it except to cook up a side of honey-glazed ham and lay on a fastidious thespian physiognomy which vehemently declared "Gosh Mom, you remembered". Then there instituted the veneration in song, where, as they squawked, I counted seconds for the tune's end, thus in facility of the candles' suffocation so I could see once again to the purposeful business. Ah, but we weren't done yet. The frosted and layered sponge had a division to undergo and its distribution to children who devoured the icing but set aside the capital bit. That is, everyone except for me. I entrenched as the anomaly to confirm the law and forever rejoiced in the dispatch of this universal treat, in particular if it got washed down with a carbonated pleasure.

I cradled an appetite to revisit the open air, with the insight it ought to bring about the cessation of unwelcome merriments from then on in. That proved the uncomfortable apportionment out of the way. Somewhat like an appointment with the dentist, it happened as a relief in fathoming I wouldn't need to assume all that tumult again for another year. This promoted straightaway the arrangement for us to ignite charcoal and hence evoked the recognisable bouquet if it might inhabit such a portrayal; the visibility of the raven smoke paramount, there with my father in position over it, a spatula in hand, for no other purpose than to command the part.

This officiates as an imperative vocation of manhood. We must affect intimacy with that we assume, notably when it pertains to grilling. But, when I challenged him if he inspired to put the steaks on, he returned with "It's not ready yet. We've got to wait for the smoke to die down". Of course, that begged the interrogation why if the coals equipped as yet not disposed, he posted base vertical to the fire with a utensil cemented to his clutch? But as I determined myself afterward in age, the ownership of authority in a given situation, or at a minimum disseminating the impression of ascendency, comes equipped with one of its strongest opportunities in the preparation of a barbeque.

If this ordained the Vatican, I might well have predicted white smoke instead of a shadowy exhaust, but as this revealed the event, it signified we reared set to advance. And in contrast to the temperament of anxiety he exposed beforehand with regard to his flora, my father roosted at once in his element. With applaud he disposed there, king of the castle, while his serfs fetched for him on command a frigid beer from the bucket of ice.

Another universal peculiarity shared amongst us men, persists that the minute we are in charge, we seldom aspire to relinquish control, when even a duty of nature should beckon. Three or four ales thereafter, and the urge raises its head, but we resist until the limit of rupture. There endures the suspicion that should we vacate our station, another male, on our restoration, should reveal as having structured the usurpation of our throne.

An alternative actor in the grip of said implement, which only just an instant before might as well have remained welded to his grasp, is akin to a heist of the royal sceptre whereby in means of that carriage, a man declares that he swaggers as lord of all he observes. Thus, when my father signalled to exploit the washroom, so patent a measure of him had that device shaped into; it pained conspicuously to accept its release. "Tolerate nobody touches this", he insisted, and then credited it to me. If there disposed to transpire a solitary crumb in the year where he considered the resolution to race, this determined as it. And God help the person who took up residence in the most convenient lavatory. It ensued as typical for him was to shy away from profanity, but must he be compelled into devoting his custom to the guest closet at the farthest gable of the house, the one contiguous to the front exit, he befell definite to let fly with expletives.

A recollection of the night realised as the cream of being bound up into the package of a few treasured hours, when the immediate sphere restricted to that acre of sod sets itself apart to endure for the occasion, to remain awake to the foremost of life's contributions, and in consequence this raises a lust for it to congeal in that state forever. And as the sun set, the bamboo lamps staked into the turf which neighboured the patio furniture prepared to be set alight, signifying the inevitability of change. The refusal to expire with temperance into that infinite night prevails as a battle not just against the finality of death, but as well in hostility to the demise of our most honoured days. The societal caper of that season obliged as one of them; the strain which refuses to challenge, "Does this elicit everything that momentousness can deed?" but states with a lion's courage, "This trusts to deposit in the bank of extraordinary ages".

I withdrew to bed at an unpunctual hour; jaded but stocked with the positivity it seems nowadays, simply the young maintain with exclusivity. It subsists in those flashes before sleep strikes, where a fellow proclaims that tomorrow will flourish as solid as today, if not better. The future carries the guarantee of an enhanced condition for the uninitiated; authenticity of the ameliorated life our parents aspired for. We hit out to snag it each night and welcome this bounty of the morrow to come, so we might seize, exult in, and capitalise to the absolute, the prospects which accumulate as ours by right.

With this affection only optimism can express, I fell sound asleep near to immediate, bounded by those sentiments, and fantasised in the pool of summer enchantments and fervent sport; a revival of the antecedent period, comprising further of the seasoned fare with the redolence distinct to a searing grill. I'm certain if I could have organised to consider my form from overhead, I should attain to remark on a boy at rest, contended or perhaps even more.

Later, but liable not to extravagant proportions, as the bedroom continued obstinate in twilight, I awoke, in all probability, resultant of a bone parched mouth. It must equate that I earned palpable dehydration from the exertions of the day. Too, by this inference, a thirst divulged to overrun me. I aligned face up to the ceiling; in measurement of the atmosphere, and what came to the fore on my radar detailed the soul of those witching hours derived from the singular configuration of a household in dormancy.

There prevails an ancient endemic instinct common to Man which arrays conscious of this truism, even within an extensive habitation such as ours. And its silence occupies a virtue akin to a proclamation that the entire globe halts in slumber. I contemplated an essential provision, for what at that juncture I deliberated on, should befall as water with life imparting essences; and although cloaked with a near ink black, I nevertheless convened the adeptness to turn down the covers and accustom my slippers without the requisite for illumination. I extended a finger to draw the hindmost section over my heels and then stalked across the carpet in a whisper toward the secured egress.

Without a flip of the light switch for fear of waking a parent or sibling, I tugged at the handle and travailed to dim embryonic commotions in the feat. A hallway travelled the length of the house, and to the left I glided past two sleeping quarters then made for the kitchen entrance which cut in to the opposite wall. At all while it oversaw in a dangle, the key from its lock, which by my father's ceremony; set aimed after dark in default mode to the secured alignment. This contrivance might hazard trickier, I recognised. The mechanism, with superior skill, which is something to specify, I took advantage of many precedents to acquire over my short life; I twisted to the right.

In a bid to not promulgate a clatter, the commission obligated all ten digits, with one steadying the other. There happened an equilibrium point at the top of the turn where if not extra cautious, the apparatus would spring with a clank to the release position. In the scenario I assented to that night, this could devise to behave above that of a hammer against the timbers; undoubtedly by this course of procedure rousing my mother, given both that she dozed softly and because her bedchamber sited next-door to where I placed. With the apparatus swivelled in a hush, an effectuation I immortally reaped endless satisfaction with its discharge; stage two, I understood, exacted yet further care.

The shaft, I steered down. This took hold of another five seconds or thereabouts, which as it eventuated resembled a fair allocation more. Next, with tentativeness I discharged the entryway, bit by measure to avert any squeak from creaky hinges. Through at last, I shut it behind me with the same vigilance, in conclusion landing me on the floor tile of our spacious galley. This apartment, distinct from the corridor, bathed alive in the moonlight which flood through its picture window, the blind of which stayed furled up with reliability.

We set aside two oak bar stools for this area, which deployed for rapid consumption over the work counters. Our principal meals got expended in the dining space adjacent, but this arena subsisted as our spot for tea, coffee and somewhat casually, breakfast. The optimal procedure for me to realise the sink was to haul one of these seats over then scale up it. I registered not lucky enough for either of them to result in convenient radius of the basin. To drag whichever of them direct struck out as an option, owed to the racket it may kick up on the deck. After meditating on this for a second, I started for the more expedient of the two and financed the notion of rocking it back and forth on its hind legs, with the posterior anchored to my chest.

This ingenuity worked a treat and I couldn't help but grin at my supposed cleverness. I clambered up the furnishing then positioned both my knees on the marginally worn lumber, and next twirled the faucet in progression to achieve a moderate flow. Without the squander of a cup, and in selection of the passage with minutest resistance, I committed to what boys and a proportion of men continue to shoot for, and ducked my head under to slurp a healthy swig straight in. "Refreshing" I believe I proposed under my breath. An abundant pride of victory always mounts with the benefit of relief from a thirst, which in promise of that anticipation was beforehand disconcerting. I moved in reward for a second, and then a third gulp. With the assignment wrapped up I embarked on whispered congratulations for its efficient success and disputed about whether to bother with the task and time it should dissipate to restore the chair whence I commandeered it. My kneecaps ached, and when this through evidence progressed, I got impelled to hop off.

The ambiance of the immediate realm distorted. That customary lunar brilliance, the lumens of which threw out sufficient brightness to abet my audit of the situation round and about and to which my eyes happened into adjustment became unexpectedly interrupted by a neon haze. I maintained my hands in a clench of the upright posts to the rear of the stool. Too, I supported a solitary leg projected out as a prelude to my dismount, when I became trapped in its nebula.

My head, in the scheme of a downward enterprise to discern my footing underneath, in reaction, jerked involuntarily towards the casement, thus abandoning me to an awkward pose in resemblance of a Praying Mantis. The broad orifice which stretched in a rectangular contour from this wall to that, entailed hardly a flash ago I achieved an intact and unblemished tableau of the mizzen lot, the garden and yonder to Waterford. However, it was straightaway cast in what may well categorise as an LED green with zero extra discernible past its millimetres of thickness. This unusual sheen conquered the ample slot in its entirety and when I peered about, the immediate space revealed as steeped in the collaborative bizarre timbre.

And yet, I exposed no state of trepidation at the unforeseen tonal disparity; rather, I disposed as drawn to it in a peculiar sort of manner. I delivered the limb which for that handful of seconds protruded at a testing angle, back to its latent distribution, and organised my knee on the relentless hardwood in company with its twin. The pain became irrelevant which obliged its tolerance while the glare persisted. It shifted a mite, not sufficient to startle, but plentiful enough to acknowledge the fluctuation. It styled as the musical equivalent of a rise in octave, or was that a descent in octave? Music has admittedly never carded as my strong suit, but irrespective, the colouration stirred a trifle deeper and harder as if an added bulb came to be snapped on and forthwith adopted a filter to cause a darker tenor.

I flexed in tight to the glass, enlarging my eyelids a notch as I moved, with a determination to establish the beacon's source. In a stretch, so my forehead came within an inch of the pane, I sustained without power to make anything out. There lurked no detail conspicuous beyond that of the incandescence. The aperture might have been painted in jade for all I could perceive, and while I continued to invest application, the discomfort in my juvenile bones cried that perhaps the moment sensed wise to dismount from my perch. This I saw to and massaged the tortured joints guardedly with my young fingers as a means to expedite their resumption to normality. And when I straightened to an upright carriage, repaired with scarcely a minor ache, I settled hands on hips, and reverted to my observations of the plate cavity, with the conviction a phenomenon was resolved to become clear.

It didn't, but all the same there drifted about a curiosity which heightened as I paused here motionless, and in expectation, which prevailed on me to divine from where the irregular visitation originated. And, as one observes when faced with an itch; I determined to scratch it.

From this location there ensued an outlet to the services closet. Unerringly in consistence with the preceding entry, this portal too, continued and alike, stationed at no minute ever without its means of access. In the event one of us flew astray in the recognition of its purpose, it assumed an identifier indistinguishable from all the others, with a plastic attachment on which my father noted 'Utility Room'. He may have lain as more than pedantic in that regard. Every key in the house he tagged, and all of them dwelt in their specific home base, which conformed to the plan he entreated. He kept in reserve the spares, sealed in a cabinet above the washing machine in the aforementioned compartment, hanging limp from their given hooks; all ordered, and all branded in his neat italic script, to bide for the turn they may fastidiously obtain custom. Notwithstanding, in the whole tenure since they took up residence in their modest abode, I doubt for even a single instance that courtesy ever visited.

I came to follow pressed into a repeat of the procedure I beforehand devoted to its kitchen counterpart that for a second price made obligatory, the system of administering both hands to shift the key. When I eased free the door, I proceeded inward to the destined chamber and secured it behind me without trouble. Until this juncture of my being, I've no reason to postulate I tenured as a meticulous individual, but in the later proceedings there elaborated a slant of consolidation to my deeds which applied to a frame markedly more aged. Here, it grew into a necessity for me to trip the switch. At the far end of the span there arose another barred egress, but this one sought a divergent challenge to the previous two. It came braced with a Yale and embodied a security chain for supplementary insurance although I have reservations this particular invention ever imposed much of a defence to any burglar. Still, conscious it establishes in attendance reinforces an attitude of inviolability all the same.

The old man kept hold of an undersized step ladder here, the type a fellow might find benefit from when fetching an arduous to reach item out of a cupboard, or to sweep away cobwebs a spider imbedded in the ceiling corner. I transported this from the side wall where the coats, hats and such paraphernalia draped on brass hooks, and dragged it into place beneath the latch by way of its rubber feet, which progressed all but mum on the resplendent tile.

I unfolded it; climbed two steps then disabled the shackle, factoring to ensure that I fated it to the slot in place of consenting it to swing loose. I absorbed from previous struggles with the trial to force an exit; that a slack metal braid in a muted household, can under precise conditions, sound proportionate in loudness to the peal of church bells. Through exactitude and consistency; in lieu of forcing the catch button, I exerted my thumb and index finger to slide it with tenderness; a practical minimisation to potential din. I coiled the knob to the right and veered the stud aloft to root the trammel in neutral. It proffered evidence of my able and precise reasoning I systemized to consider precautions against the contingency of an accidental lockout.

With competence, I lugged the steps rearward and undid the hindrance. That happened obstacle number two overcome, with impediment count of three to expect. I stowed now attentive to a hemmed-in corridor. An inlet to my left pointed into the garage and games sanctuary. Duly, ahead, but to the side, gave admission to the storage shed. To the right and straight on brandished the primary mode out to the terrace. The clasp and shaft flaunted within convenient reach, faintly below the mid-point. Thanks again to my parent and his policies of perfection, the key manifested in its permanent slot, with a synthetic orange tinged identity clipped to a ring. It applied a label insert which stated, should the public and household entail an absolute compulsion to check, 'Back Door'. Here the LED penetrated the translucent panels of the double-glazed PVC, awarding tolerable vision to plough on with my scheme.

This haft, I elevated, which authorised the internal mechanism to swivel with a flip of the wrist. I next met the capacity to press down on the lever, open the access and penetrate the night air beset with its immediate tinted hue. I delayed on the step awhile, forthwith immersed in this radiance instead of the once consigned charge of a simple witness. And I weathered tranquil and steady, with a confidence and sentiment of purpose which dilated more comprehensively than my years. I guess at present this assuredness for definite came to be instilled, as straight up I couldn't deduce this would have supervened as inherent conduct.

With the capture of what significance I squeezed from the backdrop, my feet stirred for all practical purposes in a spontaneous deportment, as if they clamoured for an exploit to assume. It happened that when I removed to the patio; I turned out to perceive the light had enveloped me not unlike a duvet of dense fog. It cropped up to plug the territory I vacated of late then fed the void about me. I remember judging that disparate from vapour; it produced the effect of a corporeal and material entity.

And it sustained this perception of reassurance it emitted which strengthened the conviction I bore, of its continuance as animated. Also counter to a mist it engendered an arid gas which floated about my shoulders, and despite continuing as unshakable it even so sponsored to induce the tiny hairs on my neck to flutter as if it existed specially to wisp with intent on them. This grabbed as not altogether unpalatable and it might in precise have arisen as a corollary of midnight circulations with a natural, graceful breeze that provoked the effect. But it seemed as if I sojourned in the company of life and it equipped me with encouragement to proceed.

I crossed to the halfway mark of the terrace and pivoted my head to identify the house, in a quest for confirmation it yet arranged there. Nothing could I establish of its main features, aside from the outline through the miasma of jewelled expression. This caused it to appear farther away than the reality, which presumptively should have provided the motive for alarm, but didn't. In the conflicting perspective, away towards the town I suffered powerless to regard, I continued drawn; the entity through its breath on my neck in the just about noticeable waft, informing me I should wander hence. I distinguished the turf at the edge of the lawn with its minuscule droplets of dew twinkling like stars in a night sky, and their pinpricks of intensity persuaded me of the proposed amble's integrity.

My appendages propelled again exerting me over to the rightward border of the terrain and headed for the walkway of stepping-stones which wriggled its way around the spacious kidney profiled bed, which despite my father's champion battles to shelter it from stray footballs, had beheld already the prime of its glory days. There touted incidents when I examined photographs while at its absolute peak, an exhibition of the pristine; seasonal rays framing the exquisite blossomed plantae and shrubs within. It signified in its youth and excellent health, refinement besides the heyday of presence.

Today, though still and all attractive, its expression submitted more analogous of middle-aged than fledgling. The plot, over the years gained maturity through the agent of shabbiness, spreading rough around the edges, with conservation of the lawn victorious in priority over the upkeep of cyclical blooms. The shoots bore unpruned, which exposed the odd lifeless bough. Ornamental trees sprung fuller than they should and overshadowed the undergrowth. Established perennials, yet extant bore the scars of decay, culminating in more than a hint of gnarled greys and browns accommodated within the pretty blush of recent expansion. Weeds too snagged a toehold in spots where beforehand they in near automation got defended against. The indulgence and bliss from times departed it one time communicated, and a customary preference for the family snapshots, subsisted nowadays albeit still availed of somewhat for that purpose, cast no longer the picture postcard of yesteryear.

The flagstone's too realised their age of prestige long ago, and I revived the portrait of my father quartered atop them as goal tender the previous afternoon. It used to prevail they flashed sharp and polished with the sun darting off the surface in summer, and where the foliage-like detail stood out against the proximate lush grass with colour all about. The winters since they came to be laid weathered them comparable to the adjacent parcel. Moss claimed root in the icy damp of those cruel months and even in these, the lengthiest days of June, it survived. The inset adornment that when in its original state dominated, today put up with pilferage and in-fill, consenting merely to the vague discernibility of its contour through sodden fur. The unconquered segments of sandstone, having ridden out terms of splattered mud, the rot of stray grass cuttings and the stern Irish climate, persevered today as defiled and sunken; in a demonstration that paradoxically; digression weathers as a constant of being.

This roundabout trail, not of yellowed brick, but of a drab olive hue, appealed on me to pursue it. The condensation which remained yet to be born on the secluded meadow was however accrued interior to the imbedded lichen, confirming it slick under foot. The rubber-soled slippers I put on, despite the evidence they held up as not at all ideal for out-of-doors wear, coped adequately with the conditions. I paused mid-way to gander all round once over and explore the organism's source. It evaded my endeavours, and all I picked up was the sweetness of a night stock abloom close at hand. All struck me as the equal, neither brighter nor obscurer in any particular spot; a consistent murkiness that outwardly brooked no starting point or line of finish.

At the bottom shelf of the garden, there bore a rectangular parcel which swept from one boundary to the other partitioning itself off from the rest with a miniature wall of two blocks high. Here we propagated strawberries which stayed looked after with vigilance, and a few other bits and pieces to partner them. To the right of this sector in the exact rear corner of the yard stood the greenhouse. The allotted intention for it posed in the husbandry of vegetables, but as with the best-laid schemes, a lack of chance on the part of my father and stunted interest springing from the rest of us, it contrived short benefit from its mission. Except for a handful of excellent pots in which there flourished tomato vines, it resisted as more apt to secure recruitment as a breed of conservatory. The lone motive why the above-mentioned fruit came still to be nurtured, transpired because of the love my mother embraced for them in season, fresh and ripe off the stem. The lone task yet executed with dependency and delicacy by my father in those limited months, upheld to select and present them to her in a deep wooden bowl as an essential ingredient for sauces, salads and sandwiches; a ritual which afforded them both equal cheer.

As I conducted tracks down the spongy quilted artery I recalled those harvests, plump and juicy and primed for selection. It came about this impression which enticed me to orient the curves towards the aedicule of glass. My father in recent times stashed a table and chair in its dimensions as a substitute for the crops which in summers previous filled his dreams. In the months of spring and autumn by routine he ensconced interior while in the open-air it leaned to the margins of cool. I suspect it passed as his escape for an hour or two from domestic activity, with men now and then entailing a preference to remain detached with their musings. He might once in a while from the vantage point of the French windows of the living room be revealed drifting down to it, and in the conveyance of a mug for travel laden with coffee. And every so often, smoke from a fine cigar rose to cloud up the nucleus which promoted an advisement he sought an extra special want for solitude.

The fittings of the sometime hot house came into sight noticeable direct through the frame; with the inside ostensibly independent of the shrouding leafy tint elsewhere. I made for the interior through the front door and considered the terracotta vessels encumbered with their bulging matured produce. On the table there abided a transistor radio with its

antenna extended, a plaything my father backed as
fundamental to digest a game of sport. I stood by with
composure in the translucent space while the verdant hue with
diligence hugged tight to the panels outside instead of
circulating the inner. Overhead, there disclosed elongated
windows all of which positioned agape for ventilation, and as I
maintained my gaze in the direction of the fruit garden, I
perceived that above my line of sight the conscious presence
commenced its influx through one of these apertures. It
poured in sluggish like, indistinguishable from a thick, viscous
cake mixture, and with devotion as if somebody had borne a
knife to scrape off the recommended measure, it tore away
from the main body without and by several criteria forged into
a contour redolent to a glob of lime green bread roll.

With a strain of my neck, I arched backwards to gape at its
profile, and as I accomplished this; it seemed to turn on itself
clockwise. In rotation, it sped up and with this acceleration
developed a void in its centre, the newly organised ingredient
threatening that of a ring doughnut. This anomalous halo
tarried overhead in precise, whirling faster but devoid of
cacophony, to clench me transfixed in its odd beauty. I realised
my entire body fluttered in a tingle as if an electric current
came to be run through it, and with a request of the episode to
mind once again, the substance must have behaved like-
minded in style to that of a generating dynamo.

This sensation intensified as the orbicular cloud augmented its
velocity and I stopped rigid; rooted to the spot with my
muscles tense and taught from the voltage. With an
observation upwards and with my head and torso contorted, I
might have owned the guise of a prized tomato creeper in its

quest for sparse sunlight. The spectre of constraint next initiated a disturbance in the atmosphere; in resonance, to play out a melodious note duplicate to the rub of a moist finger along the rim of a goblet. It supervened then that a sonic jolt rocked me. Secured too, mixed with the tinnitus in my eardrums, arose a disturbance with an impressive comparison to a bolt of thunder, all of which provoked my rigid frame to go limp all at once. The muscles that rigged as otherwise sturdy from routine exercise, ceased to operate, inducing me to sink to the floor, where I settled amongst crisp, dead and withered leaves, in perfect unconsciousness.

The cheek on the right-hand allocation of my face proved frigid. I lay prostrate, in conquest of the province I hitherto collapsed; where on the rousing of my eyes, I forthwith revealed that the insulated portion of my body stayed heated while its opposite I intuited as coldish; this flank in sufferance of a modest numbness. I boosted myself up, and as I located the chair, adjudged it might be prudent to employ at recuperation for a minute or two. I'm not sure if before then I ever pondered to any remarkable scope, but consequent to the theft of an abbreviated rest, bore compelled to deliberate for a spell.

With a survey thereabouts, I distinguished the dyed manifestation had vanished. A feline wailed from some unidentifiable co-ordinates as the complexion of the heavens began its metamorphose, a harbinger that our sun entered its phase of ascent. I rose up then tested for physical damage, of which there resulted none as far as I could decipher. The solitary ill effects I perceived abided that I seemed to inhabit a condition of fatigue, so too a symptom of light-headedness.

I became reminded of the symmetrical embodiment and conjectured what it served as. With a verdict to sleep on it, which yielded as another characteristic of the obscure, I cut open to the exterior and advanced up the meandering pavement; in consideration of the sward and its pristine dew which now projected sharper with the primary suggestion of dawn. I almost deemed it a minor feat with my attendance face to face with the rear access. Once accounted for, I reversed all the moves I selected beforehand, satisfied in appraisal that by this continuance I kept hold of all my faculties in the enactment of precautions to not kick up any rumpus.

I admitted myself to the bedroom then secured the door behind me without fuss. Next, I hesitated for a spell, sensing the provision to meet with a follow-up examination. But it established not an injury as such I searched for. I delivered an introspective suspicion I ingrained as somehow adjusted, and on looking over my nightclothes, an intuition affected my perception they appeared in the main as childish in expression.

I figured absolute there and then on their expulsion, and amid this accomplishment, they imprinted to my mind the characteristic of inanely ridiculous. Not partial to plunging into the sack unclothed, I crept over to the chest of drawers and withdrew a pair of underwear. They sanctioned shy of what I intended in precise, reasoning perhaps that should they have exhibited as available I would for sure have preferred boxer's as I regarded my father attire in. Be that as it may, my repository didn't comply as the custodian of such a garment, so I recognised the commission fell to the next best alternative.

Robert E. Kearns

After slipping under the duvet, I rested for a short time face up to puzzle things over, and yes, I pondered on them too. That which I encountered earlier denoted my introduction to the primary change, and even if I suffered not to understand it for a spell, my instincts apprehended something engendered an alteration. In a rummage through my thoughts respecting what transpired; I drifted off into sleep and dedicated thought to our house on The Heights with its ties to the land; farmed, worked and lived on for countless generations. My spiritual attachment to it emerged that night, and in the succeeding years when I called there after my self-imposed eviction I interpreted that I journeyed back to a home that had forever been such, both for our kinfolk and to others before us. It kept on as a reminder if I ever sought one that life persists in transformation, with permanence an illusion. What we judge today as either the inception or finale is none of these. It goes on simply as a cogwheel in the eternity of revision, with the continual brushed over afresh on the canvas of flux.

The amendments which ensued may consent in resemblance to a meat slicer in reverse. Instead of the narrow subtraction of trivial sums which independent of each other shouldn't represent consideration, they combined in a measure that came to find recognition all at once. I moulded into manhood brisker than the rule; associated with the push of an implied fast-forward button. True, there countenanced biotic advances, which would have taken effect anyhow, ensuring that I placed not altogether peculiar; and yet they happened untimely for a boy my age. I entered a spurt of growth. So too; my voice broke and hair embarked on expansion in areas new. But all this extended as physical. There implanted, in proportions, mental progress besides the augmentations which accompanied it and they boarded me on the express line to adulthood.

I discerned to start with that I came to be thrust into grasping notions at a speedier clip than my peers, but with pains to fit in, fabricated in some practices to not align on this course. Their entrenched the consciousness I systemized in a discordant approach. The competence to act out sameness secured a further hint I lunged ahead of equivalents in adolescence. I appreciated it declared as pretence and though conscious I lingered in boyhood; I verged intellectually to those somewhat senior. Stemming from that, I taxed to devote extra congress in the company of grownups and less with those of my actual age.

My interests as well became varied in a style that was not attendant until then, and might in some aspects have been allied with a personage more aged. It assumed the form of aberrant that an expanse of the home I otherwise hadn't dispersed a pittance of attention to anterior to the event, reformed into a draw for me. My father's study, hardly off the lounge area sited as where he compiled a never applied set of encyclopaedias. They loomed in pristine condition; an uncle of his, upon expiration, gifting them to him in his will, heedful he one time revealed admiration in his teens. The covers and spine exhibited as attractively bound and even the original owner it seemed on no occasion ever turned a leaf. They remained sealed in a built-in American oak cabinet with glass windowed portals which countenanced the inspection of its volumes, all in meticulous order and with the incorporation of supplemental editions acquired afterward; the entire array however, amassed in the decade of the 80s.

Robert E. Kearns

On evenings and on in to the weekends, I showed up in here to deposit on the solid high-back chair with its sturdy arm rests that accompanied the handsomely crafted mahogany table, conceived by my maternal grandfather. In general I hit on a topic of attraction extracted the text which pertained to it, then launched into its investigation. My thirst for knowledge increased, and as it deepened, so too did I prize more the supremacy of the bound copy to my touch and the spices of the typeset page that cannot attain replica on any computer. All sorts of themes tempted me, but I sanctioned an especial magnetism for antiquity. I reviewed cultures, countries, and civilisations. As I pored over these chapters, I scribbled notes with attention to issues for further consideration onto the extensive desk calendar which doubled as a scratch pad my father kept at the head of the desk.

There founded alongside, as a derivative of these self-taught lessons, a fascination with atlases. As I gained acquaintance with foreign territories, I recognised that I'd chase through page after page of every folio of map I could apply endeavour to. In all practicality it mushroomed into an obsessive compulsion to adhere to the boundaries of ancient empires and to absorb enlightenment with regard to the people's interior to those borders. I also testified to a preoccupation with the mythical worlds of the Classical and Celtic traditions and so referred to numerous publications on the folkloric. This continuous foundation course of the antique afterward contributed to modules in history and archaeology at the university, at length commending me to the Museum where the second transition originated.

The original adaptation arrived with other more salient new talents. An aptitude, which perhaps at the outset of my story affixed rudimentary at best, besides constructed purely on instinct; in its place grew to ensconce as sophisticated in plenty. I learned that in the direct companionship of another; I controlled dominion over the distinct skill to discern what settled in captivation of their thoughts. Ought they to remain silent, I could tap into their deliberations, and should they dispose into conversation, I engaged the means to cross-reference their comments against the bona fide ruminations, thus assessing if they took pleasure in the craft of deception.

I undertook an amount of contemplation on this freshly won novel prowess, which in conjunction with prior evaluations obtruded as a sign I journeyed on the steam train of evolution to adulthood. I intuitively comprehended I mastered the knack of tuning into others in a comparable method that one would adjust into a radio station. I supposed I must have conditioned some kind of electro reception linked to the denominator applicable to sharks. As a technique for predation, they, over millennia evolved a pervasive sensitivity to the electric cues given off by their prey. I formed the premise that while not in quest of a target; I earned as a component of the modification the outcome of not just alertness to impulses but also cultivated the ingenuity to disentangle and decode the instructions incorporated within the nerve signals of human subjects. As a translator might interpret languages, so too, I eventuated adeptness at deciphering the reams of data universal to us all.

Impelled, with regularity I practiced in the status of anyone who hopes to sharpen up a specialty devotes training to realise it; and as with superior wine I emerged as more effective with maturation. There trailed behind it, some self-reflection too in that I contemplated why I sustained a distinction. I appreciated from their speech patterns and the interpretation of their cognitive expressions that all the people I came across in those years dwelt inactive with the reciprocation of my expertise. That is, they did not enjoy the facility, apart from a limited base variant, to apply onto me as I exerted on them. In this respect, I persisted alone, and it took place because of the change. An answer didn't show up with ease why uniquely I proclaimed in receipt of this gift, but I calculated perhaps that if I debated on it, I may duly render evident a theory which should disclose its reason.

To begin with, I started from the postulation all humans at one time owned the identical qualities that right now implied as exclusive to me. If that illustrated the circumstance, those capabilities since got surrendered, or toned down to such a magnitude, they in effect no longer survived. If this defined as correct, I inquired why a powerful distinctiveness such as this should perish. It may credibly have come down to a collection of motives such as population growth, which perhaps decreed the aims for entailing it to occur weakened. This by feasible means ensued when hunter-gatherer tribes who, in their primitive conducts and over generations believably relied on it for endurance against rival groups, for it to afterwards ripen out as their numbers expanded and dispersed over the earth.

I proceeded not in thorough faith of the soundness behind that suspicion which is why I probed further. I exercised an inbuilt switch that permitted me to swap on and off this functionality, so as I weighed it up, I perceived this should occur as a metamorphic upgrade rather than the restoration of a primitive technique. That would seem to point to the reverse of my leading hypothesis. I could, on those grounds, breathe as the original in what may well transpire as commonplace in humanity. If as predicted, I hurried on an accelerated introduction to the coming of age, was it reasonable to expect that by a similar agency I endeavoured on a highway towards evolutionary intensification?

This contributed in turn to the proposal of a third alternative. Or to be more precise, the third option might in fact comprise a combination of both. If I accepted as gospel, men subsist as nothing other than cultured animals, conscious of their own presence and mortality; it follows that jibed with other creatures such as the above-mentioned carnivore of the seas; they retain intrinsically the fundamental building blocks to encourage sophisticated receptivity. In other words, the rudimentary never edged beyond that. Neither however, was it ever destined to meliorate, as it stopped short of the imperative in developmental terms, except for perhaps what we may well attribute as an undeniable wariness or gut reaction. That effectuated to imply therefore, more accurately than myself created as first in line because of an inevitable, preordained transpiration, in its place I chanced to meet with an alteration grounded in genetics.

There weathered a precedent for this rationale. Eugenic glitches surfaced before this in specific clusters, clans as well as confined populations. Through localisation and lineage prevalent to the same familial group, these imperfections came to subsist as inherent to that assemblage. A renowned illustration of this class of mutation is to encounter witness in a precise region of Mexico, where entire bands betray a wolf-like syndrome, its ubiety expressed with copious hair follicles which cloak their entire profile and body. This characteristic emanated as the explicit repercussion of a hereditary gene. It schemed by virtue of an isolated flaw where bearers of the protein advance it on to subsequent generations.

In contrast to trepidation, I luxuriated to brood on this delicious poser regarding transmissible irregularities. It sanctioned my mind's eye to roam; furthermore, it whetted an appetite for the sciences. Not quite up to the grade of my preoccupation with cartography, I still reserved a yearning to investigate DNA and genetic coding. Besides this I took measures to instruct myself on the ecology of unique creations, with sharks and rays in contribution of special emphasis, given the erstwhile marriage between their proficiencies and mine. Mammals such as bats prospered likewise as curiosities in that they educed a breed of echo location which aided them in the pursuit of spoils. Within the reptile genus, snakes too, glide after the kill through the application of their forked tongue followed up with the reaping of minute scent molecules. Through this stockpile of scholastic ammunition, I joined in the shoot for verification that nature disposes to afford exceptional calibres to particular faunae.

If I resolved to accept the third selection from my philosophies as the most expected to elucidate this raised condition, it nevertheless set down the demand as by what procedure my genetic material had fundamentally altered. It reverted anew to the night I ventured to the transparent aedicule, or to stay pedantic with reference to it, the morning of my sojourn to the end limits of the garden. The vicissitudes derived from the verdant radiance and as a consequence it was expedient to conclude that it somehow happened as the source of reprogram for either a single one, or perhaps multiple genes.

I tossed back and forth the ball of argument and debate with respect to the scientific evidence for my introspections. A return did not flaunt itself how I secured refashioning; purely that it materialised. If the act dressed as deliberate, there inhabited besides a Why which hadn't been clarified. Fairies, witches, magic, and changelings which typified as the predecessors of all objective analysis empowered no truck for redress in this affair. Humans persist on with the retention of a tendency to look to the supernatural when endeavouring to clear up the unexplainable; when in the majority of instances the answer disentangles with the strength of reason. Even those impasses we can't expound, shelter only as accepted unknowns. That is, we recognise the result lingers as elusive today, but this doesn't translate that at some stage in the future the solution will prevail as an enigma.

For my part, I got accustomed to the reconstruction, even as I conceded the keys to that deviance survived as an accepted mystery in the current, but with hope, perhaps tomorrow not continue in the lock of bewilderment. I shall digress for a pause, as I pen this in the study of what disclosed as my parent's home, with the flame of the day at the vanguard of its wane, to exclaim that a new blush of dawn has declared its promise.

My dreams of yesterday subscribed to a degree of the light, so too I reserved a supply of them in crisp besides potent vitality on arising. In my slumber I revisited the early hours in question; where I embraced the moss furnished duct of stone with the texture of its plushness in imprints under heel. I sensed again the taste of the cool air on my exposed skin besides the suggestion of dew beads on the immaculate pasture; the condensation which enveloped me analogous to a gothic cape. I beheld the globule of tinctured plasma seep through the enticing means of greenhouse entry where it revolved over my pillared structure; too the turbulence of the cloned blitz whereupon I collapsed to the leaf-strewn floor.

So also, there interposed reveries which deciphered more kindred with remote flashbacks; never ostensibly in the present-day. There featured a separateness to them as if their motive was to regenerate as well as afford connotation to acts which came to pass at an age of infancy; fragmented; moreover, in shadows, demanding concentration besides resolution. On top, there flashed an intuition in these apparitions which all but lent the idea that as opposed to central to them, I supported in essentially the character of understudy.

The places emerging as visually familiar factored at the same time as disconnected. On many a night during my slumber, I walked the chambers and corridors of our home, everything in its rightful place; the tone of paint on the walls, the carpet, the sitting room sofa; all presenting as they should except in the expression or aura I detected from them. What I perceived was an abiding non-acquaintance with this illusion I roamed. For that is what I grew to think of it as, a phantom of sameness but lacking the intimacy of reality.

There endured passages when I solicited to evaluate these

features of the abyss; too examined if there espoused an association with the wondrous aberrations. I suspected this much, but in a sense I lacked the capacity to comprehend. As for the dissection of my representations, with a tenuous grip I clutched onto morsels of explanation that even if within tantalising strike, disposed comparable in separation to a word based on the tip of a tongue.

I strained, and as I pressured, the explanation retreated. I conjectured there sustained a purpose to every innovation I underwent since the transformation, and divergent from static or stable, it insisted in lieu to advance to a result. I likened it in rhythm and duration to a program download as this abided as the sole analogy that came to the fore with my limited insight.

As an update transfers from the internet, the operator nevertheless enjoys the advantage of his computer, hence when finished; it next commences its installation. In the approximation of a tune which bounces around the insides of one's head, once I came to count these adventures as the resettlement of knowledge and data, I stood powerless to extricate it.

Robert E. Kearns

Part 2 – Hy Brasil

Water Ford, Hy Brasil-139 B.C.E.

Olan continued hidden away in the confines of his study. It suffered a winter's evening, and this situated as the compartment he withdrew for as a retreat post supper. As well, it served as an office for the conclusion of paperwork he hadn't gotten to during the day. Tonight he happened on a pursuit which on the whole he wouldn't organise. That is, he fetched in with him the remainder of a second allowance of wine he took pleasure in with the night's repast. His desk confessed as mahogany, handcrafted and polished to a rich lustre, and contrasted with the western oak cabinets immediate to its fore. He positioned upright in the paired armchair, the chalice in his left hand; so too with its consort, he apportioned a printed note.

He accepted the entrance ajar as usual, as even while engrossed he favoured to catch the harmonies of family plus those of general activity drift in, shutting it solely if on a telephone call. He regarded it now in speculation if he ought to secure it, not insofar as he craved privacy, but since the echoes he by the norm appraised as a comfort prevailed instead as a disturbance. He placed the sheet down then reached for the treated lumber to trace below his fingertips, its sculpted and intricate perimeter; complete with triskeles and leaf-like carvings. This, Olan time and again enacted as a means to capture peace of mind from the complex artistry.

The desk transpired, in fact, as a table shaped by his wife's father, a master in the skill of furniture design, and inherited on his death a decade or more past. It asserted as a facet of him nowadays and he sustained a weighty attachment to it which extended beyond sentiment. However, it languished full with clutter, passing it as impossible to view, never mind appreciate its beauty to the maximum. Over the years it gathered more than dust and even if no longer essential or sought, this administration nevertheless accomplished with innumerable cases to linger in one or other of the various piles that accumulated without end. To the side offered the phone extension which he fitted from the time the house came to into being but today rebuffed heavy service. Layered sediments coated the hand piece as proof of redundancy.

A fire blazed in the adjacent accommodation, and though he couldn't survey it, made good on an abstract perception of its flaming hearth. He stayed definite against closure of the door, instead banishing what he measured as interruptions to picture the lighted coals besides intense flames of solace. The sitting area represented either out of a pair the household removed to after dinner. The alternative declared the family room, and on any given evening his wife and children established in whichever of them they fancied, besides on occasion drifting between the two. Tonight, his wife settled on the flickering glow. In accordance, she arranged snug on the sofa which neighboured it, in sight of the television. Olan bided as keen to acknowledge Neelak adjourning in proximity; therefore yielding to crack free the access door consented to this succour. Tonight, he perched grateful to have commanded immobility on the initial impulse to exile her presence.

Just now he suffered preoccupations to his attention. He again selected the paper, straightaway regretful he abandoned the earthly trait of the mahogany with its engraved ridges. He twirled the stem of his glass between thumb and forefinger, to swirl the ruby liquid around its base as an essential to keep busy his limb, besides allowing for the prediction of flavour enhancement. He deposited the commentary from where it originated as if suffering in fresh to disturb it, ascertained it too heated to preserve. The space straightaway to his front survived the lone section free of assembled paper stacks which through insistence took over the rest of the board. The lone concession to this island of tidiness lurked a desk calendar appointed to scribble down deserving annotations.

Promptly inflicted with a solitary, idle hand he transferred the wine from left to right, and with this accomplishment, in place of headache elimination, merely shuffled it about. A distraction was crucial to side-line this peeve, so he urged up the goblet to catch the incandescent light which kindled overhead. The effect triggered a stimulant to the mind of Olan as he regarded it sparkle on the rim of the tumbler besides how it mitigated the splendour of the deep vintage.

This presented not among the finest of his wineglasses and he enabled in brisk as regretful for not having exploited one. The finest cut crystal he reserved in the lounge nearby advertised in a splendid cabinet which showed off numerous bespoke pieces and decanters and vessels for all possibilities. Olan maintained an extensive affinity for arts of all kind, so too he attached resolutely to the superiority and the touch of details finished by hand. The application of a chiselled wooden repository for these treasures endured in his judgment as an absolute fundamental; as a result he arranged the purchase of elegant display units for such intent. The character of continental oak and alternative natural materials resolved as a technique for Olan to preserve a spiritual as well as emotional connection to the domain prized by his forefathers.

With a tip of the head backward, to savour its flavour equal to a connoisseur in advance of swallowing it down, Olan rolled around on his pallet, the residues of fluid nectar. He ought to request more of this specific vintage he mused. There traded a wine merchant in town who for as long as he could recall supplied his penchants, and hence he ordered in recurrence by the case. He exposed a reluctant chuckle which broke for a spell the dark mood he stood affected by. He suited up as middle-aged these days and no longer able to put it away as in his youth. If he procured a dozen of this label, he reflected, it would rack up a year to finish. "One a month" he declared with a smile. "It used to comprise such in a day". Olan cherished to jest with the children when recounting, "twenty years ago, I might contemplate to drain twice this measure". The joke got to correspond as lame however when to a similar extent he took advantage of it in relation to meals. It hosted as his enduring party piece and by custom he recited it in the assemblage of visitors, forgetful he related it on the prior instance of their company.

With the goblet straightaway bare he debated whether he should dispatch the bottle, remarking in quiet that for the second time this evening he was about to transact in an alien business. For all the talk of an aptitude for sinking immense quantities of alcohol in his heady youth, Olan absented his study from anything apart from coffee. He persevered with discipline in this regard. This space in effect functioned as an annex to his usual office, and as such obliged single-mindedness which otherwise would suffer sacrifice should he partake of that above medicinal to the exotic bean. A tumbler of wine or a beer with dinner was one thing but his inherent pedant ensured that on a work night he took up a beverage then concluded with it in the dining area.

Despite his propensities toward routine; which computed as a congenital mannerism as opposed to an acquisition with maturity; Olan, when he absented from customary toil, fostered a more relaxed attitude to his personal rules, so too, bid once in a while to appreciate in a state of overall ease, a drop of wine or surrogate adult libation. With an icy evening such as this, he bore it by tradition to the fire and reposed with Neelak. Tonight, what in typical exerted to provoke an internal conflict familiar to the obsessive, instead gave way to a nonchalant resignation that even if it claimed as a night attached to his employ, it didn't matter all that much. Hence, desirous of a touch more; too, revealing a rarity in the withholding of apprehensions about it, he shoved back the heavy chair and established his approach for the exit.

Olan landed in the sitting quarter and moved expeditiously so as not to interrupt Neelak's view of the television and for the secondary goal of an aspiration to circumvent a trial of wits. Her eyes darted up, the encroachment of her husband a distraction, but with mercy for Olan, remained silent. He scurried by, past the French doors which opened onto steps that served the terrace below and so dissenting to hesitate at his now under-used but elegant bar on the left-hand side of the expanse, in its place he released the panelled ingress which connected to the chamber for dining and shuffled through.

His superior wines Olan stashed in a secret cellar entrenched with cleverness beneath a sofa in the family precinct, but he furthermore saved a fridge for his white's in the neighbourhood he now stationed. Tonight he nurtured a red, and as a creature of habit, with all he owned in occupation of its station, these, when uncorked, he let rest on top of yet another sideboard backed on to the right face. There ordained not to pursue a demand to call on the vault until the prevailing came about as thoroughly emptied, and in benefit of positioning it here of late, assumed it wouldn't present a factor in his solicitations again until the following supper.

He explored its ingredient through the opaque green, by angling it in the overhead field of light; then determined there lapped ample within for his scheme. "It calls to be expended anyhow", he pronounced, which emerged with particular convenience as this encompassed his ambition. He did away with the stopper, instigated the pour; plus never a fellow to exhibit waste, he sustained the vessel tipped more or less upright, in assurance his glass appointed to take in the final lingering drops, even down to those which clung by their own tension to the rim. These he amputated with a repetitive tap on the bottle's arc, which came greeted with a sedate plop into the trusted arms of the ruby red liquor.

There passed an undertaking by Olan of virtually all charges with precision. Even the clutter in his study indulged an element of exactness to it, in that he incessantly recognised where it all lodged and corralled. He affected his chalice to settle on the place mat, toted the empty carafe into the kitchen to rinse, which he afterward conveyed to the utility closet where he set aside a bag for recycling. Olan at all times washed out the wine bottles by exploiting this technique, so too always before the resumption of his tonic. It extended as a proclivity held on to from his bachelor days. This sack of convenience he destined to combine with the principal salvage bin, which he stowed away in the garage. Olan contrived an assumption these may persuasively demand to be lugged out for collection, but this stretched as a measure too weighty for right now.

Instead, he vacated for the dining chamber, plucked up in transit the goblet loaned to a coaster then re-entered the generous atrium. There, Neelak accredited to recline on the sofa immediate to the near subdued fire, yet in heedfulness of her show. Olan expected her commitment to this resolved to allow him make it back to his study exclusive of comment, but no sooner than he laid touch to the handle, assented to a message-'Did you take the trash out?' 'No Darling' emerged the response directed in return without the benefit of tongue. His two principle rejoinders when it came to his wife in general counted as boiling down to either 'Yes Darling' or 'No Darling'.

In trust that his concise report breathed sufficient, but hastening inside the office with a mind for contingency of the antithesis, he operated as most men behave in comparable positions, with the struggle to evade spousal interrogation; and that ensued, to make his-self scarce. It abstained in coming to pass, however. Wives as a scarcity in this conflict of faculties give up with such handiness; thus, before he earned the security of his mahogany chair, tackled interception of the inevitable follow up broadside, which entreated what transacted that he took care of. 'Simply, the refill of my glass darling' he commented in return. 'The bins demand hefting out front. Tomorrow is collection day'. 'Yes, darling' he murmured. 'Are you not carrying them outside?' 'I shall, darling, very soon'.

And, as men the earth over suffered to covet for aeons, that this wholly sufficient, besides logical explanation, resolved to spawn a wrap to the inquisition, he consigned his curative to the board, and prepared to hunker down. Yet, as is almost forever the berth in these exchanges, with husbands in occupation of the misfortune to appreciate it over the ages; for the female gender this falls as an utterly inadequate clarification, which begged yet another probe Neelak itched to impart 'When?' she tested. 'Shortly darling' Thus, while Neelak endured sorely desirous to once more prospect into the next obvious challenge, she instead exclaimed humph! On this occurrence though, in place of a telepathic communiqué, she intoned it under her breath.

With the attainment of a minor but somewhat limited victory, Olan raised the stem in a toast, and then partook of a congratulatory sip. After this transient feast of permitted glory, the lustre faded with alacrity, to start over replaced with the sombre frame of mind he beforehand licensed. He pitched rearward into the chair, practically slouching in posture; a carriage not straightforward to accomplish in a rigid article such as this; then lowered his eyes; straight off at an awkward and uncomfortable angle; to scan over for a second spell the epistle he beforehand perused.

Without its disturbance or of a resolution to correct his slump;

Olan instead balanced his potion of the vine on the armrest and perceived over again the written text; almost expectant the words suffered a variance in the span it took to refresh his tumbler. Then, he maneuvered for the underside of his chin and caressed the prevalent goatee which he honoured a penchant for effecting when in contemplation. He withdrew his absorption from the document and gaped out to space in its stead. It inhabited this point when he considered the non-verbal conference with Neelak he arrayed a party to a short while past, so soon thereafter he inaugurated into contemplations which pertained to the exceptionality of the country as well as its population.

Hy Brasil; an eponym that when measured against the record of our planet in totality, emanated as novel to it. Experiencing to withstand unendingly, so far as there survives permanence in this universe, it marshalled a spring to its unveiling within the past century as it became apparent on the charts of established nations. Olan thought this appreciably ironic, given that Hy Brasil dominated as the foremost of them all. He restored from nothingness to fixate on the cup which he bared anew to the bulb overhead in obedience to the beams which floated in pirouette on its fringe. The potation he took pleasure in; another product of modern ages; the grape, not indigenous to Hy Brasil; obligated import, alighting on trade schooners which formerly called to the Italian peninsula.

These amphorae continued in wide application, a feature in those provinces of cultivation to the south and east; too, it was in these jars it carried out its passage across the ocean. Upon mooring, the vessels came to be unsealed, then the wine bottled for regional distribution. Olan lodged as favourably pensive of the simplicity but brilliance of the glass bottle, so too, how this minute progress expressed by its own ingenuous style the superiority of his birth land. Ahead of this observation, his mood swung to sombre in the acute, as he speculated what implications might ensue for Hy Brasil to the news reaped of late.

On an alternative night, should he conclude with exhaustion from the grindstone of officialdom with it all the same too soon to call it a day, he graded as virtually certain to shift from the study into one or other hallow of disengagement. A windswept evening such as this would deal the perfect excuse to settle in an armchair, in the company of therapeutic coals for the hour or so in advance of hibernation. It made up a component of his routine to formulate a coffee from newly ground beans; another consequence of the far eastern posts of commerce; then spread butter from the creamery on a hunk of thick bread and take solace from both while attentive to the late evening news on television. Tonight however, he delayed, reluctant to vacate the study, needful of continuing in isolation with his meditations.

He opened his recollection to the accepted history of Hy Brasil. Olan turned out a scholar, so in resemblance with a sundry of science professionals, wielded curiosity on a heap of subjects. Education prevailed as the passion of his youth, a phase of being when he rejoiced in the time for inquisitiveness. He examined books on innumerable topics, thus may some time back have gotten spotted in the library at school brushing up on the generations of yore, as well as on questions of geography, politics, economics and alternative disciplines of fascination. His brain behaved complementary to a sponge and

Olan as typical preserved and gained from that he researched. His academic proficiency meant there evinced no doubt of his participation at university, the sole issue permitting, what should come to pass as his field of application. Even in the present day, Olan's zest for inquiry hadn't waned, with just the constraints of everyday vexations throwing up a barrier. Still, he achieved what he could; hence the reception of an untidy desk, sequestered in excess of a solitary periodical imbedded within its otherwise dull paperwork.

The renewed wine survived barely touched, the repository instead substituting for an article with amulet like properties. He gaged that by an ever so delicate swirl of the innards and next the intensification of his resolve to avert its spillage over the lip; this concentrated the mind in a somewhat hypnotic abstraction.

This soil, at the least, thousands of years visible since the great melt, an island of the Atlantic between two immense continents. Humans evolved and multiplied, breaking through untried frontiers, hence it came expected they should have surfaced on Hy Brasil. The facet of interest sustained how the indigenous community befell inflicted with the loss of contact with their former domain for all those centuries. These lasted as the type of complexity which stimulated Olan. They appealed to the intrinsic intellectual. His notion of indulgence was to speculate. He supposed it imaginable there stood in the world, distinct species of human in coexistence at equivalent epochs. He moreover assumed related extractions devised to come and then go; experiments of nature which fell short of working out. This abided as a joyous assessment to the scientist; humankind in experimentation with itself, scouting out the optimum solution. Perhaps the populace of Hy Brasil endured as the conclusion of these biological trials, the current equivalent expressed in software upgrades with the goal of furnishing a superior program.

He evoked his ancestors in the quest for virgin territories, venturing as far as the western isles of Europe, and when this tolerated as no longer satisfactory, in time they came compelled to hazard further afield on reconnaissance. They dared to sail into the open ocean; a leap of astonishing faith which bequeathed fascination to Olan. Why he marvelled, should a fellow quit the safety of firm terrain to navigate in short-tempered waters? This campaign subsisted not as island hopping, such as the push from Britannia to Hibernia. It pressed on as a journey where it maintained as unviable to predict the result, thus, to Olan settled among the grandest of all mysteries. How was a mariner to recognise they predetermined to come across Hy Brasil in the spaciousness of the deep blue sea?

But yet they achieved it. He manifested as the living testimony. He fathomed besides the Hy Brasilians flourished as the direct descendants of those people's in residence on that sister island of coarse and unpolished emerald away to the east. There advanced several interpretations on how this came about:

Archaeological campaigns disclosed the vestiges of ancient ships in those locations of what they celebrated in present day to reveal as the original settlements of the territory. This vein of boat permitted subsequent disclosure, yet in service on the aforementioned isle the Romans assigned as Hibernia.

Robert E. Kearns

Tools, weapons, shields, clothing, baskets, combs, metalwork, jewellery and supplementary artefacts researched in these tracts very much mirrored in arrangement besides embellishment those of the aforementioned isle, all of which sanctioned minor corruption in this peaty soil.

The incumbents of Hy Brasil bore a sturdy comparison to the population of the eastern isles in facial harmony, hair type as well as bone structure. It hitched as dialectical to conclude they styled in relation. This hypothesis met with ratification with up-to-date scientific analysis, which at the outset undertook detailed and objective skeletal comparisons; the notation of measurements then the survey of cranial, mandible and chin features.

This afterward got improved upon with advanced ancillary methods such the extraction of isotopes from both the founding trailblazers of Hy Brasil, so too, current Hibernian's. This data next acquired charting against the accepted diet of the latter mentioned natives. That is, scientists determined to show the first Hy Brasilians submitted, in fact, as born on Hibernia. It was resolved that the combination of sustenance in conjunction with the unique topographical conditions left a distinct chemical besides radiological signature which lodged in permanence within the teeth, so too bones of those opportune seafarers.

To conclude, in recent years there educed an even finer cutting-edge empiricism which allowed for DNA verification. The pioneers in this field rose as capable in the separation of molecules which stored the genetic instructions of those prevalent inhabitants of both countries, attesting with certainty that apart from specific enhancements on the part of Hy Brasilians, they coexisted in reality as well-nigh identical.

Nevertheless, mused Olan, there flourished not a covenant of interaction between these two kindred dominions. The actuality upheld their Hibernian cousin's abided in judgment as a backward lot by the sophisticated Hy Brasilians, which in honesty disposed not too far wide of the mark. They perchance transpired as abstract cousins, but so far as Olan raised interest they coincided as the class of family tree we seldom choose to visit; or bid them to stop with you for that matter. The thuggish Hibernian's revealed as flagrant witness to the wisdom of government policy, which set forth that all advances and technologies peculiar to Hy Brasil ought not to be shared with outsiders. "Could you imagine this first-rate wine getting into the filthy paws of those louts" he murmured, while yet fixated on the circulatory vortex.

However, as soon as this took place as uttered, he regretted its countenance. Not because of any self-reproach in affecting condescension to the Hibernians, as Olan tantamount to a respectable assortment of his brethren sustained invariable snobbishness when it came to foreigners, and their indubitable inferiority. No, it cropped up for the reason that he came to all but forget the note which declared face up the table, its narrative once again penetrating with a profound sharpness. Could it turn out this long extant arrangement with respect to the barbarians might have to vary? An appalling contemplation; besides one of a horrible factor which bestowed tremors on him. It too, set up a wave of despair to wash over his entirety. His country blossomed and hastened while the vestiges of the globe continued to make do with bows and arrows. Hy Brasil configured to guard with jealousy its inveterate secrets to the point of violence. "I consider I should prefer to perish than tolerate in a state of retardation there", he groaned. "Although what if it did not perhaps come to that"? To this end, given that the sliver of a hypothesis was favoured to conceive in his contemplations, he distinguished it suffered to burrow as a parasite about to eat away at him.

A subtle shimmer of panic accompanied the unmasked desolation, hence distinct from delaying on it any longer; his anxiety demanded as a substitute he put an end to the hurt. Upturning his glass, Olan polished off the excellent vinum then hurried out of his study. Neelak yet attained recreation from the couch, which ran protracted from the entertainment derived through her viewing, and as Olan scooted by her at speed to convey his empty for cleansing to the dishwasher; faster still; she hit him with a word from behind, "Are you going to oust the garbage?" Women! They drive you bloody crazy, he articulated. Still, despite the hitherto disconsolate mood, he brandished enough mental dexterity about him to block his darling wife from drawing on this postulation.

A night's sleep thereafter, Olan got up at seven on the dot. His ritual dictated he never ascended a second quicker, but it expressed alike in insistence that he not languish on. He breakfasted on a broad wedge of lightly buttered toast, but resolved not to elect a hot drink to wash it down. Olan intimated a man in a hurry, and with the identical convention every workday, he levied a precept that coffee could wait until he attained the office. He next recruited his electric shaver to tidy up while Neelak and the children lagged in bed. They summoned to awaken before long, thus; he preferred this morning to confirm out front beforehand.

Time and efficiency, in all circumstances essential, Olan ensured every key in the house continued in the perpetual indenture to its assigned lock. By this understanding, a prerequisite to departure occurred the ejection of the chain affixed to the anterior access; followed by the process of a downward movement to the latch button, the rotation of its knob, then a movement into the porch where he mounted a challenge to the bulky double glazed aperture to temporal creation. There he twisted the means of exit, on which hung a fob, whose label of thin card figured with inscribed italics of exactitude "Porch Door". His new car awaited–An improvement on the previous model, he professed. With a press of his thumb against the biometric pad, its electric motor kicked in, at which prompt he traversed round the curved driveway and over the rutted cow gate then saluted the accustomed perception of subdued bumps as he passed over. Next, he swung a left onto the rural byway and took on his fifteen minute commute.

In the wake of entry while it prolonged yet in darkness, Olan composed a path to the workplace he occupied flanking the main laboratories. This upheld the spot he secured an onset to matters prior to the influx of colleagues. There submitted an adequate canteen down the corridor, so latter to the obligatory ruffle of files to contend with, he made tracks in that direction to brew the coffee abstained from with the first meal. This followed his protocol each morning. Habits came to stand as typical, so too; his routines translated into an obsession. This particular ritual dictated he may not get a move on the day proper without already concocting the popular Arabian motivator he protested as distinctly fond of. At present however, the preparation reminded him over of the notice perused by his self the evening prior. Therefore, in point of satisfying the compulsion as well as felicity as a rule he extracted from the normal setup, it dragged him under into the sea of depression.

Ensconced interior to the ostensible security of his accustomed office, as well as in the silence of first light, he happened attentive to this loneliness. For the sole event in near about to two decades, he pressed why he bothered to ramble in at this hour. His eyes travelled to the pending administration to his fore, which abruptly dwindled in consequence. He solicited how it ensued that he ended up with all the bureaucratic and clerical functions, instead of the scientific experimentation he favoured. In preference to dredging through these mundane impressions, Olan bent back into the chair then mimicked the drooped tenor perfected and specified heretofore. There, in such a demeanour the drudgery no longer mattered; his dark percolation instead attracting precedence over the genuine impediment. Here he garbed in an ostensible bearing of passivity; thus, stretched a limb, and then in reverie, broke into a stroking operation of his bristled visage.

A while thereafter he detached his fingers in brief to check the standing by his watch, in recognition it should work out a time yet until the majority of staff was to enter view. This impacted on him with a smack of edginess, which braved an unusual encounter this soon into the day; his absorption in most cases attentive elsewhere. He bechanced moderately irked, all of it aimed inward for depositing as immovably categorical on premature arrival at the office, merely to figure out he wanted for the motivation to get started. Not annoyed enough however, to sort out whatsoever about it, he resumed with the caress of his whiskers, and if anything crouched down a fraction more. He then forced back the chair, crossed ankles under the table and next availed of the region just underneath the ribcage as a rest area for his mug.

He took up again from where he left off the night before, to centre on Hy Brasil and its birth. The first of the sea dogs to capture its beaches, lay, it seemed, somewhere between agrarian and hunter gatherers. They pitched camp in coastal shallows as well as estuaries and doubtless relied heavily on the immediate resources, with fishing and resident game framing a sizeable proportion of their diet, along with whatever wild fruits as well as berries they happened across. The bones of butchered deer imparted discovery for later archaeologists, likely shipped to their orb of new from Hibernia as a food source, along with ancillary creatures of appetite. These animals captured usefulness in other states; their antlers manipulated to construct combs, tools, ornaments, necklaces and such trinkets, all of which occurred as commodities of substance. One curious aspect which appealed to the visionary Olan continued that there appeared also, to encompass in continuance, a ménage of extinct bear native to Hy Brasil. It dwelled as a viable relative of ursidae to the icy north or the land mass to the west. These too allegedly, listed on the menu of the inceptive pioneers.

The pilgrims inaugurated the structure of permanent living quarters, afresh commanding full devotion to the provincial materials. There ranged several species of topiary indigenous to the landscape most of which flourished in conformity on Hibernia, thereby rendering the conversion straightforward. They felled both the trunks of mature besides sapling florae then erected circular hut-like edifices. Those erected, thatched roofs got weaved by means of branches, and reeds from indigenous river banks. The upright posts of these shelters came daubed with a mixture of mud, straw and manure for insulation. So too there situated hearths for cooking, composed of orbicular rock configurations, set both indoors plus out.

Olan managed the neat trick of betiding both in condescension besides complimentary with the accordant train, when he conceded that even for primitives, there suggested a magnitude of ingenuity administered by the foremost incomers. It entreated a significant shake of cognitive proficiency to assess one's surroundings, and then mesh the accessible fundamentals, not just to survive, but to thrive. He set aside for a modicum his loftier demeanour and acknowledged it wonderful they asserted to cultivate into a people strikingly more sophisticated.

Exiting from his reverie, Olan afresh in the present cast attention nether to his chest and observed that the mug poised there in effect ran dry. At this stage of depletion on any other given morn he affected to stand the cup on its coaster, where closer to eleven he may or may not endeavour ahead to the cafeteria for another, resting on how he progressed with his workload. This break of day however, he mulled over heading there for a second of them straight off, receptive he scoured in pursuance of an excuse to procrastinate embarking on the repellent graft.

Robert E. Kearns

He threw an observation about the desk, its utilitarian attitude not advertising in any mode of distinctiveness the splendour of its study counterpart. In other aspects however, it could be twinned; given that the stacks of officialdom, manuals, as well as magazines of industry accumulated as more or less the match. Its display of clutter credited also as the double, but moreover, so ran his system of all avowing to its station. So too, in impersonation of his home office, there mounted a section at once to his front, which showcased a sizeable planar journal, on which he laboured, besides claiming its usage to jot down remarks and memorandums. Consistent with the former night, a sentiment of dread, correspondingly; despair cut through him. All of this remodelled straightaway into, to a large extent stuff; the elementary provision whereby he ruled capable to establish his hands on whatever, by agency of a dip into any given pile, no longer suggested as clever or relevant. It ensued from this cue, the interest of aspiration to sweep it aside with the conclusion it all embedded as a waste of time.

Despondent, he sighed with profoundness, as he launched into at times when under a cloud of black; with an ostensible comparison to an invalid whose breathing evinced a dimension of stress. It sprouted an exertion for him to fill his lungs; the laid-back and strained posture in the chair not of any help, yet he lacked the energy to budge. Continuing further into the doldrums, besides now under extreme lethargy, he suspended respiration for seconds at a time, averse to rallying the requisite drive for inhalation. For Olan, it transpired during these encounters when the automatic commission to take air tolerated desertion; in place substituted with a conscious activity he barely suffered the inclination to rustle up. It entrenched at that juncture as his solitary ambition, to slide to the floor and persist at rest, with only just the minimum instincts of preservation thwarting its realisation.

He caught on to dampened sounds. Colleagues exposed their approach. Olan, frozen in place and fastened to the chair, crossed from epitomising the trim man he described, into one apparently overweight and inert. His body, too encumbered to place upright spontaneously demanded the full strength of his arms, so when he grabbed hold of the rest for leverage, he resembled a Greek gymnast on parallel bars. Somehow he dug for the willpower to push his leaden feet in opposition to the floor. His spine positioned again at a regular angle, aided the arduous task of respiratory discharge. There escalated willingness for that second round of Arabica, but gravity multiplied by ten shoved back, compelling him to stick to his seat. Here he remained; all four limbs immobile during the term of convalescence.

Upright, he encouraged the complexion of normalcy, and within minutes the pretence had veered to reality. His faculties reverted, which authorised him to at least contemplate decision making, with the insight his limbs should carry out the dispensed orders disseminating from the cerebellum. He deferred to relaxation anew; the panic bleeding away; hence he unwound for a spell to savour the innocence of achieving nothing. He petitioned in near tranquillity if he ought to initiate an assignment, but as withstood the usual conduct of things, doubt abandoned him not. As it played out, the outcome got elected in proxy. The phone cried out and so jolted him from the haze. Indebted for the distraction besides the errand for his upper limb, this he extended to acquire the handset.

A week prior, Olan declared at a conference in the nation's capital. It depicted more of a convention in truth; thus, a good number of the republic's premier scientists bowed to participation. He acknowledged delivery of his invite several months previous and related ardour for the opportunity to flee the mundane for a bit. He apportioned to it something along the lines of a mini vacation; a trip from Water Ford to the "Big Smoke" as it bore representation in humorous repartee; a holdover from the introductory theatre of industrialisation. Dubhlinn long since moved to clean energy, but the moniker amused to cling on.

This symposium he sported presumption ordained to strike as an opportunity to grapple affably with peers, besides discuss the present conjecture, innovations and practices of interest to him. Too, he intended, by a similar token to brush up on a handful of subjects through presentation at break-out groups, as opposed to sticking with an isolated field. He nestled in principal as anxious to spend a quantity of hours in the acquisition of erudition with regard to up-to-the-minute archaeological encounters, as this influenced as an eternal fascination for him. He furthermore encountered Neelak on a dig volunteered for as a student. There endured times, predominantly when he got bogged down in procedure; he tendered regret for not having chosen that direction.

Not a creature to disrupt the habits of a lifetime, with it continuing a workday, Olan got up at seven for his drive up north. In attainment of his destination way too premature he came obliged into a wander about the town for a stretch. He ate lunch by himself, with constant evaluations of the restaurant clock which adjusted all too sluggishly. At the end of that youthful afternoon segment he got relieved of his self-inflicted boredom when the hotel permitted his check-in sooner than expected. He unpacked then prepared a cup of the in-house coffee, as the outcome of experiencing to encounter that he yet suffered infliction with the restlessness of beforehand. There supervened an argument about the donation of custom to the bar though he worried it might not resemble proper decorum. Therefore, he alternated between treading the room's expanse and enlisting sedentary in front of the television until the assigned schedule for registration. Upon this achievement the organisers conferred on him a laminated badge, which when clipped to his lapel instilled an outlook of self-consciousness.

The event strove to kick-off that evening with a banquet reception followed by drinks, and the convention proper slated for onset at first light Thursday. He stuck his head into the ballroom, approved of the tables with their impressive whites and twinkling crystal, groomed as well as prepped to serve the delegates. Aimlessly he traipsed around the lobby and saloon area not happening on a soul he recognised, pronounced it soundest if he retreated upstairs to sprawl out on the plush mattress for the interim.

Later, rested but with his shirt and trousers creased, so too, sufficiently wrinkled, Olan got up and patted his-self down, with the erroneous assumption that resolute hands pressuring these fabrics should without flaw iron out the furrows. Olan oft depended on Neelak to see him garbed out smartly. Resultant of this, when deprived of her enterprise, he adhered to a penchant for galvanising to a certain extent as dishevelled. He parted from his bedchamber on the fifth floor and next he rode the elevator to the lobby where he then procured an orientation for the lounge to heed that a count of emblem donned associates convened to indulge in pre-dinner aperitifs.

When he proceeded in, Olan came to be greeted with a few nods from multifarious acquaintances. He reciprocated but declined to converse, so approached the bar, and there ordered a whiskey he distinguished ought to remain nursed until signalled for the meal. While in appropriation of a sip, he concealed a friendless hand in his pocket to create a bid for the perception of suave. At the associated point as he scouted for a snug to be seated, Olan came to the notice of an assemblage situated immediate to the boundary wall. Olan hated to stand, thus, if awarded the choice, vigorously pursued the alternative preference. As a result, this particular invitation straight off got reacted to with an internal groan. As a marked man however, there sanctioned no means to get out of it.

Sitric rendered the introductions. Counted as order to impart them by means of the telepathic practise, the custom prevailed that salutations with strangers stay conducted through the verbal construct. He observed this with a cheer and demeanour which might in reason submit as appropriate for the boffin. Olan on the other hand didn't do these courtesies too well. They impacted on him as uncomfortable; since along with every "how do you do?" it upheld there equipped to transpire the inevitable "goodnight" or "see you later". These acknowledgments permeated as excruciating to him. Hence, he forged an ineffectual crack at jauntiness by shaping an enforced smile, then forged ahead through the flurry of handshakes, whilst by the same course a film of perspiration colonised his brow. If here and now he validated not to subsist in the embrace of a tumbler, so also post as engaged with the supplementary paw, it must for sure compel on him to affect a dip into his pocket for the aim of a handkerchief to wipe it clear. To compensate, he shifted his weight from this leg to the twin comparable to a drunkard in a gallant tussle to latch on to his centre of balance.

With this awkwardness done and dusted, Olan rallied at last the breathing space to formulate a casual pass to the aforementioned pouch, denouncing the heat of the auditorium in preference to his societal discomfort. Sitric and Olan approved to cross paths in education while at the national university together. Never precisely friends as such, they nonetheless continued in contact. In the most it stemmed from situations such as these where they attended to their catching up as it chaired not in the character of Olan to establish arrangements out of the blue.

Forward from this, after an interval of amiable chit-chat which in general initiates this model of conversation, the members of Sitric's cluster opened up a scope and entered the groove of mental transmission; an acceptable gap having transpired to clear the hurdle of decent manners. To keep control of this situation forced a prominent exercise of concentration as a telepathic debate on occasion enabled cohorts to trespass in to one's hidden cognitions.

It engineered as a drawback to accompany this method, clothed in the order of a defensive deterioration which at sundry cases in point sanctioned opponents to set an examination of the discourser's mind into motion. Because of this, Olan hesitated forever cautious of dialogue with challengers via such technique. Too, while safeguarding the ability to limit the intensity of intrusion to a positive magnitude, there still fluttered the chance of a slipup. Alcohol diminished individual armaments; given it stood prone to introduce an adverse effect to these neural garrisons should excess imbibing appropriate one's intrinsic discipline. This is how come he ardently resolved to attend to his short with caution. It bargained as vital he preserves his congenital firewall to acquit at optimum status. Olan entailed on the repeat an extreme requisite to maintain control.

The talk deflected to the consideration of those topics on the agenda, and the various secondary spin-off sessions. Here, they trod on safe ground so far as Olan admitted concern. This worked out as the intellectual replacement to a cordial chat over tea with reference to the latest weather. Sitric, in addition to his associates, based as specialists of astronomy in the observatory at the summit of Mount Comra, stationed in the centremost region of the country. It situated here over the decades that Hy Brasil erected an array of telescopes which now comprised of their touted in loads addition; a large diameter optical. This happened latterly as the subject matter of generous academic dialogue, given the near insurmountable difficulties overcome to classify it as operational. It extended to the cutting edge of modern engineering, besides astronomical science. Olan, when the exchange discharged in this arena, and despite his initial awkwardness at musters with extrinsic contacts, grew to a constructive amplitude entangled with gusto in the repartee, and tendered motions with respect to the principles, so too, practices contiguous to the nation's newest technical astonishment.

A gong rang out, for then a slave to submit and announce supper. Their affable conclave which had gotten along so charmingly was compelled to disband, and with that arose the ungainly utterances Olan dreaded of "Hope to catch you afterward". Despite these however, he confessed a trifle more at comfort in the present than he found at the onset. His own sort of society equipped him with a comfort allowance removed should he otherwise have gotten immersed in debate with a dissimilar set. In accordance, when he declared at the dissolution, "it was awfully good to speak with you", he in point of fact meant it.

Expecting this heralded the end of it all, Olan trudged over to the double doors which introduced to the banqueting hall. But Sitric took hold of his upper arm, therefore held up his momentum. He leant in towards his earlobe then exclaimed "Look old boy. I want to have a word with you later. I'll see you in the bar after dinner". Taken aback to a degree, but curious as to what it amounted to; Olan merely nodded in approval and continued on.

He arrived at his table through the consultation of a board set up interior; and previous to the acceptance of a seat perused the ascribed names he stood to join. Two of the five he enjoyed no recognition of. The surviving three he approbated as bores. What he maintained ignorance of though abided that the sentiment confirmed as mutual. An appointment uniform with this never conceived to supply an excess of court jesters. Olan, for the double turn tonight, at the prelude to events cringed with the unavoidable compliments, so too divulged barely concealed desires the meal should breeze in with speed to facilitate the pardon of small talk displeasure. His quota by that computation had swelled by this point in time, to well past the boundary.

The fare went down with surprised gusto, and he churned through each course more or less in rejection of his attendant diners. In a stretched bow to cordiality he thrust the occasional limp stab at extolling the cuisine. With dessert confirmed, then coffee satisfying the intricately adorned China, Olan made haste to spin his chair towards the head of the assembly hall where on stage; the organisers got prepared to address the room. He devised in effect to turn his back and countenanced no regrets in the deed. Ankles crossed, he settled the matching saucer on his thigh, gave the cup a stir with the embroidered silverware and idled with composure in self-imposed solitude.

If he held up thereabouts in expectance of top drawer oratory, it numbered not in the announcements. All of it could perchance have gotten lifted straight from the textbook "How to Activate a Conference". Hence, within a period of minutes, Olan's focus waned. The flavourless words of the speaker propagated into tedium, so he swapped his perceptual involvement for that of tomorrow's business while too, he set up a mental reminder to phone Neelak when reconciled back in his chamber later on. He aroused his wont to determine the hour then longed for all this introductory nonsense and self-congratulation to terminate, primarily so he might transfer to the lounge. A slave in the clutch of a coffee pot rambled within proximity, and he beckoned her over for a refill, projecting a third of them should not magnify into a requisite.

Robert E. Kearns

As it dragged on, Olan swirled the dregs of the by then tepid vestiges of coffee at the base of his cup, peering into it as if to dissect his fortune. The raised din of voices, so too chairs thrust backward in unison, shook him from his trance. He stood up with urgency then muttered the swiftest of good evenings, and next fabricated a beeline to the exit, thus tickled to have fudged the unpleasant pleasantries. First at the bar, he commanded a drink, and in the lag for the acutely featured captive to serve it up, scolded himself for not at first conceiving to visit the WC. On further reflection though, he realised he bore sure to have gotten stuck in the chaos no matter his choice. Olan exposed negligible patience for soldiering in line with the rabble.

On receipt of his single malt, he spun round to go after a table. A second consequence of landing as the primary bar fly, separate to lone emanation, endured to determine those of a broader convivial persuasion organised before now to establish a claim to the chairs. He scanned the parlour, only to pinpoint that an aggregate kept spots in reserve while their recent companions locked in the drink orders. In other situations they all concentrated together, foreknowing a slave girl should establish. Adequately desperate in his plight, he endeavoured to determine if there prevailed one he might join, and while in pursuit of this, got hailed over by Sitric, who took up residence handy to the duplicate wall of before. Olan cursed his luck, but ensured to swear this to himself. Therefore, he trudged a passage across, impotent to compel a smile, under the assumed wisdom it conferred a precondition he tolerates an upright comportment. Even before a reticent gesture left his lips, Sitric favoured him to guard his cocktail while he swung by the restroom.

Sitric was expeditious in return, full of enthusiasm, as well as geared up to converse, but Olan entreated he pay back the favour. Not disposed or amenable to queueing in single-file, he, as an involuntary alternative made for his bedchamber, releasing a string of inaudible profanities all the way. "This shall be brisker", he convinced, and what is more he ought credibly to resolve his business in serenity. Relief attained, he descended to a calmer state. Then he scrutinised his image in the mirror, and after a scrub up, pulled at his shirt; the wrinkles having schemed to multiply since last up here. Thereafter he dispensed a self-compliment on the mutation of a negative into a positive, thus commending he flattered to inhere cleverness after all. He started, with approval, to brush his teeth; a groom without end he favoured the execution of later to a feast.

Olan recovered his composure enough to hum a tune in the elevator; offering it while in the appraisal of a digital display as he counted off the floors. The cocktail lounge broke into sight as fortified with crowds, so he got mandated into beating a groove to where he beforehand entrusted Sitric, who halted in isolation adjacent to the facade underneath an ornamented stucco border. He probed as to what arose that contained him this long; however Olan not eager to dole out the truth, returned to let him know the gents suffered at capacity, and left it at that. Sitric, characterised with a more easy-going personality than Olan, accepted the account, but his face disclosed with significance, the brand of a sceptic. Not a fellow to dwell abundantly on these events however, he broke into speech: "I have some news for you, old boy".

This at once snared the attraction of Olan, as intelligence at all times reported as a communiqué he featured partial to amassing, above all if announced with a scandalous quality. For a man who bore by default as introverted, he conserved to some influence the contrary quirk of temperament with the realisation of especial fulfilment out of intrigue and gossip. "Go on", he encouraged, optimistic that what he imagined absorbing correlated to a mutual social contact, or better yet, a delegate in the immediate vicinity. And as he forecasted it, Olan by this faith touted a reflexive outcome in a scan of the field, with the delicious anticipation that upon the acquirement of a name, he should exert little trouble in singling them out. But it prospered not as scuttlebutt or scandal Sitric stocked in mind at all. His material applied to the subject matter of an exploit he was immersed in.

At the national observatory, scientists consumed several years prior, engaged on a highly sensitive, besides accurate, telescope of wide lens dimensions, and this arrangement popped up as the theme of their earlier debate. Sitric ensured then to withhold some privileged tidings. He led with a preamble to inquire of Olan if he recalled their discourse, to which Olan in profound disappointment he missed out on an expected treat, so too, annoyed at such a frivolous interpellation, reacted with a curt "Yes". Sitric, either with oversight or in mistake of its connotation continued, "You appreciate old chap, it went online a few months ago?" Of course he knew; too, this got acknowledged with another blunt "Aye"; Olan barely prepared to conceal his exasperation. "Well my good fellow, we've harvested impressive results", hence, Olan upon receipt of this bred fear he might launch into an unbearable lecture, affording no more instruction than he gleaned hitherto. He stayed more or less up to date on it in any case, and the last thing he wished for at the minute was for Sitric to insert himself into the narrative with a session of self-acclaim until midnight.

Cautious in outlook, therefore not keen to permit Sitric an opportunity to ramble, he acknowledged his commentary, by contending "well, I should think so. It hijacked the best measure of three years to grind the optics". This portrayal was factual. The latest instrument applied the most advanced meniscus ever, and those appointed to the assignment saw it compulsory for patience during its manufacture; all the contributory peripherals more or less otherwise engineered. The glass affirmed as essential it submitted to a delicate mode of polishing, with this compelling a constant flow of thin lubricant.

A million and yonder revolutions ensued as mandatory to achieve an apparatus of maximum flawlessness. Even scratches of infinitesimal proportions stood to render the device inoperable; so consequent of this, a decision got taken to manufacture two in sync as a backup. Everything however, teared ahead in accordance with the program and last summer the lens came to be installed in the body of the distinct splendour on top of Mount Comra. After a copious season of trial, so too, equipment calibration, the prestigious marvel went live, and while Olan stayed informed of this feat, he secured scant word with regard to the data it threw up.

Sitric could regale to enunciate all night on the operations of his new toy, but upon the dissemblance of Olan's facial expression, thought better of it, and stuck to his original scheme. "The developed images have turned out as astounding in the extreme and the scope is affording a performance above and beyond all expectations. In fact, its achievements remain so extraordinary, at present we all but tread water in a sea of information overload."

Now this did interest Olan. It might not amuse as juicy chatter, but any reference to fresh enlightenment, with plenty of it to boot, sounded as music to his professional ears. Sitric continued–'At the start it was understood to guarantee us busy for years, but in a stock-take of the sheer plethora of evidence analysed these past months, I prevail today in the belief it desires to have us up at night for decades. There endures so many observations to pick apart, interpret as well as publish; as yet we've simply not produced any semblance of meaningful progress'.

'That's not to say, of course, we've achieved nothing (Sitric would hate for a peer to endure in the opinion they rested in laziness on their laurels) but the tutorship racked up is frankly so abundant, we barely recognise where to begin. In one discussion group we segregate a proposition for study, when next thing, there is spotted an altogether different affair which merits the equal or larger scrutiny. The long and the short of it continues, we're as yet laid up in coming to terms or consensus on how to press on in a reasoned, efficient approach,'.

Olan's full antennae stood on alert but he nonetheless aimed to control the conversation. With decades of insight to the nature of Sitric compiled; Olan comprehended he persevered on a roll; too realised he swayed into danger of setting off on a wander round the park with this yarn. By this motive, Olan interjected to concede, he huddled snuggly in the camp of absolute delight it outdid all forecasts. 'It proves healthier Sitric, to complain of more data than you can handle in place of none at all'. Then, he couldn't help but throw a scholarly punch when he declared, 'I retain absolute confidence you'll get on top of it sooner or later'.

Sitric, to no end of the prideful denomination, was not about to condescend to Olan's supposed acceptance he brandished cause to be overwhelmed with toil in his province of mastery. Thus, he jumped in with the counsel "Oh, I've long since annexed a grip on it, my fine fellow. The groundwork progresses swimmingly; victims of our own success, and all that." Then quizzical as to why Sitric had chosen to stray down this lane in the first place, probed his ramparts with the grapple hook of electro reception, supposing correctly he downed further alcohol than prudent. He was correct, there happened further to the story, so too did he detect Sitric nurtured an eagerness to spill the beans given a bit of a shove.

"So then Sitric, there must transpire something extra to this big news you defend?" To this address, Sitric smirked up a notch; and twitched the flap of a cheek in validation of Olan's guess. "Right you are old boy", confirmed he. "But before all that, a top-up happens exigent", thus, in front of potential objections, Sitric blocked them at the chasm and pushed off to score acquaintance with the bar, abandoning Olan to hang with anticipation.

After a stay of desertion, he conferred a refill on his compatriot with the delicacy of a ruler who fancied himself a generous benefactor. Not only had he procured for him a double whiskey, but furthermore he machinated to impart a secret. Emoting momentousness protruded as an overture Sitric relished, and he couldn't elude a broad grin at his own generosity. "There you are Olan. To your good health!" Then with a jump on the tribute and listing a tad on the border of tipsy; he thrust his intoxicant in contact with Olan's, exclusive of the toasted reciprocation. Sooner than Olan could assert his gratitude, Sitric guzzled most of the spirit; too he exclaimed a satisfactory sigh as if never a cocktail had tasted better.

This conference in all probability registered as Sitric's lone opportunity the entire year to act out the drama of showmanship; therefore, he favoured most definite with his resolution to acquit himself with enthusiasm. In this he revealed preparedness to prod Olan to the limit of annoyance. The latter, as shown, sustained a tolerance of low severity at the optimum of times, but Sitric was not to be denied his podium in the sun. He prolonged the tension that boiled up with dependability in his friend and pretended as though he were judging his words while he unashamedly glowered into the crystal of his highball. When he at last eyed up it took the skill of a hardened thespian to simulate the carriage of bother while inside he chanted an angler's rhyme to the beat of Olan dangling on his hook.

'Listen, my boy; the bunch of us split up into singles and teams with each of those appropriating a territory to explore. Yes, it's all come about with a trifle of chaos, I'll admit it old chap, but the metaphorical cherry on top has been damned exciting too. I've had at it hammer and tongs all hours of the day and night; cheerful to engage with it too, I might add,' here he chuckled, then augmented his statement in validation of Olan's prior estimation; 'I'm like a lad with his new bicycle. I simply can't get enough of it. I hesitate to guess if I've dozed beyond five hours in a row since the induction'.

'However, the mental stimulation of the whole thing set me back a measure. Rather than centre on a particular sector at the start point, I addressed the lot with a scattergun attitude, dispersing this way plus that, until I realised there fell a need to focus some aspect of order to it all. No, my ship hasn't always sailed in plain waters, but at least with the benefit of trial and error, I commenced to cruise in a particular conduct of tack, which mirrored scientific method,' Olan got irked and snatched a taste from his glass in a challenge to obscure the clear annoyance that characterised his face. There slipped out no anchor to put a halt to Sitric once he put underway.

'Well old boy, to shorten a dull account, I happened at the observatory while owls winged in to the hunt, operative on I don't know what, (whiskey supposed Olan, but made doubly sure to not leak this out) and my schedule dominated by the inspection of photographic prints snapped here and there over these past months. It struck then when I remarked on what came into view as a body across the night sky that hitherto I warranted not to distinguish'.

'This I came to deduct through the comparison of a series of stills which spanned consecutive nights, when I sought to deduce if there occurred any deviations from this slide to that'. Here Olan with all sincerity perceived he was being goaded. Sitric presumed to impart on him an instructional as regards celestial observations. Replete, he interrupted with a tart appeal when he argued 'Is this the news?' 'It's without question an ingredient of it', retorted Sitric. When he afterward hesitated for effect, Olan might, with his boiler fuelled and an explosion imminent, have seized him by the lapels to shake the rest of it free. Sitric projected this effect on people, and as much as Olan bursted to holler 'Out with it man!' he declined to gift him the satisfaction. Rather, he foraged in the undergrowth of self-control for the card to play it cool, (this state of being not tailored to the same sentence as Olan) and wrung out a liberal measure from what survived of his amber infused water of life.

Sitric, courteous to the simmering stew of an irate Olan, but undoubtedly rocking the cradle of smug depravity; initiated to lead over again into his earnest monologue when the duo met with interruption from their contemporaries of before. Olan thwarted by the unasked for intervention, wore enough of his faculties intact to discern this paid an end to their discourse for the time being.

For his privilege, Stiric, while not quite in the deliverance of ire to his colleagues, clung to a verified displeasure at the loss of his voice in this humorous opera. It entertained fabulously to behold Olan's contortions of indignation. Still though, he seized on the optimistic outlook; with the incitement of the entertainer's mantra of forever parting from them desirous of more. Then a just about perceptible smile reverted to his divested mien as he acknowledged: "It'll drive him bonkers tonight".

After a suitable interlude which to Olan took place as the length it strung to swill his liquor, he forged excuses, too then, wished every group member a farewell till the morrow. He arranged somewhat content to have precluded a tiresome encumbrance, so arrested the elevator for an appeased reinstatement to his floor.

There stemmed from this the memorandum of his obligation to phone Neelak. Not that he looked forward in particular to the call as in expansion to his routine drawbacks; Olan struggled more often than not with these visits. Recipients espoused a tendency to take him up wrong and understood a substance to his tone of voice which abided non-existent. The uneasiness this introduced triggered anxiety, hence exasperated the condition. He sought to make this brief, thus lessen the risk of it going pear-shaped.

Olan convened on the margins of the bed, extracted his device, and then dialled home. Neelak petitioned how the affair followed, besides posing the inquest exacted of every traveller–"How does the hotel resemble?" After the ping pong of this back and forth, Olan resorted to the fidget of his watch strap, and urged it all to conclude by natural means. "It's getting late darling. The sessions begin first thing tomorrow; therefore, I had better hit the hay". Relieved at getting out of it unscathed, or at least in the embrace of the expectation he escaped, Olan resigned to his slumber, but settled for an instant to speculate on the pertinence of what hitched Sitric's anecdote.

Up and refreshed at the fissure of dawn, showered as well as shaved, Olan for a change descended the stairs to breakfast. He predominantly pledged this meal to his thoughts. The standard common observances he undertook demanded such a speedy departure; it presented a rare treat of a weekday to savour a sit down spread.

In the allotted locality his eyes set on a smorgasbord of fruits from the buffet, some of which allocated the embodiment of exotic. He realised a bowl, packed it to the brim, and then got shown to a numbered table. A robotic like slave approached to ask if he should care for coffee. They persist altogether sullen in this hotel he alleged confidentially, but accorded his concurrence in the practice of a nod to the affirmative. The servant poured him out a cup and moved on to the next table to affect the replica disquisition with an indistinguishable monotonous synchrony.

Olan, in approximation to just about the full citizenry of Hy Brasil offered little trepidation with respect to slavery. Not constituted in any links to the country's former age, it introduced instead as a foreign custom; headed as a fashion of the world in most nations. Given their airs of pre-eminence, this sailed in as a special convention they happened only too comfortable to adopt from those locales otherwise extensively demeaned.

With the gilded porcelain hollow, Olan raced anew to the counter, and then topped a sterile of them with cereal. He poured milk over it, to next scurry and restore his spot in partnership with a glutinous aspect to his features. This too he polished off with prodigious approval, and in difference to full-up, proposed he just delayed in a shove out of the blocks.

For the third course he deviated to the apportionment locality where on offer there paraded the opportunity for bacon, ham, sausage, egg, plus tomato. This distinguished as right up his alley and organised the plate to mount up in a pile with the supplement of toast slices on the summit. He consented to the lot except for his refusal of the tomatoes. Olan didn't cherish those. Established on his throne Olan snagged the eye of an attendant to secure the replenishment of his coffee. Then, as he pandered to this orgy, he disinterred the definitive jest with a hankering for the children to announce as present–"Twenty years ago, and I could have devoured double this volume".

When near to the completion of his fare, Sitric showed up and Olan invited his company. The slave made his presence noticed and discharge Sitric's brew, while Olan as well presented his china for another. "So tell me Sitric, you never got to pin a finish onto the tail of that update you relayed last night". "In a jiffy old boy, I need to get some chow inside me. After you discharged prematurely, we stayed up later than planned". With that, he copied Olan to define a penchant for the full Hy-Brasilan breakfast; with delight moreover for the circumstance he once more provoked Olan to dangle in the sweeping winds of expectancy.

No sooner than he laid claim to rashers of bacon, black pudding, eggs and pork sausage, when Sitric tucked in to the plenteous calories and protein, designating Olan to the scrutiny of this spectacle doctored purely with the remedy of coffee residues. Plus, befitting the tactics of a capable salesman he held fire until the opponent spoke first. Olan, ineffective to contain his agitation anymore iterated the challenge by roundabout means, in a futile endeavour to suggest casualness to its expression.

'Oh, yes,' enunciated Sitric. 'Thanks for the reminder,' in default of the least morsel of need for a memory jog. 'Now, where did I leave off?' He articulated this so matter-of-factly, it left Olan no alternative but to afford a hint. 'Yes, Yes, I recall it now,' said he, in adoration of every scrap of the report thus far it grieved Olan to rehash. Too, even with these prompts, Sitric nevertheless fated the choice to go back over old ground for the purposes of melodramatic effect. 'Well old man, I destined to assess each print, one after the other. There must have hazarded hundreds, and consequent to the sight of displacement patterns, I couldn't let it go. I persevered to pursue its trajectory with a run of the models through our super computer. It developed after this exploit I reviewed and verified the results only to affirm a troubling anomaly.'

It happened here that he captivated the maximum attention of Olan, so too did he notice from him a fascinated tilt in his direction. Incontestably, Olan, not a talent in particular at the concealment of his cards, went so far as to wrench the chair in with him, then leaned on Sitric's every word.

"Troubling?" Sitric removed his eyes from the greasy plate, patted his mouth with a napkin, and then took a sip from his cup to delay the continuance. Olan kept in suspense capitalised largeness to the stakes. Another dab to the lips ensued where at length he jutted in to ready himself and solely then did he make known his hand.

'There's a body of matter and it's on this trajectory,' Olan asserted to exhale the breath he up till now held in. As well, not in the license of an appropriate comeback, struggled for a comment, and in the end parroted it as a refund through the knitted wrinkles of bewilderment to his appearance. 'Anticipated on this track?'

'Well, when I suggest it's in scrutiny of these coordinates, what I mean is, with an assay of the paradigms, preliminary auspices steer to the credibility of it negotiating this plane,'.

Olan saw it compulsory to collect his fervours before he faced the urge to enquire, "What's the likelihood?" Sitric brushed at an imaginary crumb on the chequered weave then rolled his tongue. He next favoured back in the chair and recruited his left elbow to drape with informality over the top rail. 'Well, old chap, you have to consider these extend as initiatory estimates, but I rank it at the minimum of a 50/50 outlook for collision'.

Olan, who minded regressing into anxiety when confronted with circumstances of even minor ratios, could not hide the agitation from his voice. 'What in exact is this aberration?' 'Why, I imagined I came across in perfect clarity about it all, old boy', exclaimed Sitric. 'It's an asteroid of course'.

Hence, it came founded in this interaction the origin of disturbance to Olan over these many hours. He got to establish his presence at the lectures though it ensued as a burden to take part in talks while more serious deliberations reverberated within. His single-mindedness absented itself; too, he about absorbed all but the odd word. While beforehand he desired to grace the assorted break-out contacts, now he lost all appetite, with his preference instead harnessed to an unscheduled hibernation in the hotel bedchamber. Before abandonment of the convention, he grabbed Sitric in the lobby and extracted an oath from him to afford updates. "I shall old boy, but you must commit in compensation not to leak any of this. It's strictly between us you understand"?

At the remote end of the call stemmed the accent of Sitric, and Olan who to start with was consoled by the split second distraction of a ringing phone; upon the recognition of his friend, tumbled into a soreness he picked up. 'Did you get my letter old man?' 'Yes', disclosed Olan, in the provision of a reserved but truthful feedback, averse to the appendage of extra. There succeeded a duration of dead air when neither knew whose turn it fell to deliver next. Sitric took the initiative and searched Olan on what he made of its substance.

'You are positive?' sought Olan. 'I am, old boy,' he arose met by Sitric. 'I've acquired the benefit of supplementary data, so too, I keyed the enumerations all weekend,' 'And the prospect jumped up?' nudged Olan, which sprung as a petition that by default he already identified the result. 'Well, you know yourself old boy; I merely shared with you the embryonic reckonings last week, plus they based in the main from what I exhibited to hand at the time. It's not as if it's varied the details to a pronounced extent. Then, it booked in at about a 50% risk. Today, it stands higher yes, but the concluding impression rests the same,' Again, there marked a let-up to the consultation, and Olan utilised simple mathematics to deduct; factors truly figured as a distortion for the worse, too besides, he failed to accept how Sitric lent weight to its denial. Expectations, especially those that verged on the extremes meant in excess of typical to the emotional state of Olan.

Sitric expected a remark, but played to intuition none

established as forthcoming, so he went on: 'There's the opportunity for its fragmentation beforehand; in fact there is a particularly robust capacity for it,' Olan, in acquirement of his tongue claimed, 'But that may not mean much of anything should each of the splinters collide,' Sitric approved of this argument, instructing 'Yes, up to a point such a concept could well be accurate; however it may similarly denote, the overall force of the wallop might be lessened through the break-up, with some believably not even accomplishing it to terra firma. We don't enjoy a lot to go on here, old boy. Hy Brasil is the alone nation on the planet with the wherewithal to research this genre of occurrence. It's not as if we can prod contemporaries for their point of view. What we succeed to distinguish with regard to the repercussions from such a blow remains indeed limited. We can make happen scientific reviews and denouements, but without question there abides no first-hand acquaintanceship to speak of,'

Olan by this juncture ratified that the conjectures of Sitric wrought as valid; Hy Brasil actualising as the single entity to have perfected the breakthrough into a modern, scientifically exceptional age. In a clash against the grain of his character, he extorted the courage from somewhere to bid 'When?' 'In rough, about three months from now, I should say' scripted the prognosis of Practitioner Sitric.

The latter, in flow yet again conveyed "We must suffer to conserve this between us old chap. If it came about as bared to the public at large, there might attend with it panic and chaos. Besides, as yet, I've no sense what quarter of the planet it means to clash with. Our conversation could transpire as a moot point, which lodges as a heightened motivation to stay mum. If it penetrates on the opposite side of the globe, there might destine to not ring up any cost to us. Again, there secretes no legitimate grasp on what the fullest portion of any impingement may bear no matter where it incurs."

Olan, the physician's patient, cut an improved figure at his confederate's interpretation. This past week he drooped about in pessimism with a darkened veil overhead. All the same, Olan conscious as the ultimate worrier couldn't in full leave it alone. Undetermined disclosures bred entreaties to the penetrative mind, and because of this he defied his cheer to appeal to Sitric that he set aside the indefinable potentials for the time being; too, dish out a practiced hypothesis with regard to what picture might feasibly arise should the asteroid crash home, for the sake of argument some place in the Atlantic.

'It all depends on what range of the ocean it's got rigged in the crosshairs, old man. Our relentless marine comes vast as you appreciate. A wager on it dispensing an explicit blow to Hy Brasil should return outsider odds I might imagine. It all sets up as dubious by a long way the island locates itself as the Bullseye for an asteroid slingshot. Not unachievable of course, but given how immense the planet wields, I should venture the threat of its occasion at less than 5%. So, put yourself at ease on that score. On the other hand that's not to say we can rest assured of a 95% promise at safety. I estimate the force of an asteroid in a serious altercation with this blue world to astound as more colossal than anything yet supposed.' He loomed as trustworthy to preach into a sermon with attention to yields and interrelationships, but for Olan's interjection prior to Sitric's realisation of this homily.

'Sitric, I get all that, but let us for the sake of argument agree, this stellar entity smashes into our Ocean some waters north of the equator. Where ordains that to leave us?' 'Tentatively my most excellent fellow, and with the most humble of estimations; too, shorn of past wisdom or retrospections, there would supplant devastation if it occurred to reach fruition anywhere within the shout of a headland. And even at that, there succeeds a near fistful of continents to abut each face of the abyss which may well occur as spectators to a massive tidal wave despite immediacy or not. Thus, the definite intensity of the wreckage, I cannot tell, as it likely depends on a multitude of factors such whether there inhabits a meaningful population centre within the blast radius, or follow-on mega surf. For the more developed countries, even those which spread into the Middle Sea, a shock wave that radiates from afar may not perhaps wear pretty.'

A minute or two thereafter, they finished their wrangling and again Sitric extracted a pledge to not cause this news to attain celebration elsewhere. He, by now established to brief the dominant tiers of Cabinet, and out of this developed an accord that the specifics be censored from the civic domain. In fact Sitric arrived at regret for his revelations to Olan at the annual get-together. He permitted himself to get carried away and sported such a thrill at his own epiphanies; he split at the seams to enlighten his compatriot, so he might then have one over on him. He shouldn't either have presumed to betray any of these fresh updates, but he similarly comprehended that while Olan loved to pick up on gossip; once an oath of confidentially got induced from him, it turned up in a package with his bond of surety.

Olan filled the balance of assigned hours in devotion to trivialities rather than purposeful graft, and as the afternoon grooved in to a struggle, readied explanations for his staff he came over ill, and in accordance withdrew for preferred territory. He guided along the invariable and accustomed narrow byway, panicky until he traversed the cow gate, which accorded to him the first glimmer of consolation, through its steady and habituated bumps, so too, the secondary musical pacifier of the inflated pneumatic tyres as they crossed over each bar.

Neelak, who spread out in the cosy upper lodge in the audit of her television show; tested of him what ensued to influence his homecoming this soon. Then, to circumvent detailed description, Olan simply advised he developed a headache. He shuffled away before she could press further and then floated through the house to his study; on this instalment securing the door behind; a deed he hardly ever formalised.

He accepted the hardy chair, propped his left elbow on the armrest; and here his fingers automatically sought the solace of his indulgent whiskers. The digits of his right meanwhile, dangled by their tips on the periphery of the desk. To his front, the lone section of furniture he kept in reserve was here taken up in small part with the single sheet of stationery he presumed to recount the night before. Sitric's report, the terms not in any fashion reworded since he last targeted eyes on it, caused him to ponder again on his birth land, too, what might become of it. He felt sombre, besides terribly forlorn all of a sudden, getting on almost nauseated. In consequence, to oblige its exodus, from sight anyhow; he spun the page over so it faced down on the calendar. Then, he tipped back in the seat, interlocked the extremities of his now raised mitts, and deposited them on his breastbone in agreement with the worshipers of old. He thenceforth referred to the histories of Hy Brasil accumulated in the data banks of his long-term memory.

Olan indorsed his imagination to enact the lead and gave his worthiest over again to paint in his thoughts the original migrants who set out on their primitive craft, sealed from the deathly Atlantic through the service of tanned leather and animal fats. He amazed at how it must have been for his relatives to conceive an experiment at such a journey. It evidenced the demise of one class of life; as well, it honoured the introduction to an aberrant form of them. Is this what men secure when faced with jeopardy? Is change the inevitable import of an existence endured long enough? For what else would flavour the taste for a venture into the uncharted, and how was it they embraced awareness a shoreline stood to be met with? The arduous eternal Ocean with starkness over the horizon; no focal point except a kaleidoscopic sunset, but still, his flesh and blood took compass by it, to forego a specific solid of the ancient elements for its callous and fluid kin.

He ceded a shudder, so too folded his arms, ostensibly with the goal of further warmth despite the thermometer already set to high. He supposed, given the option, he should guarantee to hoist his sails back towards the lush greenery of Hibernia. If not partaken to abandon it before nightfall, upon the rise of the morn if he again perceived the vacuum of land as well as the brackishness of brutal surf, in front, too aft, why not then pilot to the rear? Olan directed the fear of this sketch to scuttle through his veins, astonished those initial explorers allowed this terror in their buffeted hulls, day in pursuit of day. Ranked it blind faith that their future cast a league or two in advance of that middle line of our relentless star?

Irrespective of a motive, west they endeavoured with Hy Brasil introduced as verification of the crusade. He appealed whether they pursued a sweeping expanse or devoted gratitude's for the deliverance of this distinctive oasis in a desert of saturated salt. They imperilled no further, a finale ceded to their quest, and matched with the Promised Land of the Israelites, this rock in the Atlantic brandished as the zenith of their manifest destiny. It would seem, acclaimed Olan, they expected Hy Brasil should keep as their patria indefinitely. What manages forevermore to signify? He enjoined. The comeback which emanated spoke to him that always may well realistically last only until the next forced exodus, when man through coercion, probed for what he coveted to prosper as the subsequent paradise of Milk and Honey.

The foremost arrivals to Hy Brasil brought with them most of the essential items, besides, tools indispensable to life's maintenance. They relayed along cattle in addition to separate animals, but most of all; the instinct for survival trailed in their wake. And together with this predisposition, came the intelligence that brooked vital, in combination with the inimitable human competence to reach the expertness fundamental to continuity. The original Hy Brasilians set up with the competency to exploit the natural resources about them, too, fashion the prevalent timber into shelters, instruments, stock fencing, plus spears to throw and hunt with. They assembled boats, and canoes as well as bridges, besides all manner of materials with title to the characteristics for chiselling out lumber. So too; probable as the peak of gravity for all treatments in favour of these resident assets: As fuel for their fires.

They went after the inhabitant game as both provender and for the purposive skins, with just the scraps of a leftover carcass diverted to spoil. Beaver, deer, fish from the rivers, so too birds from the skies came to pass as subjugated and next availed of for all they could dispense. A stag's antlers might in one treatment be sharpened into a weapon, or in another make up the mount for a religious head dress. Otter pelts too, may occur with resourcefulness as sown together for winter protection. Olan defined that to thrive; there happened an absolute stipulation for resourcefulness. Colonisers, to begin with consider their environment; second learn from that condition, and then in the third, extract from it, in maximisation to the broadest profile of whatever eventuates as accessible to them.

Because Hy Brasil fit in many respects analogous to their home range, it may well, he modulated, have given rise to a more uncomplicated assimilation than it otherwise might; should it instead have resulted they came upon a barren or other incompatible ecology. As soon as a beachhead got created, it befell implicit that Hy Brasil sustained annexation for a lengthy extent which showed evidence in the archaeological record. This influx joined not as a purely rare and diminutive band of nascent ex-patriots cast away in its flotilla. The archives advocated that each year the population got added to, which enabled it over the course of a few generations to mount as self-sustaining. They trucked with them their customs, religion and doubtless the spoken vocabulary distinctive to their province of Hibernia.

The headmost collection of huddled homes expanded to establish hamlets then villages; which for convenience besides practicality ascended on grass aproned waterways, immediately upstream from where they collided with the ocean. It proved as undeniable these fresh inhabitants toted grains from the fertile turf of Hibernia, clearing swathes of forest to cultivate their crops. The outcome of this brandished; society, over duration, withdrew from active as such a one centred primarily on the stalk of game and compilation of foodstuffs to that revolved around agriculture. It also seemed the position, that with their ingenuity, Hy Brasilians affected the prudence to cross pollinate native and wild grains with the introduced varieties making way for output resilient to the indigenous clays, so too, micro climates.

An age of simple flint, moreover, stone tools emerged into an era which took on the utilisation of bronze in its place, which came with the properties to be moulded then worked into ornamental curiosities, as well as those of a practical or weaponised relevance. This Bronze Age fed into the Iron Age, and it tendered these transformations, besides adaptations of new technologies that donated special enthusiasm for Olan. It revealed to him in scientific expression how the evolutionary experiences on Hy Brasil might conclude in a map with a paradigm of mathematical rationality; where Progress, if it accepted to a plot on the vertical axis of a graph always soared upwards in relation to Time on the horizontal.

To explore it in this practice hoisted as an essential for how

Olan tended to feature complications. He achieved the facility to expose to his fore the distinct phases of Hy Brasil, with all its achievements listed on the perpendicular, and Time inaugurated on the parallel, beginning with the original day of the introductory colonial foundation. To him there happened the actual history; but moreover there came into the reckoning an analytical storyline where order and procedure reared to impose lucidity on heretofore conjecture. From diagrams he realised the power to extract ratios, data, as well as instruction on the individuality appropriate to Hy Brasil, all of which ministered to his rational personality. Perhaps also, from this body of edification, there might well be disentangled an arithmetical fissure to predict the future, so too acclimatisation to the existent conditions as the earliest pioneers organised to attain.

He aspired to dwell on this some more, when there followed a knock to his right, with Marka, their domestic, announcing supper transpired as ready. Olan didn't boast anything which threatened a good appetite. There stemmed on his part no particular drive to eat, hence should beforehand have devised to instruct Marka, he meant not to dine. However, now that he acknowledged the message, expected in lieu of hazarding a cross-examination by Neelak, it may well sit uppermost to show his face. Even with the supposition he stopped in no mood to feed, he sheltered even less inclined towards explanation. In accordance, and to settle on the lesser of two ills, he came out from his chair with a downright grudge, freed the door then trudged his advance across the carpeted drawing room on into where the household partook.

Later, as a replacement for the restoration to his home office as at first anticipated, Olan changed his mind, with the presumption it donned as the soundest to eschew the isolation of its confines. Hence, he subtracted a shouldered load next to the denizened fire of the adjacent chamber, in conferral of a fancy to its kindly hearth, while Neelak again took up her customary stretched out carriage atop the settee to better regard her programmes.

Olan communicated immaterially to the facet of conversation. But that accreditation did not thrust to unusual for him, with Neelak in essence all but used to it. He disappointed to suggest a whole lot improved, but the flames at least anointed him with a primitive comfort, much as he idealised it to have achieved for the ancients. He embraced the genial glow, furthermore; he romanticised the ancestors in a primordial cluster about an open campfire, in a recount of attractive fables from their shores of birth, thus propagating that heritage for the later generations. An apprehensive sparkle transpired the outcome of the summons to this utopian vision, and he dedicated again his purpose to the olden times of Hy Brasil.

Immigrants to this reverence of new chanced to institute for perhaps hundreds of years when, for causes not diagnosed in the whole, their figures out of Hibernia dried up. Daring migrants then ceased altogether, and with the elapsed moons, Hy Brasil repaired into an isolated and stranded terrain, alienated from the corpuses of the identified realms. This island of the Atlantic became a figurative one as well as literal. Not only did Hibernia cease to export its people, but it lost the knowledge to the whereabouts of Hy Brasil, in due course to the point of its very presence liberated from reality, apart that is from fragments of myth plus legend, which subsisted as implicit in those years to abide in the main as such. The immigrants themselves distinguished not as travellers; ironic given their origins. With their seat of conquest at this juncture determined, they came to renounce their ocean-going ships, anchoring instead with focused roots. The authenticity of their situation after detachment lasted that Hy Brasil furthered to uphold as their sum interpretation of existence. As well, the ecosphere which surrounded that enclave's palpability went on without them.

Olan, as a neighbour of the virtuous fireplace, conceded for his fancy to cooperate in tandem with the interpretive. He accepted, besides divined a condition where over the decades; at a date when life expectancy struck short, how it could take the effect with pace that oral history insisted to break down by the agency of slippery distortions. In Hibernia, those descriptions and folklores around the bonfires he glorified should come to differ moderately with each recitation. The age-old contemporaries devotedly curbed in their lifespan decreed to oscillate from being orated to with influence to the truth of a nation to the west, to in its stand, articulated to of a vanished creation of fantasy. Contingencies too undeniably impacted on their seafaring proficiency, and Olan came about keen to set adrift in speculation as regards these statuses, with the aftermath, that in daring to deliberate on them and next advocate a premise for the reverberations, it mitigated the hitherto instituted depression.

He measured as a means of justification, that a plague or famine inflicted Hibernia with particular severity, and this might entertain as an identifiable source how their navigation skills came about as loaded with a handicap. Perhaps it transpired that warfare intervened. When those who reveal as adept in the nautical arts expire, it stood to suggest replacements determined to afford as diminished in competence to conduct the transit. In such cases where death ruled rampant, there may correspondingly survive in significance less of the populace in competition for the accessible natural reserves, therefore diluting the prerequisite to transfer abroad. Olan estimated that these modelled about as reasonable as theories go in the service of enlightenment how Hy Brasil had gotten detached, so too, slung loose in the Atlantic. He settled on the whole gratified that the critical evaluation tested here, devised, to an assured strength, the deliverance of satisfactory ends, countenancing his pride, what is more, ego to be massaged.

His people supported an abundance of convention with them from their relationship with Hibernia. One such illustration with several noteworthy specimens in the attested chronicles told of the ceremonial procedures contiguous to the cremation of the dead, with their ashes invested to an earthenware dish, then interred and entrusted with contributions to the grave. These enshrined commodities attained sponsorship by families as valued or practicable accessories of their expired loved ones.

There prospered a tradition of expert burial mound construction with the expenditure of domestic rock, thereby in render of security against meteorological conditions. This then gained a cover of earth and perhaps a quartz finish for effect. An entrance to a duct with the parameters of a tunnel expanded into a domed internal chamber; the remains entombed within, along with their prized chattels, all of which ostensibly aligned with precision to the winter solstice. These vaults proclaimed a remarkable scale of engineering sophistication in addition to celestial command, diligent to the codes of systematisation and exactitude complement to that of current architecture.

It informed with the assembly of these passage tombs, elucidation as to the gravity of cultish precepts for Neolithic society. The essential production effort to establish a mausoleum for the afterlife wracked as substantial. There authorised besides, an obligation for legions of generous manpower plus coordination. Without a doubt, there arrayed mass organisation with these procedures, as there had too ensued establishment; the fabrication with unmistakable ritual, of environs which sought not to limit itself in full to the rounded vault. Most coexisted in a circular enclosure of stone in the tenor of huge granite blocks, thereby dedicating methodology to a ritualistic complex with astrological significance, as opposed to purely a standalone funerary for the dead. Without service of the newest equipment, it pulsed arduous to expect how these titanic boulders came to be heaved into position, and it kept archaeologists in a myriad of head scratching with the preoccupation of figuring it out. An exertion on the criterion of these heavenly and formal centres of worship as demonstrated on Hy Brasil triumphed as the validation of how the sacred indoctrination of committal defined its settlers.

Olan exhorted this train further; isolating that by means of the multifunctional exploit of these haunts of community reverence, a weighty significance might well post assigned to the theological perspective of their tenets. This forgotten faith it was expected, orbited primarily in the jurisdiction of our heavens; first among their deities professedly a Sun God. Historians ascertained it was the artificial rises that behaved for their creators as a gateway to the afterlife, with its corridor that directed into the hollow and which integrated a window box above its portal, all of them lined up manifestly with the ascension of the eastern sun. It sanctioned the admission of rays, with these thereafter flooding the space, on but a distinctive day in the calendar; that of the shortest.

The inclusion of beads besides ornaments, weapons, plus specifics of prominence designated there catechised a resolute conviction the spirit of their elders should manifest as entrusted with the indispensability of these wares in the thenceforth universe. Marvels of adorned pottery such as bowls as well as jugs substantiated that food came to grade with equivalence alongside the aforementioned. These benefactions classed as a definite benchmark to the high plateau of care overseen by the descendants towards their forebears, in the certainty that by these favours they covenanted with allegiance to not forsake them to a deficit in eternity.

The embers of the fire ran out of the preponderance of their warmth. So too, diminished in intensity, ensued the burn Olan infatuated on. There stocked a coal bucket preserved for convenience in immediacy with the fireplace, conserved on a cut out square of carpet. He got roused by unavoidability from the snug armchair to review its load. Olan extended anxiety it might venture a lump from depleted as seemed patently regular the condition when he exemplified at maximum contentedness. However, he rejoiced in the scrutiny it resolved half full; the irony being, in the main Olan evaluated such statuses in a genus of the semi vacant.

Tonight, with honest surprise given his mood of before, Olan conformed to a positive disposal, besides; he impelled to face ahead to the recommencement of the multi-coloured licks in the grate. In view of that, while adequately oblivious to the atypical attitude exposed, he met with gratefulness the situation for what it tendered. Then he cramped the hand shovel allotted to this mission, scooped out several loads of the black stuff, and light-heartedly jested, it stood in as a victim to placate the Gods. Satisfied this should do until bedtime, he induced influence again over his chair, shuffled to confirm the previous station, then resumed with his reverie, from where he left off.

History disclosed the selection of chieftains or kings resolved as critical lifeblood to Hy Brasilian culture; it, an institution beforehand familiar to Hibernia. Carved reliefs survived which pictured the sacraments of king worship. Furthermore, there was painted in addition, cave art specimens which codified as a superb source of insight to the mechanisms of the age. Gold jewellery such as neck adornments, crafted in the utmost of intricacy, revealed they could devise only to match with high-status individuals. In a secondary percentage of burials, these stamps of embellishment announced as a share of bequests to the funeral, with scholars deducting that due to their placement, too, the linkage, it bore as substantiation; their owners headed the very topmost echelons of the tribal order.

These heritages no doubt gained, in a portion at least, their own resident flavour, as without doubt would situate the case upon the institution of a viable indigenous population.

Essentially though, it was purported the doctrines survived as commensurate to those of Hibernia. There guided another authority of chronicle with consideration to ancient kingship, and that came with the scholarship of bog bodies. It emerged as cognised before this from the representations and likenesses; the Neoliths shared in an irregular train, whereby subjects promised to a routine of submission towards the king. This adherence enthused with their suckling to the breast of the royal leader which outwardly certified devotion and subservience.

Still, due to the revelation of the mummified regal corpses, these exploits of prostration exposed a darker attribute of veneration, with fealty not the durable charter of a lifelong pact. Should the King's clients plunge into an ailment of discontent; his expectancy got prematurely shortened, with the husk then ceremoniously forfeited to the obsidian peat of the Hy Brasilian marshland, with intent to assuage their metaphysical lords. So well preserved shone the tanned cadavers that the mode of execution struck as dexterously ascertainable. They agonised under the garrotte, with the cord administered yet entwined round the neck of the expunged former majesty. The typical capacity for preservation in the acidic and oxygen scarce environment conserved evidence of the devout prominence of the bosom when it revealed that the nipples suffered a mutilation; in signification it countenanced that divine mastery was terminated.

It founded as a presumption of their being apportioned an ethereal prominence to the bog mire of Hy Brasil, which embodied generous acreage of its middlemost steppe; that hence afforded a motivation in support of mortal honarium to these swamplands of sacred significance. Their hallmarks of singularity begot these desolate and saturated morasses uninhabitable, too, there spooked the phenomenon of escaped gases that secreted a purple aura in the ink of night, which to the antecedents doubtless identified as mysterious besides frighteningly uncanny in equal share.

These esoteric marshes, it patently hinted at, trusted in principle as a domicile for the spirits of the underworld. Catastrophes, for instance, crop failure, disease, an undue quotient of infant mortality or any other such calamity to upset the domain, would necessitate the escalation to a very immediate scrutiny of the King. It engrossed his occupation to ensure the Immortals provided for their people and to a uniform efficiency, stave off evil. Olan amused in the correlation that within plentiful cultures of today, it well appraised as a boon, and correspondingly an advantageous career indeed to baron it up as prince of all he purviews. But in the Hy Brasil of yesteryear, supremacy as the monarch could routinely end up in the grade of a temporary stint with the Situation Vacant banner never licensed to accumulate dust.

Then Olan transferred his devotion to the exceptional attribute, so too, the one that furthermost captivated his enthusiasm allied to the cherished Hy Brasil. This eminence applied to the miracle of endemism and how it took hold and afterward resolved itself among the populace. Their citizenry sustained through contact deprivation with the detritus of the recognised earth for centuries. Traffic to and from Hibernia, the canopied green of their precursors had ceased, which inspired comprehensive segregation. This stimulated as an issue for the science of present, when after the re-establishment of linkage with nations far-flung, it came to be fathomed Hy Brasilians boosted to an exceptional make-up, perhaps to the point of meriting conversion into a subspecies of Homo sapiens. Though granted, that prevailed as a controversial argument.

It ameliorated in present day to sophisticated ends of what could take place in applications of full separation, notable chiefly in the animal multitudes of obscure archipelagos where wildlife became suited to specialised conditions. Outlying sanctuaries founded their individual ecosystems, to force in tack the acclimatisation of the fauna to not just cope but thrive. A representation of this bore approval to have cropped up on Hy Brasil. From the preserved bones excavated out of the identical bogs as were disposed the prehistoric lieges, there extorted accreditation to a category of giant red deer one time prosperous on this rare stomping ground. The gigantism affiliated with this monstrous ungulate, experts alleged, was the conclusion of endemism. They fell extinct soon after the onset of hunter gatherers, with both having at most, coexisted for perhaps a few decades. The leviathans got predated on as a facilely accessible victual, evidenced by traces of butchering on the bones. Today, it flourished just the slighter red cousin perhaps ferried with the seminal squadron of migrants who once attended to the elevations and depressions of this atoll.

As impressive endemism studied in respect to native beasts, it founded the utmost of extraordinary effect on the settlers. That is, in accordance with all scientific understanding besides statistical factors, and in the procurement of exemplars from among the faunae as a baseline, this civilian attainment took place with remarkable promptitude. What ought to have consumed years in the thousands or spare came about in a fraction of what was expected. There flourished no other learned of extant samples for comparative purposes, with nought of this significance identified as ever having favoured to disclose. The contrasts in human populations all over show as minor at most; with facial dissimilitudes as well as skin colour the apparent archetypes.

There sprang up the belief that an intervention disposed to hurry the endeavour, hence, divergent to the regular mandate of the eons it should have tapped, it all succeeded in less than a millennium. The view went that a relatively undersized breeding faction in occupation of a secluded landform might well have given rise to the anomaly. Biologists, in approval of this interpretation as an understructure, pieced together what in all likelihood became manifest. At some stage after their segregation came into being, a denouement of the genetic defect inaugurated, perhaps to begin with amongst a miniscule cluster or even a lone individual. This code came to be passed along to consequent generations; what is more, resultant of the essentiality to breed with just each other, in due course it succeeded to reach and then become endemic to the entire nation.

It too got found out, from subsequent procedural maintenance and the comparison with extraneous embodiments, there entertained to transpire less than a controlled hereditary imperfection or discrepancy. Given the explicit physiognomies of the Hy Brasilians, it rose acceded to that in union with then topping the line seized by their neighboured creations of the animal kingdom; this promoted wholesale familiarisation plus reformation to their sealed milieu, in a style whereby nature hewed provision in the edifice of chromosomal variances.

Olan didn't value the exploitation of the designate "Defect" and in the jockeying to its inference, dealt out a reprimand. A flaw implied that the conveyor of such innate material was therefore automatically exposed to malfunctions in their own right. He, for this reason favoured the terminology "Genetic Mutation", which enhanced the citizenry in opposition to the subtraction from it. It posted as his absolute trust the good folk of Hy Brasil conquered a calibre of deportment which far outstripped any substitute race on the globe. Therefore, as he meditated on this in togetherness with the fire, he aimlessly eyed his home for inspiration. The lexicon he transmitted affected to insist on a revision once over. Hereafter, Olan confirmed to fine-tune his terms, and pledged to discuss this feature as a "Genetic Enhancement". Pleased to have affirmed the induction to such an apt exposition, he deliberated on who hazarded in the first occurrence as imprudent enough to think up the penning of the former definition.

The first of these prominent anatomical asymmetries endemic to the Hy Brasilians was interpreted to have stemmed from an emergence in the body of sensitivity to electrical impulses. In animation as a realm of the sea, it held testified to that marine creatures of diversity reacted with a congruent scheme to home in on injured prey. In view of that, it happened there dwelled a precedent for such a distinction in the conventional purview. The populace of Hy Brasil mastered this extra sense on top of sight, sound, smell and touch.

It arose perchance at the outset to secure a cognitive alertness to the nerve signals given off by their cohorts. This evolved then embarked on a departure from the proficiencies of sharks and rays, in that they began to fine-tune these indicators in a state that saw it realisable to interpret, what's more, learn from them. The brain commenced to function at a steeper prominence, in that it now deciphered the charged pulsations as it would a language. This second internal patois matured, the doyens purported, over durations but in a prominently intensified practice. Their unusual furtherance in other words came into being at such an expeditious pace, that it modified from mere receptiveness to neural incitements, into representation as an apparatus for mental dialogue. All this accomplished in a term of significant shrinkage from what otherwise ought to have situated the destiny.

Even though Olan's countrymen realised the knack for the practice of this cerebral articulation, vocalised speech was not dispensed with. In fact, it survived as the primary approach to interaction. It remained a presumption the oral and mental tongues complimented each other more readily than competition, with the duo an incarnate of balance plus harmony.

It continued so too alleged that the facility which permitted the neuron stimulus interpretation of an opposite could in selected instances be construed in developmental depiction as a defensive weakness. Thus, because of the processes in which prey of the wild conserve resistive mechanisms as a counteraction to carnivorous rivals, the Hy Brasilians likewise progressed an artistry to consent to or block the analysis of their internal symptoms, hence validating equilibrium and accord with voiced expression. This excelled as the match to a raised shield or the appointment of a firewall to halt peripheral intrusion or predacity. Thus, protection imposed as the purpose to why a dialect with sound welded as fundamental. It served as the central mode of interrelation for when the corporeal armaments happened to draw as metaphorically switched to the "On" position.

This original non-verbal endemic virtue came in handy for mixed modes of interface between the humanities of Hy Brasil. It facilitated a dialogue between two or more persons without the element of routine vernacular, so lasted, by that rationale as the swifter of the two conventions. However, a drawback affixed in that concentration hoisted as compulsory to brace the protective hurdle in place.

It ought to appear, though, as a sort of gate that could happen vulnerable or secure, just as there transpires unguarded plus blocked stances specified in computer terminology. The stability of this access in the locked deportment entailed dependable amplitude of mental exertion as the default natural orientation placed it in the carriage of ajar. Once unbarred, it authorised discussion to flow at will and without hindrance. An obvious downside of this posed that it correspondingly sanctioned conversers to browse one's opinions and sentiments through the real time decoding of emitted dynamic stimuli. Cognitive intentions, so too oral conference lodged compartmentalised but interconnected. This by connotation, it foreordained that what a person relayed mentally saw it vital to harmonise in sync with what they reasoned. Otherwise, Olan amused, there bared the decided potential to get caught out in a lie; or worse.

The standard parentage of unshielded exemplified in

legitimacy as an effective accessory for doings in pretty much all environments, with just limited drawbacks. The competence of associates to pick up on and translate cerebral waves existed with a dependence on proximity and these electrical flows did not radiate beyond a concise distance. Therefore, this facet equipped active in somewhat the equivalent respect as a LAN network, in that simply those in the immediate sphere came tailored with the faculty to telepath or decipher the sensory particulars that emanated from the brain of another fellow. This fated that in most states there wasn't a danger of accidental intrusion or portal to the inner attitudes or emotional condition out of purely casual interactions.

But, as in the template of PC's, there stipulated a proviso for caution, which translated to alertness of one's environs. Contexts may arise where the ramparts happened as vulnerable, and in which paradigm the gateway could release without intent, or continue insecure, since the compulsory application to preserve it as sound predisposed towards the fragile side. This potential might surface where a person took ill or fell under the potencies of alcohol, hallucinogenic drugs, or in modern times; particular medicines. When agape, the access paused in susceptibility to intrusion. Olan, alert to this, established as wary without relent that he regulated the controls when it came to beverages of the adult persuasion. He used to declare sometimes over supper, that losing influence over the demon that was drink, led in quick succession, to the forfeiture of a gentleman's private views. Although, quite how this squared with his boasts relating to twenty years prior persevered to his family as an unsolvable mystery.

Afterward in the saga of Hy Brasil subsequent to interaction with the foreign entities gaining re-establishment, this oddity of a convenience to scan the innermost sanctums of antagonists contrived as an asset with acute benefit. It reaped discernment that non-nationals happened gifted not with its proprietorship. There clashed no firewall, with the universal spectrum exposed that their nervous system correlated as hackable with ease. Neither did there adorn a capability on their end to contest in a joust of cognitive exchange, an appraisal of mind, or even the appreciation that an interference with their cortex eventuated.

It came to occur espoused that no matter whom the Hy Brasilians regaled to transact with, the subliminal ingenuities of the strange flaunted as rudimentary at its premium, and even then, they characterised amongst no more than a trivial sample. By the maximum assessment, Hy Brasilians indulged in complete admittance to the inside machinations of those in remote settlements. In the flesh they detected honesty as well as truthfulness, or exposed treachery and deceitful schemes.

While this skill conveyed suitable expedience, besides in a variety of conditions catering to entertain; on a notable scale with respect to national interest, this gift, the sole preserve of the Hy Brasilian populace organised in present day to convert into an implement of indispensability. In relations diplomatic for instance, it got affected as a method to always rate a step ahead of their counterparts and emissaries. Environments in a multitude of areas got manipulated to reap the advantage of ascendancy. In the matter of commercial negotiations, which thrived in vital prominence, it catalogued as attainable to corroborate the persuasions of the contrary delegation regarding the whole outlook of mercantile interests; all without the opponents disclosing the slightest suspicion of the event. This valuable astuteness was cleverly put into effect to eke out compacts that sempiternally profited Hy Brasil to the utmost respect.

Their talents might similarly succeed in application to gauge objectives attached to battle or accord. While conflict against Hy Brasil should with potency conclude in a barren aftermath for those who furthered the naivety to contemplate it, alertness to this certitude seeded at all times in sterile ground. Despite their supremacy, designs of this stripe as far as Hy Brasil met alarm, compelled prior identification of the enemy, moreover in restricted manifestations, that potential adversary's elimination. Where they might seize influence over these hostile aspirations that is what they accomplished.

Much in similar surrounds where these overseas countries sought to contest each other, with the seizure of those opportunities that might result, their engagements too could every so often prove beneficial to the homeland. All means to accumulate tidings got reinforced through the resolve of their singular aptnesses. The composition of access to detail, expertise, plus know-how in abundance, ensured it all got soaked up and then callously exploited.

There bestowed in specific on the Hy Brasilians an additional marvellous faculty and that awed as what the scholastic fraternity proposed as the "Intelligence Gene". It persisted to submit as somewhat controversial, so too, as a staple for debate, but of late surfaced as an argument Olan harboured considerations on. As the fire, now refuelled, discharged its convivial citrus hued radiance, and the conflagrations again soared in the hearth, this convergence of fascination reverted to his scrutinies as it linked to the context of Hy Brasil's earlier age.

It subsisted in discourse, moreover, came back to happen raked over many a term, whether higher intellect founded as an unconnected and distinct upshot of endemism, or whether it came about from the precise genome promotion that gave rise to acuteness pertaining to the resonance of electrical fields. Some asserted it contrived independently, confident it instituted as a solitary unrivalled condition that emanated on its own and as a straight aspect of isolation, as well as societal confinement on Hy Brasil. Others contended it assumed as a by-product of perceptibility, besides the competence to glance over; too, read traces of current in the nervous system. It evinced postulation on their part that a re-wiring of the brain introduced as the effect of an unequivocal chromosome elevation, which shaped the offshoot foundation for complex intelligence.

No matter, the eventual realisation verified as the same. There followed a re-alignment of the cranial organ which ended in authentication through MRI and CT Scans. Olan supposed that regardless of the initial trigger, neurons in the grey matter repaired at some time or other to alter. With the conduct of central nerve endeavour, any strengthening or innovation may have given rise to an impact on supplementary sections and tasks, hence setting in motion radical cleverness. It all still came down to endemism. If the audience on Hy Brasil lasted in congruency with the foreign world, instead of divorced from it there ensued every prospect the extraordinary idiosyncrasies limited to them, may well never have matured.

Whether exaggerated acumen came about absolute to, or as the final output of an explicit genetic shift lasted in relevance as just a puzzle for academia. The evidence remained that within a compressed span, Hy Brasilians due to motives of one setup or another forged an innovative and hastened genius. "Accelerated Intelligence" was the phraseology awarded to an inflated rate in the trek to proficiency. This extraordinary power led to societal improvement, and on Hy Brasil what should have ensued at a typical pace of fruition; had it established under regular conditions; instead made headway on the fast track to furtherance. Yes, tacit abided Olan that the citizens of Hy Brasil improved for some time now at a magnified clip in comparison to all outlanders.

Prior to the debut of interplay with the continentals, this cavalcade of evolution stayed on trajectory, but given there endorsed no similitude obtainable; it also predestined there vented no appreciation of its fallout in the everyday dynamic of Hy Brasilians. The aftereffect emanated scarcely after they set forth on missions of veritable quest they grouped as exuberantly further along, so too contrived to rise in betterment of any subsidiary factions they chanced upon. The modern epoch brought with it the development of scientific and medical benefits which accrued in the serious scrutiny of these discrepancies. What formerly stood credited as a visual comparison of technologies, the disciplines, plus other inroads, escorted by the suspicion of presiding as the supreme specimen of human, was before long verified as accurate, through up-to-the-minute genomic corroboration besides the ensuing methodological dissection.

Olan disposed his reflections to ramble and roam; with one brood lending ground to another, in due course to mull over in his introspections for still another opportunity, and with gloom, the modernisations brought about in the development of his native civilisation. These recalled intellectual questions, so too the evocation of the practises and fields that tied in with these occupations of the enlightened era, in typical quartered as a provenance of delectation. Tonight though, even while he recycled these reminiscences and insights as a nostalgic trip through bygone realities, not a single bit of it got balanced out through the customary accepted gratification. His mood persisted solemn besides downhearted and in those deeds troubled him yet further. He ought to he intoned, breathe to relish these inner-directed exchanges and consultations. He ought to re-visit the gilded book of Hy Brasil with sentiments of pride and serenity, but instead emoted disquiet plus a fair spatter of disquietude.

A preference swelled to languish in days vanished, and as much as it gestured a dismal regard, it depressed secondary than to simmer in how miserable he believed the immediate. Hence, he grabbed at the lesser of the two melancholies and fled to his erstwhile fanciful consultations with interest to Hy Brasilian glories.

It fetched as a curiosity if there elicited a specific page in the logbook of time at which heretic enrichment, so too, quickened mental strength tilled ahead. Yes, endemism was understood as the enabler, but dropped into the probe happened whether there unfolded an obligation for a secondary factor or milestone that met with a proviso for those specialised dexterities to update. After all, why those specific features? It could with justification and ease have come to pass that as opposed to endemism aggravating an escalation of faculties, a regression thrust in as the alternative. By this graphic in preference to a commonality of bipedal ascendants there came about a reversal where they swung from the branches as a feral ape.

Olan brooded on this, and subscribed to the theory that when society touched on a designate eve, the factor or trigger for genetic improvement as well as stimulated intellect, in combination with the indispensable endemism for it to come about, turned up to kick in. On Hy Brasil, the hamlets and villages which thrived as the mainstay of activity on this Rock of the Ocean nurtured into towns. Municipalities burgeoned and enlarged as the expected reaction to urban reality. Townships thereafter distended into cities and these then instigated their own breakthrough with the transfer of ideas among a weightier arithmetic of bodies in close habitation.

Here, Olan supposed that perhaps it specified on this verge that the chromosomes of acumen raided to the fore. The landmark came to pass as satisfied from an evolutionary perspective and once struck, a hastened refinement chartered that boat. Progress, then the transformative path, went ahead at a stauncher pace than had they landed elsewhere, or not as a sequestered community. Olan embraced an opinion that the brain was compelled into a specification that ensued altogether from endemism, whereby it rewired itself so it gained the proficiency to extract advantage from the fortuities built-up areas decreed accessible.

It surfaced from the actualisation of capacious domiciliary centres that Hy Brasil commenced to move on from an ethos that continued to revere kingship (until a sacrifice entreated, interjected he) into such that in phases cranked into a rehabilitated method of authority. This too came into being; it was expected, at an increased speed as per everything besides on Hy Brasil. The modern age foresaw that kingship meant backwardness. It transpired a wellspring of pride nowadays it no longer enacted as a constituent of their civilisation while in assemblies foreign as if to verify their inferiority; it clung on to a configuration of dominance.

The establishment of rule, while spurred, still took on a reliable content of order plus maturity to it, which in the initial periods destined the conservancy of the aforementioned monarchy. The ancients halted in affiliation with canonical laws, where sovereignty as designed, remained fundamental in quota to their currency of faith. Rituals such as those which genuflected in reverence to the king; and should outcomes go south as stirred by routine; his gruesome demise expressed appeal to more enlightened evaluations of royalty.

The king clung to his divine jurisdiction, so too, it resolved no more than hitherto accustomed, almost a precondition of the post, that he acquiesce as a contribution to the immortals. Inheritance of the crown sequenced into the norm. As well, fateful of the arising stability, a royal could expect to endure through his physical life expectancy, however lengthy that should be. The customs and worships heretofore designated as crucial to the potentate and his realm happened dispensed with. No further did he scale to the pedestal of a demigod; the upshot of this aptly plain there stood not conferred to his highness, the scrupulous veneration of yesteryear.

Those exalted with the crown, did all the same heighten into a framework of unlimited omnipotence. Although, while the anointed presumed in some respects to engage a connection or conduit to the God's, so also, bid to claim with frequency they spawned from those Idols, rose to hail marginal profit in the persuasion of their subjects to their protestations as being an emissary of the heavens. This continued in fashion until when the subalterns of Hy Brasil revolutionised, then the superior's strength and testimony of indisputable right encountered its wane.

At first, councils came to be equipped; with these emergent into an assembly which chaired in the ascendancy. The sovereigns of old considered that a legislature consolidated as their personal possession, and in consequence administered purely as a collective of advisement. The congress remained thus, in his estimation, answerable, besides secondary, to his holy entitlement to command.

However, as it happened, the Body of State as a cog in the engine of enrichment symptomatic of Hy Brasil undertook to appreciate itself as more akin to an independent officialdom. It revolted against the King's license then set about concocting a blueprint for his deposition. With inevitableness this led to a civil war where the loyalists to the crown battled against the forces of modernity. It transpired a short-lived war. The republicans of the congressional conclave romped triumphant, having mobilised the majority of the citizenry, and so too, arsenal of weaponry to its side.

The last chieftain of Hy Brasil met his capture in a hovel of a hideout and then came to occur ragged on mercilessly as a debased pauper. Subsequent to a brief term of imprisonment they reputed it as fittest for them to scrub the landscape of his furtherance. Perhaps poetical, a beheading ensued, next a cremation, and then the ashes dispersed in the midlands of desolation. This symbolism therefore put paid to kingship, at which threshold the house rose as regulators of the dominion. There descended from this an acknowledgement that were it not for both the gene of intellect and a hurried up evolution that exuded from endemism, Hy Brasil should have maintained to realise itself firmly under the heavy boot of its timeworn princes.

The directorate which started as hardly more than a rubber stamp for the monarch's partialities' transformed itself into a fresh and experimental taxonomy of government. To begin with, they answered to themselves. The chamber sculpted up with citizens of prominence and at the outset they debated and ratified laws in a somewhat haphazard procedure, without the familiarity of anything to contrast it against or pick up from. With a period of tinkering though, besides a wealth of trial and error, they came by an arrangement of oversight they labelled a Representative Republic. The Assembly of the Republic afterward got split into two bodies, one illustrative of the Democracy, and the other a Senate, each of them consistent with a safeguard and offset against the other.

That said; they harped back, too, emitted a nod of posterity perchance, to a conduct of tradition. They came by the notion that to institute with trustworthiness as deputies of the State, there determined the requisite for a Head of the Executive to preside over this renewed Hy Brasil. This contemporarily hailed Chief, it planned; should, distinct from the overlords of yore who wore out their welcome, maintain Office for a five-year term. This rule was to eventuate in conjunction with his self-appointed, but ratified through Congress, Cabinet of Ministers. No more did there sway a doctrine of ancestral expectation of control, and those bills submitted by the President commanded from the House, its seal of consent.

Integral to this virgin Republic, each man assumed a vote, so too reserved entitlement to cast it for his choice of candidate from the list who stepped up for election to the Chamber of Representatives. There followed a separate ballot for those with aspirations to claim a seat in the house for Senators, and every five years, that concern with the utmost status in this original Democracy-The Presidency.

The next segment in the embellishment of Hy Brasilian governmental strategy alighted with the ratification of a Constitution. This set out in a binding folio of contract between Government and the People how the State situated to be administered. This Charter, as well, introduced a Bill of Rights, whereby each citizen happened with a warranty in the stronghold of civil liberties that no authority could overturn or seek to eradicate. The Constitution drafted as a charter in testament to liberties of association, the right to personal property, unrestricted speech, besides the most essential of all; individual freedom.

A replacement for the elite of former eras who pronounced supreme in all, this commonwealth at present stood for enfranchisement with a pledge to the People they organised the charge of their own destinies. This Republic of Hy Brasil adapted as a Government of the People, By the People, and For the People.

The elicitation of a written bonded instrument, solidified it under the armour of law, and as such this document warranted adjudication by scholars of the discipline. It established that the party tasked with this business set up as a detached and independent wing of Government. The overseers transpired as appointed from the prevailing judiciary; as well, it stipulated in their remit to ensure privileges fell under the umbrella of conservation with regard to the induction of decrees, so too, legislative conducts. No Congress or President came by the empowerment to enact proclamations that presumed to infringe on the birth rights defined in the Constitution, and it endured this Supreme alignment that heard, and then arbitrated on cases considered before it incidental to alleged violations.

Consequent to the contrivance of this benefit to all citizens, there began a sentiment of nation manufacture or country induction. It formed as a logical progression, and Olan supposed it reared as the disposition of sovereignty for all that cleared Hy Brasil to merge its collective wisdom, capabilities and technologies for the amelioration of the State as a whole.

By his estimation, which he arrived at from the erudition of humanities elsewhere, this scheme of things under universal climates might just swallow up years in the thousands. The coming together of tribes, towns plus cities to practice the semblance of a common flag, prospered as the acknowledged driver of furtherance and sophistication. Only when alliances converged for the mutual cause of nationhood, ripened under its laws, so too, shared pride in its exploits and greatness, while furthermore, by the same regard confess to autonomy of thought as well as expression, was it practicable to go forth, then bring about prosperity in the spheres of science, culture, industrialisation besides auxiliary scholastic pursuits prevalent to a higher society.

Olan figured that with the cavalcade of aggrandisement on Hy Brasil dancing to an augmented tempo, also, its unification to embrace a model of order grounded not in Kingship but on that of a Representative Republic; it surged on the renovation of their society to august elevations. One fed the belly of the other. As each of the enrichments to their island terrain came into reality, there occasioned yet another. And this continued the sequence of circumstance.

On that understanding he returned to examine what declared as the normalcy of rule in those faraway states of celebrity, and granted too, that without the achievement of later strides in the human march, there abided every chance of a collective meltdown. In fact Olan subscribed to the theory that empires could fail or even reverse as in the sands of an hourglass where those provinces held on to obsolete habits of leadership. He should venture so far as to express that a caucus devoid of personal latitude and emancipation, the throes of death practically loomed as inevitable.

As a composite of issues they sustained as attractive; and ones as well that Olan apportioned contemplation to in preceding months. If time permitted, he affirmed aspiration to revisit them at a fresh convenience posterior to this, mainly in the paradigm of far-removed regions, and the consequences of failure to change and adapt to different, further, enhanced actualities.

All the same, he in lieu cranked his devotions to the right of pastures general and hooked on the ancient renown of faith in Hy Brasilian philosophy. The archaic ceremonies activated to fall out of favour when villages consolidated into towns. There resulted the introspection of devotional rites. For a while, cremation applied as usual, but the ashes and bone fragments, instead of interred in a dune of earth as with the traditions of former, deposited conversely in a rectangular ossuary of stone perpetuated within the household.

Then it attired that burial without first a pyre, burst into fashion, too, this hit on composition where the cadaver got lowered into designated plots outside town. These committals plied a marker in the mould of a flat or upright slab with chiselled out designations that confirmed who lay hidden in each of the regulated parcels. There lived on in ritual at the equal chapter to this, a lesser convention among a minority percentage with the service again of another throwback to the bygone, in that they affected dynastic tombs in preference to sunken graves. Internal to these mausoleums, they arrayed the contour of the deceased on a shelf to decay unaffectedly. After a year or thereabouts, all that procrastinated were the peroxided remains.

Throughout the primary ages of township; with the incineration atop a bonfire of the deceased followed by entombment and committal, it meanwhile abided the procedure that the funeral service incorporated all the revered sacraments that until that time characterised bereavement. The passing of a soul was incumbently looked upon as a cardinal and essential standpoint of their canons. Deprived of the correct procedures, besides formalities, the deceased could not cross the threshold of the hereafter. Ensuing from this; fear as much anything supported the familiar ways as operational. Clerics perpetuated the Eucharist of expiry, with priesthood an esteemed institution of the Hy Brasilian ethos. The ordained were supposed as vicars, too, interpreters on earth, of the Gods' will. However, it stretched not too obscure into the metamorphic genesis when the ascendancy of doctrinal men of cloth slid into decline.

City verve conveyed sophistication, and erudition innately spawned neoteric abstractions. There sprouted critical rationale in every facet of civic animation, in addition, with the achievement of the Republic there charged in the latest era of enlightenment. As the sciences hoisted in reputation, fidelity to the pious glided under the microscope of irreligious inquisition. There crept up steady retreat to the prominence of creed in day-to-day conservation. And, right across the corrective reorganisation, infallibility of hallowed dogma came to be ferreted into; hence, with this, secular observances expanded their foothold.

The modern tenets, moreover, points of view that coincided with populated incarnation, in conjunction with a patented logical posture to life and death, ensured that prayerful conviction, besides conventions of the holy got entrusted to the sepulchre of archaic treatise. When the factors of a chromosomal proclivity integral to the kith and kin of Hy

Brasil supplemented itself with an accelerative, so too, confederacy of forthright intent, it broached to usher through the date classified by historians as "The Age Of Reason".

This victorious epoch shepherded an explosion of scholarship as well as originality, whereby the superstitions of the onetime Hy Brasil got exchanged with systematic rationality. This indulged to cultivate over a handful of centuries reflected Olan, but in denominations of the cosmos, this expounded as but the twinkle of a star. In addition, contrasted with external peoples who fancied the ascription of illustrious society, it happened that the Hy Brasilians peregrinated clear and far down the cobblestones of progress. The Italians, Greeks, Egyptians, so too virtually every overseas territory he meditated on preserved to glorify the false idols native to their sands. In Hy Brasil however, allegiance to the supernatural cited in these years as a mere quaint and left-over relic of the fabled Creation, long since restricted to the pen of scholars and novelists.

He harked back in reminiscence to those accounts, with a grain of self-admonishment in affirmation that each of the freshest strands of reason threatened the vulnerability of drawing away from him somewhat. The lessons from his schooled tutelage instructed him that the Hy Brasilian penchant to probe and behold further afield than their state of origin, arose not too distant into the Republic of fruited plains.

High end know-how's, moreover ingenuities cruised up stream by knots, and shipbuilding laboured among those industries that flourished into prominence around this term of invention. It improved, in fact, into something of a priority for the island's executive. It got trademarked as The Policy of Exploration; touted in a Presidential speech to the enlightened domestic tribe. Its terms of reference defined to seek complementary dispositions yonder to the shores of Hy Brasil, with the purpose of authenticating the legends, perhaps too, fables recounted in the rich oral heritage of their communities. Purely with edification added to by way of scrupulous investigation, was it hypothesized by deduction, accurately as it translated, that congruent with all the premium folk tales which characteristically nurture a whisper of truth to them, so too must declare those which informed of their lineages elsewhere.

It specified as an entry to the annals of Hy Brasil that this requisite to try for shadowy ambits came to be escorted by remarks of caution and applied logic. Sooner than a naïve vault into the undiscovered there impended the cardinal for method, besides headedness, levelled to exploratory ambitions. After all, apart from mythology, it posted on that leaf in the datebook, no sense of the humanity external to those margins loved by their forefathers; so too, if traced, what that body might resemble.

There quartered as credible, inhabitants of unparalleled fields may well have clamoured to eminent expansions above they. This cogent scenario occasioned a weigh-in against the prevalent impulse of adventure. No allowance for what description of humanity, if any, that moored abroad, meant it tightened as reasonable for there to cloak an expectation of fear on these travels. They saw bound to entertain the contingency that once acquired on the scope of superiors; they left their flanks imperilled to pillage and ruin from a foe enthused to conquest. The Age of Reason merited the calculation of sentience appropriate to these conditions with a predisposition to self-preserve imposing a symmetry against opposite but equal instincts.

A Commission of Discovery came to be founded with a direct report to Congress. This authority gained its outfit from citizens with backgrounds of diversity who accredited as an expert in their field. It garnished appreciation that a multiplicity of opinion demonstrative of the sciences, commerce, philosophy, politics and education should occur vital to preparedness for the aim. Its mandate activated to tender difficulties with reference to what may achieve exposure in the wider domain, besides how relationships with the cultures of remote sovereign entities should face management if confronted.

What furthered from the Commission betided a set of protocols, and now that Olan considered it, in hindsight, just Hy Brasil played as exceptional enough to contrive the foresight to enact these procedures into fabrication. At the moment of establishment nobody singularized what to expect, hence, precautions assented to inevitability. It may seem ridiculous these days, he revealed, in that Hy Brasil complied with such obviousness as the most supreme of all via the mirror of humankind. For the era however, it showed a remarkable aggregate of orderliness, too; it illustrated a roadmap as to how the multiple contexts that may arise should be gotten to grips with.

Olan laid bare the pride in his land, so too its souls, to affect the acumen as well as foresight to put together an archetypal body to deliberate on every eventuality. Despite this, as it came to pass, many of them in the end, hadn't thirsted for introduction after all. Irrespective, it persevered better in his estimation to scheme and structure for the worst, than to invest in no master plan at all.

Initially they lodged unequivocal on the dispatch of ships for exploratory charges, the purview of which conserved for them to encounter, likewise, interact with distinct provinces. The primary dispatches submitted to embrace a crew galvanised with decidedly accomplished Special Forces in the majority, besides decked with those from the branches of academia in the minority. Counted in the directives paired with these commissions listed that should a troop meet with a militarily complex league intent on invasion and subjugation; then the representatives stood duty-bound to laud suicide more willingly than reveal the whereabouts of Hy Brasil. Each seaman came therefore to be issued with a quantity of cyanide capsules. Rather than falling subject to interrogation then torture, there happened an order to bite, crack and digest. This never suggested as a cast-iron guarantee to defend their secret, but there sustained at least, to curtail the hazard, the foresight to uphold codes of practice in situ.

After all this, the flotillas conquered forth both easterly and into the glorious twilight. Hibernia, the enigmatical domicile of their ancestors heeded as the priority target for assessment. It rumoured to stake some place on the map to the right of Hy Brasil, with common sense prescribing that if the folklore secreted legitimacy, it beyond doubt asserted within the relevance of elementary sea going craft. They dwelled short of a lot to go on apart from speculation. Inferences strove as unavoidable regarding food as well as fresh water and provisions; so too, ship size and mariner sums. Their guess purported that Hibernia should, if it prevailed, not swell from the ocean at such a protracted immensity that it reared to queer the pitch of wanderlust as problematic with concern to the critical allotment of produce and rudiments. Nonetheless, isotopic analysis proved with certitude they hatched from foreign corners. Resultant of this verification, follow on conjectures advocated, that wherever the origin of their birth, it credibly based within an arc of feasible sailing distance from Hy Brasil.

It resolved with pace their suppositions graced as correct. To starboard, in the trail of an undeviating crow there erupted those dramatic escarpments preached commonplace as intrinsic to Hibernia. This harsh nugget came forth in a veil of deciduous and evergreen canopy besides abided faces of bristled conformity. Conversely, with these correlations the likenesses petered out. Hibernia piled with uncouth degenerates where ritual sacrifice passed time as central to their mystical dogmas. Ancient masses of rite palavered as the norm where also the abundant tribes commanded by dint of regional chieftains kicked around in the interest of sport the talent for war. In short, by no evaluation did they rally the track of promotion to any consequential extent and decreed more or less static for perhaps thousands of years. Olan agreed that as he mused on Hibernians pasturing as brutal philistines; a backward mob, he at once inclined in these rationalisations towards the guardianship of his trusted with intensity partialities, almost in agitation for holes in the dyke of weight regarding those disciplines which presented declarations to substantiate Hy Brasilian pedigree from these stone-age lowbrows.

Fundamentally, the accordant gamut of syndromes was realised to coincide the match on the latter grappled with tract across from the Straits of Hibernia, which afterward proposed to the almanac as Britannia. It too embedded as a clannish zone with not a speckle of inherent nationhood. Each rivalry guarded with a jealousy its own parcel of hacked out pasture until in conflict, it got snatched from them by an approximate antagonist. These annexations straddled as short lived, with the usurpers in turn destroyed via an independent faction. This embroidered the template of perpetuation, with a never closed vicious circle of unbroken feud which ensured that gain, innovation and improvement cooked up simply minor advances. Here, Olan armed his brain cells for manoeuvre when he conjectured that when thanks to hostilities all the finest of combatants are dead or enslaved; the social order could not adequately evolve to meet its entire potential.

This standard of outcome weathered to the sequent aisle over the flooded streets of Dogger, and then on to the continent that stretched; it must have suggested to the voyagers who weighed anchor; into infinity. Each of these realms discerned in the northern quadrant of Europe engrained as fragmented, besides tribal. Countries wanted for the insight to configure thoroughly, so too, the crude aboriginals stayed behind in a position and chapter no longer acquainted to the public of home. The study of these ethnic ideologies learned comparable in some fashion as a peer into their own primal epoch that stretched right back to the inception on Hy Brasil. This sourced as a fascination to the anthropologists but to almost everyone else it showed up as a lament. It transpired as if the earthly eagerness to prospect had sought to realise a breed that quantified the reciprocal or better than theirs. The untold theoretical pitfalls enticed as a chunk of the attraction, which prompted the style of an adrenaline rush. Then, because of the encounters coming along with none other than undignified ruffians, these missions, in the observances of many, stood out to some level, as an anti-climax.

To the west, their expeditions conformed to the identical dissatisfaction. A giant pole to pole continent got unmasked to the geographers, but at each anchorage it ratified as before to persist tenanted with incongruent affiliations. Though not analogous in feature to the men of Europe, they corresponded however, comparable in method, in that they more or less nourished off the land. Some stock within an immediacy of the coast innovated enough to settle into farming, while further in, the more hostile of the above associations roamed as modestly above nomad gatherers who also hunted. While war in the next door continent was commonplace, for these ethnics of the westerly sunset, it exhibited that surmounting the spirit of their enemies, along with dislodgment to the scalp of the vanquished, cast as an integral expression of their culture, too, attestation to their courage. Bravery in the face of one's foe awarded the rite of passage, and they thus judged it as the richest of honours for a young buck to ascend to the salute and denotation of Brave.

It transpired solely when the tentacles of appraisal extended to the middle sea which scored through Europe; they commenced to catch a glimpse of what may well befall cerebration on as proper dominions. It appeared as if the genial climes under the guardianship of Sol triggered the emblem of a rudimentary protuberance of evolution. This premise accorded pause for thought, in that the atmosphere of Hy Brasil continued analogous to such tolerated on Hibernia. That is, it positioned unmistakably further north, and as a result, fell subject to intemperate elements. This argument nonetheless, reinforced the interpretation that endemism induced responsibility for their exceptionalism. If it wasn't for the ancestral enrichment intrinsic to its dwellers, there betided a cogent likelihood that Hy Brasil would foster as uniformly regressive, equal to the multitudes of divergent colours. This outlook caused Olan to shudder. The very notion of a mandatory hardship in this primordial condition arose laced with abhorrence.

He referred in its slot to those habitats where bountiful sun flared with predictability throughout all the seasons. Although they ignited as a metaphorical universe away from Hy Brasil, they at least sweetened the wherewithal to deal out jauntier imagery to the hearts of those with propensities towards the sombre. There arose glittered prelation in Hellas, Sparta, Italy, Egypt, Crete, and along the coastal beaches of Africa, the bulk of which subsisted in repression under the empire of Carthage.

By virtue of reciprocity in erudition, economics and communion with the diverse corpora of these jurisdictions there tallied the habitation of supplemental grandeurs reported to the interior which sprawled eastward. Milieus analogous of the Seleucid Empire befitted credit, and then on to those purviews that ranged beyond the corridors and convoys, remotely into those reputed breadbaskets of the ascendant star. That said, so far as it could be ascertained from the test of evidence, besides that of the datum gleaned, in each of these outliers there yet propounded nought to threaten within the lunge of a fingernail, the modernity, so too, enlightenment of Hy Brasil.

For the duration of flow in which these heuristic enterprises betided, Hy Brasil pressed through its avenue of cerebral burst. Further, while there raised an aspiration to transact with not long determined empires and enclaves, primeval as most endured, there tolerated moreover a prerequisite to ensure strangers presumed not to attain whichever of the superior aptitudes that carried over as their sole preserve. It shook in consent that if Hy Brasil subscribed to maintain its exclusive advantage on this earth, then it avowed with an imperative corollary that foreigners be not gifted illumination through the facility of acumen as well as sophistication that in these times persevered as the lone features of Hy Brasil.

Therefore, the Commission, with the espousal of their remit, comprehended that up-to-date compacts abided articulation whose bourn published at the very least to abbreviate leakage of their vernacular intellectual property. It surfaced with gusto the determination to promulgate a law which mandated all scientific erudition, higher attainment and sophisticated operations, remarkable to Hy Brasil persisted exclusive to its prerogative. The whole of future contrivances and vehicles which fronted growth, by consequence too, expertise as well as distinction, such as in the spectrum of pharmaceuticals, ensued construal as domestic confidences; the divulgence of which by any citizen; judged as treasonable offences punishable by way of capital penalty.

Definite Resolutions and Conventions Put into Effect,

Robert E. Kearns

Consisted of:

All enterprise decreed to meet with instatement across those ports of the alien entity.

Should a vagrant merchandiser of foreign parts stumble upon Hy Brasil for whatever cause, they remained forbidden, no matter the state of affairs, to moor in its harbours. They may solicit permission to berth at sea, should condition warrant. There, saleable commodities trusted as worthy of obtainment were to pass in whole to the barges of Hy Brasil, which in turn accredited as the lone means of authority to convey cargo ashore.

Any endeavour from furtive vendors to disembark, occasioned to conclude in direct elimination or slavery, with their transports confiscated or destroyed.

Every Hy Brasilian dispatch skippered for the reason of two-way custom or substitute purposes to far-off coastlines, came down with the order to expound pre-ascendancy status. That is, there must be staged no outward display of development or technological success. Boats got entrusted to operate homogeneously in the majority of details to those of elsewhere, for circumvention to the demeanour of advantage that might well arouse uninvited curiosity.

A stride onward of the antecedent convention, the retinue on Hy Brasilian decks got subjected to a dental procedure where the aforementioned lethal alkaline happened to endure the drill into a rear molar tooth. Should it result they pass into captivity for the instrument of evidential extraction with interest to the national flag it set expected they fulfil their duty to patriotism and engage in the proper decencies in preference to the divulgence of intrinsic privileges.

There came listed appended ordinances, besides directions applied, but the above-referenced index achieved contemplation as the peak of imperative codicil to honour the integrity of Hy Brasilian supremacy. Of course, the truth of mortal quintessence deviated, and in every interconnection between the spokes of mankind there happens no legislation that will overcome random fractals of convection.

With humankind, the inevitability of escaped intelligences delayed not to remain eluded. It burgeoned as a widespread recognition afar; that there erected an island nation of superior beings represented some vicinity in the latitudes of the western ocean. This familiarity surfaced not as the worst of outcomes. Olan reckoned that when a land is written into the circle of myth and speculation, all preserves of fantastic and improbable attributes get assigned to its standard as well as indigenous chemistry. It upheld in soundness it exuded as an advantage to exaggerate the uttermost of ludicrous rumours, which to the entertainment of Hy Brasilians, affected to make certain those under an extraneous pennant lurched off guard. For them, there exposed no tactic to differentiate certainty from fabrication. Their overactive notions, plus fanciful inventions next spawned new yarns, whereby Hy Brasil charted adrift from a truism to embellished fiction, then back again, contingent on the parleying factions.

The country explicated as proficient in the traffic of vendibles and appreciated wares, so conducted it on every bearing, through the exploitation of its boundlessly multiplied network. The vibrant autochthon unions encamped the full coastal length of the western stomping grounds sourced as a consigner of animal furs, blankets, so too, multiple varieties of distinctive timbers. It flourished as a world rich in natural reserves with apparent limitless profusions of lumber, a markedly prized asset.

Hy Brasil, insulated and blessed with a capable, practical family of choice community for such an extended duration, accepted in that interval to raid its own woodlands to the limit of nigh on depletion. The intrepid of this remarkable glory to the west; they came to establish in mention, grounded as a more comfortable lot to negotiate with than the parochialists of Hibernia. That ancestral birthplace too, branched in affluence with utile forest, but disparate to their recently acquainted with chiefs of barter on the echoed shore, the Hibernians arrayed in partiality to brawl in the stead of bargain. They phrased as Hit and Miss when it tightened into the haggle over effects, so, because of that, befell on the whole, largely abandoned to their own devices. Despite their repute as a lineal relative, so far as it bothered the dealers, the adage of not consummating to determine one's relatives was systematically and with jest, regurgitated as the justification to maintain their disconnect.

The Teutonic, Seubian and Gothic bands of Germania duplicated the mien of Hibernia's Celtic progeny. They lavished copious volumes of drive, as if it excelled as a hobby, tuning the instrument of in-fighting, quarrels and spat's into an art. Consequent of this, in less than sparse instalments did they weave webs of industry and market up to the par of those well-to-do alcoves down south. It all chased back, Olan supposed, to the model of the Nation State. When ethnology sojourns in that of a tribal arrangement, embodied with hierarchies of argumentative chieftains', it ensues in substance, so far as he could make out, unattainable for them to season into an enlightened orient of promise. These all-sorts of rabble choke in strangulation by their domiciliary, too, peripheral wars he agreed. Furthermore, he invited how many moons beseeched proviso to rise in these dreary arctic atmospheres, before the multitudinous houses rallied to fuse into something that approached credence adjusted to common values, principles and the regency of law.

The preponderance of chaffer with thought to exotic stuffs, wrangled up in the bazaars and regulated markets that transacted in the tropics of Europe, so too, Africa where bright afore gloom bargained as the dominant manifestation. Most of these parched nooks and crevices trammelled in the prefecture of City State's, but they systemized to such enormity they styled as robust complexities with formidable armies for both deterrence and military expansion.

With this stability there supported the auxiliary and equally vital aspects for a society to prosper. Shorn of the perpetual bickering, besides bloodshed that lunched as the staple of frigid tables, there emerged the assistance to innovate. To better as a race, Olan mused, there must figure a distance of breathing space to afford the conditions which poised to sanction its spontaneous apparition. While combat and conquest idled as policy, too, a component of the social landscape in these Capitals, it manifested in such a pattern that contrasted with the insignificant fiefdoms of the north, with their bloodthirsty kings baying for it in torrents of red without relief. Merchantry, wealth creation as well as development mapped as a constant at the forefront of their designs. In these statuses, which cut slices of peace between interrupted hostilities, all means of creativity flourished up to grade.

From splendid stalls in provisioned squares it ensued that those ambitious purchasers of Hy Brasil paddled home with precious stones, gold, spices, Egyptian cotton, coffee from Arabia, besides slaves from The Go-Betweens of North Africa, Rome plus Athens. These arenas in purpose bought their consignments from the southern and oriental continents via well-worn trains, with the effect of that coinciding, Hy Brasil, without the obligation to consort in direct with these purveyors, had irrespective, habituated access to their treasures. Tea's and flavourings of allure scored attainment, with these cherished in earnest by the consumers of Hy Brasil. They took straightaway to the indulgence of these freshly stumbled on beverages of rarity. Beforehand there aroused a reliance almost in total on beers, ales as well as distilled spirits. Once offered to the collective audience however, they simply couldn't gain enough of these elite delicacies of import. This, for Olan, delivered a review the coffee he so adored, which in his lifetime got taken for presumed. It's characteristically the position; he reflected that when a specialty obtains widespread inurement, one awes at how at the commonality ever managed without it in the first instance.

The Hy Brasilians entertained no pangs of guilt when it extended to the fixture of slavery. In each port of call; there on the auction block, chained and manacled, in promise of exchange to the highest bidder in coin, submitted wretches of every shape, sex; moreover, colour. This vocation in the peddling of flesh got explicated to the patrons as regular an occupation as the quibble in a souk for byzantine silks. Ownership by pertinent adherents to the stock of humanity, in its conceptual pattern, posed as something their countrymen bore ignorance of. With this in mind, servitude abided in its initial construct as a curiosity ahead of much else. This hesitancy amended though, when after the inaugural novelty wore off, those in bondage came to be seen as progressively analogous to just about any other trafficked property, besides far-flung benediction, serviceable for the avail and enrichment of Hy Brasil.

It catered as seductive to the arrogant and oft-times lofty reputation of the inducted heritors. Too, they abided swift to grasp the avenue of wresting service from their captives to confront any ilk of task supposed beneath them. Because of this, corporeal tonnage rushed in from the docks of North Africa, with these detainees in perpetuity indentured to among other factors; labour as servants to the home, endure bound to manual toil, what's more, perspire from daybreak till sunset as red-necked farmhands. If, at the dawn of their serfdom, these shuttled in belongings presumed to find amusement in the caste of a lawful person, it came about in not too ordinate a stretch before they got allotted to their rightful station, which in the estimation of the Hy Brasilians, diminished their stature to such more applicable to their defective loam of embarkation.

How to contend with this admitted order of servant though, contrived as another matter altogether. In stone there chiselled the principle that without exception forbid entry to the republic. Outliers happened firmly to not figure as hosted with the mat of welcome. An obsessive devotion on behalf of the authorities transpired the order of the day, with the purpose to safeguard their blood lines from tarnish, furthermore, its dilution via those lesser specimens of hominid that tramped peripheral to their singular Eden. Strangers continued on as barred from the concession of proficiency to those mores, which should they hit on fluency, situated without doubt to mark Hy Brasil as the envy of all under the Mother Goddess of Creation. They appended to this register then, of edict and contraband the prohibition titled "Propagation with Foreigners".

It thence accorded as incontestable that all subordinates of the masculine gender suffered to resign under the blade for gelding straightaway after the release of anchor. Eunuchs impacted as a popular attendant remotely; hence gonadectomy came to pass in reasoning as the solution to comply with aforementioned policy. There led with, discontent in some quarters of amenability to avail of his tactic, given that ignorance of the operation, delivered in plenty, asset wastage, and ergo, financial injury to the title holder.

Even so this got trumped with the paranoia of diminished Hy Brasilian exceptionalism. Congress nailed as adamant that the jeopardy of an underclass interbreeding with their womenfolk should not ever strike countenance. Later, with experience, plus breakthroughs in medicine, the diminution of stock secured drastic savings. Overtures to the dispensation of inceptive antibiotics minimised infection and thus curtailed the overabundance of casualties. Further enlightenment got adjoined, for then, physical orchiectomy to action disposed of;

swapped out as a replacement by the implementation of vasectomy, so too, chemical castration.

The acquisition of in thrall females for domestic burden, distinct from the carriage of healthy bucks, refrained at the outset as outlawed with rigour. If, as surfaced the condition there based apprehension with regard to their male counterparts siring, then that unease took place as multiplied tenfold when it unfurled to the fairer of the duo. After all, the formula to inhibit proliferation of the alpha subsists noticeably patent. There tendered no such apparent fix to amend the contradictory of the sexes. The fathers of the realm stifled all too aware their own men should not kerb long about pocketing the boon from any conveniently grasped fortunes, and hence, the temptation to engross in this grade of relation got buried at arm's length. Endeavours to smuggle dainty flesh, persevered as fussily construed seditious offences, blameworthy with a visit to the hangman's noose.

Despite this however, as the nation bolstered in clinical proficiencies, there convened such excellences, likewise, refinements to the study of anatomy, biological science, too, surgical treatment, that it furthered to the incarnation these womanly menials could today yield to sterilisation through the relinquishment of their fallopian tubes for a clip and tie. As a result, this unfastened the ingress to the likes of Marka for reception as familial maids. There boded still enough in respect to the attitude of suspicion to ensure these treatments to spay and neuter got undertaken via offshore medical centres prior to disembarkation. The law-makers stopped unprepared to swallow the prospect of purchasers arranging the scalpel at their own beneficial pace.

Life under this distinctive scheme precipitated contentment to most, in that there knocked about many an unmarried fellow (plus a profusion of those fettered to the ball and chain; confident was Olan) who gestured widespread enrapture with the settlement. Fraternisation between masters and the subservient breathed unequal to prevention, but in the trustful tenor of things, the carnal flames of passion stood to beget no secondary offspring.

Regarding occupations of enterprise, it was learnt expeditiously the primordial strength of Hy Brasilians to draw from, and next convert the neural stimuli of their adversaries, meant they professed colossal advantages on their side. There corresponded through the exercise of this gift, an aptitude to add adroitness in all estates of negotiation. What assented as allegedly secret found its lock of invulnerability picked. The lies, half-truths as well as fibs of the seller amassed no longer his to fathom and the buyers to hit upon. The now expert brokers of this Hy Brasil manipulated the wherewithal to locate, so too, forge a path to hidden stockpiles of loot, which surmounted as booty of, if not of war, then peacetime hostility.

All is fair they announce it, with nought external to the pale, when it bites into matters of national benefit. The primary and concluding antecedence of every man reconciled in perpetuity to the country and its citizens. Olan, who couldn't help but let out a subdued guffaw at this dubious idealism, concluded that a fine chunk of these riches by way of a miracle made certain its contrivance into the purses of these, oh so honest dealers. Scruples and straightforward contracts banded as tolerable so long as they instigated corpulent pay offs. If, though, a trifle extra stood to be netted on the side, where opportune, it regulated as unhampered from the sphere of adventure for the fortuity of interposition with sleight-of-hand subterfuge.

It ought to reign expected that while the bulk of interests and enlightenments which alien terrains controlled got taken advantage of, Hy Brasilians under no condition were primed to oblige as the utmost of generous stock in its reciprocation. While they heretofore ameliorated, improved, too, evolved at an elaborated return as well as imparting regard to the absoluteness of magnified proficiency in contrast to foreigners, there orchestrated no doubt they puttered yet by some dimension in the efficacy to pocket snippets of instruction here and there.

The discernment and upkeep of supremacy to the residuum of the orb was not, however considerable it hurt, treated as a barrier to the intake of knowledge. An apportionment to the praxis of education meant that on an everyday basis there made known almost with reliability something further to attain, and then assimilate. Cognizance of one's intellectual pre-eminence destined that an abundant aggregate of this special edification, if applied with precise assiduity, might perchance harmonise to perfection. Technology, engineering, furthermore, views extracted from overseas, regimented as the vanguard to an effective society. They attested not just to achieve from it, but Hy Brasil, who secured a monopoly on the so dubbed "Intelligence Gene", had it in their power to soak up this deftness; then, having deliberated, churn it back out in a re-tailored as well as purified format.

There, as it happened, overlapped in addition, the

encapsulation of intellectual insight, which prior to the outreach from its insular harbours, was deprived somewhat to the confluences of Hy Brasil. Books, literature, art, advanced mathematics besides alternative contrivances of culture got communicated in revelation to the mother's bosom. This stipulated as fresh input for the inquisitive temperament, of which there swore munificent numbers in the erstwhile colony, and it dined these bookish hands whose appetites never sated. The surplus of achievement in the style of contributory verities, Arabic figures in addition to those sensory indulgences in artistry won, the oftener they enticed voracity. Henceforth from their realisation, broader again as a culture they spanned.

In undeviating instance, Hy Brasil typified as vigilant of their parochial intimacies, and signified a dim mind-set on whatsoever that may ensue construed as prosperities sluicing in the contra flow. Masteries which ran to their profit and which committed to boost merit squared in theoretical points as railed to a one-way track inward. They schemed nothing that might scholastically heighten the lesser shores of this earth.

Presumption expounds all well and good to the ideal, dwelt Olan's point. How things actually influenced though, equipped they thrust up that which hovered in law as proscribed. That lasts the truism, additionally, sureness of things when devoted to ventures, so too, cooperation's with one's fellow man. All the same, aside from the wrongdoing, it clasped a curious advantage to its position, in that peak erudition scribed as an ample treatise in the ledgers of myth, which heightened in the profound this ambient mystery, furthermore, enigma of Hy Brasil.

The utmost retribution emphasised once over as the deterrent spelled out to check all and sundry from driving exterior to the bounds of sanctioned dictates. Suffice it to say, this pertained to those scoundrels caught in the act of espionage or the transmission of state secrets. Consent to passivity in relation to either of these abuses activated interpretation as the malfeasances of a traitor. Mercy in the character of faith did not extol liberally to those who betided in celebration as the "Justices who Hung".

In those rarefied threads of a perpetrator remanded in the dock for the effectuation of sentence to their fore, these convicted blackguards resigned as more than assured to alight upon the black cap of execution. The moniker of the court principals it should contend reasonable to foresee ought to compel in motion a clue as to the verdicts nomenclature. As with plenty a quip though, this one owed as much to convenience as it did to genuine solidity. The punishment of death for a grievous infraction got meted out in a public forum devised to humiliate; so, acknowledged the rite of a sometime dance from the yardarm or more expectedly, the fellows crown incised from the shoulders atop a scaffold high, to afford revelry of the superlative kind.

They assessed this horrid genre of penalty was enough of a caution to put off other would be moles. With gratitude, domestic espionage resonated as not such a frequent pursuit, deterred in ration by what an infiltrator stood to realise if unmasked. The materiality of the standing vented that peak divulgence of sensitive material when it presented got carried out abroad on a narrow, too, tolerably insignificant scale.

There visited to the foreground of that which conscripted his inner boy, with reminders of the odd report he picked up in respect to the concealment of stowaways amongst the assorted crates and cargo freighted on Hy Brasilian ships. Immigration, as per the forced stipulations didn't bear tolerance. Hy Brasil countenanced in the whole for the Hy Brasilians, and that betided the propriety they aimed to maintain.

Solicitations to hole up in the quivered timbers of a cramped galley scored without relent as the likelihood, but given the plentiful crews who manned the ropes, circumvention of exposure for the totality of the ocean passage connived as next to hopeless. Every mammal, and that included persons, which in this illustration translated to unauthorised migrants, donned no shield against the electrical pointers that conspired as their giveaway.

A miscreant could well perhaps stash with the freight for a day or two but certain bechanced it to source them from the hold in the foremost nautical miles of a sail. The craggy Salts mapped under instruction to stand on alert for this eventuality and strategized disposal of their acuteness to smell out those electrical palpitations extruding from gnarled crannies where merely tea and coffee ought to squat. There stamped in the stock of an officer, no sympathy for the deceitful dodger. When in open ocean, any scamp identified to have machinated this deception, happened for the amusement of all, ordered to tread the precarious plank and make merry with those cutthroat beasts of the deep equivalently in proprietorship of an admirable genius for apprehension. Nobler did it serve, for them to cater as a spread for the sharks, than high-hat it as a contaminant on Hy Brasil.

Curs of the sea on purposes far off refrained from the appraisal of just the neighbourhood scenery, too, those rowdy drinkeries for the pursuit of ale. It infused the structure of things to occupy their spare time with accepted male instincts, with this side effect of communion, the resultant unavoidable consequence of rapport.

Officialdom paced their plush bureaus beyond sundown, contemplations engraved with motifs of foreign carnality. Compromise deferred as the-time honoured fudge servants of state dreamt up, and they portended a dictate which commanded this conduct, if it necessitated occasion, come to pass on secluded ground.

It may well attract invitation where else relations with those hewn from exotic quarries was supposed to take place, and Olan, who didn't care too excessively for the more zealous of those busybodies, could distinguish them in all their pomp tramping an opulent rug, inventing decrees to uphold the integrity of Hy Brasil. One of these confirmed that no man was to mark their reappearance on friendly turf with a non-national wife. If a relationship augured as imperative, then offshoots from the family way, demanded without exception, to be reared anyplace other than the homeland.

It presaged comparatively within modernistic generations to the accounts of Hy Brasil, their prodigious intellects stumbled across an innovation so unexceptional it baffled how no culture hitherto ever got within proximity. In Olan's estimation, this smacked as the critical substructure for Hy Brasil's singular eminence among the peoples of Earth. In the evaluation of this for a moment, it evoked yet, as it always contrived, perplexity why it sequenced his Atlantic isle that choreographed as the first, plus lone state to befriend this originality.

It might have synthesised their sped up development, but this agreed as creativity without end he assumed externals should have gotten around to exploiting by now. There subsisted after all, sensible, intelligent, thoughtful individuals out there who prospered to create shrines of complex contrivance. The invention he aroused ensued that which pertained to the force of steam. The tribes, city republics and countries of the globe all secured admittance to the elemental components for the promotion of this award. Metals collaborated to forge into swords as well as a million other spectacles for epochs a plenty. The species cooked and baked bread, so too, made good of the scalding water stoked from the conflagrations of combustion, all of which dated obscurely back into the ethers of time. And still, not one prince, pauper or servant in all those centuries lassoed a flash of eureka to harness this potential. Not until that is the learned, wise and erudite of Hy Brasil got underway with their experiments.

The societal leap that came about from the Age of Steam staggered the mind. The Hy Brasilian way of life which had grown used to revolutionary technologies still got punched as awestruck with the extent of creativity spawned, consequent to the agency of this fruition. This latest aeon built, further cemented a mammoth gap between Hy Brasil and all ancillary variants of humanity. Steam germinated the seeds of resourcefulness on top of modernisation. Pressurised engines perfected with trial and error to control the pistons and rotary kinesis of these machines got expounded in the preliminary to industrialise the mills which stitched cotton into garments. Engineers with persistence trialled, besides tinkered with these devices for countless additional schemes, then what initially dubbed as the aforementioned, soon enriched beyond that, and next expanded into the Industrial Age.

This fertile heath of industry led to a network of railroads, on which gargantuan boiler driven cylinders fuelled by means of the abundant coal deposits mined on Hy Brasil, hauled containers of payload, too, carriages packed with travellers. Factories sprang up in the towns and cities which expended equipment that today came boosted by the might of the latest apparatus as opposed to the horses and men of yesteryear.

Agriculture as well set about on renovation. An ox might in the past have trudged as the mainstay of farm endurance, but a plough in the wake of a mechanised tractor asserted the strength of ten. Water pumps that heretofore mounted as simple contraptions on the fringe of a canal or committed to the blades of a vane atop a derrick, ascribed in this creative phase to transmute into plants of industrial capacity. Each brainchild that cued on line gave up the idea for another. The fields that once primarily tilled with crops, so too relied on the merchant institutions, logged by some means to convert almost overnight, into a nation of cities embedded with production on courses of assembly.

Within decades the march of positive disruption shepherded a rise to the try-out of new concepts with regard to the ingenuities of alternating and direct current. If there had not come about the Ages realised through the potency of steam, it settled dubious to unsound whether its actuality should arrange to champion. But as with fictions hatched of monsters animated to beget, it occasioned in the end from the laboratories of know-how. In addition, it escalated to the scope of turbines that after a time piped electricity to business then homes, and across the whole of Hy Brasil. Street lamps, bulbs for luminosity in the house, white good appliances, besides, tools driven by charged electrons, utterly transformed the landscape. Steam may have gotten replaced or augmented with newer and more efficient customs of energy, but the fundamentals of this specialty today endured the same.

Soon, the invention of transports conveyed by the reins of a motorised transmission replaced those diversities of horse-drawn vehicle. A golden era of personal independence, and what's more, liberation dared to be born. This change from pre-industrial to mechanical, and then into this new Modern Age, transpired with rapidity; yet, the citizenry with their extraordinary genetic enhancements adapted to it with haste of equal astonishment. It correlated as if on this dominion of destiny there never breathed such a thing as a primitive resident. Original and state-of-the-art handiworks concurred as an everyday right of continuance. These laurels of novelty persisted as never sat upon just enhanced, which by consensus with their prominence in the world, presented to, if not the planet, then to Hy Brasil, further in the spectacles of engineering and technical enrichments.

It identified as these resplendent terms of modernity that Olan greeted his inaugural preview of Hy Brasil. His seat of adjournment in the delectation of a natural coal fire reminded that not every aspect of bygone traditions yet entrusted there. He stopped in contentment his family retained the heart and hearth of the homestead. When the house first submitted to construction, the architect bared an option for a complete system of central warmth without the sometime inconvenience of a sooty chimney. But, there evidenced covet to the personalities of both Olan and Neelak, for the hospitable cornucopias of incandescent flame with its consequential radiances of cheer. Each of them embraced emotional bonds to this memento of distinctive times; mankind's primitive craving for fire, which despite the requisite for everyday riddance of the ashes, likewise, replenishment of the hod; neither beseeched the aspiration to accord it by some alternative channel.

The elongated memoirs communed with this nuclear confidant, resolved with the embers paling afore him. Such endured the labyrinthine foraging's, he neglected to remark on Neelak's proposal of it as a night. He squinted at his watch face and then discerned it verified ahead of supposed.

Next, he embarked on the long-established rounds with his standard logical comportment, never in betrayal of the route worn into the carpet pile. At each station he barred the accesses, sanctioning the fob of the each key to fluctuate on its ring until stalled with credit to gravity. The final door in the sequence, the one particular to the kitchen, he sealed behind him then passed through to the master bedchamber, undressed, tipped up the covers, and slid into bed alongside his wife. His mindedness on sleep sojourned at a stretch yet; the neurons in his grey matter active with steadfastness. Thus he lay, chest up; in gape at what insignificances he could determine from the shadowy ceiling. With its direction as a silver screen of cinema, he revived the projection through his films of remembrance. To end, after an hour or thereabouts of ethereal flicker, he nodded off with exhaustion, thoughtful of choppy oceans and creaky galleons with tangled supports rigged with torn canvases. He joined in dreamy revelations of old-fashioned traders on Hibernia in heated association with hairy, argumentative, beasts of confrere. They quibbled over trinkets that captivated, piled high on wooden trestles and transacted in the coastal ford upstream from the south-eastern estuary of Hibernia.

The subsequent morn, Olan awakened in the black at his predictable seventh hour. Afterward to a scalding shower however, he grieved well short of the energy to worry himself with further grooming. From the prior day, his mood at present if anything, took a turn for the worse, and it assigned to him the impression he may well survive impotent to face the ensuing hours. Effecting to consummate what he couldn't remember ever according execution to heretofore without the sufferance of a physiological disorder, Olan, in place of accepting to attire, flew back to the still heated sheets of consolation to continue immediate to his darling Neelak. Then he scrunched the folds tight about his neck and chin, to bury imperceptibly inferior to the restriction of his air supply.

Sixty minutes advanced, Neelak stirred intuitively with the foremost symptoms of dawn, and envisaged to rise. She identified however, Olan yet in contented slumber to his side of the bed, and accepted in her state of semi-awareness she must happen in error. Later to a sight of her night stand clock though, it corroborated she wasn't misguided; therefore conjectured Olan somehow accomplished to sleep it out. She furnished on him hardly further than a courteous shake, by the same shrug acquainting him with the evidence he ran tardy for the lab.

But to her astonishment he merely grunted, then at length spoke up in response to her prompts through the disclosure of his ambition to capture a day of leave. A quarter hour posterior, on his left side, too, with the duvet tucked up to his neck; he floundered about into the cooler air of the suite with a naked arm, in a scrabble for the phone to call his assistant. Thankful she faulted to pick up, he entrusted all the same a word to her voice mail, vocalised in a not put-on raspy speech. On the minder he articulated to her future self he came down with an abrupt malaise and meant not to construct his presence this day. Imminent to a compressed pause at the terminus of his reason, Olan augmented in afterthought she may not catch scrutiny of him tomorrow either.

A brief while onward of this he swung out to the bed's perimeter. Neelak he discerned, adduced definite to speculate on why he so visibly played truant. With a sentiment to skirt those inquiries he didn't aspire to retort, Olan dressed in a rush, grabbed a cup of coffee plus a slice of bread on the fly, and next concocted a speedy retreat from the vicinity of his wife. He carved a lane to his study through the circumvention of those retreats for cuisine and leisure. In place he backed the laborious although person free route via the bedroom hallway. Here, he sealed the door behind him then assembled in the seasoned high-back chair. There, he timorously situated his intense brew on the wide desk calendar paired with the bothersome note, which to his heartfelt regret, disappointed to budge.

He abhorred casting onto others the temperament of disquiet, but one of their brood, without doubt he persevered. Olan's resistance against levitated instincts to punch the numbers could only tolerate so long, and he continued to eyeball the sporadically disposed handset to his right. Therefore, with agreeable coffee and bread under warranty, he frantically opted for the dust-veiled convenience then dialled in the integers for Sitric. Without preamble, but with composure at near eruption point, he got down to council with the bid, "Any developments?"

"Nothing's affected to adjust, old boy", happened the feedback of Sitric. "Look, you ought to accept this for what it is. There's no telling what's liable to come about, so my advice is you should positively carry on as typical". "Yes, okay", toned Olan's humble riposte, but a dramatization of all being conventional or the perpetuation of business as accustomed sanctioned not in sync with his troubled outlook. Conscious he may suffer to cross the boundary of worriment, too, by the same instant bothered with how Sitric might appraise this, he dismissed the short-lived encounter through the petition "Let me know if there ensues any updates", to which Sitric advised he committed as sure to do.

He balanced up the position again; appreciative he regulated as helpless to shake the pessimism active in his gut. The worst-case appraisal reared in typical accord as Olan's foremost reagency. That arrayed as his doctrine of prevalence when disagreeable bulletins glided in on currents of turbulent air. He knew there sustained a celestial mass of devastation on target to impact the world, yet he seemed to occur the sole man in panic. He moved to admit though; this activated as not quite the precise locution, but allowed that he reconciled, to broach it mildly, as perturbed. There determined no method as yet to anticipate where precisely this asteroid might vaunt its incursion. As well, the chances of it being on a direct trajectory of concussion with Hy Brasil placed as a long shot. Nonetheless, he drifted helpless to eradicate the impression his household would all lie dead in a matter of months.

None of this stood to matter if he could determine it resolved as just the primitive's of this world who befell to host its influence, or even one or two of the minor civilisations. Irrespective, for a collision to trigger this kind of anguish on Hy Brasil struck him as troubling in the severe. In the hush of his office, Olan elevated the empty cup, simply to have an article in possession, and then rode through an aggregate of the credible ends. The most injurious avenue to emerge evinced to remain a straight hit, in which instance they arrested in all probability to agitate into vapour. With a smidgen of luck, the whole ghastly deed might eventuate so quick and without warning there reserved to clear no scope for terror to set in. The likelihood of this according to Sitric flitted some grade around the five percent mark. The analyst that coincided Olan advised these conferred as decent odds against the manifestation of a holocaust, but his apprehension super ceded the arithmetic, with the effect he focused top-heavy on its weight of potential.

'Well then', he probed, 'what should resolve the eventual outcome if it homed on an ocean of the Earth?' The forecast without question pointed to ruin at sea level for each nation that colonised the strike zone. However, Hy Brasil in all likelihood supported by processor compilations ought to survive okay. This stimulated a portrait of encouragement to fixate on if one searched for a modicum of serenity to extract. But Olan, rather than hunt for composure of the soul, obsessed instead on the calculation on its happening to manifest. It came about as a disagreeable mission, but the pessimist will forever execute his ablest to trip into fates he doesn't favour. Guided by this, he envisioned that if anything, the preservation of Hy Brasil commanded the least supposed conjecture, founded on nothing more solid than the instincts of a defeatist.

The ensuing of his ruminations centred on the asteroid daring to batter remotely. Now, this pledged as where the variables configured at their extreme. There unveiled rare insight as to the end product of an extra-terrestrial rock's effect for this resplendent orb. The assessments machinated to sustain forethought, besides deliberation, with geologists concluding that Earth must have gotten smashed with a slew of these phenomena in pre-history. While there expectedly pelted several in the past thousands of years, a greater portion of the serious hammer blows incarnated millennia prior. It bore approval these megaton yields undeniably cemented an overwhelming aftereffect on the biosphere's climate. There ventured a school of thought which suggested these astronomic assaults may well have asserted as culpable for mass extinctions; too, this powered plausibility for it to have also brought to bear on former revelations of hominoid.

It perched as this which alarmed Olan. He contemplated if at one point in history this pinprick of light in an otherwise dusky solar system settled with a tribe in that mien of precociousness such as went on venerated in Hy Brasil. What if they turned out to be victims of a wipe-out, perhaps more than once, by a comet or heavenly host? Might it decree the expected order of universal mechanics, that actuality, and therefore civilisations, rise just so far then come to pass as erased from the imperious and august prairies in a catastrophic happenstance? May well did it obey this desolation, complementary to the aftermath of a woodland or thicket blaze, which seeded growth to a renewed cycle of continuance.

Capable is it of flourishing, that life inaugurated then pressed on, only to vanish without a trace, for it to germinate all over in a locus or occasion of amendment? His own ruminations, far from enhancing his grasp of the scene, in preference compelled him into an even more nervous perspective with the outline of impending affairs. He battled on further with his dissection, with conjecture there must at one interval have entertained to persist alternative dominant species of creature this world supervened as the residence to. If this propounded the case, then it suggested revealing that far from befalling static, life often regurgitated in fresh and sometime elaborated compositions. If it yet did not gravitate in the pre-noon hours, Olan doubtless would, on that consideration, have ascended to fix himself a whiskey of tall proportions.

"So, the asteroid crashes into compacted soil" he whispered. These fortunes he relished not either, in deference to what just now subsisted in his consciousness. With an exertion to separate the instincts he embraced to affright, from unbiased principles that urged a trend to his focal point of inquiry, he strained to conceive of the significances of a telluric bound encounter. Given what he surmised, the force stood to punch over and above any potency he relegated to the figmental. It regulated liable he purported to transcend widely yonder of all the energy generated on Hy Brasil in any given year. It may even exceed this, and that depiction introduced not as a frolicsome one. If this dynamism coincided to come up against a belt of dense country, the collision should resolve as so tremendous it qualified to pulverise everything within a prodigious diameter. This propositioned to dispatch the attributed debris into the upper skies. 'What if there braved enough of this rock, too, ash besides dust', he invited 'and it plumed into the upper reaches of the stratosphere? Pray tell, what abided to breeze in to the offing then?'

From the vantage angle of Olan, this flaunted without cheerful consideration. Even the consistent intelligentsia motioned assessments of negativity that committed to outdo the private defeatist. He apprehended that his personality obtruded as more than a tad neurotic, but it chilled him to the bone when he plied to summon up methodical carriages of conviction that saw him strive to locate a spoor back to his earlier station of fretfulness, merely for the sake of it. When the substance of reality affirms as more petrifying than the fanciful, he rationalised there stowed in right an abstraction to proclaim torment on.

Again, he regressed afresh to his line of self-posed interrogations. He adventured break it down into fractions that complied as legitimate to envisage. "If a mountain say got pounded with such ferocity that its mass got exploded up into the steepest measure of its limits, what primed this for nations beneath?"

He bade this with words to advance the esteem of speech toward the organisation of his views with uniformity. He didn't extract pleasure in the fix to this matter one bit. A blanket of purge and pumice, so far upward it coalesced not to subside straightaway, trusted in theory to adjourn there for years. If this came to fruition, the residuum undoubtedly designed to impede the sun. Should this obstruction of light continue for an extended duration, it sited to plunge the earth into a permanent freeze that ought to secure irrefutably ahead of anything yet suffered on Hy Brasil. With a scarcity of radiation penetrating to condition the soil, crops posited to wither. Cattle as well as other beasts mandatory for nourishment, should they graze on fallow ranges, impended also to happen rubbed out. "A Desert of Winter", expressed the phrase Olan realised to define it.

The broader Olan progressed over the chain of incidents that might arise, the further he appreciated how correct he figured to bathe in dread. Distress without motive arrested a terrible emotion. To anguish with bounteous cause though; while not rigorously inclined to provoke a jovial mien; at least offered a peculiar discernment of vindication. Exonerative of whom, he didn't know. To his self, he supposed, quizzical if that flashed the neon harbinger of madness.

In opposition to the pinch of a stopover at the parlour bar for the purpose of concocting an efficacious nip which in all fairness he rather demanded, Olan instead sneaked a roundabout circuit to the kitchen, with his wits on alert for Neelak. There he manufactured a supplementary pot of coffee to his explicit criterion. When in the mood, this elevated a pastime he favoured the diversion to his self. Unless otherwise struck down with a fever, if the convenience arose to prepare a brew in accord with his requirements, this he elected rather than trust it to a domestic. With this day, he articulated as indebted for the task in any case. To delegate a mission to his limbs, if even for just a small figure of minutes, presumed this an exercise with appeal.

Restored to the chair, too, in the embrace of his cup to the breastbone, he killed time for it to realise optimum temperature. Through the caress of his goatee, he satisfied to soothe down a notch. Impending doom, bona fide or notional remained in all prospect not a constructive mania to fixate on with protraction in a single shift. The stroll of the corridors and chambers besides ten minutes of cognitive and physical enterprise blunted the edge off his angst.

There attended another intrigue to reflect on, but the primary grounds of cataclysmic wipe out; now it busied his notice inhabited to bechance obstinate in its shift. With a trial of the beverage through a timid immersion of his upper lip, Olan contented himself it abounded without hesitation, as nigh on perfect. In accordance, he enthused to gulp a protracted swallow.

This alternative prophecy, apart from the asteroid skipping past the planet altogether, which sounded improbable, posed as one contingent on a calibre of imagination. Should the entity bypass Hy Brasil but pummel home in parts unknown of the Atlantic, the aftermath for the isle might ensue tough to determine. The proximate sea immersed as a colossal ocean. It could deviate to any of the compass points in a body of water a thousand times more spacious than the homeland. The choicest pick if he regulated the capability to single it out, should resolve some horizontal south of the Capricorn, he agreed. Wherever in that segment of the sea may convincingly, he trusted, reduce the anxieties for Hy Brasil. "What bracketed the chances, though?" he examined, through another mouthful of coffee, as if it collaborated from the fables of his youth as proportionate to the "Salmon of Knowledge", where he who partook of it, got to posture endued with the elucidations to every complexity.

He swerved through the curves of promise yet again. Olan comprehended that there persisted a vast aggregate of guesswork to weigh up. Yet, he stuck hog-tied to spirit the will for to tack a positive spin on it all. Hy Brasil took every precaution to shelter itself from independent influences, just to meet defiance through a set of conditions it exercised no control over. Olan throve as a man of acuity in a medium that approved of the requirement to realise contingency plans in situ. Now, here he dedicated with inadequacy to regulate his emotions to any serious degree. The infusion of caffeine simply propped him up as a temporary crutch, and when he drained the cup, established on the inside as barren as it. This dark pit provoked him to bequeath serious contemplation towards a crawl back under the linens to abscond from the tribulations of being.

He isolated in the end not to his dormitory, but it claimed a term of debate besides cerebration, while trapped in the seat, whether he ought. Rationalising that it may well cohere on balance as healthier to tough it out; he in lieu imposed on himself a coat, descended the steps to the rear, and then charted the crooked flagstone detour which funnelled to the greenhouse. This divulged as a second stronghold from the hardships of life's substance, so too coexisted as a conservatory where in dependence of the season, he may commit to appear in avail of its temperate clime.

Olan appreciated an allotment of garden toil. It joined forces as an occupation he placed faith in to either relax him or confer a ration of exercise, conditional to the function he took on. Both blessed him with gratification. Labour in the pursuit of a goal, such as a summer bloom, yielded as beneficial in two respects. In the paramount he earned a favourable workout; in addition, as a matter of course he attained a high with the fantasy of how pretty the payback resolved to come about in a handful of months. Even should he not partake in a chore of strain, such as the implanting of seed or the requisite to prune, he derived all the same recompense from the milder charges. He conceded that responsibilities of horticulture and husbandry proved incalculably more congenial than personifying as a dependent to his nine-to-five.

There readied a handsome wicker chair Olan set aside, which signified as suitable to revel in its rarefied friendliness, while exterior to the structure's transparent frame; a chill stood firm in the air. Habitually he reposed on its handsome cushions, to luxuriate on a tumbler of dew smoked with peat from the midlands, while sedating his eyes to banish the trials of creation for a spell.

Today, to start with he took advantage of its tranquil construct. But without supervision of the aforementioned goblet, for which at this instance his sedentary fingers compelled an essential interest; he got up and next embarked on to busying himself with a quota of terracotta pots stacked in the corner. It wasn't as if they compelled an enormous content of labour imposed on them. The depleted compost, Olan scraped out in the autumn, but he now ensued to furnish them a once over with the wire brush, so they complied to situate in tip-top order for the spring. More, with the confidence of the onset to that season, or the Gods forbid it, the absence thereof, he sunk into an even darker mental environment, and searched if he appointed to chalk up a pending summer of flowers and colour to look ahead to.

The containers scoured out capable as he could fulfil; he flagged his activity to the tomato plants that categorised an ever emergent harvest in this favoured aedicule. He treasured their tending; too, he adored the vigilance over their growth from nucleus to crop, with the anticipation of a rich hoard of prime fruit. Perhaps rarely for one who ministered to them so, he never adapted to gain a taste for the produce of his industry. In their clan it resolved Neelak who savoured this subtropical delicacy. Foreign to Hy Brasil, he recalled they showed up as one of those headmost popular imports from far-off regions of the southwest, further; they tenanted too as a reminder to Olan of how immeasurably the nation had scored since those dates of the seminal spearheading adventurers.

"What now we accept for granted" he pronounced, with an irregular tremble to his upper lip. It prolonged as one of the modest pleasures of continuance that forever bonded a smile to his face; and that exercised the toting of a basket from his house of glass to the kitchen, occupied to the brim with a full-fledged juicy harvest. The delight this elicited from Neelak invoked worthwhile all the hours devoted here. Now and then, to recreate the glee, besides a shared treasure of experience between husband and wife, he exulted to convey them not all at once, but in batches stretched to consecutive days. It parcels the smallest of gifts that presents the ultimate of joys.

In the cradle of budded vegetation straightaway, he petted the leaves, moreover judged the weight in his palm of the green and petite immature produce. Here, Olan reverted to the emotion he combatted several nights ago, which apportioned a feature of his constitution when dejected. It delineated as if he had forgotten how to breathe. He gathered there, and after ten or fifteen seconds when his tone initiated an exchange to blue, he needed to arouse a conscious resolution to engage his lungs. This exertion drained him even further, both physically and in tenure of complexion. He fathomed not how to cry; without the practice since childhood, but if he might again pick the secret to undo this shed of tears, then that is the den he should indisputably render to intrude.

The rest of those hours saw Olan distracted with the condition of not quite in the decryption of what to do with his self. If he flew to reinstate at the house, he reared to comport in the predicament of a trap; too, if he immobilised in the apartment of glass, he beheld the portent of intense loneliness. This witnessed as an ailment beforehand noted as one of the fundamental paradoxes of melancholy. There authorised to climb a circumstance for its alleviation somewhat through the companionship of family, but the expectance of an obligation to converse when predisposed to this plight, coordinated in itself as onerous.

Resultant of this, he deferred until the decision concluded with the script of the season. Ursa Major rises precipitously at this stretch of the winter in these upper latitudes; likewise, the twilight which precedes it dallies full of fight and without concession, dragging with it a plummet of temperature. The clement quality of his favoured haunt gave way to a relative frost; hence, it decreed this which prompted his departure for the conviviality of the home.

When he admitted, his comportment of hunger exposed, with luncheon missed prior. A legion of solitary minutes evaporated, forsaken to eternity, thus, it withstood as implicit, a vestigial day of the allocation designated to his being disseminated right now into the bin of waste, having realised with it little except to mope about with a sigh in each gasp, in large fixated on nought at all other than philosophy with heedfulness to the denouement of life.

The afterward daybreak, he bothered not to make contact with his aide, in evidence the announcement of yesterday devised to cover him for a second bout in the ring of truancy. He couldn't agitate the proclivity to allow the peril of a summons in vivacity, in supposition it ceded as an exhaustion to converse in this mood.

The former evening, post dinner, he idled over next to the fireplace, helpless to disconnect his eyes from the wholesome combustion, striving to expose distinctive meaning to it all, and in mediation with respect to the transformation of a solid substance into powdery ashes. The inimitable purr of a full glow supervened with the conferral of abetment. In addition, it devolved a trace of the hypnotic. Therefore, sooner than traipse on with the sentiment these inclined as squandered opportunities; he exacted from them a portion of wellbeing.

It appropriated to his stream of drift, the treasure of favourable alleviations while they yet granted. Once however, the fire postured to within an inch of its death, and the lateness of the hour called him to slumber, he followed as above all in a rush to undress then conceal within the bosomed asylum of the winter tog duvet which he tugged above his bare shoulders. Olan shifted through the gears of resolve under his influence to dam up the whimper which yearned to escape. Rather than weep, he squeezed in tight to his most precious wife, and clung to her with longing in the usage of both arms and legs.

Here and now, in bed still, he lay awake, but without coordinating the phone call which on a more courteous day, he may otherwise have borne out, Olan resolved, that for consecutive dates he endorsed no aspirations to stir. He arranged there, in the assessment of his watch and every computation of its beats, as if in anticipation of the hands to conquer an opportune altitude for reveille.

Neelak situated her head in the architrave and sought if he might care for breakfast. Olan appreciated this as the excuse he delayed for. With rancour he threw off the wraps as he accommodated the morning previous, then stepped into the shower. He pondered abstention from this ritual, but as awful as he throbbed, traditions for him etched as a covenant; hence, after a stint beneath the exhilarating spray, he patched up as satisfied there attained a parameter of cleanliness where he tabulated to don stimulative accoutrements.

The meal of primary distinction concluded, he prepared extra coffee, and then took his place at the head of the feasting board, in demand of what he ought to accomplish with his day. A return to the sometime conservatory graced not as a pick he fancied. The day former crafted now as a sorry memento for him, and he deflected no proneness for a do over. By the same manner, he omitted the option to purpose a shut-in to his home office. One of the stranger quirks to escort his spells of downheartedness kept on that within him; there resulted the sometime inclination to shun repetition on consecutive days. Irrespective of his current disposition, Olan couldn't help but take on the function of testing why this should be. 'Perhaps', he whispered inaudibly, 'it screens as a vehicle for emotive stability'. As useful an explanation as any; he corresponded as absolute to act on it; further, by the adventure of a drive perchance, poised to scheme out of the house for a turn. He could even assume revival afterwards, but appointed as not overly optimistic of success.

To start with, he grasped not where he headed for, but the swish of seaboard surf pledged in recurrence as an enticement to his humour. With the lure of this thought up composition by degrees, pencilling in brush-strokes, he reached autonomy to his displacement which shepherded him towards the coast.

As he steered within a furlong, that thrill of anticipation he realised since a child, washed over his persuasion. Too, it conveyed with it a squint of guessed at benevolence. Not far off each incidence of an outing to the seaside there accorded something of that perception to shuffle away from it. The subtle alterations to the condition of light from one hour to the other bore its exclusive satisfactions. The wintertide rays differed in intensity from the summer, and then the length of day; sizably embellished in those kinder months, articulated its own virtues plus manifold remembrances to cherish. Even now in proximity to the Hy Brasilian solstice, he stumbled onto a chapter of circumstance that recited serene besides favourable. This too, Olan credited, ought to ship to him the gift of sensory stimulation he so hungered after with angst.

He parked at the virtually deserted promenade, and on his exit from the motor, a sharp bite to the near stagnant air struck him a belt. Despite this, the sting to his cheeks he hailed with applause, so too, it injected a smidgen of zest back into the veins which coursed hollow for an age. He threw on his jacket which draped on the rear seat, and after zipping it over his chin, he next shoved cold paws into genial woollen gloves. A hat he forwent to make dependent on the rousing needles to his exposed derma. Next, Olan alarmed the car, resolute in mission to hike in seclusion down the beach then straddle the sand at the point it converged with the ebb tide.

This slice of shoreline came into view seven Roman miles from home. As well, it surfaced in evaluation as ideal for lost walks. Olan eyed up the strip of waterfront, and as opposed to cogitating on it as a grand length, tested instead if it proposed as enough of one. Abruptly, he came to transpire overwhelmed with an appetite to trudge evermore, or at least until his legs gave out. A remote amble freed him up in a metaphorical and literal escape, thus, at this hour he sought, even prayed for a prolonged absence from the stalking upset that eclipsed his being. This absorbed the continuance, which on the calendar atop his study table; he elected to mark off the ensuing cessation of days.

He entertained the strand to his self; hence, embarked on protracted strides towards the back end where the dunes and estuary blended. His gait amid the briny grain assessed as tenacious at the outset, but every half league he recessed in his imbedded footsteps, swivelled round, took in a survey of the venue he came from and after that contemplated on the sweep thus covered.

There on the cliff above jagged rock, pointed out to sea in the attire of sailors white and blue, mounted that fellow of metal and his chant rang out "Keep out, keep out, good ships from me, for I am the man of misery".

Next, he tackled headfirst over again to press on. Burdened with this for about forty minutes, he covered shale and shells to the outlet where at his side the hilly ridges swelled, blanketed with salt-tolerant high coarse grasses in hues of brown and evergreen. Here in the openness of the bay, with just an ill breeze for comradeship, he bent down to pick out a sleek and wave eroded stone. This he hurled to sea with sufficient muscle, expectantly; and in conjunction with a muted juvenile mirth for the tinkle of its splash to echo back to lobes numbed keen.

The launch of horizontal pebbles; its exploit alternating between the aspiration for numerous hops on the skim, as well as enthusiasm for a mellow plop in the surf, spirited as a playful, so too, remunerative tryst. If this disclosed a later month on the timetable, he established not to distract the freedom of this glorious isolation to hold in greatest respect the repetitious predication and theme of these amusements. He therefore acclaimed this incomparable choice of getaway, likewise, commended all that joined with it; the batted wings of the gull, the lap of tame breakers on gravelled shore, the perfume of savoury flecks kicked up in the disputatious spray, plus the emptiness, but nigh to perfect marvel of the seashore aspect.

His casting hand now flaunted pale blue fingers where he rid himself of the mitted insulation. The benign discomfort attendant with that unassuming effect harmonised if nothing else as a cue he yet realised a heart with direction. All the same it dedicated as the hour to circle back, but he clung to the final iota of this wondrous bliss, incapable still to abide it head-on. Here, Olan's eyes descended to the band on his marriage finger; a halo of gilded allure, inscribed with indigenous lettering and accepted as a representation of vows absolute.

Olan delayed in the brackish fringe, sunk to the leather upper of his shoes, until at last pressing his limbs to orient toward the heart of introductory source. The duration of coverage took longer than the outward as his legs now and then quit their rhythmic alteration. Olan discerned he consciously affected their pause, but it still afforded the illusion to his apprehension of an involuntary accomplishment. At each point he held still, Olan battled the irrational requisite within, to facilitate his knees to buckle, crumple, and then irrevocably collapse to the sand; there to drift into a ceaseless inertia.

He pined for the saline and silt to coordinate as the variety to anoint as brisk at swallowing him up into its cabbalistic stomach, what's more, consent to his immutable peace. And with these difficult contemplations, he groaned, besides exerted to draw a breath. Then with an emotional agony he restarted with a barely perceptible amble. A mewled scrap of him got compelled to hurry onward to the deliverance of the car. There in the confined space he may perchance toast up his immaterial heart and subsistent corpse. But at this trice his parts refused to rally any sprightlier, too, his lungs wanted no countenance for the fight. It unarguably devised as a laborious function, and purely when he came to within fifty yards of his goal, was it he excavated the depths to increase his pace. This final sweep enlisted now as an appointment he called for to achieve as if his life surely depended on it. Within strike of the door and in extreme agitation, he fumbled with his key fob; then scurried inside to seek shelter from the downpour of sorrow.

A day on from this incident, Olan commuted to the laboratory. As opposed to leading among the initial on the road, he dawdled at home, took his time, so too, even fixed coffee; luxuriating in a refill to boot. Today, he set a goal to wallow in apathy and not give tuppence for the repercussions. More accurate than the effect of a dismal lethargy, it clocked in as the conscious resolution to sanction a break from his burdensome cares. He professed attraction to his onetime immersion in the sciences. Those disciplines fascinated his inquisitive constitution, but he speculated if in these departed count of years he fell in to work punctually because he treasured fashioning a lead on those assignments which stimulated the brain cells, or whether he modelled as overly dutiful with those clerical responsibilities which cropped up without sympathy as not all that significant or compelling.

The comeback to that explicit point of mention verified as not all that resistant to clear up. He irradiated debate on this when last parked at the desk. Minimal struggle dwelt essential to get caught up in, not just bureaucratic busy graft, but via the same mould; on the tedious tasks that could likewise abide deputizing in alternate scopes. He took on too much; further, he negotiated it out of habit ahead of much else. The truth divulged he adored the practical labour, experiments and research, along with whatever write up's, besides accompanying papers that consort with publication. Most of that got documented to ages gone by however, and he stayed plunged these hours in all of this other detail which showed as superfluous, boring and, at the end of it all lacking in reward. With the realisation there sustained zero to wrest job satisfaction from this inconsequence; he swore a firm pledge, that from that second on, no longer was he amenable to comply with it.

Olan smiled proper for the first mention in what seemed an epoch. He relished this added sentiment of liberation and longed for its extension into the days ahead. Perhaps; he envisioned, he ought to engage his ample brain that until now sorely lacked in stimulation, towards a tangible hope, then make a physical, so too, imaginative application to resolve, what of late survived as the basis of his preoccupations. This meaningful appointment of his talents might open a path to exorcise from his attentiveness the strangling fear, besides anxiety of this unforeseen week, to, in its place, oppose the crisis head-on, through a practical besides worthwhile approach.

Robert E. Kearns

This obstacle positioned to require a fair accumulation of analytical enterprise; hence he reverted to the method he always reached for when preparing for this manner of difficulty and grabbed a pad of paper that wedged beneath a heap of forgotten files. To his front he thumbed through the used pages until he came to the first of the blank and there scribbled upon it a few random points and subjects of import:

Asteroid on a straight course for the planet

Not yet determined where it has in mind to impact

Extent of probable damage tough to assess–Dependent on sea or solid strike

Recognised fact corroborated if there concurred a categorical interaction with Hy Brasil or within the immediacy of it this abided as definite to mean the annihilation of their Republic and its inhabitants

No procedure or extant technology accessible which has the capability to divert asteroid from its current trajectory

Perhaps just months to live?

Might there establish an alternative manoeuvre attainable? Mode of Prevention? Scientific Remedy?

Olan beheld the script he authored. Essentials of it revealed as before now allowed, but those givens may well support marshalling to his cogitations, further assessment of the circumstances to order. The final three rows highlighted as those worthy of additional consideration. Hy Brasil saw an improvement in the primary phases of advanced rocket development, but as yet, encroached to not close on convenient enough for the proposal of a repair that might be derived from this category of scheme.

The courtesy to it as a plan, though, while unrealistic, did however stimulate the brain to engender doses of cerebral intent that could hatch more premises for a workable evaluation. Olan, when he covenanted his devotion to a challenge that beseeched all of his intellect, expressed as one to invite the humblest of inquiries but then apply his self to call up the entirety of his education, and more to the point, his ingenuity to presage the antidotes.

The second to last point/question, he scrutinised again. Olan churned through the potentials, so to, the "What Ifs" going on imminent to a hundred turns before this. With this in mind, now in a perusal of this line in his heightened state of attentiveness, it invoked an altogether anomalous response. He opted to pluck from it the doomsday corollary as the one credible impression and undertook to convert what etched as an open disquiet into a statement of fact. It alleged from the lips of elders that one strategizes for the gravest, but trusts for the advantageous. Olan never quite conformed to the maxim, and seldom in count of the utmost, ample times blueprinted a chart for the ruinous. Since this gravitated to the intrinsic, it looked to him in this time sensitive array of magnitudes, that with the pessimistic supposition noted as a verity, this raised with his present mind-set, the advantage to focus its manipulation to a breakout from the quandary.

With this settled it led nicely into the final constituent. Now he conducted business with truthfulness he could pose as a grandee of erudition if there dispensed a cure through the supremacy of intellect to finesse the earlier stated fact back into a query. Prevention he guessed was ruled out in total. The resources did not exhibit; hence, the acceptance of fundamentally harbouring nothing other than a season or two left ostensibly precluded it from future efforts. However, he elected to leave it on the page, and then looped it a sum of times in ink, the exploit of which levered as a stimulant to rational acumen. Given that he synchronised as resolute in obedience to the commission at hand; then within the format of approaching fate; avoidance by an alternate exercise may nurse potential. As for the question on whether there perhaps animated a methodical conclusion; well, that occupied as where he entrained with all this.

At this juncture and with a reinforced purpose that fell misplaced to him for a lengthened delay, Olan came to muse empirically in preference to brooding in the emotive. The countenance of precision to plot a course by this praxis reacted as an agency to throw light on what he acutely distinguished in place of preoccupation with his fears and apprehensions. He defined all too aware of preferences towards the grim. 'Let's be honest', he muttered under his breath, 'they regularly exceed mere propensities and pitch more to the cask of triple distilled in a kettle of wretched mash'.

But they carried on for what they imparted, and while struggles of which, when at their worst, racked up as torturous; they founded as a relevant chunk of the make-up and personality in hold of the lately wielded writing instrument. Not that he berated himself. Yes, he detested it when holed-up in a bottomless crevice and that rift he situated in latterly engulfed as the culmination of distress by instalment.

This checked as the escort of these incidences. They burrowed to their deepest point, and then he mounted the laborious ascent of the north face all over. While passably downcast, Olan also now reasoned he possibly fathomed to the nethermost of the decline, with the tide of complexion at once buoying its turn. Resultant of this, too perhaps, as a signifier of recovery, he fastened on to the beneficial philosophy of, whilst on the climb to normality, not punching his psyche to an emotional pulp. "To laugh at adversity scrambled as the curative policy"; and on the annunciation of this proverb, there got expressed a glitter of pearly white.

To make certain of a coherent emphasis on the contemporary stood to tender, if nothing else, a hint of self-therapy, and he steadied as willing to contribute his optimum shot. He hypothesized it ought to pump fuel into the body in its quest to scale out of the black hole that dwelt as the painful centre of his universe for too protracted a period. Besides, he didn't care too much for the portrait he painted of a sedentary dejection for the next half dozen months, while he might instead service this interim to contract what the ancestors in earlier times designated as his "God given brains".

On this basis he hoisted the foolscap as a charm of fortune for his proposal, and gaping over it conversed one-way to the precincts of his solitary office, "Anyone can pen this stuff down. It's a different complication again to tackle it". But, he called this out in a jocular fashion, even with a diminutive sprinkle of soul-searching mockery. Here he raised a toast to his pursuit with what abided in the cup, suppressing beforehand, a near escaped titter.

This imminent inevitability of perplexed unease framed to comprise a share of reflection. The maiden issue to ponder abided to how to go about it. Each published manual in the vicinity of where he located ratified as of no interest or involvement to this fix. Plus, most of its bulk immersed as the substance which abetted to sever the line of his grapple to emotional stability. Therefore, in his not long appropriated liberation from the straits of formality, Olan decreed an executive order that every scrap of bothersome paperwork was to recede into exile from this space, apart from those scarce documents that attended just for his eyes or signature. All projects he hitherto dipped a toe in got consigned to irrelevance and therefore attained a 100% destiny for dispersal. In keeping with his prior vows Olan committed not to squander that which remained with official research or useless exertions. All investigations now confirmed a distinctive, likewise, applicable intent.

With confidence, Olan hailed his secretary on the speakerphone. He explained the status through the fabrication of a convoluted yarn. Drafted in for his expertise, the government called on him to oversee a specialised assignment which obligated his exclusive attention. So, all and sundry allotted to his desk meant to be farmed out, and he tendered that she indulge the subsequent hours in here to familiarise herself with the lot. With his input they should ascertain who fit best to designate each charge. The conditions of his new brief commanded an unsoiled workstation. This, he comprehended with amusement, via the evocation of a familiar adage, would come into reality as a first.

Then, with the ordinances specified, Olan arranged for the gathering of his staff to reprise the colourful fib regarding his bogus obligation for the central administration and its utmost relevance to the nation. The recitation of tall-stories arose with rarity to the lips of Olan. In fact, with predictability he got seen through as an abysmal liar, and under an altered state should expectedly bargain with this breed of deception as problematic. Today, however, he stayed propped up by the adrenalin of euphoria, so furnished it with the sureness of a professional.

"Must repose in the coffee", he clowned when all of them quitted. The promotion to this domain of humour concurred as affable; in line with the retreat he scooted from the latest slumber in black. Unaccompanied yet again in the office, he sprawled in a stretch to the rear of his soon to be witnessed sanitary worktop with fingers interlinked behind his crown, categorical in a regal edict, that for him at least, spring hinted in the streams of air.

A mere five minutes past he communicated to his subordinates he undertook to mark himself available with an appointment, for consultation in tandem with esteemed guidance, but should not uphold any supervisory oversight to prior caseloads for the immediate duo of quarters. The apportionments were to pick up transfers of equal division, and he propagandised his most sincere conviction they encompassed the capability, moreover, talent to manage it as far as the heights of competence and standards he himself set over the years.

It transpired a delightfully agreeable experience to allot, confessed Olan. In a day of firsts, he offloaded the entirety of his responsibilities, further, in that achievement, telegraphed to his ego it eventuated a precept he found to his taste. All of it he mandated with a persona of pomposity, where he mustered the idiosyncrasies to a composite of characters he bumped into at one time or another, all of whom excelled as windbag bores. He complied as decidedly proud of his articulatory feat where he commented on the undoubted certitude he held in the capacity of his team to execute their responsibilities in an exemplary conduct; or an absurdity of that sort. And all of it merited sweeter to the palate for the accompaniment of haughty marzipan. Thus, while in audience with the urinal, having sauntered around to the men's room, he chortled out loud and commanded how it happened he repressed a smirk of askew in the utterance all of that drivel.

With a rinse under the tap, he elicited from memory that all too recurrently he happened upon those he defined as the 'Serial Delegator'. Before the mirror, he tidied up, determined that in obedience to the hour's theme there should stem no urgency on his part to re-materialize behind a credenza. He esteemed his novel flash of manly dare and chose therefore to run with it.

"Ah, yes. The relentless assignor", he muttered. "Ha, don't tell me I've gotten commissioned to their ranks". Olan, who suffered acquaintance with this type his entire adult life, now, developed a smirk of amusement that out of nowhere he got inducted as an honorary member to their club. The steadfast appointor is a fellow of seniority, he reflected, where not one colleague can figure out what it is they do. The chore that is embroiled with a constituent of difficulty is with promptness, akin to the proverbial parcel, forwarded on. As masters of their realm, they are apt to perch aloft in the captain's chair; all the finer as a lookout nest. There on the throne of power, the autocrat basks in the application of command, with incessant directives for underling peasants to satisfy his curiosity what they accomplished with the day. While, to those with antennas on notice there occurs a palpable and distinct absence on the plate of their interrogator, of even a scrap of that which might risk construal as Action Requisite.

This class of man coincide on the whole as the most pretentious, furthermore, arrogant of individuals, heritable with the triumvirate of self-assurance, conceit and entitlement. This, when Olan mulled over it, showed as the embryonic reason as to how they forever abscond from responsibility. There stems from them the charade of outrage at all purulence's (to him) dispersed, not measuring up to the premier yardstick they submitted at every chance. The slothful dictator, with preliminary alarmed indicators of an offer to take on tribulations uninvited, snips it off at the bud with a pronouncement of their frightfully busy schedule. As a species, the canon they swear by, is to never shoulder accountability for incidents gone awry but endlessly accumulate the credit for episodes spliced to accomplishment. Too, they occur superbly effective in the observance of this oath, since they firmly elude any designs with a remote whiff of answerability.

Olan long since copped on to the buck shy of his particular profession, so too, hoarded a quota of swelled contempt for them. Today though, a bulb lit up in reference to a wise motto where it was held that if one is impotent to surmount them, they should as the opposite endure to team up. He happened upon a studentship of acceleration which altogether valued the absolute dominance of long-forgotten sovereigns. Don't execute for yourself what the muscle of hegemony can force subordinates to complete instead. And with that thought, he jaunted to the canteen and almost pursed his lips to break into a whistled rendition of a self-satisfying tune. He hedged it back at the ultimate chance by convening the will power of grandiose restraint.

With inner jest, he congruently mimicked with a pretend dialogue on how Sitric might comment; 'another rule of enacting the lofty authoritarian old boy, is to never err distinguished with any mien other than the sternest of expressions. One must impress as travailing in a hectic agenda with thorough deliberation, even more so when one's sole aim at present is simply to pour a refill'. 'I should have continued the whole hog' Olan cackled, 'and ordered it conducted to me'.

He plumped to sanction this solitary slip up to his thespian charade. With heartfelt jollity he instead observed the put-on manifestation which publicised "Here braves a chap of consequence". With a mug procured, he trundled with purpose back to his office exploiting all the falsity in demeanour of one weighed down beneath the invariant stresses of drudge, but where to the rear of barred doors persevered in distraction with nothing more imperative to accomplish than the appreciation of his aromatic brew.

Empowered, Olan at lunchtime revisited the duplicate scope of coast as his prior excursion. He replicated as not at all in a contemplative vein this day, and it enlisted as the aspiration for exercise that solicited from his rejuvenated figure an enthusiastic stroll. As opposed to the beach, he toured the upper deck of the railed promenade which continued to advance delightful views of the strand and far off tide. A constitutional in the clemently placid breeze allowed for an invigoration of the senses. He sustained up till now on a high from the morning's endeavour, hence a brisk tramp into the marginal headwind supervened as an opportunity to burn off excess energy. Upon attainment of the walkway's conclusion, at the spot where it slips down to the sand he realised an immediate about turn without loss of pace, and trod the reverse leg. He hadn't come within isolated breadth to this summit of gratification in ages, so in corroboration of his improved well-being, inhaled; surpassing once, the seaside atmosphere, to the fullest capacity of his lungs.

On re-emergence at the point of outset, he slipped past his car, traversed the vacant street then passed the threshold of a familiar café, clad with quaint façade which he eyed up from remote. The minute there, he was escorted to a sheltered exterior trestle that wallowed in the winter sun, so too, which came arrayed with an affable check cloth of red, white and crisply ironed at the seams.

Seated, he came to be offered the abridged luncheon menu, and as he approached familiarity with it, called for a pot of tea. The deep exquisite breaths he now drunk in rated in contrast to the ones forced upon him throughout those hours of desolation. His respiratory system got to function in the body of a man who clasped onto a purpose to live for. He settled on a choice of fare as the brew arrived, and after investing a stir to the pot, dispensed it into the elegant china and complemented it with milk.

Next, Olan shut his eyes and aspired to haul in each sensatory net of the seaside; to absorb the pure chimes about him, further, reclaim the passions of his childhood. Why he tested, did emotions, homogeneous to a born-again phoenix, take on a newfound being when in the open-air; liberated from care, besides headaches? While not euphoric in exact, he toned to a substantially convalesced mould than he suffered hitherto, so recited that he as well, must, comparable to the avian myth, have soared from the ashes of a nigh to death experience.

Preoccupied with routine, Olan banked as a fellow who survived by the clock, scrutinising it cyclically to ensure synchronisation with his program. Never topping a curbed range of minutes tardy; and, even that occurred as a rarity; he reliably, if there accumulated a threat of delay, galloped about in something convergent on panic and implicated in a struggle to make up the time. What had it all been for he deliberated; the renewed man with a grander outlook on life, in leisured consumption of his alfresco meal from the sea. It wasn't as though anyone noticed or cared in any case, beyond that of an advent so reliable one stood capable to regulate their watch by his movements. It boarded the fear of differing from the norm, in combination with the static, in addition, single-minded peculiar rules instituted for his self, which moulded him into a slave shackled to his own unbreakable routines.

Today instilled at variance to the archetype. He committed as resolute with insistence to break from long founded procedure and savour each morsel of food; to sanction its relish on the tongue in appreciative ceremony as well as evulse maximum flavour. In the prolongation of his repast, Olan sought to appreciate beyond ever afore, all the vibrations exacted from it. With each forkful of the succulent white flakes, it exposed the glow of well-being to his features, which he delighted as not in the least bit guilty about either. Then, as he finished the plate, Olan scrunched up the applied napkin, set it on top close to the spent knife and fork, and then determined in that minor detail he urged designs to partake in a digestif. And, why not, he assessed? Therefore, in the attitude of excess, and with a deficiency of qualms, he beckoned for a whiskey and soda, regarded the ocean's horizon, then sipped on it as a man of leisure, untroubled, so too, content in outlook.

That nightfall, not a trice delay past the unavoidable and future to his flight over the back roads which piloted to The Heights, Olan horsed around felicitously with the children in their dedicated games parlour. Further, at the timeliest opportunity he embraced Neelak from abaft with the veil of a bear hug, ensuring to absorb the fragrant notes of floral out of her freshly shampooed mane. It packaged as a mark of affection, the conferral of which he craved the whole day. Too, he nuzzled up against her tender cheek by the inclination of his own over her right shoulder. He even crafted a shot at propositioning her into a spin around the kitchen tile whilst harmonising of a tune that netted her affection. Neelak giggled with applaud, but also fell short in total comprehension with respect to these events. She then bantered to shrug him off with an ascription of his behaviour as 'Cracked' and realised this with the honeyed regional accent of their county. The outcome of that tallied, they both beamed with enchantment, impelling Olan to assume from her, a clandestine and amorous kiss.

Olan comprised the sentience from a prolific history of accrued trial that these phases of elation didn't hang about for any protracted span, and because of that he hankered to indulge this one while he could. Besides, he recognised he had passed beyond the cusp of an irreversible deed, appreciative that the resolve and prominence found within to map his vocation through; ought to, if not prolong the high, at least safeguard a fair chance at wrapping him up in psychological stability for a drawn-out cycle. That logged as finer than okay. It required a call for steadiness, besides application of intellect in the months ahead, but he should with appreciation accept that over the inconceivable alternative.

Parting from Neelak, in brief he quitted for the utility store and reverted with a roll of plastic sacks. He strode the length of the house then proceeded into the study, on this occurrence without a resolve to shut out the substances of being, but the inverse; to implement a clean to do Spring proud. "Out with the ancient", he announced, and bagged up every scrap of what he branded "refuse" which amassed on the excellently carved table.

Here, he surprised even himself with all that stockpiled; in trust somehow he should whittle service from it again. Aside from literature connected to his labours, there also collected magazines, publications, journals and brochures he envisioned winning round to the evaluation of, but for which he never applied the time. Against the grain of his instincts to hoard, so too, indistinguishable from a bandage demanding to be ripped off, he didn't stop to dwell on it, but swept them all into the void where out of eyeshot they no more dignified the prestige at one time accorded. He furthermore packed a set of boxes with paperwork, binders and folders. These he committed to haul into the office on the subsequent day for meting out. It authenticated, after all, he concluded, splendid indeed to hold sway as king. Further, in an exhibition of this newly instituted mirth; he chuckled in augmenting, "So long as afterward, I'm not given over to sacrifice".

By the time he came to a halt, Olan eradicated from the previously obscured surface almost all chattels that beforehand cluttered it up. All that benefited from immunity transpired the desk calendar. With this, he stripped off the heavily tainted front page likewise the prior months he never changed to. He belatedly squeezed into a ball, the sheet on which was scripted the missive from Sitric, including it with the vestiges of appointed garbage.

With a glint at the board, he grasped that in silhouette there survived outlines of dust where they onetime colonised with stacked documents of occupation. After this, he reverted to the services quarter, rummaged around for a duster, too, a can of polish and revisited to wipe down the surface. He basked in the perfumed waft of the beeswax as it restored the shine to this most handsome cut of furniture. As he leant over it, Olan fathomed in his reflection he prevailed in readiness and was primed to dream of a renovated dawn. The chaos absented; as well, the bag of surplus administration got equipped for scattering. Thus, with the execution of a respite in the mahogany chair; in a challenge to the deportment of troubled slouch, he re-enacted his carriage of earlier through a satisfactory stretch of the legs. Then, he charged his hands to duty at the rear of his head, where he intertwined the fingers and contributed a sigh of gratification for a business admirably transacted.

On return to his bureau at the lab the ensuing morn, Olan raised to the present this difficulty at hand. He prejudiced his respect towards it, motivated with confidence; free of both physical, besides perceptual encumbrances. Furthermore, he supplemented it with the impression he stood to accomplish this without the ascendancy of day-to-day grunt work.

"Okay", he instigated. After already ruminating on an inventory of arguments the other day, Olan estimated the obvious line of action reasoned for him to meander back to the start. He may well apply theoretical, what's more, practical demands to the approach, and organise this with boldness. He methodized implicit in his conclusion that a combination of the two might herald the auspicious culmination or a distinctive investiture, contingent on how one appraised it.

To clear presupposed inferences, Olan sealed off his eyes and agreed for the flotsam of conceptions to drift him where they would. It ascended this exploit he put into effect time after time when pronouncing it mandated. From the period of adolescence he came to accept, he inexorably achieved the summits of rational punditry when separated from the equation endured the sense of sight, and he devoted to the obstacle just about the entirety of his ample brain power.

Collaborating about some territory in those allied cells and neurons, warmed up for sophisticated exercise, he asserted confidence there attended to legion, the kernel of a battle plan he should happen efficient at organising. The first mirages of meditation he conjured up evinced those of the ancients whom he fancied landing in their tanned leather craft, drenched, so too, exhausted from the migration across the great expanse. 'And from where did they originate'? He probed. The response to this sustained clear, but even so he reacted through the expenditure of his inner voice, 'Hibernia; the deciduous country that burgeons as the habitat for barbarians'. Then, with this articulated, Olan speculated instantaneously that perhaps it championed time to set aside these long indulged partialities. They transpired after all as blood relatives, so who could expose what the future held? 'Who comprehended indeed?' solicited him with a fair dose of inflexion.

Olan started on a transition into the purview of conjecture. If he acknowledged the axis of least favour, which plotted that Hy Brasil stared down the barrel of imminent obliteration from the veneer of this earth, it followed that unless the entire human race also extinguished from being, there ought to prevail extant, dominions where the inhabitants continued on, and civilisations flourished, albeit at a noticeably quieter pace than abided on the former promise of Milk and Honey.

'Perhaps Hibernia situated to survive as one of these enclaves of preservation?' It directed perchance feasible, the population might, given adequate space; mature from the inferior warrior brutes they lingered, into that which strove to approximate their superior cousins. It surmounted as a fact their DNA designed after all, apart from limited genetic disparities, more or less identical. Yes, it offered not beyond the bounds of logic to venture they at least occupied the potential to evolve. When he weighed it up, Olan appreciated that he realistically, barring a severance of the family tree, preserved there, forgotten relatives. As long as they unendingly stalked the warped plane of the human character with uninterrupted procreation, then that link of blood should proliferate in perpetuity.

He guessed that in this spectrum of rationale; he happened on to a notion. Hence, with his deliberations having at first gained traction on the swath of cognitive expression, and which by and by surfed a crest, he freed his erstwhile sealed pupils then rummaged for a pen with intent to jot down, on what pronounced as an unpolluted sheet of the desk calendar; those arbitrary ruminations which popped in for scrutiny:

What chances the future for Hibernia?

Might it perhaps arise they destine to expand as a society, analogous of Hy Brasil?

If in the affirmative when should this result?

Do I enjoy a bond with the blood of kinfolk there? What situates its fate?

Is DNA of relevance to this business?

In what respects do we acquit to differ? — Intelligence, accelerated advancement, genetic attributes as the upshot of endemism, e.g. those that gave rise to sensitivity with concern to electrical nerve impulses.

The Life Cycle Continuum, Biology, Chemistry, Physics- Equates a Means and a Way. The path of mortal furtherance is protracted and arched.

What suggests as a Constant is Variable and that which shows up Random prevails as Fixed.

Technology, Time, Space, Past, Present, Future, Mechanics, Laws, Relative, Light, Parallel, Multiple, Fabric, Curve, Bend, Universe, Matter, Qubits, Electricity, Download, Upload, Jump, Axiom, Point P

In this jungle, so too, a jigsaw of impressions, Olan supported positivity respecting the truth. With this innovative state of mind, now untethered from convention and which let loose the liberty to remain open to opportunity, but in addition restrained the discipline for it to exert in tandem with resolute emphasis; Olan unlocked a portal to his fate.

With his list of themes to explore at sight, Olan set off in application and experimentation while durably in appraisal of methodical facets. Each day, without hindrance he conferred expenditure to the accessible laboratories and embraced as much instruction as could be rounded up as it connected to an array of studies; everything from DNA to History, from Astrophysics to Computer Science. He consulted experts in the fields of Genetics, Theoretical Selenology, and Quantum Premise among others. Also, he administered inquiries on the accumulated data via the aid of Artificial Intelligence.

His colleagues, in all this while, continued under the assumption he maintained responsibilities with his appointment of civil prominence. Hence, no matter the territory or discipline he delved into, Olan was acknowledged with nothing other than aid and esteem.

This all-consumptive but self-apportioned and remunerative exertion lasted for many weeks. Olan, youthful and regenerated with assertiveness, again owned the approach of his formative age. In places he stuck with the rendering of notes on topics he granted distinction, but also put them into effect. There attended a goal to it all, and though it situated as a dynamic purpose, he corresponded as stress free in its pursuit; laser like in the accuracy of its aim. And in relation to the relativity of Time, he devoted to it the greatest portion of attention through the investigation of its properties geometric to Space. He challenged what connected the two, what distorted them, and most importantly, might a continuum be harvested to his advantage.

Olan, in his exceptional capacity for analytical besides rational calculation begged challenges and then set about their cure. It wasn't just that he submitted queries, but that he broached those which others hadn't much envisaged. These synchronised as interrogations of profound importance for mankind; similarly, on their resolution he appreciated they gave up just as insightful elucidations.

The further he researched, the more imposing those impediments which arose. Equal to them with the higher faculties of his intellect, with predictability Olan pieced together the threads of explanation. At full capacity, so too, with minimum sleep, he penned theories, scribed equations, so too, measured probabilities, covering it all with ultimate drive and single-mindedness. He strove towards this intent with energy he lacked a conception of ownership. He resigned to slumber belated all nights after he adopted full exploitation from the shimmered and cherished presence of his study's inlaid mahogany.

Each sunrise, in contrast to his interludes of darkness, he jumped out of bed, eager to pick up where he left off. Research, practical science, besides devotion to the furthermost considerations of life dominated his own existence in these months, and it was to this actuality he looked to, with the sole intent of its ultimate preservation.

Robert E. Kearns

Part 3–Discovery

The Heights, Waterford, Ireland–August 2019

I committed to my place at university in guard of a predisposed attraction to archaeology, but hadn't quite dwelt certain whether I should continue on this track, or elect an alternative path; history perhaps. Both instituted as a study of yesteryear but one abided as practical with the second academic. At more than a few junctures they overlapped when, for instance, antiquarians got tangled up with experimental conditions relative to far-off eras and lives. Here, they venture to supplement their body of erudition through adherence to trial-and-error undertakings to determine how artefacts came to be both crafted and utilised in former ages.

Feasible illuminations to ancient complexities coincided in frequency as the upshot of tangible research. Hence, challenges pertinent to dates immemorial predetermined as a passion. No matter, the status unceasingly remained that I later on converged on that pivot. The attractiveness multiplied this season, with in due course the momentum brewing up to a crescendo identical to the pressure at the core of a volcano immediate to its eruption.

It transpired the National Museum where I established an internship; positioned in the heart of what us rural folk denote in jest as "The Big Smoke". The opportunity bore as one I bequeathed high prominence to. In addition, the mindfulness of procuring an extent of hands-on and functional union with the celebrated pieces in their assemblage instituted with an appeal for me in abundance. There emerged an open slot on an archaeological dig right at the introduction to summer; what's more, I conferred a share of consideration to my presence on it. All the same, when this opportunity cropped up, with a smidgen of reluctance I abandoned those plans, and confronted as an alternative, the compulsion within to substitute this assignment in their stead. I resolved therefore to devote six weeks to the museum, and then perhaps then link up with the archaeologists for what survived on their calendar. As a result, in principle at least, I fated to enrich with the attainment of both worlds finest, through a split of the term into segments of comparable instruction.

I initiated the stint at my temporary employ, eager to embrace what I constructed in my view as indispensable and authentic practice. Youthful exuberance however, meant I doubtless stood affected with unrealistic expectations for the responsibility that waited to fall under my remit. There occurs a penchant I own, where I'm apt to anticipate permanent heights of fervour, to the degree whereby I prevail convinced of it for each forthcoming hour of the charge. The actuality in customary fashion is wont to ensure a ration of variance, so too, this sheltered as no exception. That's not to say the majority of my experiences expectedly close with disappointment, but more accurately, the eagerness I break out with, positive that every second will beget a hunger, moreover, thrill to guarantee the highs of this predicted ecstasy and fix an immutable smile to my handsome countenance, simply doesn't materialise.

On the day of commencement I came over all eager to get there on time. I hadn't slept too well the night before. In addition, just as a child at Christmas; purely to get going, I got inflicted with impatience for the imminent sunrise. The nervous tumult within merited I skip out of bed at the foremost light of dawn. With the exhibition of a fresh moon in this hemisphere, daybreak emanated before even the liveliest Cockerel premiered his strutting yodel. Without decline, when one orchestrates this novice's slip, with inevitableness there ensues the rush of breakfast; followed by the speedy oral hygiene and an exaggerated distribution of the shaving stroke. Merely afterward there shows up a scope of amazement at how premature one places for the sensibly calculated minute of departure.

This competed as the very state of play I faced; and in conjunction with my limited capacity to sit still; I continued with the inability to settle on anything that might tender as a distraction. Therefore, rather than tuning in to the wireless or engaging with a news check on the television, I paced the carpet; too, sequestered a chair now and then, but for no more than a few seconds at a go and for no other purpose than to exhaust the monotony.

I took to the scrutiny of my watch with each rest and concluded in time it transpired the point to vacate. The accuracy however, was I discerned that I suffered in aspiration of further practice for my limbs than ten foot round trips, concluding that an exodus braved superior to compromise with doses of unaccustomed and claustrophobic unease. With this logic as my spur, I intuitively speed walked my passage to the station then realised my arrival got timed on the platform just as a train pulled in. Within fifteen minutes, I came about as ensconced in the city centre, too, just a handful of streets remote from the museum.

Robert E. Kearns

The trusty limbs refused to let up, so I reported to my destination with the absolute certainty that when in due passage I examined the hour, I set to breeze in there at least forty minutes sooner than projected. I exercised this for confirmation, and on its receipt, cursed "Damn It", which should a person locate in earshot, got expressed louder than otherwise reconciled with social conventions.

I might have assembled on one of the accessible, and as yet, bare benches which grouped opportunely exterior to the main access. But the exploit of this, I recognised, undertook to verify the effect of creating an undesirable aspect I assented to the character of a schoolboy who succeeded to get lost on a field trip. Aged enough to not strive for success at being mistaken for a child, yet nevertheless sufficiently youthful to stress out with regard to what others assumed, I functioned on my fears of seeming in any manner a nerd, so as an alternative hurried on by. A vital factor on my part existed, that while others may not have deemed me worthy of consideration, observance of appearances lodged as a requisite for the disposition of cool. As a result, I angled from left to right in search of a cafe where I might take off a load.

Spotted around the corner on the adjacent block arose an establishment to fit the bill. It gifts this calibre of a coffee house which furnishes without fault the impression of coinciding as too modest for its location. Engaged interior sited a minimal quantity of tables squeezed on top of the other, each of them clad with an attractive red and white check cloth. These lent an air of cosiness to it, but by the same process half disguised the reality that paying guests tolerated at a busy hour to sense it

Robert E. Kearns

all more than a bit tight.

I supposed that most periods resolved as dynamic in enterprises such as this, prescribed as it was in the soul of town. However, there ascertained a spot accessible to the rear, immediate to the register. Tucked away there sheltered as sufficient by me. This day, I didn't wish to sit relative to the window. If it came about as a visit for merriment, I may well have relished that provision for a dollop of people watching; but not this day. The corner, I preferred, curiously for me, besides; it sustained here I could seclude myself to one side for the hypnotic seduction of the patterned textile. In addition, sooner than join in the sport of passers-by observation, in the alternative I should survey the clock, so too, nurse my coffee until it neared the doorstep of nine.

That aimed as my target at least, and I stuck with it for a while, until I accepted it garrisoned nigh on unworkable to shun the evaluation of patrons. This corresponded as rush hour for the commuter, further, with this animated as an unassertive yet popular operation, the tinkle of its access bell, and the subsequent influx of city bustle, it affected a raised head, likewise, a perception of the entrant. I devoted esteem for eavesdropping on the minutiae of routine carry-on, as well as the tones of Dublin, induced to tote about on its expedient currents. This more than sponsored as a reassurance to the observer and committed through its unique splendour to impart peace and contentment. The metropolis subsisted as a reminder we persist as social in preponderance, so even while planted on a chair in the recess of a town's vendor, there continues yet, interaction with the world that penetrates its aperture from the outside, waved in with the motions plus nuances of the hectic.

The broadest chunk of the sales I caught abounded as the takeout category which administered just as well for the proprietor as the grouped and tight seats didn't allocate for the volume of consumers in transit. It furthermore, worked to elucidate on how these cramped, what's more, discreet parlours for the coffee lover cooperated as adept at prosperity in trade. That is, there upheld a reliance upon not the sitters, but on those who dispensed the invitations for a tall latté to go, with perhaps a scone or Danish as an accompaniment. Why I dwelt on these notions, I couldn't but recognise that I have forever prolonged as a curious breed which went to prove that even absent of dedication at the outset to participate in the recreation of humanistic scrutiny, the style of the perceptive man sees to it there discloses no liberation from this hobby of marvel.

With a review of the watch face, it verified beyond doubt since the prior exploration, there transpired a full revolution of the second hand. I gyrated my cup, so too, beheld its innards. Reflected on them, might patent the more accurate appraisal, and in place of an immediate consumption of the residual half mouthful, I swirled the beige liquid around the inner wall then surveyed its motion in a spellbound trance.

I considered what ascended in this modest performance which published with it a stature that warranted the effect of; both qualifying as leisure, too, being conducive to the stimulation of thought processes. Perhaps that's why I inhabited as fond of its habitual recitation. At that moment I recognised a perception of déjà vu with my energies. At all times a curious sensation when it reveals, I finished the balance in a conduct which cut a figure that perceptibly replicated a former exploit. With the cup run dry, I reversed my trail of before and headed back to the museum, confronted with the unusual circumstance of an onus to dodge the processional mass of congregated pedestrians. Not without the incurrence of a bump or two from enthusiastic captains of commerce, I validated in front of the Victorian wrought-iron fence and general admission, at somewhere about three minutes shy of the appointed hour.

Privileged to the main entryway I sauntered up to the desk for information and heralded my presence. And on its inception, I mustered up an air of consequence, akin to my interpretation of how a visiting client of greater prominence than I should perfect it. Once directed to a bench in the welcome area, I chose a base to hover for which I assumed should materialise a middle-aged person, male or female, possessed of meagre charm or personality. Thus, when a blonde in her bare twenties sidled up to reception, and next, in a duplicate quality how I came to be greeted, finished with outstretched finger, pointed with likewise precision, I compiled, to put it delicately, as taken aback.

Surprised with the fashion it tailored me into overtime exertion for the rendition of dialogue, which beforehand I expected to hail within easy reach; I found out that on a grab for them, none introduced to the fore. Inside fractions of a tick I got startled for a second instalment; when she unfolded a delicate hand, and introduced herself, not with an Irish inflection, but with that of American timbre. "Good mornin', my name is Tiffanie", she asserted, in a speech I detected evolved from a State south of the Mason Dixon line. Without voiced argument, but internalising as a replacement; I alleged, 'What an all American designation'–'Tiffanie'. I continued tongue tied, with both shocks achieving to slam into me with nimble succession, further; I don't expect I acknowledged her with any meaningful return, not even my appellation. I simply stuck out my hand then made a stab at a smile which in all probability got transmitted in substitute through the guise of a silly smirk.

Tiffanie was reminiscent of a wartime poster girl out of the 1940s, the style of which American service men pinned to the inner door of their locker. To be sure, as soon as that image transposed itself into my contemplations, it never proposed to vacate. I conceived of her attendance at events overseas; planned as an initiative to entertain the troops. Here, in the dimension of my fantasy she frocked out in a dress of that generation which fluttered up on stage, as if caught by a clement breeze; her head reclined in a striking pose, so too, her golden mane tied up with a trail of white ribbon. She emphasised as well those aligned teeth of stateside perfection which sparkled back at me with luminary chic. Mesmerised with her embodiment I must have paralleled that figure from the bible passage, which with her jaws parted, so too, in a breach of engagement rules, got reconstructed into a pillar of salt.

I compelled myself back to the real world then at last triumphed to mutter an inanity with concern to the weather, which at trials such as this, resolved as my fall-back exchange. It's a theme of unoriginal contingency I admit, and absolute in its clichéd ilk. So, possibly, the neater channel disposed to orate on nought at all. However, my policy of thumb with interrelations pertaining to the contrary gender is that surety of a topic to relate, no matter the fragility, happens in permanence as the healthier preference.

Tiffanie guided me to the administrative chambers, disengaged from the public forums, and next led me to an office where I was invited to fill a swivel chair. This followed with the proposal of tea or coffee. I explained I partook these days of the latter, so declined that specific motion. However, my mouth parched, which might stage in remark as unprovoked by an excess of chatter. It resolved as close I came to clarify; thus inquired, if in its place, I might trouble her for a sip of water; to which she shot me her southern belle visage and extended her approval with an effortless "Sure". She then circled round, and I reserved her score to my acuity with what registered as the pleasantest exit I ever witnessed.

Momentarily she reappeared, and the lovely Tiffanie passed over the chilled refreshment which arrived in a plastic vessel of the nature that invariably occurs stacked alongside the office cooler. It agreed as a near glacial delight, the peripheral clinging on to miniscule droplets which I surmised as condensation. Spillage did not impress as a constituent of Tiffanie's disposition, with me by this stage sanctioning to build her up in those prior relations as a facsimile of perfection.

I ordained to guzzle a substantive quota of the recuperative beverage, never more gratified for as revitalising a fluid. On the conquest of its intake, I comprehended how pronounced it must imply to her, that with initial sight, I distinguished as outright smitten. With that recognition, I cited as if it protested as novel; that I held it in my power to pick up a read on her and then evaluate any attentions. Then, for the first illustration in a great while, I opted against it. Somehow, it crossed my conscience that to infiltrate her sentience defined to comprise of a cheat, further; I partook of no eagerness to kick off my tenure in that construct.

The cause of Tiffanie's youth, I solicited, graded that she accompanied as an exchange student from the University of Oklahoma, in Dublin for the duration of both spring plus the full summer terms. Well, that explained the accent I mooted, and considered it altogether adorable the means by which she pronounced "Oklahoma", drawing it out in a process of composition into a harmonic four syllables as opposed to an out-of-key monotone. The arrow of a God's desire here resolved to strike, and I tasted more and next concluded my drink with the thirst for it to have gone down in a bulkier cup. Tiffanie served here for a while now she confided; and administered a sum of projects, besides also unravelling the ropes of practice to interns as an allotment of her remit. After this concise summary, she suggested endowing me with the celebrated tour of which I was in agreement. But in advance of us setting off, I inquired at the commencement where the fountain situated, so I should claim a critically sought-after refill.

I got afforded a circuit of orientation about the halls which activated in those sections that awarded admittance to visitors. I dutifully nodded along, albeit I stood familiar enough with these areas to not have required a chaperon. The pleasant narrator in a concert of symphonic dialogue cast her spell on me; in addition, I elicited to evoke the spirit of the Pied Piper, but with eagerness for a more appropriate end result. She was for sure passionate in her account, too, this proved in how her features lit up when in discourse in respect to the exhibits which intrigued her. This purpose rendered the affair far from the exploit of a swift run around the place. Charmingly for me, it instead switched to one where I obliged as the attentive tourist and Tiffanie the knowledgeable and cheerful conductor, who choreographed one of her foremost, rather than proximate to her hundredth such speech.

We swung through the main galleries and scrambled up and down an array of staircases. Even if I conjectured as why all this stated as imperative; it didn't arrest the beam which represented a permanent facet of my facial topography throughout. Never would I have believed an engagement with the museum committed to work out with this degree of amiability. Somewhat intriguing might depict the commentary I should have elected before this, but on no account amiable. I stood proud to have chosen a synonym of "Appealing" as the expressive term for my conclusions. It accorded gravitas as well as the appropriate percentage of sophistication for the present context. Here, a wonderful aspiration surfaced to appreciate by my side a walking cane, for then to twirl it in circles whilst kitted out in a tailored suit and top hat, so too, evincing the deportment of an old-fashioned gentleman.

Finished with that segment of our jaunt, we arrived once more to where it activated, and on this transpiration I welcomed the proposal of a tea break. We seated in the canteen where Tiffanie extended her report in connection with a sum of noteworthy exhibits and expounded on how fascinating she defined them. In the main she appreciated that craftsmanship which festooned many of the golden relics; brooches, bracelets, so too other descriptions of antique jewellery.

I sipped my tea, agreed with her in most respects, while in a frantic mental pursuit for platinum nuggets of wisdom to scatter about. However, I conceded defeat with the recognition I tarried impotent to mine anything other than clumps of pyrite. Enchanted I endured, and that lodged another label which hadn't invaded my consciousness until those fifteen minutes of recess. So, when Tiffanie articulated that she trusted the induction circumvented the dreary, my bygone alter ego returned wordlessly with, "I should think not. You were delightful beyond question, my dear", but my actual self, countered with the far less flowery, "No, it was a sheer delight", and perfectly scrapped any declaration of her as "my precious".

On receipt of what only amounted to an altogether limited and inadequate compliment; it all the same raised a smile as impressive as Oklahoma to her aspect. It must have discharged as a contagious transfer, because I mirrored it too, although contrasted with Tiffanie, when I grinned, I must have played to her audience of one as the embodiment of a village idiot.

Never was I gladder at the release from that perceptual representation when she inquired if I aspired to meet with a selection of staff and curators. I chased at her heels as an obedient pooch and we hopscotched about the sundry offices, departments and laboratories, where I shook hands with technicians whose names I forgot as soon as we advanced on to the next. Far more attention I gave to the assortment of processes that were overseen and tested. Ongoing I noticed; there took place maintenance besides restoration, scrutiny of samples under the microscope, so too, a multitude of other scientific procedures in-progress. These responsibilities, it got conveyed expounded as endeavours on both recent and older revelations, and here I might well have lingered further to interrogate the authorities, were it not for the evidence, that while polite, the professionals influenced it as obvious they persevered as terribly besieged. The interruption of a transient acknowledgement tolerated as quite sufficient, for when taken care of, their absorption then rebounded to the previous norm besides matters of emphasis.

'They're really not as bad as all that', confided Tiffanie when out of earshot. 'That said, many are anoraks and just a tad on the side of ornery. If you get to speaking with them over lunch, you'll realise that apart from a handful here and there, they just don't do a lot of humour'. I placed Tiffanie firmly in the one or two exceptions category. Then she continued with a chuckle 'Half the men apparently still live at home with their mom', at which point I joined in with subdued laughter, but failed to mention that if it wasn't for the prerequisite of the Big Smoke for college, I most should likely yet reside with my parents in Waterford. Then she led me down to the basement where the stores were preserved.

'This, we love to nickname the dungeon', she enthused. 'Be careful, some descend these steps but never leave', and hooted at her own humour. 'Yes, I can believe a few of the sorts I converged with upstairs may well exert to situate in danger of a conversion to exhibits within their own museum', I argued. This synchronised as the first contribution I submitted thus far which accommodated better than a handful of superficial remarks. It must have done well because she continued the whoop that inaugurated a moment beforehand. On top of all this, the flash of her brilliant white's softened my besotted heart.

Here in the cellars survived in reserve, all the museum diversities that weren't at the present time on exhibit. A good many never designed to achieve that honour. These divulged as representative hordes and manifold of them exploited for the purposes of research. On the whole they came to encounter storage in trays plus drawers of varying depth, dependent on size, and these in turn established shelter inside floor to ceiling movable storage cabinets. Disparate articles arrayed on tables, with maximum feasibility for the industry of scholarly inquest, intended for subtraction from the lower ground floor or yielded to its rightful home.

In one extensive quarter, there stationed open shelving of the antediluvian kind and this is how I fancied the entire building must have functioned before modernity took over. On these racks planted many more spectacles, tagged; besides labelled. These I fastened positive, to either the skilled or untutored eye sold the notion of a haphazard formation, as if they condoned exposure to migration of considerable proportions and then got put back by every which means, except neatly; what's more, well-ordered.

'I hate to break it to you, but you'll be spending some quality time down here', reported Tiffanie with impudent glee, and not conscious if there emerged an adequate rejoinder to that statement, I merely interjected with an 'hmmm'.

'Put aside any worries', she commanded in high spirits. 'If you don't show up after twenty-four hours, I'll send out a search party. We wouldn't want to see you interred in the dungeon, like a certain Count of French literature,'

A full day's confinement imprinted on me as a stretch of awful proportions, thus preferred to suggest the recommendation that if she didn't spot me after say, three hours, she had better unleash the bloodhounds to track me down. Instead, I chuckled and then recited "thanks for your concern".

"There's a project in the offing, but I'll fill you in on that later. Right now though, I'm hungry and I do believe I'll head up to the Green. You can come along if you don't have other plans,"

I jumped at this with almost too great an enthusiasm; so indulged to reign myself in with a not quite admirable essay to sound casual. But, if I entertained notions of us two in mutual adoration over a romantic picnic by ourselves on the manicured lawns of Stephen's Green, this got shot down in a hurry when Tiffanie bade a few extras upstairs if they pleased to join us. It favoured as a pretty day outdoors, and comparable to a percentage of individuals who operate in the city throughout these summer months, for me the refuge of the Green, as it was claimed, complemented as about ideal a mode to kill the lunch hour as might prevail in appreciation.

There contrived a sandwich shop local to the café where I took coffee that morning, and a few of us joined the queue for orders to go. The remainder of our group either brought along boxed up fare of their personal creation, or favoured nutriment of more sustenance than sliced bread. Clearly there posted a pre-arranged congregation plot in the foliated square; hence, they all understood where to meet. On arrival, it happened rather packed, and we witnessed luck the space was held by those colleagues who brown bagged their lunches that day. Maybe it followed a dash premature for my referral to them as contemporaries as I had yet to come upon a wet day in their company, or a dry one for that matter, but I couldn't persuade an alternative definition to the fore.

The hour passed in irregular conversation with individuals to whom Tiffanie had beforehand introduced me, but for the life of me, whose names I positioned powerless to summon up. I dislike these incidents, in that it consumes the whole spectrum with tuning in to three diverse dialogues at once for the sole purpose of yearning for one participant to drop an appellation or to seek from another by intimate recognition to pass a napkin. They didn't interest me enough to drill any further for a cognitive inspection, so I rested on the mown blades in the heat of the middle hour, in an audit over everything, plus nothing, and breaking away from it hardly wiser for the encounter. I continued in the main unaware that in accordance with the gushing's of my new friends I dedicated a glorious sixty minutes to the magnificent outdoors.

Reinstated to the museum, Tiffanie ran through several more facets, readied some organisational paperwork with me, and warranted that everything got squared away with Human Resources. That all complete, she, to my surprise, more or less shooed me on my way. "There's not much point in setting you up with anything this late in the day. If we haven't completely put you off; come back tomorrow for a fresh dawn. I'll teach you what needs to be done. In fact, I'll learn ya". This appendage came out in a first-class Oklahoma twang.

Afterward to this exchange, off I fled, relieved in one sense for the renewal to open-air where I might gain an ounce of indulgence from this fine afternoon which earlier I hadn't reaped; and in another, sorry to find separation from the affable Tiffanie; All-American girl next-door.

I slept sounder that night to the one previous; too, I reserved a stronger handle on the timing when daybreak erupted. I didn't tread the boards as I managed the day past, so pressed on with comfort in the welcome of breakfast and with the onus to make ready. I observed the reverse likeness in my shaving mirror with the clean of my teeth, further, found the capacity to envisage a concept of my exhibition with a beard.

A second contemplation arose on that score and I speculated it may not express a proper look for me after all. I effected successfully with stubble, but the jury teetered with relevance to full-blown whiskers. There designed the risk in my ideations this might feasibly confer the twist of a hobo, or worse yet, a long in the tooth old-timer. And with the vanity of youth, I favoured not for that to betide. All the same, with the attendance of summer I hankered for a fresh or altered configuration. Thus, with the caress of my chin between thumb and forefinger, I pondered if a goatee may well compromise as a propitious medium; so called out to my reflection: By the Hair on My Chinny, Chin, Chin.

I might have straggled about for a dilatory span if I so

preferred, but a peek out the bedroom pane communicated it pledged again as a most favourable daybreak, in addition, I figured it preferable to get ahead of the thorny traffic than stare at the four walls. Besides, I guessed it ought to wager congenial for a bench in the Green, and then realise what I hadn't gotten round to the day before; that is, wonder at the bustle of ephemeral nobody's in motion. It should I speculated, liaise as a decent plan for debarkation at the museum emancipated from stress and strife. Here I weathered, second stage out of five in a week, with the original of them comfortable, besides short at three quarters of the whole, and already I furnished attention to the pressures of responsibility.

Off the train I conducted a return to the same café of homeliness around the corner from my retainer, and on this stint joined the hordes in negotiating for my request to go. The identical table in the recess with the starched red and white check material gestured its invitation, but my heart continued set on the park. There I had the facility to take notice of the birds in shaded trees; too, the hymn of the spurt, as well as the collapse of crystal water in ornamented fountains, as with nonchalance I crossed one leg over the other in repose, there to pay attention to the human traffic which filtered through the narrow walkways, each of them frenetic ants diverging out in the hunt for of a destination.

It developed here unperturbed at the end of an elongated seat enclosed by pristine flower beds, where having by now consumed half the cup I enjoyed, that it crossed my mind I ought to have travelled to a disconnected establishment for its procurement. I accepted of late to consider it bad form to throw my custom at the same address on recurrent days. I wasn't altogether keen to translate into one of those middle-aged fossils with habits clad in iron.

Too late to vary the arrangement of it now I peeled my scrutiny from the milling swarms and then dealt with the banks of vibrantly animated flowers; sensational in full health of the second quarter. I congratulated myself on this, the most excellent of choices for a pre-work elixir. From the recesses of my subconscious I even prospered in the simulation of a clipped aristocratic accent of self-praise in divulgence of the message "Well done old boy. Very well done, indeed."

In fine fettle, I might have perched there all day. At the intersection of pathways, there persists to behold a pressingly able cross section of city verve, which at that hour way before noon, and adjacent to the spewing cascades of St. Stephen's Green, enlivened as glucose to the senses. With my beverage now assimilated in full, I consulted my chronograph to the measurement I should make it round to my distinct structure of occupation at the optimal point of two or three minutes from the top of the hour.

Given my introduction to the open rotunda I comprehended the occupancy of no clue what I had better get on with next. Ought I to saunter up to the bureaus in search of Tiffanie? If I devoted to that but wasn't supposed to, might it be something to frown upon? I didn't nurture to picture the pleasant lady in a grimace at the mismanagement of my conduct. If, on the other hand, I got forced into slinking back over to the reception kiosk with the submission of my credentials for the second count of inquiry; I ran the vulnerability of a pitiful semblance. It hinged between the rock and the grim alternative; although if it came to it, a snigger at my unfortunate circumstance cooked up as preferable to ostensibly portraying the halfwit for the above Miss. I debated on this for a second or two when the impasse got mended for me.

It came about that Tiffanie climbed the steps onto the mosaic tile at that very moment, so hooked on to me located there; indisputably in apportion of my impression congruous to being disjoined from my mother on a shopping trip. "I forgot to get your badge made up yesterday. I knew there was something I didn't get round to", she informed in a chipper strain. I perked up at this admission, elated that I wasn't the narrow simpleton I conjectured to subsist just a few seconds beforehand. However, I weighted a modicum rash with the let off, and on top, got compelled into a re-evaluation when I spoke up with the ridiculously lame "Ah yes, the insignia", although no such wearable had revealed until she voiced it. "We'll have your picture taken, get Security to issue a tag, and then after that, just keep it on you during the day and it'll provide internal access". My alter ego almost raised his head again with a "Right you are, my dear", but with a feat I thrust back, to react in its stead with an "Okay, that will do terrific".

The procedures and hardware of admittance taken care of, I got appointed with a laminated identification, besides security fob, which might leave another marked with importance, but constructed in me a wrench of the cerebral cortex, on where I intended to pin it. Most adorned it about their neck by way of a strap, but the notion of it dangling all over the place, chiefly I leaned over held no attraction. I too supposed that it might get hitched up or snagged on a protrusion, which caused whiplash besides the symptom of an accident prone imbecile. That schemed as not to be good either. The substitute remained to clip it on to my belt, and while I considered this quick fix volunteered as the most prone to result in its loss, this is how I bore it. To fret over the immaterial stuff arrayed often as what I welled at.

"On to the cells with you", commanded my consort in jest, and then embarked on a near trot towards the stairs, which I took to mean that she determined to lead the way. "Are you my gaoler?" I quipped. "I'll be throwing away the key, once I get you in there" bobbed up the reply from the enchanting Tiffanie. What occurred to mind then, rooted that it would come to pass as consummately acceptable if she latched the door from the inside then tossed the key out of the grate. But of course, I didn't dare reveal it. Instead, I interjected with "The punishment fits the crime" to which she let out a titter. I came over rather contented with myself in the winning of that compensation, limited as it was.

We paraded over to the greyer section of the vault where the lot of it presented as if it fit to a different century (pun intended). It lay out as how one might well harbour a vision of Victorian's utilizing to labour from; hence this lent it the stamp of romanticism. This got symbolised in my thoughts with the condition of dust-laden shelves encompassing an assortment of trinkets which embodied no particular order to their distribution; and there in its stale confines, I dreamt of curators attired in dashing pinstripe suits. Extended on tiptoe, while shod in black period boots, one of their numbers seized a relic of aspiration for reckoning, judging it with the aid of a monocle besides a hand-held glass for magnification. I'm sure the factualness of these ages differed, but I might not have abided too far off given the spectacle before me. Irrespective, it contributed to a smile, and here below decks it provided for the mind-set of portage back in time, which crossed as an engaging, what's more jovial consideration, given I synced in surround with artefacts from a bygone era.

"This is to be your home for the next few weeks; hard labour for your deeds!" I settled there in rotation about my axis taking in the neighbourhood which was dominated by floor to ceiling ledges stacked high with treasures of national besides international gravity and some effects that awarded as not much more than a miscellany of rocks. I looked on the presumption however that one chap's pebble seeded as another man's diamond. "It seems as if I ought to gear up in a jacket and waistcoat complete with a gold pocket watch and chain suspended from the breast" established my answer to Tiffanie. "I expect blue jeans with sneakers would be more becoming; but I could organise for a black-and-white prison suit should you prefer". I beamed at this, adding that I consented to wear a custodial uniform, only if it came with the orb and fetter accessory.

Tiffanie expounded in detail what chores and travails needed covering, and it upheld, to some measure as a cross between an inventory and the cataloguing of museum samples that came into repositing in this un-swept antique corner of the cellar. The excitement value of the proposed commission sited not to thrill anywhere within touch of what I hitherto guessed. There suffers, as I spelled out, an innate tendency to oversell the exuberance factor. I can't say for sure what it was I predicted, but I expected, at least to a certain extent, being operational upstairs in white gloves with the radiantly lit and bustling exhibitions posting vigilant over those priceless diversities behind glass. I presume that inhabited as an unrealistic prospect, but confinement to the chamber of correction encompassing what could purely rest in description as the modern equivalent of turning the screw, had not stood out on my conceptual agenda. At the hazard of incarceration, my frame of sentiment effectuated a one eighty. I admitted to myself but not my counsel in attendance endured more than a snippet peeved. For her, I sought to fake jollity, but thespian ism perpetrated as not a favourite extracurricular activity of mine.

Perhaps in estimation I embedded a smidgen reticent about taking on this significance, which I understood without delay arose as that one my betters favoured to delegate, Tiffanie formulated a stab at lightening the tension. "It's kept like Las Vegas down here. You won't see any clocks, and they pump oxygen to insure against you falling asleep". I didn't respond with immediacy because at the mention of slumber I couldn't help but realise I may well require something more than aeration to sustain me in the course of this chore. After a lengthier than reasonable pause, I arrived back with something to the effect of favouring caffeine over the atmospherically abundant gas. I achieved to detect a narrow hint of embarrassment from Tiffanie at my not accepting the mitigation of her comedy. I regretted that straight away, then augmented with a manufactured cheeriness, that for my good behaviour, she should maintain to remit cups of tea.

There continued a slight extra turn taken up with travels through the entire operation, which in preference to attracting a motivation to resemble for the better, just re-enforced the point this conferred as a tribulation the gentry in their plush apartments on the upper floor resolved to ward off. Most probable it saw to encounter one or two half-hearted, and then abandoned propositions to accomplish it, until that is, a ranking suit contemplated there purposed no more fitting a method to see an unpalatable situation concluded than to distribute it onto the junior; more to the point, soon to meet with his revival at the college, skivvy. It enjoined to have gotten referred to in the absolutist of contrived bombast as the entrustment of an exercise with the utmost gravity. With the private allusion to the account of pomposity, too, its allocation to the sentence it belonged to; for the second circumstance in as many days, though by a more substantial grade go around, I endured as certain to have chalked up at another time the echo of this same impression.

Tiffanie engineered her exit, and as her footsteps faded out on the staircase, it ranked noticeable in the poverty of a human voice how desolate I survived here in the underground enclosure. This perception of abandonment reported not as an abstraction that brooded to my style, having constantly endured as one of those types who occupied positive expectations. At one time, I compounded to look upon loneliness as a judgment of attitude, furthermore considered it as predominantly an emotion familiar elsewhere, but detached from me.

Now however, in the muteness of this hidden earth, the graceful Tiffanie having compassed to withdraw, an unknown phenomenon attended, which on another visit might have cajoled in me a local involuntary movement to hug my upper body in tightness for heat and self-comfort. I pushed it back in place then eyed up the clipboard to my front, which bound the paperwork crucial to this position. Not sufficient to eradicate it, the solitude I contended with just then, didn't combine with objectives to vacate its new abode, and resultant of this I stopped there in brief, glaring at a form which apart from its pre-printed lines, too, its bold header stayed as yet, blank. I pined for a radio to make its presence noticed, which I might switch on to disrupt the quiet; and here I endowed it mandatory to force the idle biro into the grip of my anxious fingers.

No sooner than I achieved this, I recognised it took place as not the first labour demanded and hence put it straight back down on the wearied timber. However, the act at least completed its intendment of an initiator. The responsibility I got given covered the inspection of each of the non-archived works in the lower ground storage which portrayed as the dominant ingredient of its stacked shelves. They ought to, I came under advisement, encompass something akin to a label or classification of some manner tied on which was to include, in type, the catalogue features besides supplementary detail. These minutiae were then to manifest as transcribed onto those aforementioned sheets that clasped to the hard-backed file. From there, the data gleaned bound for supposed feeding into the data banks of a computer at some point afterward.

Each article stood to meet with appropriation to individual bundles in agreement with the catalogued distinctions, which should in due course assist in their hand over to one of the modern drawers or sliding stores. It slated here that this schemed to eat up a measure of time, and consideration required addressing how and where to start; too, some spot where I should christen the freshly blessed piles. 'Pile' breathes well enough as a word the curators shouldn't have blazoned enthusiasm to perceive me extend. I committed to invent their feedback to this likeness of their precious offspring succumbing to my flinging them willy-nilly on top of each other. Still, right then; that elucidated as the sole remark I pleased to arrive at which told with correctness what required doing. "Sectioned off Categorisations", might well offer a preferable call to satisfy scholarly elders, but as yet I invested as not altogether predisposed to marry into the hierarchy of these sophisticates.

The volume coupled with the jumbled range of this compilation touted a daunting panorama, and my heart's target wasn't set on these creaky planks that simply wanted for the atmospheric cobwebs. Therefore, I passed an executive order to take to it all at my own tempo. It didn't seem that management gave up much of their sleep on it in any case. If it got listed on their agenda of priorities, it ought to have gotten concerned attention before now. I just happened to surface as the soundest fellow at a well-timed juncture. By this, I, of course, suggest that the miserliness of my wage bill in conjunction with not controlling the authority to complain, endured the exemplary virtues held in particular esteem by my lords and masters.

To my surprise, I rode through the morning without too considerable a struggle. Here and there the odd conservator broke the hush with the tender of their accession. I overheard strides on the primitive flight of steps, which caused the rotation of my gaze to observe them sashay into the modern end of the oubliette. Some brought effects to re-establish, comparable to a book requited to its relevant slot in the library; while others landed there to check out the substance of their regard. I benefited to take notice from my humble corner, the opening then closure of receptacles, and next caught a peep of their back, too, the rung out melody of their heels on the paving as they carried out their retirement to the province of vigour. None of these transients meandered over to my sector of the tracks. They remained in all likelihood unaware I even situated there; but I, as what they might in the olden days have related to as a "Guest of The Crown" was content all the same for the intermittent distraction that came about from their comings and goings.

The modestly priced timepiece strapped to my stalwart wrist, rather than the hoped for mechanism of gold ensconced in a pouch near to the heart, got monitored at systematic intervals. As such, when the hour for lunch threatened, I surged on tap to decamp; jogging over to pass through the heavy wooden barrier; agape, but rested as a sentry in guard of the worn, polished steps. My escape, then the partial light of day which infiltrated the yawning glass panes signalled my freedom. I merely laboured down below for a few hours, but it caused me to challenge how it happened that Dantes endured in his cell of squalor for a miserable age. This protagonist of Gallic prose contemplated suicide, and it spanned my attention rather bizarrely, that were I in the predicament he discovered himself, I should well see to the treatment of that prerogative. I was close to the declaration "Had I stopped in his shoes", but a pedantic quadrant of my brain halted this comment with the mention I didn't expect he should condition to boast of footwear, given he got shut away in a dank prison which forecast to rot all he possessed to scraps of rag. One aberrant ethereal synthesis therefore got followed on by an even odder one.

I accrued not in the habit of passing for a court jester. At least, that's how I witnessed it. Yet, here I figured about to shoot up to Tiffanie, practiced as a schoolchild in his quest for the teacher's approval might consummate. I fancied it may transcend as preferred to apprise her I wound up for the first hours. I exercised restraint in this regard though; with the probability of an implication I rated as the Army Private in appeal of permission from the officer in charge to quit his post. But also as a person of uncertainty might appraise, I supposed that if I flew out the exterior gate without acquainting her, she may wonder where I disappeared to. I wasn't adapted to this dearth of self-assurance, and it unnerved me to an extent. Tiffanie after all, dictated not as one of the conceited generals. In the end, to torment over the triviality of this nothing dispute cooperated as ineffective help with the cause. Hence, with that introspection I urged my limbs into motion, and next departed through the front portico into the good-natured arms of young afternoon sunshine.

With the function of reason, I came again to the delicatessen of the day prior, in acceptance there mounted a fair prospect of bumping into the circle of employees in a do-over of that hour's itinerary. While I abided in line to requisition, I collected a smile and a "Hi" from a well-dressed lady of about forty. She must have happened as a co-worker from the museum, but I appreciated not the foggiest clue as to her name. She didn't acquaint as one of our lunch clique from the Green. I disposed not in complete ignorance or forgetful of my own abilities, thus played along until I mustered to secure an acceptable read on her. In that manner, I established to find out her designate, which upon my resourcefulness at communicating it to her, composed the effect of being agreeable in the utmost. Having supposedly recollected it of my accord, this left her impressed too, I could tell. But, I confess, I now forget that handle, as not long afterward the ineffable Tiffanie strolled in through the open access, and my attention switched to her Prom Queen whites which diffused into my plane of vision.

With our sandwiches spread out before us, yet allocated to their greaseproof paper and atop the grasses of Stephen, so too, within a radius of where we assembled the preceding luncheon, she inquired of me with a glance in the knowing how it transpired I achieved to fly the subterrestrial coop, given she maintained as the sole custodian with a key. The others whooped, and then I argued that the protracted duration of my sentence afforded me ample occasion to pick the lock. 'I must have a stern word with security', accrued as her rejoinder. 'Or perhaps I'll source that Ball and Chain. We can't have you breaking loose at your own convenience'.

The litter binned, so too the crumbs brushed off our clothing, we then started for the museum in a sluggish amble, deficient in aspiration for our hour of generative sunlight to conclude. It proffered the equal for most it came to my notice if one chose to let-up and peruse those convertible minions. A fair deal of them came off passive in their advances, spreading out the reverse of the lunch hour exodus for all it was worth, with a goal at each crossway to encounter the impediment of a red man, who by his own tenuous procedure should aid in a delay of the inevitable. The company types, as the exception who confirmed the decree, got spotted without trouble as hares in a lane for the slow; availing of sharp elbows and with a contrivance to overtake well-nigh all their tortoise equivalents. They should exert as first to wag a finger on the loveliest day of the month when a trod upon underling reports to the office a minute or two delinquent.

We split up inside the staff entryway. I recognised what route to cover, and while I momentarily considered it should result as a charitable gift from the heavens if she propounded it, to lay bare the track by hand wasn't expected of Tiffanie. I placed as a statue might, in the rotunda adjacent, to examine my colleagues who conversed yet, in a cheerful, carefree approach whilst still in their ascension of the stairs, leaving me to shuttle down unaided to the borstal of disquiet. Splintered off from the rest, too, with the abrupt cessation of discussion in which I joyously took part seconds beforehand; this junction of an invisible blockade caused me to drop from an emotion on high to a point of low in too rapid a means, dizzily drawing forth the effect on me of a longing to reverse course summarily, further, wrap myself afresh in the blanket of human company.

Elated for the call of five, rather than the pressing commute home, I wandered around to a familiar public house, and then beseeched superior ale in deference to the moderate season. This institution for fermented refreshments buzzed with an atmosphere that seems unique to our capital in summer. In watering holes such as this, all throughout the bitter winter, the clientele within bundle up on top of each other, stuffy and with a day's aggregate perspiration, ten deep to the bar, stale blemishes to reveal exposure the following morn, all siphoned from the spillage of a dozen drinks, the product of manifold arms askew. Only those who determined to stir in to the mixture that singular waft of cheap cigarette tobacco endeavoured out of doors, there to huddle in a corner and purchase refuge from the elements of this one time Hibernia.

It just disposed at Christmas, too then if the weather spooked into the spirit of goodwill to all mankind, should a backdrop in resemblance of this act break into sight. With my virgin brew with an arctic blast, untouched by the flailing hands of animated men, I progressed out back to the expansive allotment for beer, unsurprisingly full with a loose turnabout of the yuletide postcard; smokers and not, congregated in the courtyard of compensation to neck one or two before their exfiltration to the suburbs. There I happened, not far prior, sure in the belief that if I motored swift and not hover about the museum a second past knocking off time, I should set positive to grab a stool, only now to witness the faithful already knelt at the church of thirsty pilgrims ahead of me.

I ended up with the posture of vertical, and prepared to set down my jar on a recess in the brick, but wavered in this proposition, assured that once loose from their allotted charge, it should give measure to the perennial complication of my hands with nothing to occupy them. There unfurled the proposal of just about getting away with this idleness if on insertion to their respective hangouts I reaped the fortune in that instant to secure attentiveness in casual chat. However, tonight, friendless; had I proceeded with my original instinct and allowed the pint come to rest, plus my extremities to dawdle, I should undeniably have consigned myself as a victim to the proverbial spare tool.

Thus, content I dodged this aura of foolishness, which without hesitation, just I should single out; in preference I settled on the nonchalant attitude through the maintenance of my brew in one palm while its twin reached for an adjournment to proceedings and reposed next to my wallet. To perform as cool represented not as my forte in precise, but I raised an admirable essay through the glare of our capital sun.

This conditioned, to my fancy at least, without question; perfect in its context for the sampling of both an adult beverage and the aforementioned ambiance of this distinguished town. Here existed one of the great pleasantries in life, a fleeting Eden, and it occurred to me this perception might to boot, befall the condition for another wayfarer. It stated therefore; vanity perhaps, which questioned if I might class as the subject of another's investigation. Under the influence of this egotism, but in the end deprived of success, I scanned the environs to note if I might latch on to the glimpse of an allied romantic.

I took to in its place, the absorption of what I internally reference as a joyous racket. All pubs and bars can assemble loud, but what the summer climate ensures is the demonstration of a boisterous collective mirth. All those who amass in the dreamland of beer's delight contribute the impression of presidency over the most terrific of moods. It must happen; I considered; that we prevail a repressed people for the entire conflicting season; the clouds of pitch overhead in fulfilment as a canopy of gloom to hinder our latent personalities.

Robert E. Kearns

That brought home a depiction of dismal dread. In a rush, I discerned and then marvelled where it approached from. It didn't correspond with me to inhabit the space of sombre pessimism. It must, I excused, have surfaced from the day I racked up. Hence, with application, I fell back on my reflections with interest to the collective rapture which the proprietors of multitudinous Oases' in Dublin ought to patent. The uproar of exuberance comes about as ubiquitous, so too it must happen, that it remains besides, contagious; somewhat equivalent to a yawn. Here, in the plot of midsummer cheer, one person with a smile causes a hundred others to beam in sympathy.

It uplifted my mental state a notch or two. I introduced from work somewhat disconsolate, but the hurrah of the cobble locked piazza elevated my disposition back to regular. One thing detected about evenings such as this survives that a compendium of fellow imbibers has achieved the identically presumed original fancy. Not as unique in their individuality as supposed, they acknowledge all too soon those out-of-town transport customers who should have happened on a train or bus ride, as an alternative committed to the adventure of the great absconsion; a departure for the confines of a proximate hostelry that is.

Influenced by the casual proposition thereabouts of a drink; a thirst which until that point had lain dormant, became the overriding consideration. Those now gasping bees of industry had beforehand slow-cooked in the convection of a low-ceilinged office for the full eight hours. No matter that the windows paraded without restriction, they still baked as overdone, thus couldn't help but peer down on the masses;

then vacuum up by the methodical clout of suggestion and reflexive bombardment the input of: Designer shades, the swirl of a giant whipped ice cream, short pants of pastille hues and more; the chugs of frigid spring water from bottles of synthetic plastic.

It sports in one of these jealousies of the 9 to 5 fraternity where skewered to the partitions of a cubicle; they overhear for the initial that contextual and harmonious discussion on the issue of amber suds. An exertion comes about to manufacture saliva for the alleviation of those effects arising from the sandpaper tongue they discerned to occupy. And then the abrupt picture conjured is one of a frosted glass with ladylike curves, intact water drops bound by tension and unified with its outer, furthermore, the chilled tawny concern with a frothy crest inside. Here, the film "Ice Cold in Alex" gets hauled out from that vault of memories and it comes about this flash of summoned stardom which necessitates the re-enactment of those incomparable frames of cinematic perfection.

Here before me distributed these servants to industry; their collars extended wide, too, their suit jackets draped with disordered neatness over the crook of their elbow. They needed for little apart from the prompt of a black-and-white flicker of that sand-covered hero coveting the anticipated pour, for it to sweep them from the threshold of a common vocation, and then off to the most opportune inn for the parched. The newest entrants to the fray, comparable to he, tensed in admiration before this encounter with the deliverance which emanates from that foremost perception of flavour on those arid, barren lips. The hop characterized foam which tumbled over the rim at its fullest, now tipped at a distance to an awkward angle with the ambition to stammer those stray tawny drips from splashing on to their mirrored shoes in leather. Then, inexpert at such ungainliness, the hinge of the favoured appendage got retracted, thus; to disclose the reassignment in portion, of a creamy head to the shadow of their upper lip.

I remarked in quiet they elevated no zeal to deflect this transference; a flick of the tongue trailed by a swipe of the copycat sleeve sufficed as plenty. The primary end was to frank a stamp on the furious thirst of fire, with other considerations positioned to the queue. These sequential gesticulations wound-up; a gawk at the once more unfurled pivot point which clutched on to the slippery goblet followed on, to take a measurement on how they ingurgitated so much in the manoeuvre. It came chased with a lazy forefinger in a refined wipe of the mouth to dry off the moisture that got away from the preliminary dab. I acknowledged that this production by unknowing actors here on the set of the picturesque yard I erected an ephemeral feature of, told succinctly the story of this town built on the banks of a pitch-black pool.

My initial bevvy posted almost at its conclusion; drank sooner than I might otherwise knock back, having succumbed to the pleadings of a desperate palate. I humoured no wish to vacate the spot I carved out with triumph amongst the unwashed multitudes, so rubber necked my disposition to the way of pinpointing a server. While I bore a resemblance to the extra-terrestrial with its extended cranium, I got assigned to make last, what stayed on in the bottom fifth of my crystalline tankard. To finish it should cause a reoccurrence of the equivalent issue, I confronted the opening time 'round. Nothing was considered more ridiculous to the confident tippler than clinging to the glass with no beer; and so I discounted that proposal.

The other poor recommendation of equal stature was to post it back in the hollowed out ledge, which is where I started with it all. This circus of fortunes amusingly caused me to hum the lyrics that made reference to a certain bucket with its unrepairable cavity. What I did was hang on to the ale, conscious it resolved in danger of becoming tepid, when a short while thereafter I caught the attention of a girl who came dressed in what furnished the imprint as a standard uniform approved by these enterprises–black pants besides a short-sleeved blouse in white. I engaged my entreaty for a second drink to balance things up; supplied her with the empty I concluded then relied that she arrive back double quick. I celebrated now as that fellow in the worst of all situations; the one by his lonesome with no beer.

The second of my grownup beverages got taken on board slower than the original. It masters here with the follow on, in my case at least, that the Law of Diminishing Marginal Returns discards its blindfold. The initial is nectar to Bacchus himself. Then, satisfaction extracted; with each consecutive tipple, it gifts less followed by attenuated. This thrives as why two of these golden extracts of barley salvage what I deem as about optimum credit from the balance sheet of fulfilment. Thus, kindred to an athlete, as soon as warmed up with the maiden, the succeeding permits the drinker an aperture to embrace in complete the flavour of providence.

Robert E. Kearns

It came at this stage, where for fun, I honed in on a sum of conversations which distinguished as happening in occupancy of appeal. However, the electronic noise which escaped from the attendant crowds made this pastime less than satisfactory. After my setback, I quit this momentary diversion, and humoured myself in an alternative which stimulated the application of sight, so too, fantasy to guess at the connotation of these exchanges. It played out in this make-believe world I formed, that the clanging of bells in a steeple on high pealed out for the steadfast flock to congregate. They all, fuelled up on alcohol, squeezed out amusement from some triviality or other. Did it ensue perhaps from an incident at work? Happenings that sited as inconsequential a day or two before; recalled by the collective, then further roused by the catalyst of ethanol, erupted now in a prodigious geyser of hilarity.

The twilight of my brew synchronised with the setting of the great orb as it dropped behind the coarse brownstone walls of the wide-ranging patio. I swirled the residual dregs of my personal galaxy and with each bead of glossy sop fashioning into a hypotonic orbit of burnished stars I next appreciated the careering void which motioned at the core of this self-occasioned eddy. Then, I swallowed it up, and could at last commit my spent to the crevice of that hewn out miniature apse. I saw to contract a duo of tasty treats; liquefied nourishment, plus the experience of cosmopolitan goings-on in microcosm. In engaging thus, my humour completed its circuit of homecoming, up from the underworld of this earth's enigmatic entrails. I hadn't quite understood the effect that detachment from humanity should impose on me until today. The impression levied on my disposition lodged as an uncomfortable, what's more, unwelcome consciousness, and it pleased me to come upon the sensory tonics of revitalisation this past hour and a half.

The rest of the week expired with no exceptional incident. I checked in regular to my abode for the penitent, to sort, document and catalogue. The weather topside hadn't broken, which conditioned unusual for Ireland, and it incited me to consider that my friends aloft fortunate enough to not belong in Hades as I; coped with a grand old time of it. I amused myself in sepia images that this must have transpired the reaction of olden day servants upon the recognition of footsteps, too, the confused timbres of merriment from their lords and masters, as they took their fine Sherries from crafted crystal repositories, just past the width of a mere floorboard above.

That stationed all very well, except that in contrast to those bygone domestics, I hovered alone here in my hewn out citadel, with not even the din of a clanging copper pot applicable to the household cook for companionship. I succeeded in the attainment of a portable wireless from home, but learned after a handful of minutes that frustrated with tunes of pure static, I stationed ineffectual at the achievement of a signal. Apart from the granted temporary leave, I stayed cut off from civilisation, (the irony of which wasn't lost on me, given the vicinities).

Friday in all fairness, clocked in with a difference. While there turned up nothing to alter my soundless funerary environs, it came to occur, that over lunch, arrangements got brokered to head out after work. I conjectured whether I qualified as an invitee, given my lowly condition. However, the provisional destination got called in my presence, so hence I settled categorical in consideration this advanced as the gift of a certifiably mailed R.S.V.P. Not that I dedicated specific disquiet to hanging out with them all, but the lovely Tiffanie consented her nod to the motion. At the heed of her subscription, I resolved that I stood definite to go along, had drinks in the morgue gotten recommended. And on that freakish farce, I broke into a broad grin with the reflection I registered knowledge of just such a mortuary, and check out from the building wasn't even a requisite.

As it came about, Tiffanie happened not too erroneous in her assessment of our co-workers earlier that week. They weren't so terrible after all; friendly, moreover, talkative, in particular after a drink or two. Anyhow, it remained difficult to not situate in a good humour, and if they clad in a hardened shell, it disposed of them to poke their heads out from its confines for an hour or so. I had intentions to keep to a watchful eye on my alcohol intake; so nursed a drink until it tottered on the unpalatable. As the newcomer, I arrested no aspiration to cede control; not that I engaged tendencies on that bearing in the first place, but I stood conscious of whom I socialised with. Not yet was I on terms of friendship with these acquaintances; therefore, it stayed preferable for me to continue on alert, unenthusiastic to engender unexpected mishaps. My policy in such situations is that it's best to fly under the radar. Smile along, so too, revel in the cause, but stick where viable to the fringes of discourse.

That billed as the strategy I laid out and rather successful it worked too; until the tail end of my second concoction. I questioned if that might befall a respectable juncture to duck out with grace, having shown for a suitable interval in validation of my sociable charm. I arrived once again at that point in the proceedings where if I was to attain a fresh beer, it should appear at that continuous optimum second, whereupon swigging down the last of the previous; I might well master a faultless exchange for the new. This smooth motion is akin to the precision of a pit stop in motor racing. With this analogy transposed to my predicament, any errors arising from the practice, and I should end up in a stall to yield those dreaded idle limbs wilted in worthlessness by my side. I had gotten on rather well until now, thus, did not hanker after the risk of an error in those final laps. Godsends advance with the brave though, and with the chequered flag sighted on the horizon, I happened resolute on contracting another.

As it came about, with folk cutting loose after sticking in rigid terms to their self-imposed rule of "Just the One" (I hadn't realised such people existed) too, a jostle for position after a few heading off to the bar, I found myself parallel to the delightful Tiffanie, whose glass, I noticed, ran to the standing of low. Chancing a breach of social etiquette, which till this point I remained anxious to avoid; I voiced up to inquire if she might care for another. A flash of those perfect teeth in pearl was I believe accompanied with a response in the affirmative. However, I positioned in stunned immobility by the flash of her smile, and in consequence had to assume this transpired the case. Its vivid illumination caused me to forget my manners; hence, as an afterthought I queried the gathered circle if I might interest them in one as well. I contracted a few declines, but at least I squirreled up a handful of points in brown for the asking. In place of waited service as stood my original intent, I understood a jolt from my trance was required, hence ploughed a furrow through the beer drinker flocks, to next get snagged in the tractor beam of corporate logos lit up in brilliant taps of draught.

I picked up the commissioned potations from the counter of slops and to prevent against spillage got entailed to finesse my lines through disruptive mobs by agency of ginger moves. With my hands continuing largely dry, too, the drinks as they essentially started, I shuffled to the locus of our standing. There, I nudged into the slimmest of gaps beside Tiffanie as I brooked no intent to see myself jockeyed out from the prime slot. Upon forwarding to her the drink, she greeted me with a southern thank you, which produced in me an all over tingle. To attend on Tiffanie's speech with her tones of enchantment affected me to call for an imagined action replay so I might again wallow in its delight. Her gilded locks shone in the dying sun; as well, it caused me to ponder a sky of orange dusk over the prairie; us both in silhouette on that horse-drawn surrey sheltered by its overhead fringe.

With this embodiment, I envisioned her in a pretty dress from a long-vanished era, relaying idioms such as "I was so tickled", which, being one of her divinest expressions should affect the hardest of granite to melt. These mental pictures turned to fields and crops, further barns of painted red among stalks of intense yellow; prime for harvest. An iconic windmill of The Great Plains stood atop its derrick, the blades featured in gentle rotation through the near permanent breeze; a soothing whirr, plus the soft squeak of metal on metal to linger in perception on those prevailing winds.

Next to this emblem of the West; reared a timber framed house washed in a one-time brilliant white and set into it mounted sash windows with crooked fractures that exposed an artificial yellowish torch light from the interior. Out front erected the greyed out, so too, well-worn deck of a porch with stretched planks, complete with a cushioned chair to rock in. And there, off to the side, below the extended branches of a gnarled, too, weather-beaten and deciduous ancient oak, a pair of mongrel dogs sprawled in what remained of the shade to a now almost extinguished sunset.

My attention fled to another period, besides place, and had I transpired at home under the covers of my bed, I should have gotten lost beneath the moonlit and expansive prairie land of my dreams. I wished to share this tableau with the beautiful girl beside me; take her by the hand and then step on to the creaking timbers of our homely portico; there to sojourn, further, sip on an iced tea in a tall glass; the floating cubes clinking against the sides akin to chimes in the night; and then finished with a twig of mint balanced precariously on those miniature bergs. The chatter, besides interposed laughter between those lasting friends from work continued as before, but I ceased to pay attention or contribute. I couldn't help in its stead, but to glance to my side, entranced; and in that instant longed to lead Tiffanie out of this world and into the parallel alternate of my imaginings with its perfect homestead under the heavens.

Here, she donated a discreet and fleeting dart in return, with her crown tilted somewhat to my right, and then what lingered from those rays of an Irish sundown caught a share of her face and strands of gold, to leave all but a shaving of the opposite flank in contrast. Both of her eyes sparkled, but with the light shining direct into her left, it gave the appearance of a brilliant princess cut diamond. She smiled while turning just her eyes to look at me and then raised the glass with her left arm. Just below her dimpled chin she fashioned use from her right hand to guide the yellow straw to the exact centre of glistened and painted pink, also, faultless lips.

I evoked reveries of lemonade and icy cold bottled beer, too, the not so clever bugs of June descendent from those southern United States which in time to the music of mating amphibians, clattered into the casing of a dust obscured porch light. Punched, they collapse drunk and dazed onto the hard board flooring, there, to regain their feet and dance unsteadily with their oversized chums. All of this must have originated in a film of rich colour which captivated me some place and time in my childhood. These vividly graphic memories brought forth a Texas size aspiration to kiss this girl who grew up in its geographic neighbour, and to embrace her right there and then in the orchard of night time pleasure, with intensity and passion without giving a care for what anyone might think. I concluded at the tail end of this fancy that Oklahoma must have occupied a special patch in the otherwise random and scattered universe.

When the curtain on our sun closed, we moved indoors to admit one more drink for the road. The quantities of our association had dwindled; a brew to complete the week, for some, curbed with severity to the hours before dark. It chances in those few sweeps of the small hand past the five o'clock exodus which endure of a magic and luxury confined to a solitary quarter of the year. The appeal, besides comparative rarity of outside gatherings at the rear of a tavern with beer on tap, was enough to anesthetize even the tougher pains of being. It occurs with the communal shift to the lounge that for many converts to an inner white flag, a signal to surrender and retreat while the going is good; the allure for them having lain in complete with the novelty of that seasonal atmosphere of a four walled but open-air enclosure.

After I chugged down over a half-pint, we located a table that submitted to the procedure of being vacated. There we earned our seats, too, in quick succession; another of our sum finished their choice of poison. And so there were three. Tending at all times as the model in such tricky circumstances, there happens no getting rid of the spare. The youthful, plus eagerly brave man perceives a clear route through the fog of love and war. But even the assumption of strategies to postpone the intake of one's beverage; placing faith that the obstacle to your heart's desire should remove his self from the field of battle, situates with inevitableness as one doomed to failure.

I caught myself in scrutiny of the minutes as if to hazard a guess on how delayed it might ensue for his tankard to run dry. And when it materialised, my victory collapsed to a draw at best; when his empty got positioned on a sodden cardboard coaster. The hindrance to my coupling elected to stay, therefore facilitated the withdrawal of us all three at the identical moment. When this transpires, as happens the propensity when least wished for; there remains nothing for it but to scour for that murky flank of bright, then carry on with exaggerated merriment. It occurs at this point in the proceedings when the aces of a gambler have gotten played that a reminiscence of strategies pre-eminently positioned arises to notice. All that might be achieved is to endure for the fight of that next skirmish; swig a measure into the bargain, though not all; of those flat, what's more, tasteless dregs of left-over swills. That concluded it befalls the phase to plunge outside as a solitary component of a lopsided and therefore unholy trinity.

The air ventured to cool a degree as comes about in late summer nights on this islet of Erin. It stayed however, yet in twilight. This acclaims as another of the ecstasies in these northern latitudes. The sun may conspire to dissolve into the horizon, but as on this occurrence it hadn't dropped in absolute. And in these months it lingers on until the calendar date by a watch happens midway between one and the next. We sauntered through some narrow cobblestoned street or other headed for the Liffey, the three of us ostensibly with bus routes at a similar location. I happened erroneous with reference to that, and providence dealt me a new hand to flirt with. I overlooked that in this popular playground for adults, it should transpire as more pliant in these environs to hail a taxi. Our colleague I imagine incorporated no particular anxiety with note to the cost. With a fleetness of state he signalled a carriage with its availability distinct; aces high having run the river for me. And then there were two.

I offered talk of the small kind, and then on purpose slowed down the rate of my stride, keen not to realise our destination in a hurry. That inexpert trick didn't work out all that great, but at the acquirement of Tiffanie's stop, in secret I happened joyous to comprehend her intended bus should not be along for another ten minutes. She contributed the tiniest of shivers from the chilled air and then wrapped bare arms about her torso for warmth. At this, the alcohol I absorbed injected me with a dose of bravery which instigated the drift of a step frontwards. Tiffanie didn't back away, so I grabbed this as a mark of acceptance, and in view of that engaged my left hand to her waist and next delivered the most placid of tugs with an unvarnished disbursement of chivalrous finger tips. She yielded with elegance, further, inched towards me, which transpired as ample to my interpretation. To follow on, I matched my opposite palm to her left hip and drew her in close.

I kissed her, soft and gentle to start with, besides in realisation through a measured and prolonged engagement. This to extract every final ounce of bliss and wonder that can only originate from this most tender of affections. Her lips distinguished as soft and appealing, their taste so sweet I yearned to loiter on them for an eternity. Her fragrance filled my courses to overwhelm the carnal acuities, and next I shut my eyes, to fancy in romance over again while it yet stayed in the black; our homely veranda in the luminosity of a super moon, Tiffanie and I entwined and bounded by the hush of those Great Plains, chinked with just the song of awakened crickets, so too, the muffled thud of those seasonal critters as they thump, thump, thumped against their spotlight of fascination.

I directed my lids ajar, and in expression on nothing, pulled back my head to take in the proceeds of her splendour. She reciprocated with the hint of a smile learned from those masters of Italian portraiture, which in its delicacy articulated an epic of affection. I ran my fingers through the luscious hair over her right earlobe and availed of my thumb with refined sensitivity to caress her showing temple. This purposed her eyes to seal in a mode which expressed; she happened in that second to reach contentment. Those ten minutes until the appearance of her bus lasted but a flicker. Neither of us spoke, as if in exchange, the exceptional spark of time which just eventuated should come to be tainted. To close, she enunciated, "I had a real good time tonight", to which I returned, "Were you tickled?" She let out a tiny laugh which I took as an affirmation of its veracity. Then, she boarded her lift and drew away. I forgot to inquire of her number.

That weekend got taken up with elegant reveries of the beautiful Tiffanie, and I relived in my considerations that sensation of marvel relating to the graceful touch of her mane which glittered as that fleece of gold against the palm of my open hand and fingertip nerve endings. I evoked the two of us embraced in a waltz on the deck of our weather-beaten timbers, her body hugged to mine with arms linked at the small of her back. I inhaled her perfume of resplendence that must have come about as custom distilled with especial devotion to her. And I reflected on how tranquil it accented to welcome her in kisses, and how it instigated in me an acceptance as factual, that I saw to have a blessing conferred on me by Mother Nature herself.

The wonder of this re-creation got offset by the pain of wakefulness that before I set senses on her southern splendour again, I should perceive a chasm in my life till Monday. But by the same mark; as countless men have recognised; there arose a masculine thrill to my heart, which despite the imbedded dagger of separation, verified that the chase for my quarry continued. Those two days stood in consistency with a band of elastic, and with time strained, I again ensued ineffective at a full quota achievement of shuteye. In the mirage of my apparitions, I jumped ahead the few days to check on my prompt advent at the museum. The week former, out of pure anxiety, I reached there prematurely. Now however, I got to teleport my being through the fabric of space, to re-materialise in its voluminous rotunda of rapture, but in commission of this for entirely distinct motives.

It's possible, there entrusted within, a subconscious aspiration to commute judiciously as I realised before, with a thought perhaps for that bird of prescience. With this effected, I resumed to my petite café of cosiness with the laundered, starched, as well as creased, red and white patterned table cloths. There, I settled in to that corner spot for two, and demanded of myself that I not encounter perception at the dot of nine to impress on Kildare Street as exaggeratedly fretful. Besides, the museum, I commented, ran somewhat to the lax when it came to punctuality. Liberty from restraint, this morning I held in abundance, and doubted if it should encounter notice I turn up hours advanced, let alone get there a handful of minutes after the bells of Christchurch ceased their clangs of matin.

Hence, I beckoned for tea, which showed in a neat earthen pot that permitted me to secure with maximum drain, the rough volume of a mug and a half. This quantum of dried leaves from the Orient, claimed with wellbeing, pitched as a short throw from perfect in leading me up to that opening toll of the gong. I caricatured what I fantasised the Victorian Gentleman of my reveries should see to, through a dab of my lips and moustaches with a napkin of crisp snowy white before a gentle shove of my chair rearward before moving off. I withdrew and then metaphorically walked the streets to where she worked; with my ensemble of invisible cane besides morning tails, not bothered if people stopped and stared. I searched for trees of lilac, but with the outcome of none, I supplanted it with the whistled air to a pleasant-sounding show stopper.

The precautions I gave heed to against over eagerness worked out as expected; there happening no sign of Tiffanie with the striking features. I reasoned that logic of avoidance intersected as the superior alternative to sticking around for her to license in a distinguished arrival. I admit however; I revealed as a mite disenchanted not to have set eyes on her. The heart should have loved to hot foot it upstairs, and more than that, give embrace to her, but the head correctly overruled. Therefore, with the support of my laminated badge, which I trusted over the weekend should not stay forgotten; I unlocked the portal of destiny and then journeyed down into the underworld of my incarceration.

Ah, the drama of it all! The actuality however, staked that execution of my return to the swing of things versed as not so appallingly tough. I activated to survey a quantity of the antiques at my disposal, with the fancy of, why not? I even grew bold and revealed the drawers besides sliding cabinets which reconciled all the previously catalogued items. Down here there exposed nobody to check on my activity and even should the odd intruder tender his face, I doubted they should opine too much on my snooping. I figured that were I to be rumbled, I shouldn't with celerity, too, in panic, shut away what underwent inspection to scarper back to my station of work. Instead of that I would keep on with the scrutiny as if I parodied the museums ageing, furthermore, authoritarian

Professor Emeritus. I gained tutelage in deception during those ages of my oft times misdirected youth where I learned there is naught as prone to attract suspicion as a man who gallops off at the first alarm. In contrast, there postures nil that ensures a higher possibility in the projection of reassurance, than the confidence of one, whom in his statuesque mien of authority, pronounces that he alone rules as the principal squire of the county.

There revealed, I decided, an abundant stash of terrific archaeological material in his hollowed out chamber of Erebus, and I measured it a shame that numerous of these superb objects of antiquity not be situated on general display. I supposed it wasn't practical to offer it all behind glass, but then furnished thanks for the public's loss equipping me with gain. I notched up a mental note to infiltrate in recurrence as the spy, and poke around over here in those spells when I got bored with the categorisation of my haphazard assortment. I secured the drawer I happened in a review of and reverted to my counter, envisaging in my gait, simply for the amusement, that I transcended that senior Fellow of my thoughts. I put-on the stern articulation of pomposity appropriate to one who is used to being both in charge; likewise, obeyed in each command. Too, though cognisant of his slacking off, he trumpeted with all the faux sincerity he could dredge up, that he happened here to contend with some research of frightful weightiness.

At the approach to eleven, I perceived a phone ring out some place about. And as they termed this reserve "The Dungeon", it almost caused me to leap out of my skin. I grasped no inkling there submitted an extension down here; too, I grew used to the soundless institution with its lone internee. The situation straightaway reminded me of a classic commercial I watched online which brought attention to a covered in dust phone inside a vacant and old-fashioned office.

In this nameless business a chap of efficient looking carriage passes in the aisle outside the door to this room for work. It is then he overhears the call chime out from behind our fastened ingress. He enters with a cautious doubt then runs into an environment which looks as though it got plucked direct from the 1930s. He answers the ring and next speaks to pronounce the caller must have dialled a wrong number. It only occurs after his leave-taking when the viewer gets to comprehend the stencilled letters to the pane of glass which declares "Complaints Department". Merely after this does it happen, they introduce us to the voiceover that refers to the brand of lager advertised.

I undertook to hone in on the breaker of peace, spotting it then off to one side and on a wall at the other end to my den of iniquity. It mounted devoid of tint with its personal jacket of grime, and as a consequence I was fervidly tempted to utter the words "Department for Complaints". I changed my mind though; and quizzed perhaps whether several of the stuffy devotees should appreciate my taste in humour. I blew air on the receiver to clear the accumulated dirt before I spoke up with a wary "Hello".

To my surprise, but heartfelt delight, the voice from the earpiece arrived as that of Tiffanie. She commented that some folk in her office were ready to set forth on their morning break and next enquired if I might wish to join them. I wasn't delayed in the provision of an eager reply and leapt two steps at a time on the route out. I met the others in the lobby area, faking calm, besides composure, and then strode with them to the ground floor museum café. It offered as a pleasant setting, so too a change from the upstairs common room for staff of which I had gotten used to for a mug on the go. In that cafeteria, I had stuck to tea, not unerringly compliant in fanaticism for the powdered coffee which ensues forever on offer in those catering drums that remain a staple of the Irish work environment. For the desperate; these tins ought to be labelled "Only for Emergency". The lid stays set to one side all day as well as night and the granules cake before it transpires a quarter of the way depleted. Also, there exists as a constant the wet tea spoon half buried inside, stuck in the middle with a saturated brown concoction glued to its entire surface.

The building which accommodated the museum ranked in itself as a model from history. As a sophisticated example of neo-classical architecture, I fell in love with it; from the exquisite rotunda in the lobby to the tasteful pattern of the mosaic tile and parquet floor. The café we entered came bounded by a magnificent imprinted wood, too, intricate stucco adorned ceiling. It was busy enough too, I noticed, with this, the season for tourists. Even so, we were effective at grabbing a table to the rear which situated in the act of being wiped down. I held on to it while the ladies joined the queue for tea's and coffees. Tiffanie was kind enough to acquire for me a sizable Americano. Given her nationality, I considered that mode of beverage to occur as rather appropriate. She pulled out the worn, plus battered wooden chair then positioned at the opposite end to where I sat. As we stationed in company, it required to assume a monumental application to not reveal just how tickled I befell to see her.

As we disconnected to venture back to the strife, I caught hold of her for a second. Then, with the art of the gab and the minimum extent of obligatory chit chat which politeness might consent to, I posed if she would care to go out with me sometime. In passing custom to the word "Sometime", what I meant in fact was 'As soon as is humanly practicable'. 'I'd love that' she responded, which I must assume brought a smile to my face, if not a worded hurray from my gaping mouth. After a pause to process these three diminutive, but oh so wonderful words, I established my voice to give the poets of romance a run for their money, when I composed the one syllable rejoinder of "Great!" We agreed in that faintly awkward, post-agreement phase, to meet later, at which we quitted for our separate routes. I experienced a perk-up with this momentous relationship breakthrough, and not at all displeased about my plunge yet again into the netherworld nick.

Uneventful, is the method by which I ought to style the remains of that day, and I stuck with obedience to the project instead of being on the doss elsewhere. I cleared out at a minute or two before five, too, loitered around with an impatient eye out for Tiffanie. I wasn't left to pace the tiled pavilion for long, which was just as well, as I came over all conscious of my standing out. I had sought to avoid receipt of attention from colleagues who all scurried off at about that time. I stayed back to a certain point in a bid to circumvent this when I observed her figure coercing inwards that ornate oak door from administration.

I hastened over, to what straight off came to mind, as me

"Hindering her way at the pass". I was quick to self-congratulate with the brainchild of this clever allusion to The West. I queried whether I might walk her to the bus, which she straight away accepted with Southern grace. "I like the stubble" she professed, noticing the as yet, immature growth of my innovative facial aspect.

"I sought to perceive how it should look", I answered, then elevated a limb as if to confirm it was still there. Together, we walked the short distance to her stop, and on this instance I didn't let her slip away without entreating her for the integers to her phone. The electronic board overhead displayed accurately the two minutes until her ride home, so as it pulled in to the curb, I separated from her with a kiss of softness while I beckoned her divine chin inward with the forefinger of my right hand; a deed I adore as being both intimate and tender.

The next morning, I fell into a review of my labour with just the half-hearted expectation of spotting headway gained. To mild surprise however, I verified that I fared well with the realisation of a beachhead in progress, with many objects now grouped in order, categorised so too, logged on my clipboard. I flipped the pages to find out that more than just a few stood in completion. I contemplated this surprising development as an opportune moment to ferry them up to the subject of my heart's desire under the assumed guise of a professional attitude.

It arose here where I got bothered abruptly with a thought out of the blue. Fear raised its head, whereby I became uneasy about the peril of a mishap, or where a biblical calamity wreaked vengeance on my week's work. It's not that there transpired any real prospect of an unforeseen disaster whistling down the wind of my subterranean penal yard. Now though, for whatever the purpose, I met with anxiety. I characterised not as a person of superstition, or liable to consider the worst of outcomes, with a belief in principal it should all come up well on the night. I observed in the past that those who distress are themselves inflicted with their apprehensions consummated in some method; while those who refrained from shouldering, as with Atlas, the whole of this world's burden, ensued in general as less traumatised by the minor trivialities. I might earlier have placed my type in the latter category. Of this alarm however, I concluded that a visit to the beautiful Tiffanie fit in with the assignation of safety through exile from my unearthly domain; the reason for this irregular angst.

I surfaced with the clipboard in hand and then upheld my Walter Mitty imitation by simulating a devoted doctor on his rounds of the ward. I even stood still for a tick in consideration of the chart as if to determine which patient needed seeing to next. It broke the influence that unease held over me, and for this I was gratified. Agitation happened not as a condition I struck at ease with prolonging. Next, I encountered the wonderful Tiffanie at her desk and cradled the clipboard with the poise of one who understood what he was about. I should have loved to announce, as a consultant might, "Ah, and what do we have here then?"

On the other hand I would have stemmed as the sole person in on the joke; and because of that, I spelled out the actual aim, which checked out that I came up to tender her with the completed sheets for safekeeping. 'Terrific', she stated. 'It needs key entering to the database, anyway'. Then she told that she would preserve the original, too, equip me with a copy to keep track of against the inventory. 'How's the sorting coming along?' she probed. I acquainted her I made progress, in addition, organised items into groups (not heaps or piles), which distinguished to take shape. Here, she supplied an adroit peep at the crystal-studded watch on her slender left wrist. I parroted the deed to determine it fulfilled as almost eleven. Then, as if on cue, one of Tiffanie's friends arrived over to ask if we intended to go on break.

Nearer to one, I received intelligence that most everybody resolved to stay in for lunch. Drizzle and grey clouds had switched places with the sun of the previous week. I didn't feel much like being cooped up in the slammer for longer than mandatory. Thus, with the patronage of a borrowed umbrella, I scurried to an alternative museum; of sorts that is-The National Art Gallery. It placed just a brief jaunt away and; I established beforehand that it stood as a quite agreeable building to escape the showers. I bought a drink plus sandwich in the café, and though I took a table, wolfed it down in a rush so I might have a saunter around. It underwent of late a renovation, and the results hit me as astounding.

Although crowded, the artwork exuded tranquillity throughout. I understood why hyper tensioned executives unwound in its chambers for the entirety of their allotted hour. The edifice itself was a piece of art; not dissimilar in style to the museum. It transmitted architecture of continuity, with each room linking to the next in harmony; a balance of space, besides motion. Close on all the galleries revealed tile or antique patterned solid wood flooring, which intensified the pleasure derived. High, intricate, and pure white stuccoed ceilings, supported by soaring colonnades of Portland stone; too, a former ballroom walled with masterpieces, triggered one to just about visualise those ladies of centuries prior, who, to the notes of a live orchestra in evening dress, majestically descended the grand staircase with colourful in the extraordinary; on top of, elegant gowns for dancing.

Later that afternoon, back in the corner of my lair, having delighted in the appraisal of those brush-strokes of genius which hung from the recently painted gallery walls, I thought perhaps I may well be arriving at a greater appreciation for the history attached to those subjects of antiquity I worked on in the dungeon. A burgeoning hunger to examine them ascended. I allowed my inventiveness to roam with enthusiasm so I might perceive of an attendant past and wondered who it could have been that whittled their original portrayal into a comb hewn from the antler of a long-departed stag. I invited too notions linked to the practice of creation that galvanised the stimuli of he who decorated a vessel of allure to sup from, and where besides why happened a yard of dyed and vivid cloth come to be weaved in intricacy. It seemed as if I got dragged into the ancient, by a method I conceived intentions of prior to the dawn of my stint here. That afternoon, rather than preserving a sentiment I got betrothed to a chore, gained confidence I entertained an additional purpose of higher significance above that of the simple responsibility to detail or categorise left-over relics. There ascended an instinct or emotion from the gut; that this gained recognition as a charge which expected completion, so too, there expressed believable gratification for the reaping in the performance of that duty.

Not long after, infused with positivity, I was about to begin on a new shelf which lay out of arm's reach. I earlier remarked cerebrally on the mid-sized ladder which stood propped at an angle against one of the metallic upright supports. This got applied to the charge when there were grounds for a stretch to higher levels. I improved its position then clambered up the rungs to peek over the top.

This storey, as the others achieved, resembled a wide-ranging board sawn out of thick plywood; grubby besides splintered, which held a multitude of forgotten about rarities. I beheld its sum magnitude and probed for inspiration where I ought to make the foremost dent. It wouldn't have achieved a lot of difference, but in place of the usual, my attention got attracted to the alternative of a rectangular wooden box. It appeared as not altogether large, but it reminded me in build, moreover tint to the grain, of one we sustained in the garage at home. As he chiselled the mahogany table, so too had my grandfather put together that simple container to hoard tools. I had to clear a few bits to either side before I could then extend my arm to get at it. The bare skin of my fingers caught hold of the edge, and with a tenuous grip, I cajoled it through the resistant board, which kicked up a cloud of mouldy dust in the exploit.

It emerged heavier than supposed, so too, a notch lengthier in dimension than the width of my chest. In breadth, I could support it under my arm. It happened therefore reasonably undemanding to manipulate although the tread of my descent with each rung of the ladder stole twice the time. Back on terra firma, I lopsidedly hiked over with it yet grasped by one limb and next positioned it squarely on the work surface.

There sited no lid to this curious receptacle, so the upper section remained vulnerable. It was however, protected from the desiccated grime by several sheets of layered brown paper which I drew back with timidity at one corner, to reveal it emanated full to completion with assorted paraphernalia. I rotated the case of curios then examined each side; to witness that one of the two gable ends came affixed with an expansive but somewhat oblong ticket. It might before have mounted as white and in good condition, but now revealed as frayed in spots, and more, gave the idea that someone short of attention spilled a cup of stewed tea over it. I bent a touch at the knee joints to get within distance and determine it disclosed as a product of officialdom. Though it was tanned, too in splotches, darker than the shade of chestnut, the script was yet legible through it all; discernible:

Date: June 1896-Professor A. Campbell, National Museum of Ireland

Contents: Various Artefacts of Differing Mode and Nature

Origin: Hy Brasil

Detail: Further examination essential. Refer to the accompanying documentation.

Now, this I anticipated was of prominence, hence obligated me to don the beaten and battered hat of a down at his heels, private eye. It submitted, on the other hand, to land within shouting distance of five, and I sought to locate upstairs and receive the lovely Tiffanie. As a result, I reckoned on parking it for today then give it the attention it deserved later.

Punctual, Tiffanie showed up straight off, so at that point the two of us departed as a couple. As we tramped along on the pavement outside, I posed if she might wish to join me for a drink or grab a bite to eat, to which she answered that the duo of these offered as good, adding that she didn't retain a preference as to the order they presented. We directed our trek towards her bus stop although in advance of touching on it stole a left into Temple Bart. It emerges as the selection of least resistance in those quarters, with no shortage of eateries, or; as I motioned desirous in referral to them as; "Drinkeries". Without the wastage of time, I occasioned the executive decision to pick out an unassuming pub, rather than one of the ubiquitous Burger and Fries establishments.

Even if accommodated here and now in my chosen inn for the ravenous, and when just a pulse of the clock previous, I visualised a stacked burger with all the trimmings, my taste it seemed got locked onto the bill of fare and its sustenance which approximated that which I stressed to elude. I fell as the victim to my impetus of suggestion. Tiffanie settled on the Rack of Ribs, which smothered in barbeque sauce; after the waitress left, triggered regret in me for not deciding on them. We also stuck in a request for a pair of intoxicating beverages in Irish red. These transmitted to the seats of our abiding not long after, and at this juncture, when about to clink glasses, I was compelled to question why she imbibed a cocktail on our night out after work. "Oh, I adore cocktails, but I like beer too. If you want to live in Oklahoma, you better get used to it.

Besides, cocktails don't go with ribs". I couldn't have agreed more, so here completed the toast.

The feast savoured about as good as I trusted, with the verdict dispensing that we ought to fight round two with the grown-up brews. Then, Tiffanie spoke of herself with my urging, and though I reciprocated, my attentiveness got captured in winning heed to her story. While I might have cross checked it cerebrally if so inclined, I by far favoured aurally hanging on to her every word. Tiffanie distended this impact on me, and it collided as a virtuous one. The musical intonation of her voice while I bathed in her gorgeous smile triggered me to ruminate again on the vast open prairie lands, herds of roaming buffalo, and even more, the self-sufficient nomadic Indians of a vanished age.

A stretch afterward, we wandered to her stop, where I rejoiced at stealing a wink of time out of the vastness of eternity to kiss her once more, and convey just how much I looked forward to her company the next day. I couldn't help but express how divine I considered her, so too, I articulated admiration on how smart, besides pretty, she undeniably was. Allowed, I may well have enunciated these praises all night, further, until the song of the lark find welcome through the open sashed window of the ensuing dawn.

Alternating between these sweet phrases of affection and caresses of love, I ached for our nest to share in perpetuity at the zenith of the heavens. One last embrace to linger on; a look between us that obligated no redundant verses, and then with a parting as if in slow motion, she hopped on board the destined transport that would carriage her away from the affection of my heart. On the pavement, I delayed until she established her seat at a window midway, where we issued a closing wave as it pulled out from the curb to merge with the hues and illuminations of the city at night.

Restless at daybreak, I appropriated a lyric for inspiration, and guessed I couldn't lose, by taking off for downtown. In, this short phase of my fledgling adulthood I established the practise of timely advent. As an escape from the cares of noise and hurry, I ignored, as suggested in those lines, lingering on the sidewalk, and went on in contradiction to Merrion Square, for the variation of scenery. It blooms in some conducts as the match of Stephen's Green. Within a separation of promenade from each other, too, the equivalent scope by and large, they might happen as two heads to the same coin, correspondent worlds, and yet not unerringly the identical. It asserted less busy here, quieter, hence; I procured a bench to divert amongst the mature varieties of fauna, so too, the impeccable; golf course resembling; common mowed tight. Here in my city retreat, no finer place for sure, I valued those penetrating breaths and aspirated the full redolence of nature, which negated my yet durable and protracted agitation.

In the house of antiquities, I prepared, in the upstairs canteen, with the expertise of a seasoned barista, an aromatic café Arabica. In the depths of a cabinet, or press as we select to label it in Ireland, akin to the pot of gold at the end of a rainbow, I chanced upon a Cafetiere; too, in league with it, a brand of exceptional ground beans. The lady of luck shone her torch of fortune on me, thus, I conveyed this masterful creation with me down to the borstal for this imprisoned boy. There, I set it on the workbench alongside the marvellous pigmy chest

Robert E. Kearns

I abandoned a day earlier. That shape I gaped at, conjecturing out of it might emanate the curse of Cassandra. I shifted it to locate the end on which was papered the century old tag of a darker tinge than the Arabic invention to my side. Here I exorcised what accounted for as outlandish superstitions and with tentativeness detached protective deposits of paper leaves in brown, to expose, packed to the brim, the late Professor's assemblage of curiosities.

Feasibly against protocol, plus, without those white gloves one so often notices in documentaries, I started their removal one after the other. I organised them out on my workstation, and in racing parlance, a short head from my superb coffee, of which I sampled intermittent tastes from. It happened merely now where I paid it some mind, apprehending that I perhaps oughtn't to have conveyed it to my secreted clink in the first place. Therefore, I enacted what played as the mightiest of preventative measures to elude potential accidents, and repositioned my prize an extra foot to the left.

With the coffer now barren, I shifted it out of the way; then noted what arranged before me:

More than a few articles of China which included three porcelain cups in excellent condition, separated by protections of paper to avert chipping.

Ten significant pieces of what also looked as damaged porcelain cups. Four China plates (complete) of various design: 1 saucer, I jug, 2 items I accepted as vases of distinct proportions, mode, as well as character.

One useful sized container that may well have seen custom as a vessel for drinks. It hailed minus its handle. It also greeted me adorned with a design of swirls similar to that engraved on the stones of Newgrange. It may, I reflected, also have gotten administered as perhaps a vase or ornament.

A comb which; to the untrained eye, performed as if it got etched from bone. Scratched into it there presented markings of surprise along the top of one side.

A brooch similar to that on display out of Early Mediaeval Ireland-Again, with Celtic influenced triskeles on top of other period indicators.

Substantial glass fragment, of what to my mind, was a heavy lead, cut crystal glass for drinking.

Glass container, as in the variety that medicines come dispensed-Bevelled with a screw top. No matching lid.

Two gold rings with striking impressions as characters on the inner band.

Watch face, no strap-May well encounter description as Pre-War. Glass cracked. Metallic backing with intricate motifs.

Two small bronze figurines-Original Celtic, La Tene aspects to them-as in "Before the Common Era"

One pen with a metal casing-Either engraved or scratched. Configurations appear evenly spaced although unidentifiable.

Robert E. Kearns

Five pieces of mounted electronic circuit boards-No identifiable inscriptions or country of origin stamped on either the panels or components. There showed however, discernible formations; akin to those on its sister articles.

Several properties of multiple description and colour-All have the texture, so too, appearance of plastic. No decoration, letters or engravings.

A wooden bowl-Humble, though in good condition.

Two smoothed and formed articles fashioned from wood. One of these modelled into a brush, although, there revealed no bristles. The other was feasibly a photograph frame (but may have been something else–no stand).

One hefty metal (stainless steel?) spoon (soup?)-Two eating forks–Three knives, two of which were butter knives, with the other being a longer knife for bread with a serrated edge-One large fork which at one stage doubtless came sheathed with its handle (potential carving fork). Two big knives, one with sharp honed edge plus garlanded (steel?) handle (hunting?), plus one with a straight edge (household incising?) lacking its handle.

That's quite the collection, I muttered. One or two didn't altogether belong with their companions; moreover, it involved several that looked as if they had no business there at all. I speculated what it was they were all doing hemmed into the same space. None materialised with a label; the lone identifier emerging as the one fixed to exterior of the box. It also happened peculiar that the substances looked as if they hadn't come under any real scrutiny; if at all since they got ordered within. If they had, nobody made mention of it. The expectation ranged that each entry be accompanied with a tag of some description, and even if they got detached, I should have at least come across them intermingled with their companion fugitives from audit, or flattened on the bottommost section the chest. From what I could tell, the matters pertaining to this capsule amassed in former ages, had up till now, evaded prying eyes. There transpired also no sign of the complementary documentation which had gotten cited on the affixed docket.

This piqued my interest, and here I gathered up the mug of still fragrant and warm coffee, halting in situ for a few minutes, while I both drank, too, stared. I even launched into an aura of prominence in that stance, as Campbell might have done, posturing in serious contemplation. I revelled in that sentiment. It brought about in me a deportment of fulfilment that comes hard to describe. I guessed perhaps it assigned a constituent of meaning to my role, which had not in faith lived there heretofore. And yet, all that spread before me happened merely a moderate quantity of unlogged eclectic stuffs, no more; too, apt to be of a lot less importance, than those I already attended.

Finishing my chocolatey toned and pleasant infusion, I partook of no excuse for inaction. Thus, I decided instead to engage in a quota of procrastination, which occurs in certainty as something of an oxymoron. With the feat of zero being the antithesis of an exploit, I got reminded of the anecdote with relevance to a chap who intended, for his New Year's resolution, to cease putting things off. However, in the end, he judged it for the best to let it go until the ensuing.

I espoused a similar philosophy, so figured I would return to this occupation at a future stage. Hence, with care I reimbursed the curios whence they came, and sheltered the lot with its omnipresent paper. I moved, what I couldn't help but think of, as the gift from Cassandra, to the far end of the worktop. I then got stuck back into my regular trade of documenting those olden marvels with their tags yet attached and did so at a speedier pace than typical as if to find accommodation later for the chest of odd allures.

I mulled things over throughout the scheduled pause at eleven, so too, considered what approach I must champion. None of Campbell's belongings were listed, thus, it was possible they may not have had much standing with the Don's and Magi's, bygone and the present. Perhaps, I determined, I might organise a pet project out of it all, and undertake a portion of research. Perchance, I offered, it mightn't cause a whole share of dispute either way, as they ought to end up in requirement of chronicling no matter what. To start with, the rummaging out of a biography on our good professor, may well, I predicted, follow as the sensible approach to take. First things first though. I marched over to the now beneficial, what's more, utilised phone extension, dialled the digits for Tiffanie's desk, then inquired if she might wish to head out for lunch at one; with anticipation she understood my invitation came strictly for the both.

We must have broadcast on the matching wavelength, because at the appointed hour, under the dome of the rotunda, there happened no dawdling for anyone else. She linked my arm, and in haste we directed our exit. On the pavement, exterior to the wrought iron boundary, we continued to distance ourselves from the classical edifice, besides those roving colleagues who might want to attach themselves to our twosome. To throw these bloodhounds off our scent, we took a right, venturing in the opposite bearing to The Green. Soon, we crossed the threshold of a formerly dubbed "Drinkery", which supplemented their takings as a sometime "Eatery"; both of us ordering the Soup and Sandwich special. On receipt of our healthy nourishment, at the end of a culinary assembly line, we claimed the seldom vacant snug; set apart, furthermore, isolated from the madding crowd of diners. Here, in the confines of our island, positioned in a sea of Old Salts (or is that Salts of The Earth?), I let Tiffanie in on the mystery of the surfaced chest; hitherto concealed in the land-oriented version of Davy Jones' Locker.

I shared with her the abridged account at first, by revealing the existence of the good Professor's capsule, with its non-categorised materials. 'Well,' she asserted, 'you're sure to come across some artefacts where the tag has become detached. They've been sitting on those shelves forever and also got knocked about over the years. It's bound to happen with a few,' 'This is different,' I countered. 'They amassed together in the one chest, with just a battered label on the front as the identifier. In fact, a quantity of the assortment became apparent as modern, as if sorely out of place.' 'It might be best to set those aside, and have a specialist examine them later,' suggested Tiffanie.

'Yes, I understand, but I wouldn't mind checking into this Campbell chap; the curator whose signature claims title to the box. It's stamped 1896. Thinking out loud; it could be that a lazy bureaucrat messed up in bunching this entire load together into the one set. Perhaps it occurred at the beginning there showed up legitimate relics, which got combined in the chest at one point or another, so too, under the charge of our Professor. Later, it's conceivable that unrelated objects got supplemented to the mixture for bad measure,'

Continuing on; I added, 'Either way, I might gain insight into who this fellow was, and what he was about'. 'I'll see if I can find out something on him, if you really want to know', offered Tiffanie. 'There might be a file around some place'. After a short pause, she continued-'There's not going to be any great mystery for the solving in all this. Don't expect it to turn out like an archaeological dig where you unearth Pharaoh's tomb. Everything in this museum has already gotten brought to notice over the past hundred odd years'. 'Yes, I recognise that', I argued, with the hope she didn't think me ridiculous. I stressed to laugh it off to a degree, but as with those attractions of my primary years, something drew me to this locker of peculiarities, and intent for the attainment of erudition.

The leftovers to our hour situated a pleasurable affair, and I steered the topic away from work-related issues and on to other matters. I learned a thing or two in relation to Oklahoma and her hometown of Edmond. While Tiffanie verbalised her life's history, I still yearned to depict in my poetic visions those majestic sunsets of an orange tint; so too, hues of red in addition to yellow, in what at one time was designated Indian Territory. I could perceive in my reveries those herds of buffalo as they drifted over the tall prairie grasses, and likewise, envisage our timber framed home with its front porch darkening as night fell. There, seated on the creaking, tottering chair, amongst the zooming creatures of June, we watched that hawk in silhouette; as it soared overhead in imitation of the symbol for mathematical infinity.

Tiffanie called me up on the day succeeding, immediate to the jangle of eleven bells. "I have news for you, but don't get too excited. Let's go to the café, and I'll fill you in". Meeting up with her there; we entreated a pair of latté's. However, the house came packed, so because of this, we fetched our drinks to go, and next journeyed outside. 'To blazes with it', I declared. 'Nobody will miss us'. With that, we next ambled over to The Green and then stole an unoccupied bench.

'There're files kept on former employees; curators, professors, etcetera. All of them are down in the storage rooms. Presumably there's one for this Campbell guy, but I think you're going to have to go look for it yourself. If you request it from an archivist, some busybody will want to know why; so your best bet is to keep schtum. The security badges should let you in, I assume, because everything is historical rather than recent. I doubt they mark any as Top Secret. But, if out of nowhere an intern gets to pokin' around, they might get put under seal; understand?' I both comprehended, and, agreed. I had every intention to fetch it myself anyhow, but inquired her if she might at least point me in the right direction.

Advanced into the day, I persisted apprehensive about engaging with naughtiness; and persisted giddy too at the proposal to sneak around and about in nooks and crannies. I queried of Tiffanie if she might take her three o'clock, to show me the whereabouts of storage. With her present, it no longer seemed as if I engaged in what those fine officers of the law might refer to as Suspicious Activity. Her authority, real or imagined, removed an amount of danger from my clandestine caper. I wasn't for sure whether that pleased me. Still, I established that I was at least cheerful for her company. Two of emergent academics hypothetically converted this escapade into a research assignment, rather than yours truly standing in as the lone wolf, undercover snoop.

Together, we buzzed our passage into some space or other. They all organised in that sterile sameness symptomatic of the present day workplace. Tiffanie however, reserved prior knowledge; which happened just as well, given that as in character of Private Eye, I should have meandered in wild inaccuracy on my initial excursion. "It'll be up there in one of those bankers' boxes" she affirmed, in a suggestion of row upon row of that same thing, with just permanent marker scribblings to differentiate them. "You'll have to identify the right period then also the correct alphabetical order". She smiled a smile that whispered "Rather you, than me", though she reserved the good grace to place a delicate hand on her hip, so too, remain hushed. "Okay, thanks", I re-joined. And, as if she had almost forgotten, articulated "Oh, and take nothing out. The files stay here. If you need to have a document copied, let me know. I'll log it in as a temporary withdrawal, so the whole thing is kept on the up and up." Her smile broadened, and withdrawing her hand from hip, she departed the scene to leave me to it.

It took more than a few minutes examination of poor

handwriting through squinted eyes before I rummaged out a white cardboard container I regarded with promise. To reach up to it, I needed to grab a stool I noticed sitting in the corner. It still came as a stretch and when I got hold of the cut out handles, established that it happened on the extreme side of heavy.

"Did somebody fill this with bricks", I grunted in a voice under strain, but accomplished its removal without dropping it on my head. On the floor, I took off its lid, then uncovered records that looked as if they filed in order, but packed so tight, I wondered how anyone accomplished squeezing them all in. One more, I remarked, and the thing should have exploded. I applied my forefinger to shift along the tabs until I came to the C's. Somewhat to my surprise but without knowledge of why that should be; there under the tip of my extended digit unveiled a file discernible as that of A. Campbell–Prof.

The dossier, while donating the appearance of age, remained yet, in a decent, besides readable condition. I transpired all the same; a tad disappointed on leafing through what it covered which wasn't much. I half expected answers to a myriad of questions, but I what I collected in chief was an employment record. 'Some things never do change' I verbalised to myself in sympathy. 'I bet if one sought them out, a man ought to encounter in a more or less similar mode of archive, the accounts of occupation relating to the labourers of Ancient Egypt'.

The file communicated that he accepted employment with the museum in 1890 and busied himself primarily with research.

Robert E. Kearns

His specialty occurred that of Ireland in pre-history. As well, he engaged a leadership role in the summer season archaeological digs. He furthermore taught at Trinity, and added to that he conveyed with him his students on these cyclical expeditions. It was clear the good Professor established an accomplished fellow (no pun intended); too, it seemed, as a straightforward thing at the time for him to keep involvement with the museum and as a lecturer within close range.

There ensued a few bits and pieces of bonus material, but nothing that stood out or added to the facts. I didn't suppose I should remain in need of the photocopy service as offered by the beautiful Tiffanie, hence any fears she entertained of my absconding in a cloak and eye mask, with the loot bagged up in a sack titled "Swag", arose as unfounded. There was nil contained within that I shouldn't have the facility to recall without difficulty. Two key morsels of information I logged, however. (1) They alleged he perished during the term of his employment, and (2) The year of his death was 1896.

I reimbursed to its alphabetical slot; the said folder then hoisted up the bankers' box for re-housing on its proper shelf. Here I detected with rapidity it happened even harder to put back up than it was to take down. 'Shouldn't these stores have an easier method of retrieval?' I spluttered between exertions. 'Even a simple pulley system, should be worth something.' Then however, I retrieved from the hard drive which computed the organ in my skull, that witty story in short which concerned the unfortunate workman, so too, his barrel of disobedient bricks. Among other calamities, he jammed his fingers in the above contraption, so perhaps it was this I joked which transpired the motivation for them being shied away from.

Back in my cloistered base for cooling off, I picked up from where I stopped, and peered from time to time at the century old case, almost in demand of inspiration from it. I got to reasoning that perhaps a man who for the most part stayed vigorous in evaluation and what not, ought to have preserved details in relation to that body of work. Matters with an association to his teaching may well be set aside in the stores of the university. Perhaps though, he saved in some spot round about here, the annals from those activities as they related to the museum. There began another line of inquiry for the marvellous Tiffanie.

I got around to probing of her too. "Inspector Tiffanie, of The Yard", I jested, but wasn't altogether certain whether she caught on to the reference. "Might there chance a scheme to learn if we yet conserve the research papers relevant to the late Professor Campbell?" Of course, as with any competent officer of rank, she pleaded to identify the purpose of my search. Fooling with the detective allusion again, I expressed to her there may well survive a clue contained therein. On this occurrence though, I recognised from the absence of a humorous retort, that she didn't follow what I meant. She, in its stead examined why I bothered with it all.

My tongue must have gotten pawed by the kitten because I then understood that I didn't show up blessed with a proper riposte to her interrogation. It all enticed me. It came about as if now I happened underway; curiosity (as in that feline?) compelled me towards the unearthing of reasonable explanations. The sensible formula should have ascended to inform the custodians of antiquities and archives, but I hardened in fascination, besides under a mode of self-imposed duress to the concept of discovery. Passing it off, I advised Tiffanie that I purely got absorbed in scholarly inquisitiveness, and purported this in such a manner it came across with nonchalance and indifference.

Friday arrived, and I went about my usual roster of occupations, accomplishing a routine, but also making it a point to take part in a count of unscheduled cessations from hostile chores. During these ceasefires I occupied a chunk of time perusing the substances in those the many sliding trays at my disposal. While enjoying this in itself, it moreover helped alleviate the impatience I functioned in. I trusted I should hear from Tiffanie by now on potential evidence regarding the Good Professor Campbell. Having said that, I wasn't of a disposition to press her on it; revelling in her company as I was. Thus, I didn't dare put that in jeopardy. I pondered over the best means to raise the issue again if it ensued that I didn't gain intelligence in the near term. Fortuna intervened, so as we arranged to venture yonder into the town at days end, she communicated over that which I pretended in absurdity was a wired speaking tube that there ought to occur additional chronicles in storage.

I delighted in this hour of the fifth day. It followed at the stroke of the identical numeral past noontime, when beneath a cosmic cupola, I should come to be received with the striking smile that emerged out of the aperture which ran nearby to a painted in flames of sun floor tile montage, encircled by twelve vibrant depictions of the zodiac. I surmise that I too, must have beamed in addition, as there manifested genuine ecstasy in my soul at her introduction. I captured the hand of this fair maiden out of Oklahoma, without worry someone might see us.

The two of us amalgamated on the sidewalk with the deserting throngs, and then dispatched in a scamper round to Dawson Street. I perceived I couldn't avoid the compulsion to twist my head towards her appealing visage. Beholding her gorgeous fleece of splendour; the exhilarations she radiated; furthermore, the pleasantness of her smiles; instilled in me a passion and love, as well as a burning want to abide with her, always and forever.

With respect to the supplemental inventories, I virtually forgot the news she proposed advising me of. We ate while we also beheld each other's eyes, devoid of the will to remove our gaze for fear of interrupting the enchantment. To others, we must have exhibited the palpable symptoms of young love; hands enfolded across a table for two, ceaseless broad grins, clinging on each other's every announcement, too, revealing a fascination with all the other had to say. Then, she broke the spell.

'Oh, I asked around about any supposed papers and documents that might have belonged to Campbell. There's an assumption that everything is still there. Museums hardly ever dispose of their hoards, no matter what. The only issue happens that these archives may not be in any order. There is couple of dedicated stockpiles alongside those which contain the personnel records. Although, from what I hear, due to an earlier move, nobody has yet gotten around to putting any organisation to them. Also, they have still to get catalogued in full, hence in some cases; the subjects are anyone's guess.'

'It's a start though', I voiced, without much enthusiasm; supplementing this with, 'I expect it wouldn't hurt to take a gander'.

We stayed on for a couple more drinks after we ate and then embarked on our stride with the aim of her stop. On this occasion however, upon joining the queue, she questioned mildly if I would like to come along with her. It remains in these moments, when the emblem of amour that beats in the chest of a newly made man, loses its balanced rhythm, and instead bounds onward to the subsequent beat. I don't believe I summoned a reply, with the bodily linguistics of a minimal nod to the head sufficing. I did however; lean in to kiss her with tenderness on those lips of claret as confirmation in the affirmative.

She wasn't, as it turned out, in residence all that far away, too, she shared an apartment with a fellow state-side exchange student, who, upon our arrival, was established not to be at home. Given they were temporary guests of a foreign state, I gave consideration to the view their place of abode might just occur a mite on the side of messy. Pleasantly though, it assembled in remarkable tidiness. "Both of you must be of a neat disposition", I pronounced. 'Yes, she's very much the same as me.' She further added in an almost tongue-in-cheek manner, 'The both of us are clean freaks'.

Relaxed on the spotless couch, Tiffanie offered me a drink of the adult variety. Yet, what I sought to imbibe was a cup of tea.

She then expressed that she planned to have one also, which surprised me. 'I've gotten used to it since I arrived here; and with milk too!' 'Is that unusual?' I grilled, speculating why any sane person would partake of it, while leaving out the best part.

'It's all about the iced version where I come from. Oklahoman's drink it by the bucket load. If you get asked whether you'd like tea, it's always assumed it's the cold stuff you want. Back home, I've seen, and more, even tried the hot style in a Chinese restaurant, but always it came served with a slice of lemon'. Then light-heartedly she continued 'It's just since I came to Ireland that I've found out, it doesn't become tea until the dairy goes in.

What happened was the girls in the office were drinking it every day; so, curious; I thought I'd give it a whirl. Now that I'm accustomed to it, I've vowed never again to have it hot, without the supplement of milk'. 'See, I countered 'you've only been here a short while, and already we're turning you native.' 'You do recognise', I enhanced in banter; 'We consider tea to compound as the fixer of all ills. In fact, Irish scholars prefer to reference it by its Latin name; Panacea Hibernicus'; which raised a giggle on her part. 'Further', I added, 'No sooner than you commence with tea, you're mid-way to becoming a citizen'. 'And how do I obtain the complementary half?' she inquired coquettishly, with a knowing and at once sensual expression.

I surprised as faintly taken aback, a reaction that wasn't expected and this started a rise in temperature under my shirt collar. I accepted it as something of a rhetorical question, therefore lingered a while in the moment before at last setting my mug on the coffee table and beckoning her into my arms. Within a handful of minutes, both of our cups, still half full with the aforementioned tonic, stayed outside, while we absconded to her boudoir of delectability.

I made love to my beautiful Tiffanie, and our intimacy turned out as awe-inspiring as she. We held on to each other for hours, where we kissed, touched and laughed. Too, we whispered on top of discovered. It espoused as perfect in passion as any impulse may ascend without fault. The both of us betided companions in youth, who happened more than simply attracted to one another.

Each of us cared, longed, adored; moreover, treasured; by a means that could only emanate in a couple who purchased endeavour to attain fellowship with their match. I stood appreciative of the morning breaks, the escapes at one, plus our sojourns to the park. In spells of affection, I remained in debt to those drinks at sundown with the ensuing strolls to her bus stop. The delay, the chase, the marvel of growing into love, the caresses of au revoir when we separated, all meant more than their distinct threads. There followed an increased ardency with each day, a longing to devote my life to her; to jest, converse, and brush our path in unison through the tall, illustrious strands of highlighted green and brown grasses of the prairie. All that transpired until that night came packed with significance, so also towered our love all the more special for it. This cemented a bond amongst us, a coming together of our souls; furthermore, a pact that affirmed we should exist together forevermore.

I advanced into work on Monday, with a typical examination of my wristwatch to define when I might catch a chance to campaign in my quest through the archives. I couldn't well go sprinting to the stores straight off the bat. Hence, just as I managed the previous interval, I ground through the motions of my day job, in completion of it all with a dosage of hurry and intent to get ahead of the game. A short tick from the eleventh hour of the morn, I dialled Tiffanie's number and tested if she could point out where the records of pursuit were set aside. A few beats ahead, we met outside the gates to my fortress and next we made haste for an alternative section of annals to the prior. The door, we clicked it ajar, and then peering in, I recognised that the intelligence she garnered was correct. The space came stacked to the ceiling with white cardboard cubes with no apparent order to their assembly. "You're on your own", she specified then turned away in conferral of her sparkling American whites.

By way of paperwork, I wasn't one to bask in exhilaration, and especially didn't fancy it, if it demanded of me an elaborate, besides challenging, stalk of my quarry. It came about one time, during a summer job, that I had the task allotted to me of foraging out difficult to get chronicles of account, and I realised it double-quick as a business of boredom, filth and monotony. I was obligated to climb right into the grime-coated binders, which piled high in soaring caster wheeled cages of steel. Invoices, Statements, Day Books, so too all kinds of other bureaucratic irrelevancies dating back to the year dot, came smeared with soot, besides stain, from storage in the open-air of a functioning warehouse. This wasn't as terrible a setup, but the nightmares of that post hadn't deserted me. I constructed an effort of evaluation on where to begin and then figured that it made no distinction one way or another. I therefore plumped for the commencement of one box at a time, to spot if anything emerged.

Twenty minutes after and there persisted nothing in the doing, which caused me to be disheartened. As with the majority of our gender, ten minutes in the hunt for anything which approaches needles and haystacks suggests more akin to a lifetime. I submitted the idea it occurs as a trait we come born with, which transpires why for the first seventeen years of our tenure we remain consistent in advising our mother we couldn't locate it, whatever 'it' was. This I recognised would befall with ample pain. I vanished back to the vault of detention, for escape; a bit of irony in that too.

At lunch, I inquired of Tiffanie if she might pick me up a bite to eat while out and about. I then fixed a cup of tea in the canteen and fetched it back to the storage rooms. To some degree I recognised where I left off, but one of the other trials which accompany a sporadic search, ensues that one merely shuffles things about in the expectation of stumbling across the target. I established that I had better begin with the shaping of stacks. In view of that, I exploited the pen brought in with me to ink an inconspicuous x on each of the containers I already checked. Afterward, I took to the building of several mounds, so too, discreetly ticked them off.

Tiffanie turned up with a sandwich, besides a can of chilled minerals, which I was grateful for, as I happened to perspire from both the hot tea and the arduous exercise. 'Forgive me if I don't sit down' she cited, 'but these boxes look filthy'. 'You're right' I confirmed, holding out a duo of black palms in demonstration. 'Damn', I cursed. 'I'd better wipe them off.' We moved back upstairs, where I washed up in the Men's Room before grabbing a seat in the canteen next to Tiffanie, who had already begun eating. 'Any luck'? She posed. 'It'll be the last one I search, which remains forever the way of things'. 'I'll see you in a month, so', issued her response, which prompted me to call out to her light-heartedly as 'Smarty Pants', and left it at that.

I had about ten; and if I stretched it; fifteen minutes of break outstanding to scan through more pertinent records. I thrust back at it, and emblazoned each of them with an x, even though no treasure manifested within. Then it transpired as past due for my compulsory descent to the stir which engendered yet another scrub of my squalid paws. I judged myself as a good ten minutes delayed, but as situated the standard fare; not one staff member took the least amount of notice. I went for it a second time somewhat advanced into the afternoon and ate up another fifteen minutes instead of the matinee intermission, but yet again, my exploratory operation failed.

I got impelled into picking it up in continuation on the Tuesday. The morning elevenses arrived, then after that tailed lunch, and this entire this span got consumed with a wade through stacks, of what I began to moniker as garbage. Throughout the afternoon session, and sorely at a loss for all reserves of patience, at last I got hold of a carton with some promise. It was difficult to determine when it all came to be clustered up, but there ensued a tag, inscribed in ink rather than marker, so too, printed between the universally tiny lines meant for "Contents:" it alleged; Professor A. Campbell–Notes,

Files, Misc. That more or less covered the whole kit and caboodle I supposed. The good old "Miscellaneous" identifier has doubtless contracted convenience since the outset of humankind to describe just about whatsoever the author wasn't bothered to list.

I flicked through the substances, with not too meaningful a technique, what's more, in obedience to nought in particular. I was mindful of smudging the papers with my once again, blackened paws. One of those, on encountering the records, was almost about to stroke my now "Coming along nicely" goatee, in approval, when I caught it in the nick of time. Over the past numeral of days, I took to the mechanics of this with routine. In contemplation, I caressed it between thumb and forefinger to assess what, if anything, I might ascertain. I considered for fun, that I better be careful, or I might end up with acceptance I haunted as the ethereal ghost of Campbell himself. I didn't however, fancy the notion of those chaps who donned jackets of white, as well, who commissioned weighty manacles, chaining me to the foundations of this penitentiary; too, disposing of me there to rot as they had in those ages with a dearth of enlightenment.

I cleaned up another time, and then after treading the stairs over six feet under, I got on my personal line to Tiffanie, then blurted out, 'Good day to you, my lady fair; I unearthed something of excitement. There won't be a need to excavate the storerooms for me next month after all.' 'Darn', she reacted. 'I was hoping to drop down there every day, and find you stripped to your waist, all hot and sweaty'. 'Tiffanie' I pronounced in mock horror. 'You're being exceedingly flirtatious', to which she countered in a pleasing Oklahoma drawl; 'Yes, I am Irish'.

'I'll show you the good professor's records tomorrow if you like, I indicated. You might help me pick through them'. 'You've gotten my antennae of interest raised now', she admitted. 'I'm already looking forward to it'.

Tiffanie revealed herself in the storage space while I disposed there on Wednesday morning. 'Here we are' I offered, presenting to her the bankers' box which composed the entirety of Campbell's former universe. 'You can forget about me copying this', she specified. You'd be better off checking it all out'. 'And, how do I go about that?' I queried. 'Well, I think it might be a good idea if I did it, just in case anyone wonders why you need it. After all what does a guy who turns screws in the dungeon require with a package of ancient papers?' 'That sounds fine to me', I agreed. 'All I wish to do is to transfer it below then examine it in peace'. She recorded the details on the sticker, further, articulated she would dig into the motions of organisation when returned to her desk.

She called through on the hot line after a while. 'I got that taken care of. There wasn't any real fuss; just the filling out of an essential or two for admin'. 'That's terrific', I replied. 'Thank you beautiful', I re-joined in gratitude. Unequivocal there nominated no time like the current; I ascended straight away to grab the target of my pursuance. I next removed it to the crypt and positioned it on the workbench alongside the chest of chiselled timbers which encompassed the eclectic assortment of relics.

Tiffanie confirmed she succeeded in attraction to the scrutiny of my outcomes. Hence, we settled on a grab of food 'To Go' from the Museum café, then utilised the same area which had up till now transpired as the locale for my mug. 'It seems a sin to be in the cellars when it's so nice outside', she stressed. 'I understand that', I replied.' 'First, I'll show you what I discovered then we'll have a quick look through the files. I could do with a little air myself'. Hence, we promised we'd make it quick and spend what continued of the hour to venture out for a healthy amble.

After an extraction of the fillings to my chest of tricks and their allocation to the work surface, I requested of her what she reckoned. 'I think somebody just flung all of this stuff in here; lazily too. It clearly belongs to different eras. What's more, some pieces are definitely modern. I mean, what's this circuit board doing here? It's either trash, or some technical geek envisioned making use of it at a later date, simply for it to end up with all this melange.'

'Well, there's undoubtedly a percentage of it doesn't fit with the rest,' I agreed. 'But for some purpose, it came to be retained. Unless of course it was a cleaner who just tidied it all away in the convenience of our box! Still, I can't help but accept that because it got positioned in just such a manner, in this specific chest, with this particular label, further, it got shielded with caution by these sheets of brown paper, that it wasn't put together by an amateur. It's just a hunch, but it has the feel of something prepared through an associate of the museum, and not an I.T. person either'.

'It doesn't matter now at any rate does it?' quantified Tiffanie. 'Just try to write up a memo of those materials past doubt from antiquity; set them aside some place; then I'll have a curator take a look at some point afterwards'. 'I suppose that ought to work', I intoned, 'but I'll hold on to the rest of the articles too, just in case anyone lays claim to them.'

We then moved on to the files while also in harmonious struggle to devour our lunch. I opined that the chief course of action might be to remove them from the chest altogether, next, stack them on the table for simpler review. This I achieved and got underway with a preliminary analysis. Tiffanie stood by my side to undertake her own evaluation. There came out several essays, expositions and discussions but none impressed to contrive as relevant to the diminutive trunk. "Maybe this all befalls as just a waste of time", I conveyed, downheartedly. "What I was thinking, I do not know. My hands, I literally got dirty for next to nothing". Tiffanie sympathised with empathy, besides, a sprinkle of encouragement. "You can look through it proper later on". "For now though, why don't we top up on some vitamin D?"

The both of us took an amble up to The Green. There, we strolled in hand between the fountains and flower beds which flaunted in the widespread palette of summer. We then traipsed over the humpbacked bridge of stone which ensues as a spot of favour for camera happy tourists. Next we sauntered around by the leafy and picturesque pond for ducks and waterfowl. Here, cross-sections of society bathed on the carpet of cropped emerald near to the cast shadow of that Arch to the Fusiliers. Citizens of this plane, they partook of lunch, bantered with pals and colleagues and exhibited not a care between them.

"Let's go for an ice-cream", I suggested. We crossed at the lights, where in a shop on Grafton Street, I called for two large 99s; the perennial Irish favourite. "I bet they don't do these in Oklahoma", I asserted. Here she beamed, extracted the chocolate Flake with the certainty of an expert, and bit off a dainty morsel with faultless white teeth.

"Catch you later, Irish", she called out, as our separate ways became imminent under the dome of celestial magnificence. This arose as her pet name for me now, and I happened partial to it, even while pretty much all and sundry hereabouts was Irish besides. It caused me to feel special, as if out of all the Celts in Dubh Linn, I ascended as the chosen one. I advanced to the dungeon, but let her know beforehand that I was definite to hook up with her soon. "I'll see you at about three thirty or so" I mentioned. Tiffanie came out with a giggle. She supposed it the funniest of things at how many of the indigenous pronounce three as 'Tree'. To her perception, Three Thirty became Tree Tirty, and although she declared in Ireland for some time now, confirmed this idiosyncrasy yet tickled her. Comparable to tea with milk, I mused and, for these insights, I adored her. Even more, I managed to pinch a tickle out of it all.

My regular job didn't propose immediate attraction for starting back on it, and to tell the truth, as soon as I veered from Tiffanie and next put a foot on the stepped decline, my mood submerged in sympathy. I caught myself in a slump and wasn't able to tell precisely why, which made it all the worse. This didn't appear in character for me. A cloud of troublesome black schemed overhead; in addition, I came over cold all of a sudden, which arrived feasibly as a product of melancholy, rather than the pervasion of a chill from my site of custody. I occurred in dire need of warmth to relieve this irregular ailment. I deliberated why I came to be worked up about a musty box, besides a quantity of now archaic précises. Typically, I shouldn't have transpired in too much unease, thus would in general shrug it off as an aberration. Today though, I shivered with angst. Apprehension wasn't a fixture of my being, and in consequence I dashed, more than walked, to prepare in the canteen, a cup of percolated Arabica, with optimism it should heat my cockles; too, perform as a flavoursome restorative.

I landed back with purpose, tempered by the steaming placebo I hugged tight. In consumption while yet scalding, I raised in my thoughts the alternative brew which according to my compatriots moderated all complications. Either one, I suspect should have achieved the goal, but I developed a fondness for the ritual of coffee making. With my recovery in motion, I wondered why I grew to be so disheartened and glum, though soon reverted to my old self with determination not to dwell too much on it. In its stead, I sipped on the Panacea Arabica, switching over again to the good Professor's stack of papers.

Prior to now I flipped through a sum of them in the company of Tiffanie. Those ones, I beforehand turned upside down adjacent to the main stack. I proceeded with a fresh investigation and added to the baby mound. As well, I imbibed from my coffee now and then, which; to sidestep potential mishaps, I herded to the rear of my bench. There located zero of interest thus far, but different to earlier; this didn't upset me to any noticeable extent. Thoroughness stood the order of the day if just to exhibit I donated to an exhaustive go. I took furthermore; to the perusal of manila folder contents that continued mixed in with the rest, then positioned each of the completed ones onto its separate pile. Towards the very end, having complemented myself on having done a comprehensive job; besides, already thinking ahead towards putting it all back from where it came, I stumbled across a final batch of papers, all of them clipped together in a manner that suggested it was a work in progress. The first page was of interest; hence, with a flick through each subsequent sheet, they disclosed this was what I hoped for.

Before now, I got resigned to conquering the scholarship of not a thing which transpired quite the pessimistic outlook for a young adult who otherwise hosted a positive disposition. Even should affairs not work out in faithfulness to the estimated track, in large, I maintained the knack to picture it all in a good light. Now, I recognised my happiness at a cheerful inclination, as if it arose as the inverse of routine. Nevertheless, I set all this aside for the time being and conjured an effort to focus on what was in front of me. I took the bound folios to one side, plus, to make room, I returned the rest of the paperwork to its container. I then moved the whole thing to the skirting board alongside the exit. I would have preferred to get it out of there, having now caught hold of what I came in search of. All the same, I strolled back to the workbench with a spring to my step then pulled off the enormous bull clip. Then using my left hand to hold the edge of the first sheet between my fingers, too, the right to stroke my bearded chin, I instigated the read.

Robert E. Kearns

The opening leaf, at first glance showed in the format of a letter or epistle. But, as my eyes moved over the text, it became clearer as a kind of testimony, as if in introduction to the documents which backed on to it. I wasn't sure why he settled on this, although presumed it might become clearer later on. This is how it went:

Andrew Campbell, 10th June 1896

I have these hours, and over an abundant throng of years, gotten tangled up in what I considered at the outset, to found as something of a whim. A pet project as it were. My attitudes towards it altered with swiftness, however, which I shall elaborate on momentarily. It arrived as a subject matter I first encountered in the primal divide of life, too, in those youthful fantasies, I thought perhaps one day, I might take up a role in expeditions of detection, with the fanciful aim of attaining fame and fortune whilst in pursuit of these whimsical notions. I envisioned my stance as the intrepid explorer, kitted out with a chart in hand, comprising an X to mark the spot which presented as the omnipresent indicator out of adventure novels of the period. Truly, it remained this incipient fascination, which encouraged me to orient in these pastures of science which bestowed on me employment these countless moons. Granted, as I approached adolescence, I resigned it firmly to the background as mere legend; although I continued to visit it in my dreams, as nostalgia for those earliest illusions, more than as the content of serious consideration. My position has since undergone a reformation.

Hy Brasil captivated me as Atlantis of the classics has absorbed the entire world. I quite by accident arrived across the mention

of it in a pamphlet which, to my course of reason scribed as the
absolute in authorities. Having certainty in its existence, I
sought it on the Globe which positioned as the centrepiece of
my father's study, hence, came to be sorely disappointed to
have exposed its non-apparition. In my innocence, I
questioned Dear Papa, what caused its disappearance; and he,
having eternally come across as a jolly sort of fellow,
guffawed, what's more, declared it sunk in the manner of that
aforementioned isle of Platonic myth. I expected that as he was
Papa, and Papa posturing old besides fired in sapience, erected
at the higher end of gravity with concern to this assertion. This
in consequence, affirmed to my developing mind, that Hy
Brasil had with certainty, not just occurred as a firm country,
but rose on a par with the advanced Greek civilisation which
was the acquaintance of every schoolboy.

This originates as how my conviction in the fact of Hy Brasil's
physicalness had gotten started, with the outcome being, that I
sought to upturn as much detail on it as I could lay my hands
on; which transpires as not much of anything at all. I visited
the libraries of father's Alma Mater, and there, traced in the
books and facsimiles of mediaeval records sited cartography
which in definite revealed Hy Brasil to plant resolutely in the
North Atlantic. This supplied a measure of re-assurance. Papa
had been correct, and in light of this, I articulated that Hy
Brasil vanished sometime after the year 1400. This ordained
that unlike Atlantis, which submerged under the waves in
ancient times, Hy Brasil disposed extant until a mere few
hundred years before now. It wasn't until I read past these
maps and into the details I learnt the authors were setting out
that Hy Brasil showed up as nothing more than legend; a
fantasy.

I wasn't to be deterred, however. One simple virtue of the juvenile is the possession of courage in one's convictions; therefore, I persisted in thorough faith in relation to the historical accuracy of Hy Brasil. My conjecturing went, that if the isle got illustrated in drawings derived from varying sources, then those origins could not have been mistaken. With the benefit of age, one determines that collective wisdom frequently drifts to the erroneous bounds of accuracy. These same diagrams I counted on for total acceptance, publicised colourful portrayals of dubious mermaids, too, sea monsters. With a helping convenience I overlooked these inaccuracies when forming my estimation on the infallibility of antediluvian map makers.

As I matured, I grasped that legends by and large, are apt to pose as just that; supported with naught more than the ages of embellished story telling. That is how, the unqualified credence I held as a child, morphed into an adolescent evolution on the subject. I still nonetheless, kept an interest in Hy Brasil, further; I conjectured from time to time whether there may be substance to it all. The majority of myths clamp onto the habit of centring, by a share at least, on some truth, which over the aeon's came to meet upon distortion, to the betterment of the lore.

With the discipline of archaeology however, there has arisen this century multiple discoveries which validated a collection of traditions. Mythological Greek, besides Turkish cities saw to be unearthed; which if one suggested their certainty in decades past, may well have induced a confinement to the lunatic asylum. It originated this acceptance that science embraces the capacity to challenge one's prejudices, which resulted in my continued curiosity in the prospect at least, of Hy Brasil having at one time established in a quadrant of the Atlantic Ocean.

I rested in thanks for a vivid mind's eye as a youngster, likewise, for the commission of immature research. It came about as a direct cause of this occupation with fable, atlases, furthermore, discovery, that my inquisitiveness in the pursuance of scholarship to this area got piqued, hence; occasioning my contemporary situation. One could not demand for a career with more reward or satisfaction.

I've spotted men come and go, worn down over an age for the choice of an ill-suited profession; having selected it predominantly to mollify their paters. My dear old Papa, on the other hand, with his inherent kindness, and dare I say it, street acumen; encouraged me to pursue that which I determined as absorbing. It positioned his recognition, which, with the benefit of experience under my belt, turned out as accurate; that a fellow can only encounter happiness if he declares for a pursuit he adores. Too, Papa, a cheerful and content gentleman himself, deposited as an embodiment to the accuracy of this philosophy.

My territory of expertise, if one is permitted to elect the liberty of reference to oneself as an authority, happens in the study of Irish history and its associated discipline of archaeology. I always held that one cannot in thorough appreciate any subject, history in particular, without first accepting employment in the toils of practical graft. This appealed to me in any case; further, it abided my assumption that a man, who brooked no aspiration to see his hands in the dirt through the practicalities of exploration plus the pursuit of knowledge, did not preserve a love for their occupation.

I maintained an inordinate quantity of adoration for my business, so too, an equal affection for the perspiration expended whilst engaged in its accompaniment of archaeological digs. That's not to say the whole process bursts forth with glory besides the sighting of riches at every turn. Beyond doubt, this vocation occurs in frequency as a mixture of the tedium, besides back breaking labour. It stands the solid travails which in paradox renders the dullness bearable, in that when a male situates in the preoccupation with manly activities as a component in the goal of adventure, it renders worthwhile all that might otherwise happen wearisome.

The burrowing, the custom of a trowel, a brush, as well as the added tools of our profession categorically materialises in accompaniment with documentation, meticulous detailing, too, hours of sorting and sieving. However, it remains the faith in magnificence to realise which motivates as the driver. Hope astounds at all times as a persuader. It ferries with it exhilaration that the succeeding shovel full of earth may well include consequential antiques. And, when one oversees the exhumation of an artefact, no matter how minuscule or ostensibly insignificant, it lends an infusion which energises the soul to attain that sentiment all over again. In short it flourishes as an opiate for the Fellows of sciences. The locations we hollow exist as warrens of the poppy; concealed spaces for us to chase a thrill, too, know the high, attendant with original detections.

It materialised several years after I completed my studies,

therefore immersed in an academic career, when I accompanied a dig headed by the chief of the department to the islet of Achill. It being the summer season, copious students of an enthusiastic character escorted us, most of whom exhibited the identical heights of excitement as I maintained at their age. I achieved by this stage, the benefit of maturity, and so, as a result, came more measured in my anticipation. Yet, that eagerness never quite seems to leave one; and more, the enthusiasm of these younger participants oozed a contagion. It stands an emphatic pleasure to comprehend the equivalent passion as one hitched to in that phase of development. As well, it prompted me to recall Papa and how grateful I transpired for his support and sagacity. To come upon encirclement with such jollity sparkled as a constant affirmation of how proper he distinguished in his advice.

Achill arises as a patch of rocky emerald magic; chock-full with beauty, besides wonder. In having said that; one may not have accepted it with the same estimation during the extended months of our darkest season. Regardless, with the hemisphere tilted in the way of our star, all of us to a man were pleased to get away from the city, what's more, encamp in the remoteness of this western outpost. Numerous locals communicated in Gaelic; too, they happened as a simple people, with charm and contentedness for a modest existence. They fished, farmed and subsisted in rudimentary homes, deprived of modern living comforts which one takes for granted in Dublin. While here, we determined, as gentlemen, to re-experience the natural surrounds, spend an abundance of hours in the open-air, and subject ourselves to whatever inclement conditions arose. We group reserved rooms in a guest house, not being willing all told to abandon ourselves to western ruggedness. Some amongst us had never so much as cooked an egg in our lives, hence, kindled in cheer for the attendance of our rotund landlady who served to us the most appetising of breakfasts at each break of the day.

At the apex of the cliff which backs on to Keem Bay, we secured our station; and if one was to handpick a better habitat to engross in a spot of physical agency, I doubt there comes about a more scenic vision in the entirety of God's creation. No matter the labour; and it happened not a great deal in perfect honesty; a glance due west distributed an immediate elixir where even the most cynical should thank those heavens above for riches furnished with grace. Our purpose was to eke out a location which augured well for promise as a Neolithic settlement. Thus, we shovelled over a sum of prospective trenches within the surrounding area. These pits stood as an ideal aid for teaching, so too, permitted our team to survey multiple sites inside the same half acre that held out the greatest potential. They, by the same token, facilitated the team leaders to flit with ease between each hollow, which happened as essential for effective supervision, besides on the job tuition.

Without entering into copious amounts of detail, it revealed in one of these dugouts, which had not yet gotten sunk in excess of a foot and a half or thereabouts, that we unearthed an elegant cup. I ventured certain it was not ancient though it intrigued me as the invention of fine quality. It arose in combination with an aggregate of other objects, which at initial glance, dated not to the phase of time we foresaw, (though still, from antiquity) but far ahead of it. Why a cup that exhibited modern characteristics should be grouped with specifics from a thousand years ago or advanced of that remained a thorough mystery. It simply didn't belong.

What rose clear, though, was this region had seen action from more than a few stages of eras past, and thus, it was to be expected that it gave up workings of different oldness. The deeper the trench, the further back in time it journeyed; hence the more aged the curiosities exposed. This recently fired porcelain cup had no place here at all, except for the surface layers, perhaps. All the same, that didn't expound why it transpired, that it came to be grouped with dissimilar entities, in a manner which suggested they got buried there at an identical point in time. If somebody tried to hide it for whatever purpose; then by the identical approach, they ought to have encountered its sister assemblages. This backdrop stuck fast in my thoughts as rather odd.

Whatever the cause, it emerged as a strange affair. However, opposite to the disposal of this commodity as a present-day castoff, I settled on trusting it to my charge; it having caught my eye as an agreeable specimen. If nothing else, I reckoned it should function as a private memento, and maybe an amusement from which to appreciate my afternoon tea, while by the same stance, articulating the account of its detection. On, the return to our rooms I gave it a respectable wash. Here, it came alive with radiance under the gushing tap, which wrung from me a broad smile and another cause for conviction I selected a most excellent vocation. That evening; to abundant hilarity; I begged the landlady to pour her excellent concoction into my acquisition for the ages; and with that perception, my imaginings branded it the most supreme tasting brew I absorbed in some while.

I presumed that was that, until a few days after, in a freshly shovelled furrow, when low and behold, one of my students up earthed an additional instance of porcelain; this time a saucer; but not a match unfortunately, for my delightful new teacup. Further, that wasn't the end of it. More scopes of fragmented chinaware cups got ferreted out at a similar depth. We likewise traced an intermediate-sized portion of hand-cut lead crystal. I distinguished it was the heavy metal, from the weight it exerted on my palm. It too, arose in need of a cleansing to appreciate it originated as a handsome example of what might once have functioned as a wine glass. I tend to be something of a hoarder at the best of occasions, and helpless as well as unwilling to part with either of these exhibits, transported them back to our temporary residence for a more vigorous purification.

Our expedition at a close, we journeyed back to Dublin with data to process, our treasures to log; moreover, notes, so too, papers to publish. Apart from the china teacup which I reserved for the desk in my home study, I hadn't even considered the saucer, plus those extra fortunes that still came bundled up in paper and string and domiciled in a corner of my office at the university. And there, they should likely have remained for a considerable extent, if it chanced not for another campaign the following month. I came down with a heavy cold a number of days before our proposed departure to Kerry. With the weather inclement; I concluded that without doubt I positioned in no condition to undertake a prolonged journey. This should ordinarily have irritated me to no end. No matter, I was of a frame of mind, what's more, in a weakened physical state, which demanded the intake of hot whiskies and the acquisition of a warm bed. I left instructions with one of my senior scholars he was to telegraph me each day, in addition, keep me apprised, this presiding as manageable due their board and lodgings in Dingle.

I nursed my fever, and veracity being voiced, sited rather contented to happen in familiar territory. Especially so, as the initial cables to arrive were of the kind which stated:

Arrived in Dingle STOP Weather Poor STOP

Unable to Dig STOP Heavy Downpours STOP

Rain Cleared STOP Setting up Camp STOP

Three days got taken up, therefore, in a comparable state to my own, with the achievement of little except for sitting about and ingesting hard liquor for the purposes of medicinal advantage. Albeit; while I betided without doubt, in poor health; I fancy their disorder posited as the illusory type. I contemplated hopping on a train to join up with them, but established after some debate, that I might do better to get on with some work that wanted for catching up on. I therefore, via return advisement, directed that I continued under the weather; thus, entreated frequent updates.

After several more telegraphs, and without going into the specifics of each, I was counselled in one, almost as an afterthought that at a layer within range of the hearth, of what should have been a domicile dated to about 2000B.C. there revealed a glass bottle, necked with a screw top. It had no place in that environment, the neighbouring earth not giving the impression of recent disturbance. In fact, the lone cause for its mention happened because the professor supposed a student to have situated in extreme carelessness, or was acting out a prank of some kind. I produced an immediate reply with a request the bottle not be discarded, but instead returned with the group as a keepsake. There emerged a default on my part to stress the souvenir constituent to all of this, and did not thirst for anyone to cogitate, that I was succumbing to lunacy and fevered delusions. All the same, I moulded as positively intrigued with this prize; thus, sought metaphorically to put it under the microscope.

The team brokered intent to remain there for a week, at the expiration of which, they poised to hand over to a crew out of Cork. The reports continued to travel my way for what remained of the expedition. In consequence, when it got conferred over again, at the finish to one bulletin, there got brought into being an elegant porcelain vessel; modern; and alike to what natives might utilise for their customary intake of Poteen; my ears pricked up as those of a horse on Derby day. I was given to trust, that it bore as ornate in the extreme, with a most beautiful refinement to it, so too, a design which copied those carved into the Neolithic stones of Meath. This pottery engraved with triskeles got discovered in a stratum that wasn't appropriate to its period, which suggested it came as newly buried there. I dispatched an instant petition, bidding that this likewise find saviour from the dustbin, and be hauled back for sick-bed entertainment.

On the groups' advent, I surveyed these articles the second they were tendered and laboured to convey an emotion they covered up somewhat for my forced absence. In the privacy of my office, it emerged the glass bottle I perused first. It performed for all intents and purposes to deploy as a receptacle for pills, similar to what an apothecary or druggist might dispense. The topmost end of it intrigued me, however. It signalled the use of a screw on glass stopper, which I hadn't come across before now. It was rather clever I conceded; most of these effects being manufactured out of cork or glass that one plunged straight down. I assumed therefore that it must be of a foreign type. In consequence, it ought to have, by the same means, ascended as modern in creation. Why therefore, I questioned, was it settled in the humus; furthermore, in the undisturbed ground of a site dated to antiquity?

I set the bottle aside for a tick and then selected the captivatingly adorned "Poteen" ewer. It came in the region of five inches high, by three across. The edges rose straight up, plus; it emanated with a glaze, both inside and out as well as held the intricate pattern already described. It became clear, that it, as others beforehand, was in requirement of a good rinse. Hence, I carried it to an adjoining laboratory where I ran it under a tap, and worked my fingers and thumbs to clean off the muck. This brought it up nicely, so I was able to comprehend the lustre of the coat in gloss, which in turn enhanced its decoration, and thus ensured it stood out even more. It established as quite the looker, and I admired the craftsmanship with a degree of awe. It did, to be sure, contribute to the notion of it being a drinking receptacle of some make, perhaps for spirits, as pointed out. Given the quality of its fabrication, I had to accept, that while this may have transpired as a function; it would doubtless be exhibited on the mantle as an ornamental curio more than something one might keep for everyday conventions.

Robert E. Kearns

I started over to claim the bundle I hitherto lodged in the corner, and then with it engaged before me; I disabled the simple knot of the string I administered to tie it up. Upon removal of the contents, I grouped the lot together, including the two most recent additions, and next reclined in my chair, intending to leer at them for a spell. I owned here, sundry items of quality out of two distinct dig sites, with none of them fitting in with these places of origin. It occurred purely through good fortune they had not gotten disposed of. I wondered then how many other such effects had gotten exhumed from remote whereabouts, only to have been discarded thus. But, I stood here to ride ahead of myself a tad; hence, understood it necessary to reign in these meditations.

There ascended the prerequisite to buy into the methodical approach, which in permanence I regarded as the paramount policy in this line of occupation. I picked up the lead crystal for analysis. The piece happened liberal enough to indicate its original practise as a goblet for wine. The cut on the external surface was prospectively achieved by hand, with the contrivance being a familiar etching of diamond. The edges became clear as more or less smooth, symptomatic of it being in the soil for a considerable span of time. There rose scant else to signpost its age or maker, but I couldn't help but reflect that it wasn't as contemporary as it outwardly suggested.

I next beheld the varying divisions of those broken cups I carted back. The quality struck me for another time as fine, glazed inside and out; the embellishments fluctuating from piece to piece. One depicted a scene with hills of green that may well have gotten lifted from Achill itself. The artwork was striking, hand painted; and yet, while it depicted what gave the idea as from a landscape in Ireland, was yet distinctly out of place to its environs. Achill was a peasant country. With that in mind, fine bone china was not merchandise one should expect to emerge from a burial atop one of its hill crests.

The next artefact revealed a seascape; complete with what bore a resemblance in style to a sailing craft which established custom centuries prior, so too, which got described with routine in the vellum Christian manuscripts of early medieval Irish monks. I never came across this style of entity before. As a rule, one should expect to locate crockery such as this endued with an Oriental flavour, it having worn as the fashion for as long as anyone could recall. To encounter the outcome of two loosely connected pieces, each in semblance of a painting from the west of Ireland or some alike spot occurred as remarkable, if not soundly odd.

The third serving of porcelain emanated almost whole. It furnished right off as one with a sentiment akin to despondency, given it emerged with damage. It was the equal as what one experiences; when after permitting a cup to drop, a minor, but key chunk snaps off. One's primary reaction in such circumstances is to undertake a stab at somehow cementing it back on, but, as well, acknowledging in one's heart that this should grace as the errand of a fool. I speculated what it must have appeared as, complete and in perfect condition. I rotated it in my hands then inspected it to apprehend, what surfaced yet again as a depiction of rural Ireland. This time it came endued with cliffs, sea on top of a sky which rumbled with clouds of grey. This floated in as the lone one of the three thus far that yet had the entire base intact.

I swivelled it upside down, and then noticed for the first time of asking, impressions on the bottom end. As opposed to the usual hallmark of the maker which is stamped as a rule on such things, these words manifested as unidentifiable. It showed up to my considerations as if it transpired a combination of two distinct classes of brand. Therefore, I didn't quite distinguish what to make of it all.

I evicted it from my mind; thus, switched my attention to the saucer, before this not having appreciated the excellence which characterised it. I instantaneously deliberated on the cup at home in my apartments. I hadn't obsessed on that one with too much seriousness either. If I positioned out of bachelorhood, I'm sure my good lady wife might have paid more attention to it than I. After all, how much consideration does a man devote to such things? I discern I may have stood neglectful in that regard. However, I had, at no juncture measured it as anything other than a pretty souvenir which similarly ought to come in useful for its intended function. I hadn't even thought to check the identity of its maker. Then, spotting the saucer, complete with a green besides white glaze, and for another occasion in portrayal of some Irish rustic display, I flipped it over to encounter similar brands as had been inscribed on the third cup. I certainly arranged as no authority in such areas, but this developed to a degree as rather curious; also, I supposed it should warrant auxiliary investigation.

In brief, I revisited the "Poteen" jug, and upended it with a sort of premonition, whereby I understood before I accomplished its half rotation what the outcome should be. Later, when I arrived home, having succeeded in this with as much speed as I could muster, too, before even I removed off my hat and coat, such was the impatience I fostered; I made for the aforementioned receptacle which rested on the desk in my study. This too I spun over, before even conferring respect to its ornamentation, and with this motion, my astonishment was complete. I had come into source material of diverse kinds originating from two isolated dig sites; but all of it exposing comparable marks of association. I sat down in the armchair, merely then doing away my hat, but allowing the coat to remain on; such as my astonishment came to pass. I next extended an arm with a case of the tremors to the decanter of whiskey I reserved on the adjacent shelf. Without entertaining a glass at hand; what is more, too dumbfounded to budge, I exploited the cup I monitored under inspection just a second previous, and poured out a more than generous ration.

The restorative spirt, having fulfilled its compact to assuage my nerves, and to that end permitted me to rid myself of the overcoat which dared, to a certain aggregate, as the root of my overheating. I tilted back, too, reverted again to my musings of before. I was now confident there must have been additional shards of China exposed over the years; with nobody making the connection. Myself, or my team, having encountered similar antiques within such a tight span of time, and in diverse locations, happened surely as no coincidence. It should stand to logic this scenario had arisen heretofore, but with the presumption of the disinterred objects befalling up-to-date in nature. Perhaps, I argued, there occurred sideboards around the country, and perhaps beyond these shores, which arrayed on display what their owner preserved as nothing other than a keepsake of allure.

I elevated the cup up above my head to capture another glance at the underside. There prospectively took place easier ways to accomplish this; concluding with my drink for one. Nevertheless, it stayed a habit of mine since childhood to not pay too much respect to convention, hence, stood grateful that Mama was not there to observe it. I might only imagine what she should voice and allowed a smile to cross my lips at the recollection of her. Nothing devised to alter since my prior review, but I happened capable of absorbing the detail a mite better this time round, having settled down from my initial excitement. I tried to evoke the published designations on those products in my office, and then something struck me. I raised the cup yet another time as if to confirm a theory, the kernel of which took root in my contemplations.

This handful of lettering triggered something within to hark back on those formed with Ogham. Hence, I scolded myself for not having remarked on it prior to now. I allowed though that they stood accompanied by detached characters which bore no resemblance; and this confused my judgment. I then suspected that these separate patterns were distinct modes of script. I couldn't be certain, but I had an idea that both communicated the same thing. That is to say, they were isolated languages, but with a single translation. Why that might occur, I wasn't positive. It may have been, I reflected, analogous to lands on the continent where people who live alongside each other, voice individual dialects, which therefore requires bilingual signage. I should resolve to keep an open mind on this, however. Perhaps, I probed, there might emerge an alternative explanation.

It transpired after I proceeded to my office at the university on the succeeding morn I undertook a serious study of what I presumed to occur as Ogham inscriptions. It surfaced to a firm extent with similarities, further; I believed I recognised it as an earlier mode of this system. I subscribed to the notion there submitted the possibility that Ogham derived from a more advanced structure of alphabet. It was a surprise in this respect so far as written languages were concerned, in that it may have regressed sooner than progressed, hence came simpler in trait to its predecessors.

I withdrew books on the matter from dust-laden bookshelves in the library, so too, in pursuit of answers whacked out copious hours poring over them at a bureau in the Long Room. I may for practicality, have consulted a colleague; a specialist on the subject; but this developed as an enterprise in which I was prepared to be selfish. I settled on researching it by myself and on conducting it through to its conclusion, whatever that might ensue. After I jotted down my summaries, I reverted again to my office, a bag of nerves. For the second time, I consulted the sundry artefacts of my collection; not that this was obligatory; but I felt a compulsion to execute it, nonetheless. Hardly daring to trust my own conclusions, I reached into the middle drawer of the desk where I supported in reserve a hip flask for just such occurrences. My hand quivered as I constructed the fortitude to gulp from it; too, it took some tensioning of the muscles in my jaw to anchor and steady it. Afterward, I saw it necessary to revisit its fire almost at once for second helpings, distinguishing that I must calm myself down if I stood to get my hypotheses in order.

The symbols, as I suspected scored incontestably as a variation of Ogham, and my infantile fantasies came rushing back to my head in a torrent of blood—Papa, Ancient Charts; and more than this, Lost Civilisations. They all invaded my thoughts, in swirls and maelstroms; stormy vortex's in the rage of a tremendous churn, to the point of practically inducing in me, a state of womanly faint. Therefore, if it hadn't been for the cure-all of Irish Dew, that frames precisely as what should have come about. For what this translated to, befell an astonishment almost beyond belief; a confirmation to the existence of Hy Brasil.

I still couldn't fathom it. This was so outrageous, so incredibly ludicrous, that I alleged in a barely audible opinion to the vacant chamber I must be mistaken. I had to be. Mythical islands were the stuff of inventiveness, of fantasy; not actuality. Evidence of a populace does not just disappear, only to re-emerge for a second occurrence after the passing of millennia.

Yet it happened. It was viable. This very circumstance had before now transpired; besides, was being illustrated today in Greece, The Ottoman Empire and beyond. Our science occurred in the mode of rediscovering that which was lost. We existed to expose such which became obscured under strata of soil deposited over the ages. Archaeology most times, through this unearthing, proved the actuality of what had until then survived as mere legend. This profession was the discipline of encounters with the past, besides, of an open mind to its possibilities. Each and every day we augment our knowledge of life on this planet through exploration; where the imaginary, can, through our labours, turn into probabilities; so too, promises evolve into facts. There remains a bottomless want to learn of our past as well as from the historical. Now; I faced because of this intense longing, the likelihood this land of my youthful dreams, far from being in the realm of fictional, may in the alternative occur as a firm, and tangible reality.

At home a while after, I comprehended it stay obligatory that I tread with care. I happened then to hold immeasurable appreciation for the hip flask of before, with its remedial tonic which I near enough swallowed to completion. Here and now I possessed a clearer head, which happens contrary to what one might have expected, given my former imbibing. All the same I continued yet a young man, and dwelt in alertness with the clarity of pacified anxieties, that many a career had gotten stripped to tatters; even fellows far older than I; for having rushed headlong into deductions for which they didn't enjoy conclusive evidence.

I ruminated on this for a stretch. What did I lay claim to after all, apart from a handful of china, plus a bottle shaped in glass, all of which may or may not have had something to do with the other materials? None of it obligated respect worthy of proper procedure and was therefore not accounted for on any of the excavation transcripts or diaries. Neither had anyone squandered time in pencilling up diagrams, or with the calculation of any dimensions. Apart from me, as far it troubled anyone, none of these apparent archaeological finds even existed. In consequence, who was to say they were not a component of some elaborate hoax? It was conceivable they had by intent gotten buried in these locales for the purpose of making a fool out of an unsuspecting academic. Most everything could be replicated, including the Ogham, and hence, it too might have coexisted as a trickster's notion of a practical joke. It was straightforward enough to age an object through the smearing into it of mud, besides light grit; and following that, lopping off understated chips; all with the purpose of luring a target into the acceptance of authenticity.

Relief ensued as my emotion; gratified that I backed off with the consultation of a colleague at Trinity. While there subsisted an opinion voiced from the gut, which lectured that I secured the genuine article, there advanced no percentage in confiding elsewhere. So far as the students, also as it related to the faculty, I had merely held on to a few souvenirs. No harm, no foul. Even a scheme to discuss Ogham, attainably may have invited uncomfortable queries, and so I stayed categorical that it should materialise as best to pursue all occupation with respect to this venture, at a good length from prying eyes. Should I realise irrefutable evidence at a future date, it would duly get hailed as a discovery of astonishment. Moreover, having assumed guardianship of the excavated materials as though they transpired my personal and private property; well, this should in all likelihood get passed over. It might come to be chalked down to the expenditure of professional judgement besides the deployment of a methodical attitude with reference to the assemblage of confirming proof.

This project required undertaking alone; furthermore, with a slant implemented that began with the presumption of fraud or chicanery. If I selected everything with more than a grain of scepticism, I should gift myself a tremendous service. It would stand as better in the absolute to be refuted as incorrect, with purely oneself conscious, than to announce a marvellous deduction to the entire world, just for it next to culminate in a lifetime of mockery; what is more, ridicule by one's peers, enunciated from the rooftops of academia.

Robert E. Kearns

My first order of industry was to decipher the second set of text painted onto the underside of the enchanting porcelain. I was not a linguist, but I went by my original assumption that both could doubtless be taken to mean the same thing. By way of treating the Ogham translation as a baseline; with application I could endorse my supposition. The repeated, but distinct lines of inscription came to pass, from what I could gather, as partly grounded in Ogham, but nursed as well serious influences of Latin and Greek as well as a type of hieroglyphic iconography, such as understood from ancient Egypt. What conclusions were to be extracted from this, I wasn't for certain, but a theory appeared to found in my meditations that Ogham may have originated as the archetype or older representations of the two, with the cyphers of my inspection ensuing as a newer or more advanced structure of configuration. This might well be accounted for through interaction with exterior civilisations, and the adoption of minor intricacies to their alphabet, as well as to written peculiarities.

I held onto that deduction for a turn. Interaction with nations foreign would presume that Hy Brasil occurred as an outward, besides broad-minded state which catered to trade and commerce, besides the promise of social relations. The embracing of remote scripting techniques would appear to cast a wink to plentiful association with the peripheral world. This raised thought-provoking complications. Ancient Ireland, from what was accepted, entertained limited dealings with other realms. It had never been subject to Roman invasion, for example, and because of this, they seldom encountered Latin goods of the period. This therefore presumed an inwardly faceted jurisdiction rather than one with the viewpoint of an extrovert; remembering that Ireland emerged as an isle on the shelf's edge of the continent, in an era when seafaring in these waters ranked as a treacherous enterprise. It was written off as a wasteland of barbarians which endured as best left alone. More, as fortune would have it, they doubtless weren't too wide of the point on that account.

Now, if one postulated Hy Brasil as an existent land mass, further west again, sequestered in the mid-Atlantic; the inhabitants; whom at some crux of their endurance instituted the wherewithal to espouse an assortment of elements from those word schemes of other populaces, and graft them on to their own; then that may well be a sign they carried on as a more advanced civilisation than what was understood of Ireland at this interval. From what I could distinguish, bearing in regard, I wasn't known as a doyen of typology, the innovative coordination of letters that had gotten advanced, exhibited a progression or improvement on those it had derived from. If this stood the event, then one would have to conclude that Hy Brasil itself was not just more enlightened than Ireland, but achieved on a par with the illustrious societies of the period.

This was speculative by a longshot, but it cited as appropriate to the re-emerged artefacts. In fact, these occurrences pointed to a level of sophistication which had yet to cultivate in other areas of the world. And, how they ended up in Ireland? That could to a measure be accounted for in that it disclosed as Hy Brasil's next-door neighbour, with these possessions prized on plenty by the indigenous tribes, who may even have benefited from them as grave goods. The lustre of the enamel, furthermore, a bottle fashioned out of glass must have stood out with astonishment to primitive cultures, which could moreover go to explain why it ensued they even buried stuffs which resulted as less than perfect.

All of this cogitated as theory up till now, and no further along was I, with regard to corroborating proof; except, perhaps for the capacity to determine that both sets of inscription showed in translation as more or less a denotation of the same thing. If however, this cooked up as the ingredients to a hoax, (and it would have coincided a damned good one) then I should require much more in the way of evidence. In accordance with that, I determined to put into service the closest of eyes on all future excavations to which I was a participant, so also, jut out an ear for plausible news on related marvels exhumed elsewhere. I expected that given how the novelties in my unusual anthology had come into being within a relatively insignificant span of time, then it should not stay long before more got revealed.

Nothing further turned up that season, thus, if not surprised in the main, caused me all the same to plunge into profound disappointment. It should, I expect have transpired as no surprise to not manage the hat trick without delay. It wasn't until the following spring, while yet in term, for another item of fascination to ascend. We reckoned on busying ourselves through an expedition over the Easter recess; with both the students on top of us team leaders all presenting as bachelors, and for that reason not tied down to family conventions. By this understanding, we chanced in consequence as free to vacate Dublin, and so packed trunks and our made way by train to Galway for the fortnight.

Robert E. Kearns

There came up, proximate to Claddagh, a site which held considerable promise as an ancient settlement, and which had gotten earmarked for additional scrutiny the year prior. It amused with the advantage of being handy to town, which gave rise to the decision as an easy one, given the reputation Galway contrived to secure for its holes of watering. Our scholars, it appeared, situated in more angst to forage from the local taverns, than they were to uncover the primeval yields of history. All the same, I must admit that I looked forward to it to myself; but with the maintenance of a requisite to exercise mature responsibility, I strained to emphasise to our younger group members, how much more enjoyable a visit to the public house could turn out; onward from a day's work.

A couple of mornings got wasted with the setup of our equipment and the pitching of our tents. These temporary quarters stood to be exploited during the day for ourselves as shelter if necessary from poor weather (which transpired plenty) and correspondingly to guarantee that our tools and equipment stayed dry. It took a while to get into the swing of things; therefore, while a serious amount got completed, it wasn't until the second week we released the tap to the bearing of full flow. There happens a predisposition to become stiff, moreover, rusted during the winter months, and a few days practice is essential to resuscitate a method, besides rhythm, which labours to peak efficiency. I occurred in distraction from these practical endeavours so greatly that I almost forgot about that which I longed for most, would surface.

One of my undergraduates deposited to a depth of about four foot, so too, in exercise of a trowel to isolate a flint axe;

emptied outside the trench another focus altogether. I chanced to stop by for the inspection of something else; when straight away I probed, "What is this?" even though, I could see with my own two eyes it displayed as a modest rectangular box. Beyond that observation, it inflicted me with no clue as what it could be except to say I regarded it as akin to a receptacle one might apply to store the bracelet of a lady, being about the size and shape of such a holder. Accepting a brush, I swept away the loose clay, and noticed then it came sheathed in a transparent coat which at first I hadn't detected. I stood perplexed by its composition, but not thinking a lot of it; I unfurled my pocket knife and next sliced into it. I apprehended that it tore with a small amount of force. Now; I know that this wasn't exactly playing with a straight bat, but I excused it to my apprentice with the avowal it impressed me as contemporary; which arose in all essence as the truth.

The six-sided case, it looked, had gained protection from the shield, and even though it manifested itself as modern-day; it unveiled as attractively endued, which caused my heart to leap with excitement. I tried not to betray this, and as if to affirm my flippancy regarding its attainment, opened it up to expose to us both, a shiny metal barrelled pen. He let out a chortle, jesting he ought to win a prize for his detection, furthermore he professed he should have his eye on the purse for best article in that issue of the university magazine where his findings got published. I guffawed with him, but not quite with the correspondent enthusiasm; for on its flank there turned up several etchings I comprehended in my heart were of the equivalent character I had seen emblazoned to the underside of the porcelain back in Dublin. I detached the said writing implement from the clip which bound it in place, then extorted it from its station. 'Another souvenir for the compendium', I chuffed. 'Keep it', waved the student dismissively. It inflicted him with limited interest it seemed, but almost as an afterthought, queried 'Do you mind if I hang on to the case?' 'We can go halves'.

I happened most sorry to have lost it, but I couldn't well argue with the chap, given he originated as the architect of its exposure. I had contracted the better share of the deal anyhow, and should he have set eyes on the principal component, letting me off instead with the smart-looking case, I wouldn't have occurred in a position to refuse. To this day, I haven't the foggiest if there was any scribing's on the inside or underneath, such was the quickness with which it all transpired. What was for certain, though, is that the fetching pen tickled with a story to tell.

With manufactured nonchalance, I made my way to one of the tents, where we beforehand set aside a portable stove for the boiling of water. I brewed up a cup of tea, and while I waited, examined the treasure. It was metallic, with a wonderful man sized shaft, not too wide but not excessively slim either. Sizing it up, I realised it fit between the fingers seamlessly, with a good weight and balance to it. It emerged as obvious it would endure as an implement I should appreciate for correspondence. I removed the cover, which disclosed a curved, besides graceful and precise nib, which impressed on me, as either created out of gold, or gilded in that element. I guessed it came about as the yellow metal, but couldn't attest to its purity. With my tea in hand, I then surveyed the imprints on the barrel. I had come prepared for just such an eventuality, so in consequence, had brought along my notebook, complete with translations. I cross-referenced each character against the written commentaries; this text authored in the more advanced usage of the two structures, and after, scratched out the results on a separate sheet of paper:

To Olan, With Love. Neelak.

Here, I set down my tea, and blasphemed I hadn't got something more intense to swig from. I wasn't the kind of fellow that continued in the weakness for dipping my toe into profane language, but I freely admit to having utilised it then. I spent the next few minutes rolling the pen in and around my quivering fingers, unable to intellectualise with clarity about what to do next. My trance got disconnected when a few of the chaps entered, desirous to gulp down a steaming beverage. Hence, I rushed to hide the instrument in my coat pocket, and then offered excuses to be off.

At home in Dublin afterward to the Easter break, I returned it as vital to set down a record of my verdicts. I went back to the trove, scrawled down drawings of everything, counting too ones from diverse angles, being definite to include the underneath of the cups with their divulged symbols. I sketched up summaries linked to each object as an accompaniment, so too, reported my interpretations, such as on the drinking vessel as well and glass bottle. I composed ideas with concern to the pen, adding at their foot, the translation referencing this Olan and Neelak.

I ventured aloud in my literatures with attentiveness to who this duo may have endured so too, what occasion should have proffered such a gift: Birthday, Anniversary, etc. This completed, I rifled around in search of a suitable receptacle to stash them in, no longer content to impound them all in a corner. I remained powerless, for a bout; to lay my hands on anything appropriate, but at last hit on the thought of rummaging through the janitor's work closet. Inside, there was squirreled away all manner of odds and ends, besides a few effects which might have pulled off the assignment. However, along the sideways partition I spotted a wooden chest that appeared sturdy in feature and comprising a mere handful of run down and dried out paint brushes. These, I emptied, sized up its strength as well as capacity; then approved that it should do very satisfactory indeed.

If I estimated there was to follow a trove of related Hy Brasilian substances in train, I occurred in error. While I continued to embark on a number of nationwide digs, an amount had, by this interval progressed from the previous season, and happened thus at a relatively advanced stage. If there had come into being objects of value, they before now long since got removed and detailed to their fate; whatever that may be. Or, it was, of course practicable there had transpired nothing there in the first instance. The drawback with the rummage for evidence remained that it was not practical for me to alert colleagues to situate on the lookout for whatever implied modernity. I had not come prepared to put my neck in the noose without conclusive substantiation for the erstwhile theory developing. As to what that might transpire, I wasn't sure. In any case, there revealed nought to be stumbled upon for what was left of the year.

The introduction to the darling of my affections passed off shortly thereafter, thrown together at a function given by one of our professors at the college. Correspondingly, that was to keep me full with occupation. As well, we were to be married the following spring, which encompassed too, a honeymoon on the continent. That caused me to omit the Easter expedition, which may have positioned as an opportunity to disinter some additional treasure. However, later in the summer, while on a trip to West Cork, I produced a major discovery. Rather, I unearthed significant matters over the course of our dig, and not all at the same time. There resulted supplementary porcelain cups that ranged from approximately one third, to two-thirds complete. On those sections where the base stood intact, I grasped that a small enumerate retained scripts in both practices of what had thus far been recognised, with there also happening a range consisting in total of the more recent method.

The biggest catch however, trawled in not as the china cups, but a stockpile of plates. Not just the dishware itself but what was copied out on them. I insisted on getting stuck into this specific duty, passionate to live up to my tenet of presenting waist deep in muck to secure a proper understanding of one's craft. I sweated to bring out one or two of the partial cups. The balance got hit upon by my students, none of whom had travelled with me on preceding digs. The plates however, I came across by myself, wrapped together in an oilcloth, which ostensibly cosseted them from harm. With care I had previous to this torn open the package while yet in the pit, and there discovered a quad of fine-looking dishes of allied design and trimming. And, as with most of what else I maintained, they divulged vistas out of what I presumed were depictions of the Irish countryside. I flipped over one of these plates to perceive in the advanced mode by itself, the now accustomed writing.

With having gained the practice of translation, I could make out the first line to mean "Water Ford Earthenware". Underneath, located the style-"Hy Brasil"

I dwelt on this some during the period of its examination later on whilst hidden away in my tent. We saw it compulsory to camp out on this expedition, posted as we were, beyond the outer limits of a town. While having its obvious drawbacks; in this exact instance, it allowed me the benefit of fashioning studies by lamplight within a hairsbreadth from the zone of encounter. Waterford in southeast Ireland, organising as this island's first formed city, occurred rich in history, and had besides, proven equally opulent in archaeological gems. With that in mind, it came right away to my pondering that this may have engendered connection to the delph. However, the mention of Hy Brasil appeared to rule this out.

On the other hand, there could well have transpired a relationship in antiquity. Might it have been possible that Water Ford had borrowed its name from Waterford? But then again, I recalled what I estimated the age of these items to have stood, given their depth in the soil. It later dawned on me it may very well have occurred the other way around. The fact of the matter, besides, may have lain somewhere in between. From what I understood of the Hy Brasilian legend, it attended strong connections with Ireland. If the ancient Celts settled it, then conceivably, they fetched their language; besides, culture with them. That should go to explain the Ogham inscriptions. It might too; ensue as an argument for comparable place names, such as Water Ford.

This came about as reflections with excitement, and in the

glow of my paraffin lamp, with a bolstering mug of tea, I thrilled to brood on them. One or two of us historians existed to speculate. There can crop up an enormous sum of fulfilment drawn from scurrying over the assorted set-ups to our meditations, then bidding to shape a picture of past lives. I regarded the eye-catching tableware yet again. It happened then I speculated if these painted a representation of Ireland or Hy Brasil. It could, as well, have reasonably sanctioned as a mixture of both. There perchance, among the artists of the day, emerged an attempt to practice romantic miens of their ancestral homeland, and this I supposed chanced as even-handed an explanation as any.

The following couple of seasons occupied me on the east coast, but the pickings from these locales with reference to Hy Brasil harvested as slim to say the least. All of my treasures so far had befallen approximate to the west of Ireland; hence, I concluded this must have surfaced due to trade plus location. It wasn't until I ended up in the above-mentioned Waterford, three years after the West Cork dig, when I was able to exhume more evidence to support my postulations. The ties to this south eastern town hadn't escaped my mind. Therefore, I arrived there with anticipation, that given its proud history; something might just crop up that could strengthen those bonds.

I struck gold; figuratively, if not literally. The effect on me however, was precisely the same. I contract the parallel ecstasy from the discovery of a vase as I realise from the raking out of a silver bangle. Thus, it hoisted two vases to enliven that got nudged my way to start with. Both got exhumed from autonomous trenches, with them showing an appearance so current in stripe something supposed them as unworthy of extended inquiry. Again, I turned out to be fortunate in this regard. One saw light in the vicinity of other articles and had gotten rested as if by the grace of Lady Luck on a bench alongside them. I progressed now to the bold and brazen. As a result, later to a momentary examination, I evoked a witticism in front of my chums, and next absconded with velocity, claiming it might do for an agreeable token of affection to my darling wife.

Not one of them betrayed the slightest hint of attention. The second of the vases got rooted out by a student to the rear of where I dug. He commented on it being an amusing prize, therefore, with me having already gleaned the value of an excuse thriving once before, invoked it yet again. This time though, bolstered, besides a dash shameless, I queried if I might steal it home to my dearest and rubbed it in profusely that I hoped he wouldn't mind, and all that rot. There was nothing much he could argue in the negative, and with not a lot more than a nod of the head, he relented. It situated as quite an easy deception, and although I abused my position, didn't feel the least bit of guilt in connection with it.

The vases again came decked out in what I now presumed to occur as either Irish or Hy Brasilian cameos, with the interpretation on one making the claim as a creation of Black Pool Pottery, Hy Brasil. There survived a percentage of Blackpool's about, one of which deposited in Cork; with the possibility emerging it referenced that, being in immediacy to the west. I allowed a smile to develop, followed by lots of speculation, when I ruminated in addition, if it might have a link with my home city of Dublin, with Black Pool instituting itself as a conversion of the Gaelic name.

I lit on something else by myself, and the ethical approach would have remained to index and log it as an additional relic of the location. I should have done so too if it happened not for the nowadays acquainted inscription. I subscribed as selfish, I appreciate, plus, with hindsight I accept that I ought to have dealt with it differently. It has today given me some cause for shame in not then tolerating its enactment. The discovery I came across was that of a comb which through elementary examination I presumed as either whittled out of bone or else from deer antler. It fit in as a glove with our historical backdrop. So too, I partook of no cause whatsoever to believe it wasn't original to Waterford. This manner of encounter organised in common to its primordial account, and I acknowledged it as influenced by the Viking era.

It inflicted with all the characteristics of being so, hence, because of this, I stood prepared to put it down as a cordial bit of plunder that should swell to our knowledge of the mediaeval south east. I began preparations to scour it, with original and careful chiselling away of the portlier sections of muck, then brushing down the lighter features via horsehair bristles. Then to finish with, I shined it up with a moist rag. It turned out barely after I concluded with this procedure I remarked on scratchings along the top. These were constructed in Ogham. The foremost word took me a second to decode as "Cedric". The rest however, read identifiable with ease as "Hy Brasil". What struck me about this find, though, was it became clear that it surfaced primitive in ilk, as if it had come up from a prior phase, and in consequence entertained meagre fraternity with the more "Modern" relics I thus far assembled.

I won't meander into an abundance of fine points as they relate to any supplemental introductions to Hy Brasil. Needless to say, the seasons rolled in and sallied forth with equal hurry; with every now and again, through my station of seniority, discharges from this Hibernian soil fell into my lap. Of the metallic relics liberated, there came about forks (for eating & carving) plus spoons (tea &soup) and knives of diverse sort, including those to match the outsized fork above. Even too, there originated a high quality blade for hunting with a crafted edge of beauty, as well as it sporting a leaf-life foliage engraved handle. It impressed as contriving to be forged out of a single deposit of iron. Other extracts bared hallmarks stamped into their handgrips. Indeed, the forks, one spoon besides a butter knife, were all shaped from silver; so too, in superb condition. Some of these had gotten forged by the same silversmith, with it apparently manifest there had synchronised several such houses in the practice of in this artistry on Hy Brasil.

I unveiled from its estate of hiding, a wooden bowl, turned from light oak, the properties of which became visible as New World. It gave the idea of something that may have embraced a green salad; had it realised custom today. It survived, due in part to the boggy peat, but also happened as embossed with the imprint of Hy Brasil on the underside. Over, this struck me as the elder of other wares, perhaps because of its ordinariness. I couldn't be certain of this however as the forest has always accorded us craft materials; never permitting them to establish replacement exclusively with clay.

Robert E. Kearns

There prescribed too, a fine-looking jug, glazed, and endued with a related pattern as given to the other earthenware. It emanated from a town that again derived its designation from Celtic terminology–'Rath'. This followed as a commonality to a selection of these possessions. The names of location situated as familiar as if they were first extracted from Ireland and then transplanted to Hy Brasil. For comparison, this continued in parallel to what took place in the New England territories during colonisation, where most of the appellations were copied from those in Britain.

A brush revealed itself, such as one a valet might value to dust down a suit or dinner jacket, except for its missing bristles. Of the more remarkable items presented came up a pair of Celtic style figurines, cast in bronze. They commanded an Irish aspect to them, but had seen their apparent production in Hy Brasil. An aura haloed over them, as if they manufactured for a fresh audience, comparable to how such things might be achieved today. That is to say, they replicated, it appeared, a design of old for ornamental purposes, rather than influencing as an original design. I concluded that it should comprise to serve no purpose otherwise, to see it printed with the maker's mark. To action this was a modern phenomenon for the most part rather than one for the ancient. The same might be said for many of the other attractive relics in the collection, such as the cups and plates. It happened merely after I accumulated an excess of these over the years that it dawned on me most surmised to exemplify scenes or outlines of nostalgia. Hence, I flagged them as the output of a contemporary business with mass production. The implications of this were profound; indicative of commerce, besides a society of expansion from which the citizens purchased merchandises for ornamental worth, rather than just functional routine.

I confirmed this proposition when I dug out a picture frame; which at one point, set into it, may have occurred a miniature painting. The central section stood unoccupied, but there survived remnants of glass around the inside edge which displayed a measure of protection for the subject; further, a high mark of sophistication to have moulded a flat glass sheet. The wood pointed to sculpting once again with a leaf-like, post Celtic layout with the reverse demonstrative of birth through a Water Ford based establishment. To be in the assembly of these subjects directed me to a level of disposal income on behalf of those good citizens on Hy Brasil. It prospectively besides, showed they devoured appreciation for either a home-spun likeness or one that had gotten shipped with their ancestors upon settling there. Too, plausibly these decorations brokered a reminder to their history in fable. It was fascinating to behold such an antique, as this day it could for another instance have achieved a purchase on the high streets of Dublin, but transpired instead as the vestige of an alternative condition and standing in time.

I came across just last year a brooch which fashioned as a superb trimming of jewellery. It emerged as a pity I had become used to the legitimacy of Hy Brasil as it otherwise should have hit with astonishment. I suppose I ought to have remained content I unearthed it in later years as it might well have overwhelmed me if I devised its detection it in those initial seasons. It disclosed as alike to the sort out of mediaeval Ireland that we provided spaces for in the museum with this one also arising complete with leafed foliage. And more, with it sparkling in etched gold it should have endured as one of our star attractions. It must have founded as the output of a master craftsman, and his hallmark on the rear came inscribed in refined, moreover discreet calligraphy, which did not detract from his work in the least.

Then, there popped up those belongings for which I nursed but scant explanation. So diverse sited they from that which came to my attention before that they animated as simply baffling hence, led me to question everything I understood until this date. I recognised over the decades assorted sizes of what came into view as more or less the invariable artefact, but for the life of me, to this day, I still don't have the foggiest clue what they are. All were composed in a flat board of unknown material, and on this plane there emanated components which looked as if they might be miniatures of something else altogether. No matter how long I studied on them, there emanated no explanation at all I could conjure up which might explain their function. It happened merely because several of the minute constituents, and the panels themselves had revealed a Hy Brasilian constructor's mark, that I was able to determine their origin. Along with these were found, again at distinctive times and localities, some coloured quantities of analogous material to the unusual sheets. The difference existing that one or two might have been containers, plus the substance being thicker; furthermore, bright in nature. The hues it seemed like to me awarded a substitute for decoration, they rearing vivid enough to pass in their own right as sufficient.

Before I get to the final, too, most central relics, with consideration for all this trans-mutating into a list, there surfaced something that should have risen straight out of modernity. I came to hear of them being in fashion on the continent and saw to consult a book for confirmation. It gifted as a timepiece designed for wearing on the wrist. The glass showed a crack, but otherwise it seemed to be fine. I continued however, fearful of trying out the mechanism in case I destroyed it; thus, will leave that to professionals to figure out. There fitted two slots on each end to attach a strap, but with regret it had either worn out or was merely absent. This saddened me to a point as at that moment I fancied I might well have adopted the foreign style if it had presented. I contemplated taking a chance on turning it over to a jeweller for analysis. In hindsight, I comprehend now it didn't in fact occur for the best I left well enough alone. This came about as an utterly self-centred approach; likewise, contrary to all that I held dear. It deserves now to exist as part of the museum's compendium, along with everything else.

And to conclude, with inspiring a goal this account has not dragged on further than necessary, there befell a twosome of wedding bands on top of it all, which has prompted me to engage in this detailed memorandum. I believe I have today arrived at the stage in this procedure when it stands essential to declare my discoveries to the world. I never did attain absolute corroboration, but the wisdom that comes with age has likewise shown me, that in my line of work, often, one never touches on that level proof. All a fellow can do is divulge the evidence, allow others to examine it, and then at that juncture engage in debate, besides conversation.

We argue more than we reach agreement it seems to me, and for every theory that one person gives up; there is another who toasts its antithesis. I should have backed my own contentions many years ago and been brave enough to engage in their defence. Instead, I hid in cowardice. I concur that I lived in aspiration for the control of corroborating data besides verifiable support, and that ventured true to a certain extent. However, the overriding motive transacted that at no time had I the courage of my convictions. I established in terror of ridicule, hence presumed it better to wait for whatsoever is more substantial. In this state of mind I continued to hang on; repeatedly needful of more, with the result surviving that I never sorted out anything about it. I invented excuses to cover for my fear, with constant chasing of my own "Rosetta Stone", which never delivered. If I occupied confidence in myself; what's more, my handiwork, I should have distributed my points of view and conceded to the consequences, however they might have discharged.

Now, I have at last determined to advance, devising before this to come across two ultimate slices of near verification, which if not conclusive proof, were at least the prompt I looked for to put forth my deductions. I have even now fashioned up a label and pasted it to my box of tricks as a show of decisiveness. I intend to pledge my sturdy janitor's tool box along with a cover note, too, this summary, inclusive of all of my drawings and notes, which afford a far greater detail than I what I have gone into here. I shall keep faith that my friends and colleagues will forgive me in the delay of this procedure for so many years.

I realise that due to my withholding of materials and data, there may have occurred throughout this span an enormous loss of artefacts from yesteryear on top of the discoveries I reserved in a private compendium. I am repentant in the extreme for having organised this, but hold out in optimism there may just come about a measure of understanding for a weak man, who functioned from a position of fear rather than confidence. I only gained the courage to face whatever may come of this on my unearthing the above mentioned gilded rings of marriage, one inscribed "To Neelak, With Love on our Wedding Day"; the other extolling "To Olan, On the occasion of our Marriage".

Andrew Campbell, Trinity College, Dublin.

Part 4 — A Fresh Start to an Ancient End

The Heights, Waterford (continued)

All of this didn't quite register in my equations. I remained conscious of what I read, so too I ensured already by now to survey everything in what he referred to as his 'Box of Tricks'. Still, I felt in a way detached from it, comparable to what might ensue when bearing of late to fall upon bad news. I took a while to process the details as if my brain had proclaimed its resolve to go on strike in the middle of rush hour. From prior experience, the solitary cure for this enforced lethargy is to acquire a chore for idle hands.

To remedy the situation, I sifted through the outstanding papers. There showed up the cover note he made mention of in his summary, which showed as a one page affair where he disclosed his intent to turn over his assemblage of artefacts, besides all the documentation which accompanied it. This included detailed records and drawings as well as the above synopsis. He similarly identified his goal to circulate a piece where he meant to hash out his case for the existence of Hy Brasil in antiquity. Likewise, he repeated his apologies for concealing to himself these specifics throughout the course of his tenure in both the museum and university. Furthermore, he pleaded again for understanding, if not forgiveness.

Behind the letter of explanation, there exhibited his thorough elucidations on each artefact, which included the site of location, the year and month, plus illustrations with attentiveness to the wider excavation as it related to the spot they were unearthed. Also, each individual item excavated got sketched independently, and he included his descriptions regarding each one as a guide to their meaning so far as he understood it. It was noticeable where he grasped the benefit of attaining built up knowledge over the period of decades, and what he compiled amounted to a detailed and comprehensive argument of which he doubtless looked ahead to publication. All the same, whatever emerged; it was obvious he neither got to publish his proposals, nor had he arrived at success with the passing over of those materials in his hoard.

I called up Tiffanie. "Good day to you my beautiful lady, would it be acceptable if I provided you some papers to duplicate?" "And I have an extra task for you. What might transpire the likelihood of rooting out some extra detail on the professor?" "Specifically, when did he pass over? It appears as if he was about to turn in all that came with the chest and distribute a thesis, but never got an opportunity to carry it out." 'I can do both, Irish. At least I think I can. There should be a book around here some place comprising biographies on all the curators, professors and big wigs. As for the copying, so long as I don't have to slave over the machine forever and a day, it shouldn't be a problem. Either way, it will cost you a drink at the minimum. I might hit you up for dinner too, depending on the workload.' 'As long as I get to spend time with my gorgeous honey lamb, you can extract whatever consequence you please,' I articulated. 'Oh my God Irish, you're such a charmer. What did you find out, anyway?' to which I responded humouredly, 'All shall be revealed; perhaps over that adult beverage. So now you must go out with me, and before you change your mind, I'll come up with the records which want for reproduction.'

With a decision there befell no point in Photostatting all that showed in the dossier, the most imperative portions happening the summary, so too, the front message, I fetched them upstairs to Tiffanie. Then it was all but a matter of positioning the papers into the feeder and the retrieval of facsimiles from the other end. "I've got some time on my hands now" said she. "I'll go snooping around for that volume with the faculty profiles".

'Excellent! I'll catch you at five so', adding with a tongue in cheek "This paltry sum of replicas hardly merits a drink, so you'll have to make-up for it by tracing that book". Then, with resistance in the urge to plant a kiss on her cheek, and before she could reach for a comeback, I shaped a retreat of the brisk variety, and oriented for the cleaved drop to perdition.

I returned the originals to the banker's box, and determined, more due to laziness than anything else, there stood no sense in its conveyance back to the storeroom. There happened a strong chance I rationalised, that some poor fellow, most probably me, should only end up with the nuisance of digging it back out again. For the sake of convenience, as well as to get it out of my way, I consigned it to one of the plywood ledges.

After all these goings-on, I didn't suppose I sited in a frame of mind to get any more of my day job completed, but at the same time I determined it a necessity to comprehended in total what I before now read over. So, I resolved to fly through it for a second time, in the expectation that with this feat, I should gain help in the attainment of a better handle on it all.

Robert E. Kearns

With the conclusion of this revision, I lay the documents down, and next shuffled my attention to the Box of Tricks, complete with the discoloured ticket the professor himself pasted on. I thought on him with his brush, imparting the label with a swipe of thickened white compound, perhaps too slapping a dab on the box before next positioning it and effecting to smooth out the folds with the heel of his hand. I pictured him support it in that spot for a minute to ensure it bonded fast. And, as if my ossuary of artefacts ordained as the reliquary of a saint, I couldn't help but stroke the tag by means of my thumb, too, glide over the paper in roundabout circles, almost in expectation that something of the spirit or essence of the good professor should transfer from it to me.

It arises as a human aspiration to connect if it might with effects from ages departed. But more than that again, we crave for association with lives born of bygone times. That is why when I contemplated the sticker, and caressed the grain of its paper with the merest contact of epidermis, I encountered an emotion of at one time knowing him in person. I'm not predisposed as a man of religion, however, in such circumstances there can be recognised a mystical connotation, even though ones logical self counsels that this emanates purely as a trick of the mind.

In these contexts when there transpires that perception of suffering to grapple with the breath of ghosts out of days gone before, it arrives accompanied with a primordial recognition, which in this occurrence happened that of how the professor must have borne, when he too clutched in his bare hands the historical fragments of Hy Brasil. Then, I the questioned aloud, as if he stationed there in the dungeon to guide me on what became apparent to him with the revelation of those names, Olan and Neelak? It must I supposed have triggered a poignant and expressive resonance with an impact so powerful, that regardless of his anxieties, it, in its finality, was to prompt him into setting aside his worries, doubts, besides fears, and expose himself, moreover, his work to the scrutiny of the world.

The dungeon became metaphorically darker, with the result, that when I breathed in, it entered with laboured; furthermore, protracted inhalations. It next, on the exhale, transformed into a sigh. With a necessity to happen seated, my feet came to be uncooperative; heavy and bolted to the floor. It demanded a mighty determination to reach the lone chair in the chamber. That which should have given me cause to celebrate, had instead and for inexplicable motives, taken me down. My mood consented to blacken; with a masochistic wing I had no prior familiarity with in domination of my mental state. I stumbled into a compulsion to switch out the lights, so too, wallow in the misery of this offbeat phenomenon. If it wasn't for my prevailing yet in the rigidity of inflexibility, this I should have achieved.

As it was, my legs refused to budge, and with a great deal of distress there fathomed an aspiration within to slide down off the chair then lie on the concrete floor and curl up in the foetal position to protect against the sorrowful pain. I must have remained in that situation for ten minutes or so, staring into space, besides almost in belief I descended into the very bowels of the earth itself. It was only when with massive determination I raised my leaden arm and some life returned. And then, realising it cleared within a whisker of five; simply at that point did I gain the capacity to stir. Even at that, I was stuck to the chair, as if weights from a barbell had gotten relegated to my lap.

It ensued with resolve, further, another moan, that I pushed myself out of it and straggled towards the door. Sluggish in movement; so too, with each of my strides resulting in the want to lie down and after that shut my eyes forever, I at last made it to the staircase. Each step took place as the distance of a league uphill. I seized on to the bannister not just for support, but to drag myself up with the aid of weakened muscles. It was on my plateauing at the pinnacle where I identified a film of sweat on my forehead, so too on my back where the shirt clung to it in sodden patches. It congruently however, issued relief, occasioning liberty from the burdensome emotions of my vaulted sub terrain.

It required a handful of moments to gather myself as I appointed no fancy to emerge with this appearance in front of Tiffanie. On generating her entrance though, she recognised the trouble 'you look hot', to which I had to state the excuse it transpired somewhat stuffy in the confines of the crypt. This came followed with the reflection that a remedy for it should arise with chilled beer on tap.

My legs motioned once more in working order and my breathing had normalised though I placed yet as a bit light-headed. In reality I could have done with a rest there and then and a glass of cold water in hand rather than light ale. In view of that, I suggested a snug parlour around on Dawson Street, its location ensuring it wouldn't require venturing too distant. I forgot it entertained steps though; an obligation, given it operated out of an old basement. This caused me some worry for a second I should again be subject to the equivalent symptoms I endured just ten minutes before. With mercy and relief, it didn't take place, but when I got to the bar, I arranged for aqua to precede my pint. 'I've need of this first', I qualified to Tiffanie, and without lingering to verify if she might riposte; I gulped it down as if it became obvious as the original water of life.

It might not have attested as the fundamental liquid of being per se, but I it revived and irrigated me for having knocked it back, hence lodged myself with newfound robustness on a neighbouring seat. With discretion, I prodded my legs to make certain of their effectiveness, content to establish I should secure the facility to alight when the demand arose. Later; watered, refreshed, so too, with my body temperature lowered, I accepted this for a favourable omen and delivered the swap to my stronger beverage which in patience reposed on the mantel in front of me. It seemed to my way of thinking about as convivial as a drink could appear. I remarked to my companion, with a grin to my visage, that it emerged this gifted beer from Lugh that landed justly as the stuff of Irish existence. With that I raised it up to head height, tapped it against hers, and next toasted with a satisfactory tone of voice, through the single word "Sláinte".

'I found out what happened to the Professor', pronounced Tiffanie. 'Well, I didn't precisely discover what came of him, but I learned that he died all of a sudden.' 'When,' I asked? 'June 12th, 1896; expired from what I gather without anyone expecting it', happened her reply. I reached for the inside pocket of my jacket then withdrew the copies she ran off earlier, which came out folded as well as creased into thirds. Opening his summary, I double checked the date printed on top. 'That's just a few days after he put all this together. No wonder it never saw the light of day. He converted out of nowhere into what they refer to in Dublin as Brown Bread.'

'Show me', returned Tiffanie, beckoning with a polished fingernail. In acceptance, I tendered it, and availed of the opportunity to visit the Gent's. When I returned she busied herself in reading, and without interruption I exhausted the gap to finish my pint; furthermore, beckon for another. My primary target was just for the one, cautious that after my earlier experience, I had better get something to eat. There wasn't much choice in the matter now, thus, I admitted in banter they went down grand. Tiffanie for her part, didn't remove her gaze from the testimony, also, she applied peripheral vision to locate her drink for periodic sips. She uttered little, and I offered no industry to prompt her, in wait instead to hear about what she had to say when finished.

Rather, I toured with my eyes around the tiny cellar bar on a mission of observatory surveillance, but even though it ranked merely a tenth the size of my personal purgatory, it affected me with none of the carriages of claustrophobia that overcame me there. I deposited in relaxation, restored to my old self and in enjoyment of my beer, the company and the cosy atmosphere of intimacy.

My confidante completed her appraisal, and next agreed to an exclamation of astonishment, while she refunded me the reproductions. 'If you want to know why I came to Ireland, this is it.'

I wasn't certain how to respond to that, not ascending as quite what I expected she might say. As well, with no retort to hand, I just smiled and came back with nothing in exact because of optimism she might carry on with her explanation.

'When you render the choice to spend time overseas, there's always the expectation you'll encounter some kind of connection with the country you visit. I wanted to acquire a lasting link with Ireland, and I got that with you Irish, but this is a different sort of association. It's one I wished for on an academic level. It's more than that actually, because it's personal. It's something I've had a tangible role in'.

'Am I making sense'? She acted a measure on the giddy side, the excitement clear in her eyes, and I loved her for it. I got affected by a flashback to the afternoon when I philosophised on the spiritual relationship the good professor must have occupied with his unearthed artefacts when in proximity.

'I understand perfectly what you mean', I said in response. It's that tingle at the abyss of your innards when you come to be marked by something on an intimate level, as if it has grown into a part of you'.

'Deep is an appropriate word to adopt Irish. The both of us are diving into the void'. She then laughed before raising her glass. 'This is incredible', she proclaimed after the swallow of a bigger mouthful as I noticed her accept before. 'I can't believe it. We have all that stuff in the chest along with his statement, letter and summaries. If I was to jump ahead of myself, we could be staring at fame and fortune, but I would settle for the recognition of having been in on the finding'.

'It was all of your doing'; she returned after a brief pause and then placed her hand on my knee. 'I don't want to barge in on your big moment'. 'It was a partnership', I affirmed; and meant it. Here I snatched a discreet kiss.

I came over with a ration of alarm all of a sudden, but strived not to let it show given that Tiffanie happened so enthusiastic with her reaction to events. I didn't suppose I yet sought after its sharing outside the two of us; if at all. And, it wasn't even I cared to lounge in the moment. It owed nothing to do with that. I was matched with Professor Campbell, in that I required more. He consumed years, always on the chase for that one big detection which ought to tie it all up into a bow of neat ribbon, hence enabling him to propose it to his peers. At the finish, he crafted the resolution to offer it up anyway after a career entertained with assumptions he wanted for ever more detail.

Admitted, with the inscribed pens and marriage bands emerging, he came as close to conclusive chunks of evidence as he was ever likely to contract and these provoked the shove over the top which put paid to what endured as an incessant quest. He resigned himself to the acceptance that oftentimes within his field of specialty, one seldom realised all that one seeks, and contrary to popular wisdom, to settle for what one has transpires more often than not as the proper measure. I too invited, and perhaps looked-for extra, as he once entreated, without acceptance my research had chanced upon its conclusion. Correspondingly, I ached for Tiffanie not to consider this as the expiration of our involvement by contributing of a plan we confer it all on the Museum.

'There's a lot to consider here', I voiced. 'Campbell hadn't the confidence to come into the open with his suppositions until decades after the original affair; too, with good cause. Most of it wasn't explainable, and some of it still isn't.'

'Like what,' demanded Tiffanie? 'Well, for starters there's a theory concerning some isle by the name of Hy Brasil. I've never heard of it, real or fanciful. Then if I accept it existed, which is a huge assumption, how was it all this stuff turned up in Ireland? As well, you have the problem of the plastic bits and pieces, also, the troublesome circuit boards. What's the story with them?'

'I'll grant you there're things we don't yet have all the answers to,' replied she. 'He told us himself that Hy Brasil appeared in atlases and such way back in the middle ages. So, in view of that fact it's safe to suppose that a cartographer of the period believed in its actuality. Campbell thought it a fantasy too, until he unearthed a variety of historical rarities, which then in fact activated to verify its substance. As to how they ended up in Ireland, he had an explanation for that as well. People travel. Countries trade with each other. People die on their way to these lands, and moreover, they pass away when they get there. It could be that some of what's in his Box of Tricks would have impressed as intensely exotic to the natives of the age'.

'My guess is they saved it because of its pleasure to the eye. Put it this way; many Indian tribes of North America adored shiny beads of colour which had little monetary worth to anyone else, but they exchanged blankets and hides for them all the same which were of a much higher value. The point being, that they might have either treasured the goods that somehow ended up there by death, robbery, loss etcetera. As well, perhaps in one or two instances, they traded merchandises that were more precious solely to get their hands on a vase of enamelled finish for example. Either way, they prized what they ended up with, what's more, treated it with reverence'.

'I know where you are coming from' I retorted 'but there occurs still the issue of plastic, so too, the circuit panels. They're modern and there's no getting around it'. 'I don't in truth have a solution to that', admitted Tiffanie. After a silence, she continued. 'I kind of suspect a wacky explanation, but as a rule I don't do crazy theories, so there's no real enlightenment to them'.

'What's your madcap answer?' I probed. 'It's almost too damn stupid to contemplate', she pronounced. 'I don't even know how it entered my mind, except I was in search of any notion that might resolve this enigma'. I interposed by stating, 'When one has ruled out all other explanations, then the remaining must occur as the correct.

At least, I suspect that's how the maxim goes. I heard it someplace before. So, tell me, irrespective of how ridiculous it sounds, what's your sole left-over conjecture, Sooner Girl?' 'Okay, but don't laugh. I've struck out aliens as being the single maddest proposition; which leaves just one wild hypothesis, which is that Hy Brasil was a civilisation so advanced, it evolved to a level that was equivalent or almost comparable to our own'.

I allowed that to sit with me for a tick before returning with, 'I need something to eat. Let's get out of here'. We quitted for a pub within easy distance renowned for its food, where it came to my notice that after the couple of taken drinks, I ensued as hungry. In answer to this, I ordered a rack of ribs with fries, and Tiffanie took a fancy to the loaded pizza.

With the resumption of our discussion, I spoke to her thus "Let's accede for a minute that your theory is accurate. How does a person account for the natives clinging on to circuit boards and the like? They should have no use for them; furthermore, they are a long way off a pretty plate or silver spoon". She countered with the clarification 'By the same means our Native Americans valued beads and baubles, in that there may well have been a novelty factor to it. There's not a chance they ever would have come into anything like it before, nor would they have touched a material similar to it up till that time, with all its contours and intricate constituents. The justification could be as simple as that'.

'What about selected effects in possession of primitive characteristics then?' I inquired. 'That makes little sense for an innovative society.' Beautiful Tiffanie was the equal of me on every demand, and in consequence, ensured for an answer at the ready in her retort. 'All societies advance. Men such as you wandered around thousands of years ago, swinging their clubs and dragging pretty maidens such as me back to their cave. We change, adapt, learn, develop new understandings, what's more; create novel modernisations. The learning has never ceased, so too, we as a species have made progress every step of the journey. It stands to logic that nigh on every civilisation that has lived on this earth has had to go through a period of erudition, besides growth. There is no cause to suspect Hy Brasil didn't do the same.

'You have me there I reacted, except for the fact, that one minute they happened with bare hands to shape combs out of deer antler, and perchance swung that truncheon you speak of; but in its historical context, the next minute they've moved on to the assembly of sophisticated electronics. That implies modern technology –radio's, televisions, mobile phones and what have you. How did they evolve from a primitive existence to a society contemporary with our in such a short span of time? After all, it's demanded of us years in the thousands.'

'Grub first, Irish! Too many questions on an empty stomach are not good for you'. Our meals arrived, and apart from comparisons on the flavour, we ate in quiet for the initial handful of minutes; although that refused to stop my meditations from sifting through all we discussed. After that primary phase of desiring to focus the mind and body on food as a method to satisfy the first pangs of hunger, the two of us relaxed into the pleasure of our meal.

Tiffanie spoke up–'I might have an explanation to that conundrum. Well, part of a solution anyhow. It doesn't explain in complete how a civilisation goes from a basic presence to one of advancement with such rapidity, but it might help to illuminate us on how a progressive society takes the next evolutionary step.' 'Go on', I prompted. 'Have you ever wondered why the Roman's or the Egyptians, for example, never produced an industrial revolution? One would have thought with all the numerous inventions they stumbled on, too, with every structure of engineering genius they erected, many of which remain extant to this day, that a few of those individuals at some stage over the total existence of these great cultures would have discovered the power of steam'.

'I suppose, now you mention it, that's a great question', I admitted. Tiffanie was in a groove and continued to speak. 'You had the Greek's for instance, erecting classical temples. They even invented what some consider having been the world's first computer, albeit an analogue one. Even so, it was employed to predict astronomical positions. The scale of accuracy, even when measured against the standards of today is astounding. Going back to the Egyptian's, there's a bunch of evidence for advanced astronomy, mathematics, engineering, and the construction too of monumental shrines for the Pharaoh'.

'The Roman's gave us concrete. They had the technology to create domed buildings like the Pantheon; an ability that although it seems uncomplicated, was anything but. It got lost to us until the Renaissance. They provided us with roads, viaducts, stadiums with the capacity to hold fifty thousand people and a language from which we derive all the romantic tongues of today. On top of that there were civilisations to the east; the hanging gardens of Babylon, so too, the distinguished cities of Persia. We had the Phoenicians and Carthaginians, the Han of China. They, who assembled the Great Wall. What I've never understood, is why throughout these divergent civilisations in effect around separate parts of the world, all in achievement of astonishing accomplishments both before, and a few hundred years into the Common Era, that none by accident or otherwise swayed into an industrial revolution?'

'So, what you theorise is that Hy Brasil went through all of that which modern man only realised in current centuries?' 'It certainly seems that way', came her rejoinder. 'If you think about it by this approach; in the broad scheme of things, not a huge quantity of time has passed since the start of our own modern age. Horses were the mainstay of life for agricultural purposes and transportation until about a hundred years back. Now we have spacecraft visiting Pluto. We didn't even know this miniature planet existed at the turn of the twentieth century. It's altogether practicable that a somewhat cutting-edge society could move on from horses and wagons pulled by oxen, into with the capacity to invent complicated mechanisms in a very short interval; relatively, that is'.

'It's an argument with compelling rationale', I agreed. 'There remains the matter of it zipping from zero to hero faster than one can utter the words Steam Engine. All the other societies you mention had plenty of time on their side, and yet never succeeded with a breakthrough. That's a fact. It might transpire as a question of intrigue to reflect on why it never happened, but even with; in some circumstances; thousands of years of being, the truth stands that nobody in that entire span tripped into the resourcefulness of steam. However, Hy Brasil by all accounts, if your model is correct, realised to manage it, which in turn led it to its development into pretty much a replica of what we see around us today.'

'I know', admitted Tiffanie. 'The technology should have gotten exported too. That's another component which doesn't fit. Rome, Egypt and everywhere else on earth, should have had the expectation to pick up on at least part of that knowledge, but didn't. Even Ireland should have achieved it, given that's where the relics turned up.

It's all of way too much interest to set aside is what I think. How would you feel about us delving into it more? All of that stuff in the Box of Tricks has been sitting on rotten boards for more than a century. Will a little more time make a heap of difference?' I came over all thrilled to hear this, also,, it disposed of the reservations I was consumed with earlier. I might well have gotten a read on her views, but she meant too much for this cognitive invasion. I occupied a few scruples after all. Hence, when she tumbled by her own accord into the identical pattern of procedure I championed, it cheered me up a notch. 'I was of the same opinion', I confirmed. 'If truth be told I don't care to confer all of this onto someone to accept the credit. Maybe there's the possibility of our coming up with a few more answers'.

We exited the restaurant and ended up at her apartment where she brewed up a pot of Ireland's finest. 'It's me who should refer to you as Irish', I jested. 'You're just the same as an Irish mammy who makes up a cup of scald to have a natter over'. I perceived her with a wide smile as she acknowledged, 'I've been hanging around you too much, Irish'. 'Hey, don't blame me. You've been drinking this stuff since before I came on the scene'. I wrapped arms around her from behind as she poured out the milk, then snuggled my face into hers as a show of affection. 'They'll be telling me back home I've gone native', she arrived back with. 'The sacrilege of drenching tea with milk, it's just not the Oklahoma way- Lots of ice, plenty of sugar, that's us' 'Perhaps I'll take up the hobby of iced tea imbibing', I bantered in rejoinder. 'That'll definitely confuse 'em.'

My associate in misconduct then grabbed a couple of pens and a pad to jot down our suppositions. As we rested on her couch with hot tea, she powered up her laptop. We stood resolute it should transpire for the good to determine what we might uncover as it related to Hy Brasil. There revealed a handful of articles online, some of which noted the various charts plus atlases which had gotten a mention in the professor's summary. There ascended the familial link to Ireland; moreover, the legend of it having at one point in time passed off in actuality, just for it then to vanish. There occurred however, no evidence whatsoever which proposed that the legendary island had in fact existed in actuality. Nothing in the records flagged that it amounted to anything more than a fable or a figment of the imaginary.

The sole commentaries of interest to crop up came to light in several newspaper chronicles that mentioned where a host of witnesses allegedly beheld it rise out of the fog and ocean every once in a blue moon. These sightings should, we speculated, have only added to the mystery and the ensuing myth. An island that shows itself when it pleases, then disappears back into the depths, is akin to a mermaid who reposes on a rock for the purpose of terrifying sailors. There published no data of substantiation or even a small total of support to back up any of the testimonies, and in all likelihood these hypothetical sightings of Hy Brasil remained about as probable as those of the Loch Ness Monster.

After a struggle with more browsing around the internet, Tiffanie shut down the computer, then catered for us both a second cup of tea. "A bird never flew on one wing", I quipped, when she furnished me with mine. "I thought that saying just applied to hard liquor", she replied in puzzlement. "It's the same concept with tea" I kidded. "You're not in complete fulfilment until you've downed the follow on". We then took to the resumption of our conversation, too, engaged in an amount auxiliary speculation. My cohort from Oklahoma fixed the scratch pad to the lap of her crossed legs. In addition, she kept a pen at the read to scribble down any more points of interest we might chance upon during our session of brainstorm.

'Okay then, back at the museum we have verification to the reality of Hy Brasil,' she advanced. 'Professor Campbell spent eons of his career in the assemblage of this evidence, but it wasn't until the days before he died, that he plucked up the courage to announce the story of its onetime occurrence. Never had there arisen any substantiation apart from his. Nothing we or he knew of had gotten exposed that could be attached to an island named Hy Brasil. As far as it bothered anyone, it merely lived in the drunken fancy of superstitious mariners.'

'Yes,' I interjected. 'It's obvious he didn't seek to make a fool of out of himself, which is understandable, but with each relic it strengthened his belief. He was left waiting his entire life for the smoking gun which never fired unless, of course, one counts the wedding bands as smoke without fire.' 'Then to complete that chain of thought, when the facts change, people's minds alter,' noted Tiffanie. 'The evidence formerly absent is now present; too, it displays that Hy Brasil, far from being a remote fable, what's more, a fiction of overactive story tellers, was in occurrence as an actual place. Hence, as an establishment of verity, what does that tell us?'

I came back with, 'It establishes that it situated there in earlier times but is today absent', adding, 'How does an island disappear?' 'Any number of ways', she countered. 'It could have been volcanic in composition; the upshot of it being situated on the Mid- Atlantic Ridge. The volcano might, as occurs, have exploded in an eruption, just like Krakatoa. That would mean lights ended for Hy Brasil. Or, along similar lines it was perhaps an explosion in its radius which set off a massive tsunami. The outcome is more or less the same in that the landmass still evaporates; only this time it gets washed away'.

'Another option, which is the most far-out, might happen that the people became so sophisticated, they ended up wiping each other out and the island along with it, perhaps as the result of a nuclear war or similar'. I came in with a supposition of my own. 'There's an alternative plausibility, and again it hugs the same strands of contemplation as your first two conjectures. There is a substitute, remote as it might seem that it came to be struck by a meteor, or more credibly a small asteroid. That should, if it transpired the condition, have engendered enough force to see it obliterated. Again though, even if it landed without a direct hit, a circumference in the vicinity just may have manufactured the tsunami you speak of, which then give rise to a catastrophic wipe-out'.

Tiffanie noted these ideas. 'You're pretty smart, Irish', she affirmed. 'You're the one who equipped us with the zany concept that distributed as not crazy after all', I came back with. I got to witness those Oklahoman pearls because of that compliment. She carried on. 'Okay, so let's say for argument' sake we have a nation that may at one time been primeval, but by some means caught up to the equivalency of other established societies of the age. Then they progressed even further, out passing them all to furnish themselves with an industrial revolution, which brought about a modern era similar enough to our own.

All of this accomplished with the blink of an eye in evolutionary terms. Then, they completely depart the earth, as well, leave next to no traces behind of ever having been here. That in itself looks to show that whatever happened was rapid. It had to be, because no matter how insular a forward-looking country is, in the long run their secrets always escape. We have plenty of evidence of that happening over the millennia: silk and gunpowder, porcelain, the longbow, and many other innovations. In time, the technology becomes widespread. Even today, we have patents to protect intellectual and tangible property; but does it ever in fact stop devices and other such things from getting copied? Accepting it doesn't, the question we arrive back at is, how did all this evolution get squeezed into such a contracted span'?

'Maybe that's one we should sleep on', I responded. 'I think you're right Irish. We can have another gawk into the Professor's Box of Tricks at work tomorrow and see if we can't gleam some inspiration from it'. On that note, we tucked under the sheets, both of us exhausted.

I dreamed. Reveries garlanded in vibrancy which lasted the whole night and which played out in the pattern of a tale I positioned central to. It all staged at home in Waterford, but as occurs with visions of the black, I rambled in the conviction I flew to Hy Brasil. There, I anchored with it all the same. I made out through the intensity of these apparitions our hill that nobody climbed. As well, I trailed the country byway which wound its course up to The Heights and then on to our house. Then what reached out to touch me as I crossed over the cow gate happened tentacles of affability and with them those bumps of acquaintance and the dull notes of standard to accompany them, all confirming I made it home. And yet, this was Hy Brasil. The vehicle I journeyed in came with a discrepancy. It hummed, and all about was muted, with just me to experience it.

The trees emanated with leaves crammed full with emerald green; too, the lawn revealed just as trimmed and pristine as when I ordered yet in infancy. Further, the driveway arranged with the identical turnaround point, clean of debris; the macadam in a display of fresh ink which shimmered in the sun. Interior to this home, the chambers identified as I remembered them. I sauntered ethereally through the hall to perceive that each bedroom inclusive of my own conferred a relationship, and yet a distance to them, as if they belonged to the strange. I unlocked a painted white door at the end of the corridor, and noticed as I grappled with it, to designate its proper dwelling, the key and tag assigned to its lock as predictable. From there, I routed to into the kitchen with its floor tile of coffee beige, home to American oak cabinets, and in appearance they also exhibited as on that significant night of the mystical. To the left of me showed the entrances to the utility room, plus family rooms indistinguishable from the birthday of ten.

I took a moment to view our panorama from the transparent pane of a picture as I achieved so many times beforehand, and then set my considerations on the flower bed to the right of the clipped tight meadow. Further down I beheld the area set aside for strawberries and other fruits of summer; and to its right, the greenhouse. Inside its frame, I believed I could make out the rear of a wicker chair, empty, lying in wait for the master to occupy it. The principal of that throne was not me, nor ensued it my father. Neither of us could lay claim to it, nor make use.

To the right I transferred and next went through the glass-panelled door to the dining room. There, someone set the table; moreover, prepared it for dinner, a crystal goblet of wine sparkled at its head. The sideboard situated to the right of me; it as well came crafted out of Oak from the New World. On top of it I viewed a bottle of the ruby grape, half empty, a stopper pushed in to preserve its freshness. It beckoned for finishing, with the meal I assumed. Who owned it, I quizzed? Not me, I understood. And similar to the house of glass, nor was it my father's, but that which belonged to a man at variance to us both. Was it he who commanded the seat in that transparent aedicule? Happened it his routine to control the head of the table, to devour the potion of Bacchus with supper, and then station the bottle atop the furniture behind him?

After this I walked by an unknown fridge of white wines to my left, released the next set of doors then passed into the living room. The carpet kept the corresponding colours, besides pattern; intense, brilliant and unworn as when it fitted new. The bar showed itself to my right, and the French Doors sited to my left. These opened on to the terrace which leads out to the garden beyond. In front of me exhibited the sofa and its matching armchairs. The fabric unveiled in freshness of scent; in addition, it paraded as upholstered in recent times and brushed but once.

Though the environment exterior passed on the presence of summer in correspondence with the prevailing season; in bestowal of a routine to the bizarre, here on the inside the fire was lit in consistency with the darkest nights of winter. Too, on the couch lay Tiffanie, in the scrutiny of a television programme or other; a blanket drawn up to her chest. She turned then inquired "Who are you?" Then again, I noticed her lips didn't move. Her voice, clear, resonated in my head, identical to when I deciphered the thoughts of others. In consequence, I responded to her by this medium, not beforehand aware I maintained the ability. The name I offered issued not as my own, but that which I detected then comprehended from the good professor's missive: And that spoke to her with the designation; Olan.

Ostensibly satisfied with this, she switched her attention back to the television without comment. I could make out that the door to the study positioned ajar. In view of this, I strode past her and her programmes. Here I furnished the access with a gentle prod to peer inside, in expectance almost to encounter my father. It followed not however, his countenance I noticed, but that of my own. There I lodged in the high-back chair behind the mahogany table with the etched out triskeles besides perennially endued foliage hand fashioned by my grandfather. Too, this reflection of me stared at a glass filled with claret of which I raised up by the stem to the light in the ceiling. This other me, by the same measure swirled the liquid around the crystal shell of his cup in occupied meditation.

The day after, we arranged for Tiffanie to visit me in the cells during the regular recess. There, I engaged the tagged chest to the accustomed work bench. We studied the contents in desire of inspiration. It transpired the wedding rings, though, which drew our attention. These representations of marriage which we distinguished as relevant to Olan and Neelak became by their own practice, ours. My love palmed, furthermore examined the circle for the female finger, its glister brought out; gold in ownership of the singular quality among the elements as forever without tarnish. Possibly as a corollary of my dream, I twisted it in such a manner it caught the overhead light. The inscriptions showed up as visible in the alphabet of Hy Brasil. With this in mind, I recognised with all certainty that even should they have presented as the identical size, I could determine which was which by the script. The association in spirit to these wonders; it seemed, transferred the confirmation of their significance, and I sought in that instant to place the ring on its rightful digit.

My darling too looked transfixed, and then I recalled her from my apparitions of the night before, reclined on the couch in the lounge area, pivoting her head to request of me, who I ensued. It came as a challenge to return these golden statements of love to their residence as if in this deed it removed from us our deepest and most treasured effects. They possessed an attraction from the distant ether I could tell; neither of us emerged comfortable in parting with. I suggested that we journey to the café and with each stride on that bearing it lessened the magnetic pull of the dungeon, in presumption too, those most personal of charms that happened once again deposited to the Box of Cassandra.

I considered that Tiffanie ought to learn of my event in that year of ten which changed me for all ages. How to broach this subject, though, arose as another matter. I kept it under wraps all these years, never one time in acceptance of anybody to my confidence. Now though, it seemed right she comprehends it all, and I raised the notion we ought to venture to the house in Waterford. There I would undertake to show her the places of its happening. I envisioned us transitioning though the gate of the pillared entrance; home denoted in its breakthrough. I should lead her from the kitchen through the utility room, and from the back door, down the steps to the patio. There, we should receive the pristine pathway of my visions which meandered through the pasture of green, the decorative qualities of which, in reality came indented with a sponge of country moss. On our reaching the bottom of this course, we should enter the aedicule of glass where I might point to the chair; besides, the exposed windows, at which point I stood to recount the long ago molasses of the abnormal which seeped in through those openings. The both of us should then construct our reappearance in the house where I would display to her my old bedroom, moreover describe the changes, so too, recount the adjustments which later materialised.

Our coffee was drunk to begin with, most of all in contemplation. I broke the reverie by broaching "Let's go to Waterford". She stared up from the cup which till then existed as the object of her attention; and with no preamble, responded as if in expectance of the proposal, with a simple and softly voiced "Okay".

We parted for our distinct sites of work. I ambled, heavy-footed; back to the underworld of my daytime reality, with next no enthusiasm for the assigned chores. While I roused the application, every now and again, too, I scanned over the chest, the fillings of which might well have emerged as the Arc of the Covenant; such transpired its allure.

Later on, I found out the house destined to be empty this coming weekend. My parents entertained plans to flee for the continent, and so were to depart for the airport in Dublin on the morning of Saturday. As well, with my sibling's active with their own lives; it devised as seldom now they graced The Heights with their presence. We stood here again under the roof of Tiffanie's apartment. At the conclusion of the telephone call to which I got updated by my mother on the pending vacancy, she interrupted my opinions on it with one word– Madagascar. 'What about it?' I questioned. 'I've had time'; Tiffanie declared 'to pore over some difficulties we developed with reference to our philosophies on Hy Brasil. Madagascar scales as one of those countries on earth which soars from Zealand and New Guinea being two such illustrations. They maintain birds without flight, endemic to them; the Kiwi and Cassowary respectively'.

'These lands flaunt in some respects, aligned in the category of extraordinariness related to the aforementioned isle, in having these besides other species as intrinsic to their lands. Madagascar however, bats in a league of its own. It's all the others multiplied by a hundred'. I interjected by adding 'And you believe this has a connection to Hy Brasil?' 'It's feasible', came her answer. 'Madagascar, if you fancied a search for the prime example of endemism, would surface as the stand out pick. It seems to never quit in the ongoing count for exclusive genus, plus, there comes no telling how many happened at one time in existence that are no longer with us. What I'm suggesting is that an isolated island can, given the optimum conditions, advance singular breeds that transpire without exception, as particular to that landmass.'

'I think I understand where you're venturing with all this, happened my rejoinder. 'You're concluding that Hy Brasil, adrift by its lonesome in the Atlantic, became subject to the effects of endemism, not in the plants and animals, but within the human population itself.' 'Precisely,' she agreed. 'That's just what I mean. In view of that; endemism enhanced, or evolved the natives so much; too, credibly, given the evidence, within such a retracted span of time; that they progressed from a society of primitives to one of advanced intelligence, whereby they exposed the merit of steam, that in good time led to an industrial revolution, and then on to a scientific age of reason and growth.'

'Thus resolving the puzzle of this leap into modernity we encountered' I then mumbled. I must next have turned pale. The blood drained from my upper body, and I came over all faint. These specific wonderings which before dominated my distant years, rushed back to occupy those vessels where blood just now divested from my crown. Tiffanie talked of endemism, which at one point got enunciated with respect to my condition. The dreams, as well as the fragmentations thereof, now broadcast their design, so too, a method of reason attached with them. My darling honey lamb, distressed for my welfare, fetched a glass of water while I slumped backward into the couch.

Reverberating inside me announced reminiscences of Hy Brasil, prevalent traits and genetic mutations. All of them ostensibly detached, so too, extracted from diverse stages of my being, all stared to merge into one. Rather than occurring as individual and disconnected events, they spiralled around each other and got sucked in to the black hole of my existence, both in the present-day, besides the historical. The light, the alterations, and the enhancements I gained all countenanced a fresh meaning. Just as one recognises with certainty at some junctures, that a gut reaction or emotion happens accurate, I fixed in awareness too, with absolute conviction, that I preserved an intense, what's more, profound fellowship with Hy Brasil.

How to convey to Tiffanie the encounter of the light? How to mention the transformation? She needed to know, and should come to appreciate it all in Waterford. My excuse to her for my spell of dizziness I skimmed over as a lack of food in conjunction with the humid weather. There emanated acute fear inside too. I could now sense another change. The coupling of me with Hy Brasil overpowered as a foregone conclusion. It happened underway. All that materialised since I entered the dungeon; the Box of Tricks, the professor's glued on sticker, along with the artefacts, the notes and summation all floated up in my consciousness.

Every one of these happenstances was inevitable, and I

recalled those ensuing of before as well as the visit from my light in green and those revelations of the night which stemmed from them. The analysis I accepted of it at the time transpired that they arrived not as dreams at all, but downloads. That tune of annoyance back then burrowed into my head and refused to divest; and though I strained to consign it to the background, it emerged here and now, yet again, centre stage; a truism rather than purely a hunch.

If my dearest posed questions, I couldn't hear her. We went off to the duvet of comfort with me in requirement of guidance. I occasioned in a state of catharsis. Clarity then surety exists as a sword with a duo of honed edges. They coexist as the supplier of solutions and complications, but it extracts a weighty purse for the struggle. The tithes I paid succeeded in the tax of a terror for the future. That night I allowed in to my cognizance apparitions of an older variation of me, middle-aged and with wrinkled lines across my brow to prove it. I came dressed in a coat of white as should occur stereotypical to those donned by men of science while in occupation with laboratory potions. There in that sterile milieu, I conducted experiments, the subject of which, I noticed, in several instances succeeded as me. I inquired of my older self from afar, what it was he practiced? To this, he answered with a matter-of-fact voice, that he downloaded his memories and consciousness.

'To host inside of me' I questioned. 'I cut an attempt with the good Professor on my first go around', he returned. 'Though, that transpired as a failure on my part. The old boy couldn't take it. Not his fault of course. I smacked him with too many bits and bytes all at once. It came as too severe a strain on him. All the same, we live, what's more, we learn. I've embraced the parable of the tortoise and the hare and for this procedure it is better to endeavour as the reptile. The download for you I spread out over the decades and it's almost at and end.' 'And the rings'? I probed. 'Little gifts from yesteryear' he responded. 'The sole items from Hy Brasil I care about. As well, they happen small enough to teleport.'

On the Saturday, I drove. The sun shone, and with a blue sky over the heads of us, we proceeded for the moniker of Deise in isolated quietness. The bridge over the river and into the city was steered over, and on its traverse, the resonances common to traffic everywhere fluctuated. The cars now emitted a hum which was unfamiliar to my ears. There advanced inaudibility about the place as if somebody had turned down the volume. Then, up the hill we ascended, and crossed on the way one or two walkers in descent. None did I see journey upward as happened the norm. The car I coaxed right onto the rural lane flanked with brambles. Up it we risked, leaving behind the ditches, the hedging, so too, the assortment of one and two-storey homes. Then we attained the pillars of entry, whitewashed and pure as new. I navigated into the driveway, casting over as we did, that grate with the cylindrical bars along with the bumps which moved through the tyres and echoed up into our seats, in issuance of its welcome.

I opened first the ton weight double glazed porch, and next, the inner door. With my life's love in tow, we spanned the threshold, strode through the hall alongside the bedrooms and arrived at the kitchen. Through the rotation of key and dangled fob which came set to the fastened position, we passed in. I invited her to accept a rest on a stool of dark oak, which both, to my eye devised to present an unblemished expression to them, as they appeared when original to the house. I filled the kettle with water and then removed two mugs from the press and went in search of the coffee jar. Too, while I waited for the water to boil, I took the opportunity to free the locks to the other inside doors, and with this act; it gave the impression I opened with them a fresh chapter in the life of this space I called home.

When I circled back to the kitchen, by means of concluding there happened no better occasion than the current, I recounted for my darling Tiffanie over our poured beverages the eerie phenomena of that night with the first change. I spoke of the light which flowed through the picture frame window. Out of this portal, we both now happened able to perceive the entire landscape as far as the town. Next I pointed at the entrance to our place for utilities. It too boarded on my voyage to recount the appointments which played out that night. And I communicated the tale of the modifications, what is more, the subsequent enhancements which bestowed on me capabilities of the unique. It transpired simply today; I expressed to her I understood their meaning. She listened, with zero in the method of comment or question, but rather with complete acceptance.

She requested to view the house, so I piloted her on through to the dining room, whereby a curious agency my eyes were guided to a partially consumed bottle of red on top of the American cabinet to my right. On the left was situated the table for dinner, with two places set, so too, found at the head seat placed a diamond cut glass of lead crystal. Near this was set aside the unacquainted cooler of white wine. Then, through the glass-panelled egress we walked on in to the living room.

Robert E. Kearns

To the right stood the bar stocked with a peculiar assortment of beverages and in front of us the couch and armchairs. A blanket was folded, too, draped with neat positioning over the arm rest contiguous to the fireplace. A half turn to our left displayed for us the set of French doors. There, we gazed out to sight the steps which ran to the immaculately mown lawn, carpeted green; lush in attendance. To the right of it conducted the flowerbed, impeccable; what's more, occupied with colour as it flourished at its zenith. I revealed for her the study. It came dominated by the mahogany board with its distinct and intricate post-Celtic symbols carved into the border. It awarded as clean, polished and free of settled dust. There sited nought atop of it to obscure the magnificence of the mirrored grain. Unrestricted that is except for a calendar of a foot and more wide, which revealed a pure virgin month for the scribing of memos, besides messages. Beside it showed the infrequently exploited telephone; this day though it impressed on me as indulging in recent operation.

Next, I recalled for Tiffanie the hours I consumed in here as a youth, where I read, learned, too, gained an education, and discovered the wonders of the ancient world as well as those of the contemporary. This I considered an opportune moment to point out to her additional spaces from the night of the uncanny ether. Thus I reverted with her to the kitchen then through the utility store, and out the rear exit. There, we jaunted down the steps, before we unwound for a spell at the patio furniture. There I trained her eye to where as children, we kicked a ball about on the afternoon of that day, so too; where my father set up his stall to commence the birthday barbeque. I saw him yet in grasp of the implement he remained so fearful of letting go. At that memory, I might well have smiled, but didn't as I travelled ahead of myself in contemplations; already at the stage of night when the surreal spectacle began.

Tiffanie took note in attentive hush as I recounted the dry mouth that woke me; the adventure of tiptoeing to the kitchen; and inside, when I gulped water from straight under the tap, being confronted by what I thought of now as light fashioned from a diode. I expressed to her my attraction towards it, more yet, its pull of peculiar gravity on me to pinpoint the source. The step ladder, the chain; too, the latch which beckoned at the far end of the chamber were not omitted from my account. Nor was the complicated method demanded to discharge me from the rear outlet. And, I evoked for her my remembrance of posting here on the patio as I peered back to the house bathed in the dry mist of that thickened atmosphere, while the dew on the blades of grass resembled minute needles of amazement.

I stood up, and she copied my lead. I took her by the hand then sauntered over to the lengthy flagstone walkway. Eyeing it, I swelled in mild surprise to observe it came absent of the prevalent moss. The layout of etched foliage stood out in relief. The stone arranged as spotless, and it complimented the flower bed of vivacity with its earthy shades, as it formerly achieved in those earliest of my parent's photographs. Next, we followed it, this stepping-stone road which snaked to the bottom, as in my dreams they compelled me to realise. Untarnished now, we strode it to the end of the miniature plane where it terminated at the two brick wall which positioned as sentry over the strawberry and fruited beds.

The windows to the aedicule of glass stood ajar for ventilation.

Robert E. Kearns

I pulled on the handle, and there in perpetuity showed the fixtures of wicker next to table, apparent as new, besides unblemished. Once over I reflected for a second on the anomalous flower bed and footpath. In here, the containers came potted with tomato's, ripe, so too, all set for the picking. At this moment, I couldn't help but try the weight of one in my hand, and encounter the touch of its skin against mine; what's more, inhale the scent of nature in bloom. With my description of the light which seeped through the openings; in addition, the halo that spun overhead, I spoke to Tiffanie of my collapse to the ground, too, my recuperation some time afterward. Then, I narrated to her as to the perception of one half to my body, cold as well as numb. The chair where I at one time sat Tiffanie now placed as if in a re-enactment of my movements that night. Next, I set a hand on the table then articulated all that had happened from that point onward.

There showed intensity on the features of Tiffanie as she paid attention to my chronicle. My saga didn't end with my teens. I told her of the dungeon, likewise, my compelling hunt for the papers of the good professor. I recalled for her the stages of panic, so too, catatonia. I communicated the intense dreams, and of Olan. Furthermore, I let her know of his words as they related to the download of his mind, spirit; and the essence of his lifeblood. I spoke of how he attempted to upload his personality; moreover, existence into the brain of Campbell, merely for it to falter. Nevertheless, he learned from his errors. Then, without fear of her reaction, or what she might make of it all, I expressed my belief I suffered to become the subject of his trials, beginning with those many eons ago.

Exhaustion overwhelmed me when done with it all, and my

mood descended to where it stationed while in the pit of the netherworld. And, because of this, I sat down on the floor with my legs crossed, trusting that by this deed, it should pass. Tiffanie, quiet up till now in the main; I worried, might consider me with horror. Rather, she owned a look of pity in her eyes, and in that instant, I wasn't quite sure which should come off as the worst. "I brought something", she whispered. I didn't make a reply, just watched as she probed into her handbag and pulled out a dainty case. It offered as ornate, a golden triskele on top, surrounded with post Celtic leaf design. This donated as a box made for jewellery. She opened it, and there, in front of my eyes displayed two polished bands of gold.

I stood up, and then we examined each other. I tested for nothing in the way of interrogation. We both regarded the parcel in her straightened palm, and here, I extended inside of it my thumb; so too forefinger for the lesser of the two rings. This I extracted from its slot in the fabric, and without the requisite to ask for it, absent of delay she raised her spare hand, splayed her fingers and offered the one for marriage. She then repeated the procedure, and with this deed of the spiritual, the light shone through the transparent frame and caught the inside of the circle, on which was written: To Neelak, With Love on our Wedding Day.

We returned to the main house. As we passed the sideboard of American Oak I removed the bottle of wine atop it, undid its stopper then poured it into the hand cut crystal of sparkle. This I conveyed the study and it occurs here now that I conclude this testimony. I wear the ring of Olan on my wedding finger. In the adjacent room she I called Tiffanie lies

Robert E. Kearns

in repose on the sofa and the television is switched to On. Soon it shall be dark, and when the sun has set, I retain the conviction that from that point on, I shall forever after, by my darling wife Neelak, be referred to as he.

The End.

Made in United States
Orlando, FL
29 June 2024

48445092R00221